A native of California, Darian North now lives in Brooklyn, New York, with her husband and four children, BONE DEEP is her second novel, and her first, CRIMINAL SEDUCTION was an Edgar Award nominee for Best First Novel.

# Bone Deep

## Darian North

# KNIGHT

ISBN 1 84067 256 0

Typeset by
Letterpart Limited, Reigate, Surrey

Printed and bound in Great Britain by
J. H. Haynes & Co. Ltd., Sparkford, Somerset

Caxton Publishing Group
20 Bloomsbury Street
London
WC1B 3QA

To
Lance Gidel
Clay Gidel
and
Claudia Gidel Fugate

My brothers and sister.
My valued friends.

So this is what we shall collect then,
      The decipherment,
The clarification,
      And the explanation
Of the mysteries and the illumination . . .

*The Popol Vuh of the Quiché Maya*


On that day, a strong man seizes the land,
On that day, things fall to ruin

*The Books of Chilam Balam*

# I

*Moonsmoke*

# One

The underground chamber smelled of damp mossy dirt and rocks crumbling to mineralized powder. It smelled of twining roots that had crept down deep to suck nourishment, then died, replenishing the soil with their decay. It smelled of life. The cycle of life. As though it was a part of the earth's womb.

And so it seemed fitting that the bodies should have been placed there. Returned to an eternal womb where blood and flesh melted into the earth and became part of the cycle.

Iris Lanier stepped off the crude ladder onto the packed floor and breathed deeply of the musk. Even though the chamber was familiar to her now, there were still times when it affected her as it had in the beginning, when she felt her own smallness, her own insignificance against the continuum of human history.

At her feet lay the five women. Their bodies were arranged like the rays of a starburst, emanating from a center oval paved in smooth flat rocks. Two of the women had been decapitated. Three had damage consistent with having their hearts ripped out. Brutal deaths. But they had occurred nearly two thousand years ago and were now just scientific curiosities.

Iris had finished the fifth woman the night before and the pleasure of completion was still with her. She stood a moment, surveying the project as a whole, trying to

3

see it with a critical and dispassionate eye, taking in the fine clean lines of the bones and evaluating her own competence.

When she began in the chamber, the women's bones had been deeply embedded in the dirt floor. Her digging and scraping and brushing had stripped away the dirt and left them lying bare, preserved in position but no longer cradled in the earth. Soon they would be taken away completely. She would excavate the final skeleton, an unknown that was represented only by a pair of feet and legs protruding from the tunnel at the front of the chamber, then all the remains would be photographed and recorded in place, and then these six citizens of an ancient world would be packed in bubble-wrap and lifted out into the twentieth century.

Carefully, Iris edged around the women. The underground room was fourteen feet wide by twenty long. Her entry hole and ladder were at the back. The star-ray women filled the center so that she had to press against a side wall to get around them. At the front was the original tunnel entrance that had sloped downward from the surface. The tunnel had been completely filled with dirt and debris and it was this fill that had partially buried the sixth skeleton.

'Hello . . . Dr Lanier?' a female voice called from the overhead entrance hole. 'Can I help for awhile?'

Iris wanted to say no. She had been looking forward to beginning number six alone. But she could think of no acceptable way to refuse.

'Come on down,' she answered.

Linda eased herself through the hole and descended the ladder as though she were wearing a tight silk dress and high heels instead of jeans and sneakers. Iris watched her, thinking that any of the male members of the team would have rushed over to give the archaeology student a hand. The men were transformed by Linda's helplessness. They

4

tripped over each other in their efforts to render assistance. And though it was all exasperating at times, the performances were so amusing that Iris hoped Linda would last longer than the other work-study volunteers who had passed through camp.

'So, everybody's done but number six?' Linda asked brightly as she stepped off the last rung of the ladder.

Iris nodded. 'Stay close to the wall,' she said, indicating the path she had taken around the star-ray women.

Linda stepped daintily along the wall but stopped midway to kneel beside one of the skeletons.

'Is this one of the ones who got—?' Linda drew a finger across her neck.

'Yes,' Iris said. 'That's number two.'

'Even after you showed me where the injuries are, I still can't find them on my own. It's amazing the way you can see so much in bones.'

'Just practice,' Iris assured her.

'It's more than just practice,' Linda said with a note of resignation in her voice. 'Dr Becker says you've either got a gift or you don't. And I'm beginning to wonder if I have it. I mean, I've always done well in class, but when I'm working in the pyramid Dr Becker makes me feel so stupid!'

Iris considered how to respond. Linda was twenty-five, an adult, and only four years younger than herself, yet the woman seemed childlike to her.

'Maybe he's testing you,' Iris suggested.

'In more ways than one,' Linda said with a touch of sarcasm. She pulled her trowel from her back pocket. 'Where do we start?'

'Don't they need you in the pyramid today?' Iris asked.

'Maybe, but Dr Becker's in a real touchy-feely mood.' She rolled her eyes. 'I just had to get away.'

There it was. Daniel Becker's weakness. Every female was a sexual challenge to him. Iris was the only woman

5

who had lasted on the project.

'Did you tell him he was annoying you?' Iris asked.

'I'm not going to tell Daniel Becker that he's annoying me! Please! I just hope I make it through this dig without sleeping with him.'

Oddly, this childlike woman seemed better equipped to handle Becker's advances than some of her more savvy predecessors had been.

'If you don't want to sleep with him then don't allow yourself to be bullied into it,' Iris said.

The young woman gave her a sideways look that dispensed with naiveté and helplessness. It was wise and shrewd and secretive. As though they shared some ancient feminine knowledge. Some deep primitive bond.

Iris turned away, disturbed by the sudden intimacy and by the assumptions held in that look. She studied number six. The feet and legs were visible to mid-thigh but the rest of the skeleton was buried in the mouth of the tunnel. She would have to move a lot of dirt to free the upper body.

'I'll bet he's never tried to bother *you*, has he?' Linda said from behind her. 'You've got them all so intimidated.' She chuckled softly. 'But doesn't it get tiresome? Being so untouchable? Being the great scientific mind all the time?'

Iris stared at number six's feet. The delicate phalanges, the slender reeds of the metatarsals, the complex jigsaw of the cuneiforms. So perfect and timeless and familiar.

Linda sighed in an exaggerated and vaguely petulant manner. 'Oh, well . . . whatever gets you through, right? Whew! It's warming up early today.'

Iris nodded and began rolling up her sleeves. Immediately Linda too began turning back her cuffs.

Every day Iris wore faded denim jeans and a man's chambray shirt over a tank-style undershirt, knotting the long tails of the chambray at her waist. When the morning chill wore off, she rolled up her sleeves. When the dead heat of afternoon settled in, she took off the chambray and worked in her undershirt. It was all part of her routine. Devised for efficiency and comfort. But Linda made her almost self-conscious about her routines.

The woman, who had arrived at the dig with three large suitcases full of designer casual clothes, had managed to put together an imitation of Iris's plain work uniform, and she dressed in that every day. She had also changed her hair to a single braid down her back, just like Iris wore. Becker and the others teased about Linda's transformation, referring to her as Iris's little sister. Iris didn't know what to think of it. She supposed it was flattery, but she found it disconcerting.

'Don't let me distract you,' Linda said, moving up close as Iris toed off her leather sandals.

Iris didn't bother with a reply. She wasn't distracted. The work was pulling her and she was eager to jump into it.

Linda's presence faded completely as she concentrated on her final subject in the chamber. Mayan ceremony had commonly called for tossing a slave into a burial vault before the outer entrance was sealed. When the team broke through into the vault beneath the pyramid they had found several unfortunates huddled in the doorway to the king's tomb. She and Becker both suspected that the chamber's number six had met a similar fate, probably tossed down the tunnel entrance just before it was filled with dirt.

She studied the bones, absorbing the details of angle and placement, imagining the position of the skeleton within the sloping tunnel, noting that it was face down, guessing that it was lying straight rather than bent or curled from the waist, picturing it beneath the dirt – waiting, patiently waiting. And the work took her, as it so faithfully did, took her into a magical oblivion – like sleep – where the work was a dream of work. And the dream was all there was.

Some time later a soft *whump* and a piercing shriek jarred her back to reality.

'It's after us!' Linda screamed, leaping toward Iris and clutching at her arm like a drowning swimmer clinging to a lifeguard.

Iris saw the snake then, a dark ribbon of movement against the dirt floor. It streaked through the bones of the star-ray women, into a chest cavity and through a pelvic opening, under a scapula, and finally into an eye socket where it disappeared from view, curled into the brain cavity of the skull.

'Quiet!' Iris ordered, covering her ears against Linda's continued screams.

'My God, what are we going to do! We're trapped down here with that thing. It could be poison! It could—'

'It's not poisonous. Don't you know what a coral snake or a *Barba amarilla* looks like? Besides, do you think someone would use a poisonous snake as a prank?'

'A prank?' Linda's eyes jerked upward to the overhead entrance hole. 'You mean it didn't just fall in here?'

'No.'

'That rotten Tim! I told him at breakfast how scared I was of snakes.'

Iris rolled down her sleeves and pulled on a pair of gloves. She didn't bother slipping into her sandals. They might trip her and they certainly offered no protection for her feet.

'What are you doing?'

'Covering up in case it tries to bite me.'

'But you said it wasn't poisonous.'

'Just because it doesn't have venom doesn't mean that it won't bite.'

With a little squeak of fear Linda backed against the wall, furiously tugging at her rolled-up sleeves and pant-legs. Iris ignored her and poked through the odds and ends in her toolbox. What did she have to catch a snake with? Nothing presented itself.

The skull where the snake was hiding trembled slightly, then rocked back and forth, as though the skeleton was saying no.

'Damn!' Iris muttered under her breath. She crouched down and moved toward the eerily animated skull.

'What are you doing?' Linda hissed.

'Catching it,' Iris whispered, though she thought she remembered that snakes had no hearing. 'Before it displaces the bones.'

'Oh no. Oh my God. We've got to get help. Let's just leave him where he is and tiptoe up the ladder for help.'

'Don't move,' Iris warned.

She closed in on the shivering skull and slowly lowered her gloved hands toward it. The snake darted out through the right eye socket, threaded through ribs, crossed the left ulna and radius, then streaked away. Iris scrambled to follow while a new burst of screams racketed through the chamber.

When it reached the smooth center stones, the snake doubled back, nearly smacking into Iris's instep, and, without thinking, she stepped on the head, pressing just hard enough to keep it trapped between the ground and the ball of her bare foot. The body writhed violently. Stooping, she grabbed it in her left hand and was startled by the rippling strength in the slender creature. The tail whipped around her arm and squeezed. She could feel the reptilian pulse beating against her wrist.

*He's more terrified than I am*, she reminded herself, swallowing hard against the panicky realization that she had a snake's head under her bare foot. Linda's screaming went on and on like the insistent blare of a car alarm.

'Quiet!' Iris shouted. Linda's mouth snapped shut and Iris added, 'please . . .'

She drew in a deep breath, flexed the gloved fingers of

9

her right hand, lifted her foot ever so slightly, and grabbed the snake's head as it pulled free. Her aim was slightly off. She had intended to grip it so that the mouth was locked closed, but the snake was fast, nearly too fast, and her fingers slipped and she ended up clutching his neck, or what would have been his neck if snakes had a neck, and his head swiveled free and his flexible jaw slid sideways and he bit down on her index finger.

Linda emitted a sound that was closer to a hoarse bark than a scream and Iris felt the sting of the needle teeth penetrating her skin through the glove.

'Damn.'

She fought the urge to fling the creature away. Pulse galloping, she stepped carefully over the skeletons, one hand entwined in coils and the other held by sharp insistent teeth.

'Steady the ladder for me,' she told Linda.

'I'm not getting near that thing.'

'Linda! Hold the ladder. Or do you want me to let it go?'

Sullenly, Linda moved around the star-ray women, staying as far from Iris as possible. She gripped the vertical poles of the ladder, turned her head away, and squeezed her eyes shut.

Iris inched upward, one rung at a time. When her shoulders were clear of the hole she stretched her arms out along the ground and relaxed her hold on the snake. The creature didn't budge. As far as the snake was concerned she was the prisoner. She shook her hands. Still nothing. The teeth and coils held firm. Then suddenly, in one sinuous motion, it released her and disappeared into the dead leaves carpeting the forest floor.

'Oh my God, oh my God,' Linda was whispering over and over as Iris went back down the ladder.

'It's gone,' Iris told her.

'I thought I was going to have to have a heart attack!

My God, when he chomped down on your finger . . .'

Iris stripped off her glove and examined the bite in the brilliant light streaming down through the entrance hole. Tiny dots of blood marked the entrance of each tooth.

'Are you all right?' Linda took a step toward her and Iris quickly dropped her hand.

'It's nothing.'

The temperature was nearing ninety. Iris folded her cotton bandanna on the diagonal, rolled it into a long strip and tied it around her forehead to keep the sweat from her eyes. Then she stripped off her outer shirt and hung it on a ladder rung.

'You're going back to work now?' Linda asked in disbelief. 'After all that . . . Aren't your nerves just completely frazzled?'

'I'm not ready to go up,' Iris said. 'But why don't you?'

'No, no,' Linda insisted, beginning the process of stripping off her own shirt and rolling her own bandanna. 'If you're staying, so am I. I don't want all those guys to think I'm a big baby.'

Iris settled back into position and picked up where she had been working. But it wasn't right anymore. Her movements were mechanical. She troweled away the dirt in firm rhythmic strokes, rough cutting and clearing away the outer layers, periodically carrying buckets of the accumulated dirt to an empty corner of the chamber. She went through all the motions but the magic wouldn't come. She was trapped with Linda and with her own erratic thoughts.

She tried to focus on the dirt she was moving. The texture of it. The weight of it. Later, the archaeologists would sift through it for artifacts but right now the only concern was that it be moved. That it be chopped and gouged and chipped away until the rough outline of the skeleton was revealed. Until there was only a thin cover of earth left on the bones. Like flesh. Like the earth had

11

given new flesh. If she could get there then she knew the magic would return because that was the best part. That was her favorite part. When she wielded the brushes and picks and spoons, delicately peeling the earthen flesh away, scooping out the hollows and crevices, unveiling the final mystery.

She glanced up at Linda who was working on the opposite side of number six. Their trowels bit into the earth in unison, making a soft chuffing sound. Like breathing. Occasionally the shrill screech of a parrot or the racket of the howler monkeys drifted down from above.

Four months she had spent in Guatemala. Longer than anyone had thought she would last. There was only a month and a half left in the digging season so she knew she would make it till the end. How much more did Becker have to see before he made his decision? Was he delaying for some other reason?

From the beginning, Becker had indicated that there could be a place for her in his ongoing projects and research . . . *Provided* that he was impressed with her work at the dig. But with only forty-five days remaining, he had yet to make a solid commitment.

What would she do if there was no position offered? That possibility was too terrible to consider. She had given up a decent job and an affordable apartment to join the Mayan dig team. She had sold most of her possessions and put the rest into storage. If Daniel Becker did not take her under his wing, she would be left with nothing. She would be directionless. Homeless. Worse, she would be workless.

Since earning her doctorate at the age of twenty-two, Iris Lanier had been constantly employed. She had reconstructed the faces of Egyptian mummies and crafted diorama figures from fragments of early human bones. She had studied bone collections, measuring and sorting and cataloging, then using the information to create computer data bases. For seven years, five and often six days a week, she had worked in a museum basement – different museums in different cities, but with basements that ran together in her memory so that it seemed like one unbroken line.

The idea of leaving Guatemala without a job to step into was unimaginable to her. The concept of weeks or maybe months without work was inconceivable. Work was the glue that held her life together.

Though she was not usually given to self-examination, she wondered what had possessed her to forgo security and follow Daniel Becker. She had been content. Her days had had a soothing pattern. And she had considered herself lucky because there weren't that many options available to a PhD in physical anthropology with a little pre-med and a lot of human osteology thrown in.

She was not an impulsive person at all, yet she had behaved impulsively. Or so it seemed in hindsight. She had attended, by chance, a museum fundraiser where Daniel Becker was the featured speaker. Becker was a legend: a brilliant archaeologist, a daredevil explorer, an author, and the host of a television series about the Maya. He was a trim, compelling man in his late fifties with an infectious enthusiasm for his field.

That night he spoke at length about how he had researched and explored for a decade, and finally, finally he had found an uncharted Mayan city, northwest of the long-established site of Tikal. The new city was not as striking as Tikal, an enormous ruin of three thousand major buildings and the remains of additional thousands of lesser structures, but the new city had something of unimaginable value to offer. Unlike Tikal, whose towers and spires rose like ghostly fingers above the treetops, the new city had been hiding, swallowed so completely by the forest that it had slept for centuries unnoticed. The new

13

city had never been looted. Never been probed. It was waiting, with its treasures and its secrets intact. Even its name was not yet known.

He then told of the team he hoped to assemble, a multi-discipline team of scientists – not just archaeologists but epigraphers and anthropologists and conservators. A team that would gather information on every aspect of Mayan life and preserve the cultural riches of the city.

At the end of the presentation Iris had sought Becker out and asked him about joining his research. She still didn't know why exactly. It was as though she had been gripped by a temporary bout of insanity.

She had told her shocked museum colleagues that she had long been captivated by Mayan culture and she thought travel would be nice and it would be a refreshing change to work outdoors and do excavations. But while there was truth in each of these reasons, they had not been in her mind when she approached Daniel Becker. The disquieting fact was that she couldn't now say what had been in her mind. She simply could not explain it. Nor could she explain the fantasies she had indulged in as she was in the process of dismantling her contented life. Not since early childhood had she succumbed to such rosy flights of imagination.

She had imagined fieldwork would have a richness, a significance and substance that her museum work lacked. She had imagined that she would find dignity and a primitive purity in the third-world country. And she had imagined that joining the team of esteemed scientists would put her into a charmed circle of camaraderie and shared grandness of purpose.

It had all been nonsense of course. Completely irrational. Guatemala was a troubled and depressing place, beset by corruption and incomprehensible violence. The team of scientists was awash in petty jealousies and competitions, and more concerned about oneupmanship

14

than about any grand purpose their work might have. And the leader, the great archaeologist Daniel Becker whom she had admired since childhood, had turned out to have unpleasant personal flaws that were hard to reconcile with his brilliant work.

Still, even though her joining the team had been inexplicable and impulsive, even though her irrational fantasies had been foolish, still, she had no regrets other than those concerning the future. She was happy. She liked the challenges Becker threw her and the autonomy he allowed her. She liked doing physical labor that left her aching and exhausted at night. She liked living in a tent and being greeted by the sounds of the rainforest every morning. She liked feeling distant from everything and everyone she had ever known. And, most important of all, she liked the intimate nature of the work. The way she got to know the bones. Examining them on her own terms and within her own time frame. Coaxing their secrets from them carefully and slowly rather than rushing to reduce them to statistics.

She desperately wanted to continue with Becker and with the style of work he offered. And she was afraid, deeply deeply afraid of the void that yawned beyond him, a void that was made more disturbing by the knowledge that she had created it herself. She was afraid of life without work. She was afraid of failure. Afraid of going through her meager savings and being forced to ask for help. She was afraid, period. But then she supposed that the fear itself was unavoidable. Wasn't fear a part of her nature? Wasn't cowardice in her genes?

Iris paused to stretch her arms and shoulders. Linda followed suit. As the digging progressed upward into the slanting tunnel, the angle and position of the remains became more awkward, forcing her to alternate between kneeling and squatting, and to work with her arms at shoulder height when she was used to digging downward. Muscles she had never heard from before complained. The temperature climbed. Sweat trickled beneath her clothes and soaked the sweatband at her forehead.

'It must be getting close to lunch,' Linda said.

Iris nodded. She had smashed her watch weeks ago but she could chart the changing position of the sun by the angle and quality of the light slanting down through the hole in the ceiling.

'You don't have to stay, Linda,' she said, blaming the woman for all that had gone wrong with the day.

'Oh no! I want to stay. I want to see you check out the pelvis.'

'I may not be able to tell anything from it,' Iris warned her.

'I'm betting you will,' Linda grinned. 'And I want to watch.'

Linda's enthusiasm instantly wiped away Iris's annoyance. 'All right then' – she smiled – 'let's go ahead and take a look.'

Linda pulled back as though alarmed. 'But you said never to go deeper before you've roughed out the whole figure. Isn't that what you told me before?'

Yes, that was her usual rule and yes she had always been firm about the need for rules and structure and routine, but she felt oddly detached from all of that. As though she had strayed outside herself. Without replying to Linda's question, she bent to work. Nervously, Linda followed her lead, and beneath their tools, the rough shape of the pelvic girdle grew more refined. Iris took smaller and smaller bites with the trowel and then switched to brushes and spoons.

With the body lying face-down, the pelvis was less accessible. Her knees ached and the muscles in her neck felt close to cramping as she bent and peered into the pelvic hollow, scooping it clean of packed earth.

'Now,' she said to Linda, 'use that.' She pointed to a narrow brush that had been intended for painting window trim when she bought it in a hardware store. 'Brush the entire area as clean as you can and then tell me what you see.'

As she spoke Iris reached for the battery-powered miner's lamp. Even with sunlight streaming through the hole at the back there were too many shadows for fine details. She switched on the lamp and pointed it directly at the pelvis.

'I wish I could pick it up,' Linda said, as she bent closer to peer into the pelvic cavity.

'It would be easier,' Iris agreed. 'But we study everything *in situ* first. The way we find it.' Iris traced her finger over the flare of the iliac blade. 'I know it's hard to see much under these circumstances, but look closely. The shape and flare of the ilium, the rounded pubic arch – it all says female. And the pelvic cavity . . . I don't have a male to show you for comparison, but if I did you'd see that the female has a much greater pelvic capacity and a wider opening with a nice oval shape for giving birth.'

'Wow,' Linda breathed, 'another female.'

'Yes, and a mother. She has parturition scars.'

Linda wrinkled up her nose. 'Scars on her bones from having babies?'

'Oh, yes. Our bones are engraved with the stories of our lives.'

Linda looked down at the brightly lit pelvis for a moment. 'Another female . . . Six women in here . . . That's really weird, isn't it? I mean, it's not an ordinary family tomb, it's not a royal tomb, and it's nothing like any of the slave burials they've found. How was it discovered and what made you decide to open it anyway?'

Iris considered her answer. Even though Linda was not officially studying under her or even in her field she

17

felt an obligation to teach the younger woman whenever possible.

'I had done a number of family tombs, and I'd studied the bones they found in the well—'

'Sacrifices?' Linda asked eagerly.

'That's what the evidence indicates.'

'Tim told me there were remains buried at the ball court, too, and that you thought they were sacrifices at first, but then you guys decided they were the losers of games.'

Iris picked up her trowel and began digging upward into the tunnel again.

'Yes, there was a mass grave at the ball court. All the remains were male. Most had been decapitated. Two of the skulls were missing, and of those present all had sustained forceful traumas.'

'That is so creepy, isn't it? They must have kicked the heads around in place of the ball. There was something about that in one of my textbooks. A painting from somewhere . . . or maybe it was a carving . . . that showed them using a captive's head to play ball. So creepy!' Linda wrinkled up her nose in delighted disgust. 'But you never said how you decided to work on *this* chamber.'

Iris kept digging and considered her response. Experience had taught her that people seldom wanted to know very much about anything. They wanted short and simple explanations. Sound bites. Surface gloss. Like the stories on television news coverage. But few things were ever so simple. Because of this Iris usually chose not to attempt explanations at all. It was too frustrating. Too discouraging.

She glanced up at Linda, trying to gauge the depth of interest. The woman seemed to be waiting. Sincerely curious.

'There was an epigrapher,' Iris said, 'who was here for a

18

few weeks. He roamed all over, finding odd broken bits of carvings and trying to fit pieces back together. One of the things he found was a pile of stones that were overgrown with vines and looked like they might be the remains of something that had been scattered or partially dismantled. When he pulled off the vines he saw that, even though the stones were almost crudely stacked, they had glyphs and figures carved into them and they were very purposefully placed. They were either marking a spot or blocking the entrance to something.

'His translations revealed that the stones were marked with warnings. Things like DO NOT ENTER, BELOW LIES THE BAT ROOM OF THE UNDERWORLD, ALL WHO ENTER WILL NEVER RETURN. And they were decorated with vampire bats and other underworld symbols.'

'Vampire bats?' Linda asked.

'Have you studied anything about the Mayan concept of the underworld?'

'Not really,' Linda admitted.

'It's fascinating. Xibalbá they called it – Place of Fright. They believed it was grim, watery, and disease ridden. Full of torments and tortures. The average person was doomed to spend life after death there, but it was possible to escape. And they had myths about heroes and heroines who fought or tricked or played their way out of the underworld.'

'How did the bats figure into it?'

'Xibalbá was multi-leveled, with lots of rooms. And one of the most terrible places to be was the Bat Room. Imagine it, a dark, fetid cavelike room full of vampire bats. Pretty terrifying, isn't it? So, essentially, those stones were supposed to be guarding the entrance to hell. Or the Mayan version of hell.'

Linda seemed to be transfixed, so Iris continued.

'Everyone else was concentrating on the pyramid and clearing the way down the staircase. I wasn't needed there

19

so' – she shrugged – 'I decided, why not go to hell?'

Linda laughed. 'Couldn't you come in through the tunnel though?'

'It's completely sealed and will be a big excavation job, so the size and depth of the chamber were mapped with testing rods. Then we punched out a back door.'

'God, it's all so exciting! Sometimes I have to pinch myself because I can't believe I'm really here. On a dig with Daniel Becker and Iris Lanier! My parents wanted to give me a cruise for Christmas but I talked them into paying my way here instead.'

Iris was amused at being put into the same category as Daniel Becker, but she didn't comment.

'You know I majored in archaeology because of Dr Becker's television specials. I mean I was never a whiz like you were in school.' She chuckled. 'Nobody ever wanted to give me any big awards like that Kaliker thing you won. But I've always been determined . . . you know? I've always known I wanted a career like this. And then when I had my chart done last summer the astrologer told me some things that . . . well, it was just obvious that I was destined to come to Guatemala. My astrologer helped me convince my parents.'

'You have your own astrologer?'

Linda shrugged as if to say, *Of course, doesn't everyone?*

'And you actually base your decisions on what this astrologer tells you?'

'Sure. Nancy and Ronald Reagan used an astrologer while he was in the White House. I mean, I'm not saying that those little generic horoscopes in magazines are worth anything, but real astrology is serious.'

Iris didn't want to say how ridiculous she thought that was so she didn't say anything.

'I can tell you don't believe in it. So . . . what do you believe in? Religion? Transcendentalism? Reincarnation? Divine destiny? That prophecy thing everybody

20

was reading about?' Linda grinned. 'Fortune cookies?'

*Privacy*, Iris thought to herself. Why did people think they were entitled to that sort of private information?

'Everyone believes in something,' Linda prodded. 'I took a philosophy class all about how there's this human need for mystery. For beliefs.'

Iris stopped and stared down at the tool in her hand. She didn't want to answer. She didn't expect herself to answer but somehow it happened. 'I believe in science,' she heard herself say. 'The power of science. The power of facts and knowledge to make the world better.'

Linda sat back on her heels and regarded Iris with a searching curious gaze. 'Yeah . . . but beyond all that. I mean, what kind of mysterious magical things do you believe in?'

Iris lowered her eyes again. She didn't like this sudden intimacy with Linda but she had to admit that the conversation was intriguing. It was as though she didn't know the answers herself until she heard herself speak them.

'Magical things? My work is magical at times. I believe in the magic that comes when I work.'

'Oh, come on. There's got to be more.'

'When I was young I believed in all sorts of things.'

'What happened?'

'Nothing. I grew up I guess. I learned to rely on my intellect rather than my imagination.'

'But Dr Becker says that imagination and intuition are part of being a great scientist.'

'Dr Becker is a showman.'

'He says it was imagination and vision that led him to this city and to Jaguar Eyes' tomb down inside the pyramid.'

'He knows how to tell a good story.'

'But I've heard others talk about having hunches and visions, too. And Tim says all the time that epigraphy is eighty percent art and only twenty percent science.'

'Maybe they want to give their work a mystique,' Iris said. 'But there's nothing supernatural about it at all. They studied hard. They learned. And now they're good at what they do.'

Linda shrugged, obviously unconvinced.

'I overheard Tim talking to Dr Becker this morning,' she said, lowering her voice to a confidential tone. 'Whether it's imagination or not, he's made some real breakthroughs. There's still a lot left to translate – with so many glyphs on the walls and all the carvings and everything – but Tim says he's got the story on Jaguar Eyes. The king was a real warrior type. Most of the writing in there is about his great battles with other cities. Which is pretty much what you'd expect. But there was something about his wife . . . Tim thinks her name was Moonsmoke. Lady Moonsmoke, I guess, since she was married to the Sun Lord. Anyway, Tim told Dr Becker about how Moonsmoke and Jaguar Eyes had several kids and were a real popular ruling couple.'

Linda paused for dramatic effect.

'Then the story gets really good. Things were going great for Jaguar Eyes until he lost a big battle and was captured and presumed dead. Moonsmoke took over as ruler. The people loved her. Life was better than ever in the city.

'Then one day Jaguar Eyes returned. He had been a captive and had escaped. There was a happy reunion. He took his place as king again and everything went back to normal, but then he started planning another war.

'Suddenly, Moonsmoke disappeared. Vanished. Poof. Kind of a pre-Christian runaway mother, I guess, except where could she run to back in those days? Anyway, her husband and kids were devastated and the whole city went into mourning.'

Iris froze in place and studied Linda's face. 'Why are you telling me this?'

Linda frowned, uncertainty in her eyes. 'Because it's really hot news and I thought you'd be interested.'

Iris stared into the woman's face, searching for some sign of evil intent. She felt suspended. Paralyzed. Unable to do anything but drag air in and out of her lungs and stare at that face. Was Linda mocking her?

'What's wrong? What did I say? Was I talking too much or something?'

'Please . . .' Iris had to force the words out. 'I need some time alone. I—'

'Sure! No problem.' Linda stood and pocketed her trowel. 'I'll go on up to lunch.'

After the woman was gone, Iris leaned sideways against the chamber's rough wall. She was shaking. Her heart was pounding.

Huddling against the wall, she pulled her legs up and hugged them to her chest, pressed her face against her knees, squeezed her eyes shut so tightly that she saw patterns and colors. Then Mayan bats and demons. Then a strange woman's face contorted in pain.

'No!' Her voice echoed hollowly in the burial chamber. 'No! No! No!'

# Two

Some time later Iris opened her eyes and lifted her head. The chamber was just as before, silent and comforting, unchanged by the burst of human emotions. *Was she losing her mind?* The absurdity of her behavior filled her with an embarrassment that verged on shame. She leaned back against the wall, feeling weak and spent, as though she had just outrun a monster.

Number six stretched out beside her. The skeleton looked very odd, lying half in and half out of the tunnel, lower legs and feet bare, upper legs cloaked lightly in earth, pelvis naked. The effect was undignified.

'We can't leave you this way,' Iris said.

She pulled herself back into work position, grabbed a trowel, and leaned forward, toward the solidly filled tunnel that still imprisoned six's upper body. Starting at the outside, she worked inward, shaky at first but then gathering strength and chopping at the dirt with swift, vicious strokes, sinking the sharpened blade into eons of hardpacked dirt as though it were the enemy, hollowing out the tunnel and roughing out a shape for a body that no longer existed. When the fire in her muscles had burned away the last of the nightmare, she put down her trowel and took a break. She stretched her neck and arms, rotated her shoulders, shook out her hands. Then she moved several buckets of dirt to the corner.

It was time to go up. She was hungry and tired. Lunch

25

was long over but she could at least find a snack. She untied the rolled cotton bandanna from around her head, shook it out and wiped the sweat and dirt from her face, lifted her heavy braid of hair and wiped her neck, then swabbed the cloth across her chest and down between her breasts.

She tilted her canteen up for a drink of tepid water and thought of ice. What a luxury ice seemed to her now. She closed her eyes and fantasized about all the luxuries of civilization – ice cubes clinking in a glass, bathtubs full of hot water, real beds. But she had to smile at herself because the yearnings were not really wishes. She did not want to leave the dig.

She turned back to number six, finished up to mid-back. As always, there was no good place to stop. She hated to stop. If she could just do a little more. Maybe up to the shoulders.

She picked up her trowel and began again, slow this time, but steady, pacing herself. Dig. Dig. Dig. Suddenly there was a jarring crunch and the twang of stressed metal. Iris felt the jolt all the way up her arm. She had struck something. Something very hard. Probably a rock that had been mixed with the fill dirt.

She reached up and explored with gloved fingertips. Yes, it was definitely a rock. Oddly shaped. Narrow and flat. She dug on each side of it, thinking she would free it and then use the trowel to lever it out. But it was long. A long shaft of rock positioned vertically and very solidly.

She stripped off her cotton digging glove, reached in, and explored again, running her fingertips over the hard, cool surface. Then she jerked her hand back and spun to reach for the miner's lamp. This was no rock. It was a tool. Something shaped and elaborately carved. She sighed impatiently at her own carelessness. The dirt had been so clean that she'd become inattentive and now she might have damaged a valuable artifact.

She positioned the light and worked the object with a short-bristled, medium-stiff brush. Then she pulled her magnifying glass from the case and leaned close. It was a long shaft carved into a twining design. Like two snakes wound around each other.

Iris considered climbing out and asking Becker or Tim or one of the other archaeologists to come down and look. But she hesitated. They were all so busy with the king's tomb and so enchanted with the treasures there that they probably wouldn't want to come down. They wouldn't want to be bothered.

Excuses. She admitted to herself, almost as quickly as the thoughts formed, that they were really just excuses. The truth was that she didn't want to involve the others. The chamber was hers. She didn't want the archaeologists to decide it was interesting and take over. Let them stay in the tomb with Jaguar Eyes. These women in the underworld were hers.

She bent feverishly to work with brushes and picks, cleaning not only the object but the portion of the skeleton that was below it. Finally the nature of the carved shaft was revealed. It was the handle of a knife. A small portion of the top of the blade was visible, too. It was quite beautiful. Crafted of obsidian. Broad and flat, with a hand-chipped surface that gave it a faceted gleam. The balance of the blade was still buried in the back of the prone woman just as it had been when it was plunged into her. Earth now held it in place. The earth that had filled the bones as the flesh decayed.

Iris repositioned the lamp and sat down on the packed dirt floor. She stared into the gaping maw of the tunnel, illuminated by the glaring light. The woman had obviously been sacrificed, like her companions, but there was something odd about her position in the tunnel and about the method of her death. Iris couldn't remember hearing of any other sacrificial victims found with knives left in them.

27

Lightly, she ran her fingers down the elegant shaft of the woman's femur. 'What happened to you?' she said, feeling as if the answers were there, but just beyond her reach.

She closed her eyes and tried to imagine the long-dead woman as she'd been in life. A textbook image was all that came to her mind. Even in her imagination she could not breach the gulf of time and culture to see the woman as a real human being.

But then that was the big reason she had specialized in historical remains. As long as she couldn't imagine the people, the bones had no power to haunt her.

'All right,' she whispered and reached to turn off the light. But another irregularity caught her eye. There was an edge of something peeking out from underneath the chest.

She worked it with a brush. It was a curved edge, one-quarter-inch thick, and it seemed to indicate that the chest of the skeleton was lying on a disk-like object. Damn. She'd have to call in the archaeologists if this was another artifact.

Before she could wrestle with her conscience any further her thoughts were interrupted by an incongruous sound. It was the sound of a vehicle. Faint but unmistakable. She cocked her head and listened. The weekly mail and supply delivery was not due for days. No one was scheduled to leave. The ruins were too remote to attract curious tourists or spontaneous visitors, and volunteers arrived by invitation only.

Maybe it was one of the project's benefactors making a surprise inspection of the progress. That had happened once before. Becker would be in a panic if that were true. Not that they weren't making progress. The work was going well, but Becker would be frantic if he didn't have a prepared song and dance to launch into.

She stood and slapped the dust off her faded jeans. It was

settled. She would go up now and worry about number six later. The engine sound died. She pictured a fancy Land-Rover full of overweight men in safari suits and women in fashionable sun hats and heavy gold jewelry.

Quickly, she toed on her sandals and climbed up the crude wooden ladder, through her own personal rabbit hole and into the still afternoon air. The light made her blink. There was always a moment of disorientation when she came out. A momentary half-blind dizziness that came with re-entering the world of the living.

She skirted the tumbled stones around the tomb's true entrance and started toward the tent compound. The compound had been erected on the outer edge of the central plaza, on the flat remains of a broad roadway. Military-style tents marched down the road in a line, pitched on wooden platforms so that the ground beneath wasn't disturbed and so crawling slithering things were discouraged from visiting and they were above the rivers of water that ran across the land during tropical downpours. Off to the side was one jumbo-sized tent, nicknamed the Club, which served as the communal dining and meeting area. Along with cooking equipment it held several long hand-hewn wooden tables with benches. Three of the tent's sides were kept rolled up and hung with panels of white mosquito netting. The netting floated with the slightest stir of air, like long sheer curtains around a garden-party canopy.

From a distance she could tell that there was no one at the compound or the Club so she turned and headed toward the city center. She passed a battered Jeep, obviously the vehicle whose arrival she'd heard, but not quite the luxury transportation she'd envisioned. Some of her eagerness dissipated. A Jeep like that hadn't brought the kind of visitors she'd imagined. She considered going back to the Club and looking for food, but a slight curiosity remained.

She cut through the forest. Huge multicolored parrots screeched overhead and streaked through the trees, flashing brilliantly against the dark leafy canopy. They were the same kind of birds that brought thousands of dollars in US pet shops. Birds that would soon be on the brink of extinction in the wild. Here, in the Petén of Guatemala, they were frequently the main course for Sunday dinner, roasted and eaten by families whose income for an entire year of backbreaking labor wouldn't buy a pet shop parrot in the States.

Parrots were not valued here in this land of fearful ignorance. A land where human labor was cheap. Where life itself was cheap.

But who was she kidding with her arrogant North American assessments? Life was declining in value everywhere. Hadn't she read that the average victim of a robbery-murder in the States was killed for less than two hundred dollars?

The spongy forest floor gave way to hard paving stones and she entered the central complex, a collection of buildings and plazas where the city's population had gathered to cheer decapitations and heart removals and various other community activities. Though the paving stones were still in place, tenacious little trees and vines had managed to sprout anyway, covering everything with a layer of green. She cut between two structures, then turned into the heart of the complex. Everyone was there. They were standing in a huddle near the largest pyramid. Becker was in the center. Off to the side a man she assumed to be the Jeep's driver was laughing with the project's two hired natives. There were no patrons in designer denims or safari hats.

She saw Linda and wondered if the woman had told everyone of Iris's strange behavior in the chamber.

Becker looked up then and spotted her. 'Iris!' he called. The urgency in his voice carried across the open space between them.

The huddle opened and fanned out, and she saw that Becker was holding a yellow piece of paper. It was the standard yellow of a telegram. Was that possible? A telegram delivered to the rain forest in Guatemala?

She wondered if their permission to dig had been revoked. Or if one of Becker's key benefactors had withdrawn financial support.

Becker waved the yellow paper in the air. 'This is for you, Iris.'

'For me?'

Rather than hurrying forward she stopped. Everyone's eyes slid toward her in guilty curiosity. She had the irrational urge to run away and hide in the jungle.

Becker came toward her.

'Iris, are you OK?'

He took her arm and the contact startled her. She wasn't accustomed to being touched.

'Here,' he said, forcefully placing the telegram in her hand.

It was addressed to Dr Iris Lanier.

JOHN LANIER CRITICAL CONDITION.
MORNINGSIDE HOSPITAL. NEW YORK CITY.
COME IMMEDIATELY.

She read it through three times, then turned and started toward her tent, walking slowly at first, but running by the time she reached the compound. Becker must have been running too because he ducked through the tent flaps right behind her.

'Iris! Iris! Who's John Lanier?'

She faced Daniel Becker in the confines of the tent. There was only a narrow area down the center where an adult could stand up straight and his presence in the small space felt like an invasion of privacy.

'He's my father,' she said.

31

'But . . .' Becker's authoritative manner dissolved into puzzlement. 'I thought . . . On the forms you filled there was no next of kin listed.'

She turned away so she wouldn't have to meet his eyes, then bent to pull her large suitcase out from under the cot.

'What do you intend to do?'

She put the suitcase on the cot and unzipped it. Inside were more chambray shirts and jeans identical to the ones she had on. This was where she stored her clean clothes. All she had to do was add a few things and throw her toiletries into her carry-on bag.

'Damn it, Iris! Talk to me!'

She faced him. He was close to her own five foot eight and they both had to stoop slightly to stand in the tent.

'I'm going to see my father. There's nothing to talk about.'

'Wait a minute.' He held up his hands as though stopping traffic. 'Will you just calm down and look at this logically.'

'I am calm, Daniel. The telegram says to come. I'm going.'

'There's no allowance for extra travel in the budget,' he reminded her. 'Your trip here with the team was paid for and your return trip with the team will be paid for, but that's all.'

'I realize it will have to come out of my own pocket,' she said.

'You think you're just running out of here? How do you expect to leave?'

'I'll ride out with the driver who delivered the telegram.'

'He's staying the night.'

'I'll pay him extra to take me to Flores now.'

'Even if he will take you . . . there's only one flight a day out of Flores-St Elena. You'll probably miss it. Or it will be full. And then you still have to get a seat on the flight out of Guatemala City.'

32

'I'll deal with the problems as they arise.'

'This is insane. It's too big a risk. A foreign woman traveling alone . . . Don't you remember that European woman who was stoned awhile back because some mothers thought she was giving the evil eye to their babies?'

'I have to go, Daniel.'

'All right. But consider this. I'm due in Guatemala City next week for a series of meetings. You can go with me and I'll make sure you get a commercial flight out. I could even leave a day early. That would put you in the air, safely *en route* to New York, in just five days.'

Five days. She didn't know when her father had been hospitalized or how long it had taken for the telegram to reach her. Five more days?

'I'm going now.'

'Christ . . . You don't know if he's still in the hospital. You don't know if he'll be discharged by the time you can make it there. You don't even know if this is legitimate!'

She ignored him and surveyed the tent. Her dirty clothes were in a bag in the corner. She would leave them and her other suitcase.

Becker was silent long enough for her to hope he had given up and was about to leave, but instead he moved some of her books and sat down on the extra cot. She was uncomfortable with his presence in the tent, even with him sitting quietly. During the entire four months she had never had a tentmate. It had just worked out that way. She was the only woman on the team and female volunteers had always seemed to arrive in pairs so that they shared a tent separate from hers.

She could feel Becker's scrutiny. She didn't like being watched. And she didn't like it that he'd moved her books without asking her. Everything was arranged just so – her stacks of books on the extra cot, her laptop computer and disks on the small table against the back. It wasn't particularly neat but it was the way she wanted it and she

33

didn't like someone else coming along and making changes.

'So you have this father in New York whom you don't think enough of to put down as next of kin, but you're willing to drop everything and put yourself at risk just to—'

'California,' she said, without looking up from her packing.

'What?'

'My father lives in California.'

'Damn, poor guy must have been on his vacation.'

'My father doesn't take vacations.'

'Well, business trip then . . . Whatever. My point is that it was bad luck for him to end up in a hospital clear across the country from his home.'

She stopped and pulled the telegram out of her pocket to read again. New York. She had read the words but hadn't absorbed them.

'New York,' she said in disbelief. 'He's never been out of California before.'

'Well, there you have it,' Becker said smugly. 'Something is fishy. I'll get on the radio and arrange for a call to the hospital in New York. Find out what's really going on. You never know. It could be a prank. A false alarm. A mistaken identity. By this evening we can have the real story and formulate a plan.'

'I have a plan, Daniel. I'm leaving. Now.'

'Oh. Well excuse me. I should have known you'd be too stubborn to listen to a practical solution.'

He hesitated, then asked her the question that she suspected had been foremost in his mind all along. 'What about the work? Everything has to be done and moved out and sealed up before the rainy season. If you're not going to finish that chamber you're working on . . .'

His words trailed off but she completed the threat in her mind. *Then I'll have to get someone else who's more*

34

*dependable. Then you won't get any of the credit for the work you did. Then you won't have a place on my team anymore. Then there won't be any job offers.*

'I'll come back,' she said.

'We're out of here in forty-five days.'

'I know. I'll be back in time to finish my work on the last woman.'

'Woman?'

'Yes. I did the pelvis today. It's clearly another woman.'

'A young virgin who died a gruesome death?' he asked hopefully.

She felt a twinge of conscience. Should she tell him about the knife in the woman's back and the mysterious disc beneath her chest? If she did she had no doubt that the work would be taken over by someone else.

'Sorry. She's closer to a middle-aged mother. Nothing to attract the media for you.'

'Ahhh, I'm not worried. Jaguar Eyes' tomb will knock their socks off without any virgins involved.'

There was a weighted pause. She knew what was coming before he said it.

'You realize we'll have to open the sarcophagus without you if you're not back in time?'

'I'll be back,' she assured him.

Daniel Becker was a thorough and methodical researcher. When they opened the king's burial vault he made everyone hold back, approaching the treasures slowly, one by one. Iris had photographed and recorded and examined the skeletons crouched just inside the outer door and then packed them up for removal. After that there was nothing more for her to do because Becker insisted that all the clay figurines and carved jade discs and painted polychrome vessels be attended to and that a cursory study be done on the wealth of glyphs that adorned the inner walls of the tomb before the heavy lid of the sarcophagus was moved and Jaguar

Eyes' remains were unveiled.

The king's bones were still waiting, undisturbed, and she was determined to be the one to study them.

'You know you missed the big announcement over lunch, Iris.' Becker's demeanor changed, as though he had accepted her leaving and dismissed it. 'Tim has finally found the missing pieces to that biggest stela and he's discovered that the figures definitely depict Jaguar Eyes and his wife. So we have a good portrait of the old boy. Much better than the one on the sarcophagus lid.'

Iris stopped what she was doing and stared down without seeing. The stela he was referring to had been found months before, toppled and broken into three massive chunks, apparently the victim of a collapsed wall from a nearby building. The middle and top pieces had sheared off cleanly, but the bottom one had fragments missing and the glyphs carved into it were unreadable without those fragments.

She had watched as a group of men struggled with pulleys and winches to lift the huge chunks of stone, fitting them back together so that the column of stone stood upright again, intact except for the splintered-off areas near the bottom. Viewed as a whole the stela was stunning, a grand piece of art by any culture's standards. The sculpting was deep and intricate and precise. The large central figures had an awesome power.

She had assumed immediately that the male was a god or a king. He was standing in semi-profile, decked out in fierce war regalia, his bearing arrogant, his body sturdy and well-muscled. He had the high sloping forehead, strong beaked nose, and tilted epicanthic eyes that were the Mayan male ideal, and his well-defined mouth was curved into the faintest suggestion of a smile, victorious and mocking, cruel in Iris's opinion, though no one else had agreed with her.

He was looking down at the female figure who was

kneeling and facing forward, gazing out from the stone as though watching all who came to stand before her. She too was dressed in elaborate finery. Intricately woven robes and heavy bracelet cuffs. Large earrings, a necklace as big as a breastplate and a spectacular headdress. Her hands were delicate and her fingernails long and well shaped. Her face was round and symmetrical, her eyes perfect almonds, her mouth full.

But it was her expression that haunted Iris. In the woman's face the artist had captured something unforgettable and timeless. A wisdom. A sadness. A solemnity that was almost Zen-like in its intensity.

Iris was so eerily affected by the portrait that she could not look at the stela without emotional discomfort. She was drawn to it, yet tried to avoid going near because she found her reactions unsettling. In all the Mayan art she had studied or seen pictured, she had never felt anything but a scholarly curiosity, but this stela, this sad wise face, had even entered her dreams at night.

Now the face had an identity.

'That's Moonsmoke,' she said, more to herself than to Becker.

'Right! How did you know her name?'

'Oh . . .' She shrugged. 'Linda.'

Becker grimaced and shook his head. 'I should have known. That girl is quite the disseminator of information, isn't she?'

'Woman, Daniel. She's a woman.'

'Right. Right.' He studied his hands a moment. 'I can get someone else to finish out the chamber, Iris.'

She swung around. 'I know you can! But I'm promising you I'll be back. You can trust me to complete the work I've started.'

'Jesus, you're difficult. You know, it's not enough to be talented in your field, Iris. You've got to learn how to play

37

the game. Or . . . you'll have to find someone who'll play for you.'

'Please, Daniel. I don't have the patience for euphemisms right now. What is it you want to say?' She waited, expecting him finally to admit that he'd decided against offering her the position. That he didn't want to work with her anymore. That she could take all her belongings and leave because he didn't want her to come back.

'Forget it,' he said, and leaped up off the cot. 'Bad timing on my part. But you're coming back, right? So we'll have plenty of opportunity to talk then.'

'Right,' she agreed, feeling relief.

'You're leaving your computer and your books?' he asked, looking around the tent.

'Yes. There's no point in taking it all if I'm coming back.'

'Right. OK then.'

He edged around her toward the tent opening, stopped, and for a moment seemed as though he might try to hug her. Quickly she lifted the suitcase from the cot and held it between them.

'OK then,' he repeated. 'I'll go fix it with the driver for you.' He took the suitcase from her and ducked out through the opening of the tent.

Iris hefted her carry-on bag to her shoulder. It was heavy. Crammed with computer backup disks as well as her personal items. She would leave the computer but she had to have her backup disks with her for peace of mind. She turned and surveyed her tiny living space. There was nothing left to do.

What if he was dying?

What if he died before she could get there?

She had been concentrating on the details of leaving and refusing to think about her father, but suddenly it broadsided her, catching her unprotected so that it felt like a sharply delivered punch and she clutched her stomach against the pain of it.

'Hey!' she heard Becker yell somewhere outside. 'Get that driver down here!'

She stepped out of the tent into the still afternoon heat. The forest was quiet. Even the tenacious green tendrils choking the ancient stone demons looked as though they had wilted and given up. She was fearful. Both of the trip and of what she might find at the end of it. She palmed the sweat from her forehead, adjusted the weight on her shoulder, and started forward.

# II

## *The Jungle*

# Three

'Don't touch the dog,' growled the uniformed handler at the end of the German shepherd's leash. The dog himself wasn't growling. He was eager and enthusiastic, thoroughly enjoying his work, tail waving and eyes bright.

Iris watched the shepherd slowly sniff his way toward her, poking his nose at one traveler after another in the customs inspection line. It was one of several lines that snaked through the chaotic international arrivals area in New York's Kennedy Airport. The only happy face in the crowd was the dog's. All the humans looked as tired and impatient as she herself felt.

The dog drew nearer. He reminded her of Togo, her father's favorite dog. Long dead now. Hit by a car when she was twelve or thirteen. It was the only time she ever saw her father cry and she still remembered the astonishment she'd felt at those tears. And then the resentment. She had actually hated poor sweet dead Togo as she watched her father hold the limp body and weep into the fur. That night she had crawled out of her window and met Jeff in the orchard to drink a pilfered bottle of cheap whiskey. She had been sick for days afterward but her father hadn't noticed.

Another childhood memory.

Under normal circumstances she rarely thought about her childhood and she seldom had an unbidden recollection that predated her graduate days in college. But now

43

she felt besieged by memories. They heightened her anxieties for her father, or maybe they were caused by her anxieties for her father. She wasn't sure. Either way, her customary calm was wearing thin.

She had called the hospital from Guatemala City and they had verified that, indeed, John Lanier of Santa Clara, California, was a patient, but they would give no further information over the phone. Nothing. Not a word about his condition. Not a clue as to whether he'd been in an accident or had a heart attack or contracted a disease. In desperation she had called Yoshi Hirano in California to find out if the old man knew anything.

'I can tell you nothing more,' Hirano said gruffly. 'I thought about going to New York myself, but who would look after the orchard?'

And that voice from the past had added to her turmoil. It had struck her like a stone falling into still water. Sending out ripples that circled and spread. Stirring up sediment that had lain peacefully on the bottom for so many years.

'Oh, Christ! I just picked all the hairs off my suit from the dog who met my plane,' a man in back of her complained as the German shepherd moved closer.

But the dog stopped just ahead, intent upon a young pregnant woman. She was cinnamon-skinned with vaguely Mayan features. Iris had noticed her on the flight from Flores-St Elena and again on the flight from Guatemala City, and had felt sympathy for her. She appeared to be nervous and possibly ill. On both flights she had made frequent trips down the aisle to the bathroom.

The dog became increasingly animated. He danced and yipped and lunged toward the woman while she backed away in wide-eyed terror. Suddenly, she spun and ran. Uniformed men materialized to chase her, their expressions grim yet infused with excitement.

The entire room went silent and people pulled back,

44

creating an open area that set her flight apart, as though it was a spontaneous performance, a drama for the distraction of weary travelers. One pursuer grabbed at her clothing. She jerked free, then slipped, and fell forward. A collective gasp escaped from hundreds of throats as she pitched toward the floor. When her swollen belly hit, there was a crack, like the breaking of a ripe walnut. Then the dark uniforms descended, vulturelike, and she was obscured from view – either unable to get up or prevented from it by her captors.

Heart pounding, Iris scanned the room for signs of emergency help on the way. Anger combined with her concern for the woman's condition and she thought that she should do something. Someone should do something. But she didn't move and neither did anyone else.

A phalanx of uniforms cut through the tense crowd and hurried toward the trouble. Reinforcements. *How many armed men did it take to subdue a four-and-a-half-foot-tall pregnant woman who was lying on the floor?*

With the arrival of help, the small knot of men surrounding the woman relaxed. They straightened and stepped back, giving Iris a view of their captive. The woman was still on the floor. Curled there like a wounded animal. A low murmuring swept through the crowd, intensifying as she was roughly pulled to her feet.

Then, in an instant, all of Iris's anger and sympathy turned to disgust because the woman's swollen belly was now flattened. Plastic tubes of white powder dropped from beneath her dress, landing at her feet in a pile of fat pale worms.

Iris turned away, annoyed with herself for falling prey, emotionally, to the subterfuge. Non-involvement was always the best policy. She had learned that long ago.

'He made me do it!' the woman screamed in broken English as she was taken away. 'He says he will kill my kids if I don' do it!'

45

What would happen to those kids now, Iris wondered as she continued on toward an inspection station. But it was pointless to wonder. There was too much. Too much wrong. And the only way to stay sane was to ignore it.

Hours later Iris finally stood in a wide, brightly lit, hospital corridor, holding her luggage, staring at a door marked NO VISITORS EXCEPT FAMILY.

Her father was behind that door. Her father who she hadn't seen in six years.

'Hey! You can't go in there!'

She turned her head toward the source of the warning and saw that the voice belonged to a janitor with a mop in his hand.

'It's my father's room,' she said.

The man jammed the mop down into a wheeled metal bucket and walked toward her. He had the small mean eyes of a bully.

'Did you check in with the charge nurse?' he demanded.

Had she? Her thoughts were disordered from exhaustion. What was a charge nurse?

'You gotta check in and get clearance before you can go in there.' He pointed down the hall. 'Nurse's station is that way. Go left where the halls cross.'

Dragging her wheeled suitcase, Iris went in the direction he indicated. She turned left and saw a carpeted visitors lounge with a large coffee urn on a back table. She stopped. One of the naugahyde couches was occupied by a forlorn looking woman in clothes that had been attractive before they were slept-in. The woman had long grey-streaked hair drifting loose from a knot atop her head. Her turquoise-braceleted hands were folded in her lap and her eyes stared sightlessly at the floor.

Iris hesitated, considering whether she could get a cup of coffee without disturbing the woman. Leaving her

46

suitcase in the hall, she walked quietly across the carpeting toward the urn. The woman did not look up.

There was a tabloid newspaper on the table beside the coffee urn. It was the first Iris had seen since returning to the States. Quietly, she flipped a few pages.

LOCKET KILLER CLAIMS NINTH VICTIM
MOTHER HANGS BABY
OMAHA STUDENT BLUDGEONS COACH
SON BEHEADS FATHER
DENVER COUPLE SLAIN BY MASKED JOGGER.

She hadn't seen any US news the entire time she was in Guatemala, yet somehow all the headlines were vaguely familiar to her. It was like turning on a television soap opera years later and immediately knowing what was happening. The peaceful order of the dig and the serenity of the underground chamber seemed like a dream from another time.

She put the paper down and eased a Styrofoam cup from the stack next to the urn. Then she stopped. What was she doing, reading a paper and having coffee? She was stalling, that's what she was doing. She had traveled so far yet she was afraid now actually to see her father.

From behind her came a hollow female voice. 'It's empty. I've been here for days and there's never been any coffee. You have to go down to the . . .'

Iris turned.

'. . . cafeteria . . .' The woman's voice trailed off as she looked into Iris's face. Her body stiffened. Her eyes went wide then skipped away as though she was embarrassed or offended, or even frightened.

Iris glanced down at herself. She knew she was travel worn, but she did look bad enough to cause alarm?

'Thank you,' she said and hurried back out to the hallway.

47

When she was almost to the nurse's station she glanced back over her shoulder and saw that the woman had moved to the lounge doorway and was standing there, staring after her. The bizarre scrutiny made her want to drop her luggage and run.

Behind the nurse's station desk was a sturdy, broad-hipped woman in a white pantsuit. The woman was talking on the phone.

'Can I help you?' the nurse asked finally in a no-nonsense, almost impatient tone.

'Yes. My father, John Lanier, is a patient.'

The woman frowned. 'You have identification?'

Iris took out an expired driver's license and her passport. Immediately the woman picked up the phone again, pressed 0 and said, 'Page Dr Milford for me. I need him in 408.' Keeping the receiver at her ear, she consulted a card taped to the side of the counter and dialed again.

'Hello, is Detective Kizmin or Detective Barney there?' The woman rolled her eyes at whatever she was hearing, then said, 'Yes, it's important. It's about John Lanier. I was told to call if—'

Iris could not make sense of the conversation. A detective? Why was the nurse calling a detective?

'Yes. Yes. I'll wait. But I'm busy. I can't wait too long.' With the phone cradled between her ear and shoulder the nurse bent over and began making checkmarks on a long list.

'Would you please tell me—' Iris started to ask, but the nurse began speaking into the phone again.

'Fine with me,' she said belligerently. 'Just don't go saying I didn't call.' She dropped the receiver and studied Iris with a critical gaze.

'You look beat,' she said.

'Yes, well, it was a long trip.'

The nurse seemed to be wrestling with a decision. Finally she said, 'No rule in my book says I can't take you in,' and she moved out from behind the counter.

Iris followed. They passed the visitors lounge and she saw with relief that the strange woman was gone. She concentrated on her stride, staying slightly behind the nurse, letting the sturdy professionalism pull her along. The woman's white synthetic clothing made swishing noises. Iris wanted to ask what was wrong with her father but she felt guilty for not knowing. *A good daughter would know.*

As they approached his door panic fluttered in her stomach and she thought that maybe she shouldn't go in. Maybe it would be a shock to him. Maybe the nurse should tell him that his daughter was in the hospital – ask him when he wanted to see her. Whether he wanted to see her.

The man with the mop nodded and said, 'Hey Helen,' as they passed.

'Hey yourself,' the nurse returned without enthusiasm. She jerked her head toward Iris. 'This is Mr Lanier's daughter.'

Iris could feel the man's eyes on her.

The nurse hit the door with her shoulder. 408. NO VISITORS EXCEPT FAMILY. It swung open with a snicker of pneumatic hinges. Iris followed in the nurse's wake, eyes riveted to the white-clad back, heart roaring, palms damp, feeling like she had stumbled into quicksand and was being sucked down. Back down to childhood. To a time when she was eight years old – overwhelmed by emotions. Devoured by emotions.

The nurse stopped. Iris stopped. The door closed behind her. There was an unnatural stillness in the room punctuated by rhythmic beeping. The pattern of a heart-beat. And there was a bed. White sheets. A form on the bed.

'Hi John,' the nurse called heartily. 'I brought you a surprise.'

Iris let go of her suitcase leash and stared.

'He's been through a lot,' the nurse said. 'You OK?'

Iris didn't bother to nod. Of course she was OK. It was the man in the bed who was not OK. The desiccated husk of a man. The caricature of her father.

She had come assuming that he was sick, that he was critical, but this . . . this was beyond anything she had imagined.

The nurse briskly checked the various wires and tubes snaking from his body. Iris could not bring herself to move closer. One side of his head was swathed in white gauze so that only a half-face rested on the pillow. A bloodless, pale, half-face.

The visible eye flickered slightly but remained closed.

'Is he asleep?' Iris whispered.

The nurse regarded her with a puzzled frown. 'He's in a coma. Nobody told you that?'

Iris's knees gave way and she sank into a chair beside the bed.

'You know what a coma is, right?'

Iris nodded. Of course she knew what a coma was. But now, looking at her father, she wasn't sure exactly what it meant. Was he unconscious? Had his mind gone into hibernation? Was his brain still alive?

'What—' She had to stop and clear her throat. 'What exactly is wrong with him?'

The woman's frown deepened. 'I'm not supposed to do this king of thing. It's not my job.'

'What kind of thing?'

'I shouldn't have let you in here till you talked to the doctor.'

'Please, here I am, right beside him, and I need to know what's wrong.'

The nurse's eyes darted nervously toward the door. 'He was shot.' She adjusted the pillow beneath the bandaged head. 'Got yourself shot in the face, didn't you John? But

50

you're still with us. You're still in there fighting.'

'Shot?' Iris repeated the word in disbelief. 'Someone shot my father?'

'He probably didn't want to give them his money, but who knows. Sometimes they shoot you anyway. For no reason.'

'He came here, to New York, and someone shot him?'

'It happens. Tourists are just as good to rob as anybody. Probably better.'

Shot with a gun. Shot at close range by someone who had looked into his eyes, possibly spoken to him. Iris could not get her thoughts around it. She could not take it in. A stroke or heart attack. Cancer. Even a car accident. Those would have been terrible but they would have had a handle of familiarity. Something to grasp. But this. Her father being shot?

'I don't understand,' she said to herself and was surprised to hear her voice repeating the words aloud.

'Who does?' the nurse answered sadly. 'So many bad boys with guns. No one's safe anymore.'

The woman lifted John Lanier's arm free from under the sheet and gently straightened it. 'Pat him. Talk to him,' she urged.

Reluctantly, Iris extended her hand, but she pulled back before her fingertips touched his flesh. He had avoided physical contact with her when he was conscious and there was something obscene about touching him now when he couldn't object or move away.

The nurse frowned and started toward the door. 'I'll page Dr Milford again,' she said, and then she was gone.

Iris stared at her father's half-face against the pillow.

Shot.

Shot in the face.

She closed her eyes against the fluorescent brightness.

Shot in the face.

51

There was a lingering bitter scent, a blend of disinfectant and medication and urine. She had never been inside a hospital before. Doctors' offices yes, but never a hospital. Even her birth had been at home. She had never known her father to visit a hospital either. Did he know that he was imprisoned in a behemoth of a big city medical center? Did he know that someone had fired a gun at him? Did he know that she was there?

Her eyes stung suddenly and her throat closed so tightly that it ached. She pushed out of the chair and prowled the room, examining the tubes and wires, the labels on the liquids dripping into his veins. She flipped through a clipboard hanging from the end of the bed. The pages were full of cryptic notations that meant nothing to her. She began to pace. Back and forth. Back and forth. Eyes fixed on the bandaged half-face, the parody of her father.

A stomach churning dizziness came over her and suddenly she couldn't get enough air. She had to drag it into her lungs. And she realized that she was sobbing or hyperventilating or both, and she bit down hard on her knuckles for control.

There was a brisk knock at the door. Before she could reply, it swung open. She scrubbed at her face with her hands, trying to compose herself. A man walked in followed by a woman.

'I'm Detective Barney. This is Detective Kizmin. You're the daughter?'

The man was big and soft with sandy red hair atop a droopy scowling face. A bulldog face. His tan trenchcoat hung open, revealing a brown suit that didn't quite accommodate the heft of his belly.

The woman was hanging back a little, letting him take the lead. Iris hadn't caught her name at all. She was the opposite of her partner in more than just gender. Everything about her was polished and hard. Her severe hair.

Her prominent cheekbones and raven's-wing eyebrows. Her sleek charcoal suit and coat. The coat was wet on the shoulders. It must have started to rain.

'You've got identification?' the man asked, making the statement into both a question and a demand.

Again Iris pulled out her passport and license. The man glanced at them and passed them to the woman, who eyed them as though capable of seeing through the paper.

Iris watched her. The hardness was intriguing. It was uncommon to come across true hardness in a woman.

The woman had an interesting face, too. Iris tried to imagine the skull beneath the tan-gold skin. What a fascinating puzzle that skull would be. The narrow nasal opening that would indicate Caucasoid on the race-estimation charts. The high, straight forehead that would fall under Negroid. The cheekbones, with their distinctive zygomatic arch that so often signaled Native American or Mongoloid blood. Howell's Multivariate Test would never classify her. Maybe the woman's hardness came from her attempts to classify herself. Or from other people's attempts to classify her.

The passport and license were handed back abruptly and Iris said, 'Could I please see some identification from you?'

She asked mostly because she wanted to get their names straight, but she could tell immediately that the man took it as a challenge to his authority. His scowl deepened as he grudgingly fished in his pocket.

The woman showed no reaction at all. She waited until Iris was finishing examining her partner's ID then she held out a badge wallet. The gold shield was impressive. It looked newer and shinier than the man's. Maybe the woman's hardness had grown in the course of earning that shield.

Detective Barney and Detective Kizmin. Kizmin. An unusual name. Both of them detectives. Iris had to shake her head. It was all so unbelievable. Her father shot. Detectives studying her passport.

'OK . . .' the man said as though dispensing with formalities and signaling the true beginning of their interaction.

The woman produced a small notebook and clicked a ballpoint pen into writing position.

Iris straightened in her chair. It was ridiculous to be nervous. She was the daughter of the victim and not a criminal. She took a deep breath and clasped her hands tightly in her lap.

'How did you become aware of your father's circumstances?' Detective Barney asked.

'I got a message. Here, I have it.' She pulled the tattered yellow sheet from her pocket.

The detective scanned the sheet without touching it. He looked over at his partner who leaned forward to read, then took the sheet from Iris and put it into a small plastic bag.

'Who sent this?' Barney demanded.

'I assumed it was from the hospital.'

'Were any other relatives notified?'

'There aren't any other relatives.'

'No one at all?'

'No one.'

The detective wrote something in her little book.

'What's your permanent address?'

'I don't have one at this time.'

Barney glanced at Kizmin with an expression that was almost gleeful.

'No permanent address?' he said. 'Are you telling me you don't own anything? You don't live anywhere? You don't get bills or have a bank account?'

'I have some things in storage,' she said. 'I have a bank account, and my credit card is automatically paid from that account. I've been in Guatemala for four months

54

and— But what does any of this have to do with my father getting shot?'

'Where is this bank account?'

'Here. New York. I mean I opened it in New York but the bank has branches all over so—'

'So you're from New York?'

'No. But my first job after college was here. I don't see what—'

'You've been in Guatemala how long?'

'Just a little over four months. Since November. I was supposed to stay till the rains start in May. That's the end of the digging season.'

'Digging season? Is that the same as planting season?'

'No. That's digging as in archaeology. Mayan ruins. Not farming.'

Detective Barney's eyes narrowed a fraction as though Iris had said something suspicious. The woman made a note in her book.

'Travel back and forth to Guatemala often?' Barney asked with a casualness that was so contrived it was almost laughable.

'No. This is my first trip home.'

'Your father visit you in Guatemala?'

'No.'

'That's a long time without even one visit.'

'Exactly what are you implying?' Iris asked. 'That I didn't see my father enough, or that I'm lying?'

'I'm not implying anything,' the detective said. 'I'm gathering information.'

'Not very relevant information.'

The detective shot a glance at his partner as though to ask if she was hearing the same thing he was hearing.

'Revalent, huh? I'll be the judge of what's *revalent*,' he said, and she doubted that the mispronunciation was an intentional part of his ridicule.

'That's my job, lady. Collecting information and judging

what's what. Now, are you going to let me do my job?'

Iris nodded.

'So you're in archaeology?'

'Not really. I'm in physical anthropology . . . osteology.'

'Any friends visit you in Guatemala?'

'No. I'm living out at a dig site. The conditions are not conducive to having guests.'

Kizmin made notes. Barney went on.

'Why was your father in New York?'

'I don't know. I was hoping you could tell me.'

'Did he come to New York often?'

'I didn't know he'd ever been to New York. He . . .' They didn't understand. They didn't have any idea who or what her father was.

'My father is a fruit grower. He never leaves his orchards. Not for one night. Certainly not for days or weeks. He . . . he has routines, habits, ideas . . . that are cast in stone. I can't imagine why he's here. I can't imagine him here, period.'

Barney waited until she was finished then asked, 'Who would he have contacted in New York?' making her wonder if he had heard anything she'd said.

She sighed. 'No one that I know of.'

'Friends? Relatives? Business acquaintances?'

'No one that I know of.'

'So . . . Your father traveled to New York on an open-ended ticket and paid in advance for a room that rents by the month, and you're saying that you had no knowledge of this?'

'A room that rents by the month?' Just when she thought she had heard every unbelievable thing, there was something more.

'In advance,' Barney said smugly.

'I . . .' Iris stared down at the detective's scuffed brown shoes for a moment. 'My father and I don't keep in close contact.'

56

Kizmin made more notes. Iris wanted to grab the little book and read what the woman was writing. Undoubtedly it was all critical. *Unstable, immature, bad daughter. Certainly guilty of something.*

Barney leaned his forearms on the end of the metal bed and Iris realized that the man had not once glanced at her father's still form.

'Why would your father go out without taking his wallet?' Barney asked.

'He didn't always carry a wallet. He sometimes kept his money in a clip.'

'A clip?'

'A silver money-clip.' Iris made a vague descriptive motion with her hands.

'Did your father own a gun?'

'Only a shotgun. He used rock salt when there were stray dogs causing trouble.'

'Was your father a homosexual?'

'What kind of a question is that?'

'Just a simple yes or no question.'

Iris hesitated, then said, 'As far as I know he was straight. He hasn't had any kind of relationship since . . . since losing my mother.' She stopped. They had no business knowing any more. 'How can all these personal questions help you catch my father's mugger?'

'Who said your father was mugged?'

Iris rose from her chair. She knew she was gaping at the man but she couldn't help herself. No words came to her.

'Where can you be reached?' Barney demanded and Kizmin poised her pen to record the answer.

'If it wasn't a mugging . . .' Iris shook her head and looked from the man to the woman. 'If it wasn't a mugging, then what was it?'

'That's what we're working on,' Barney said, leaning toward her in a vaguely threatening manner. 'And we're gonna find the answers. Even if we have to go to Guatemala.'

Barney straightened the lapels of his coat. 'I need some air. Find out where we can reach her, Detective Kizmin.'

Iris stared after him, speechless. She watched the door swing shut on his exit, then she turned and looked at Detective Kizmin.

The woman was nearly six feet in flat-heeled shoes and she had the striking angularity of a fashion model, but there was no frivolity about her, no posing, no preening, nothing at all self-absorbed. She was as still and sharp-eyed as a perched raptor, with a seriousness that verged on menace.

'Where can you be reached?' the woman asked and Iris realized it was the first time she had spoken.

Iris drew in a deep breath. She wanted to sound steady and reasonable. Surely this woman was capable of listening to reason.

'My father is a crime victim, detective. He is not the criminal and neither am I. Now, exactly what happened to him and what are you doing about it?'

The woman fixed her with a penetrating stare, but Iris refused to be intimidated.

'You have no right to treat me like this.' The stare did not waver. 'I'm warning you . . . I have important people I can call.'

Even to her own ears the warning sounded half-hearted. Which it was because the last thing she wanted to do was call the Kaliker Foundation and ask for help.

'Oh,' the detective said, a dark wing of eyebrow shooting up in mock alarm. 'Then I'd better tell you what you want to hear.'

She flipped back several pages in her notebook and began to read.

'The victim, John Lanier, was shot in the face at close range, approximately two a.m. on 13 March in Riverside

58

Park.' The detective lifted her gaze from the notebook to Iris. 'That's not the kind of place where nice people go sightseeing in the middle of the night. That's a place to score drugs or sell drugs. Or to find a hooker. Or a victim.' She dropped her eyes to the page again. 'Thirty-eight-caliber slug recovered from victim's brain. Assailant unknown. No witnesses located; however, the ambulance driver saw someone hurrying from the scene as he pulled up. A woman. Possibly a prostitute.

'All the victim had in his pocket was his room keys so there was no way to identify him. Or to notify family. We had to trace the keys to locate his room. Found his wallet on the dresser inside or we still wouldn't know who he was.'

Kizmin focused on Iris, studying the effect of the information. 'The investigation is still in progress,' she said.

Iris tried to assimilate the terse recitation of facts. Nothing made sense to her.

'Anything you'd like to add?' Kizmin asked as though daring her to lie. 'Anything you haven't told me?'

Irish shook her head.

'Now, are you going to tell me where you can be reached?'

'I don't know yet,' Iris admitted.

She remembered all too well how expensive it had been to survive in New York. During her brief working experience in the city she had had to live like a pauper in order to make her salary cover her basic expenses and she knew that the city was even harder on the pockets of visitors.

The detective's gaze sharpened. 'You said you worked here after college. You probably have friends who can put you up for a while.'

'No.' Iris had to turn away from the piercing stare. 'There's no one.'

'How about all those important people you said you

59

could call . . . won't they help you find a place to stay?'

Iris ignored the sarcasm. 'I'll probably be here at the hospital most of the time. If not, I'll tell the nurse where I've gone.'

The detective handed her a business card, then glanced at John Lanier's still form. A minute softening occurred in her eyes. 'Most of your father's personal effects have been released, including the keys to his room. The nurse out on the desk has them. No reason you couldn't stay there. From a police standpoint, I mean.'

'Thank you.'

The detective walked out and the door settled shut behind her. Iris sank back into the chair. Carefully, so that she didn't touch her father, she leaned forward and rested her forehead on the bed. Her thoughts drifted.

*'Any fool can plant a tree. Squirrels plant trees when they bury their acorns. But grafting . . . grafting is something else. Grafting takes skill and faith, knowledge and commitment and patience.'*

*John Lanier was standing in the yard, bearish and tanned, his clothes streaked with rich dark dirt. He had led her to a tree that was split open right to the center. She wanted to please him and tried to stay focused, but it was hard. There were so many other, more enticing competitors for her attention. The baby owl she'd found that morning and was trying to feed, the snake skeleton she'd spotted in the grass as she was walking with her father. So many distractions.*

*'For the orchard we buy trees already grafted and growing. Trees that will give us a quick sturdy start. Remember I told you about the Colt Root Stock System?'*

*She nodded.*

*'These trees in the yard are the ones I've grafted myself.'*

*She nodded again, picturing him with his glasses on, and his sharp little knife out, concentrating hard so that she wasn't allowed even to tiptoe in that direction.*

*She studied the split tree. 'Why did this one break, Papa?'*

*'Remember Iris, we graft when we have something unique and beautiful that can't put down strong roots of its own. Something too delicate or too damaged. Something that is unwilling or unable to take hold. We graft to give it the strength and sturdiness to survive. But sometimes the graft union doesn't hold – the cuts aren't sharp enough or the rootstock isn't strong enough or the scion has been too badly scarred – and this is what happens.'*

*With his fingertips he traced the pale green cambium beneath the bark, the lifeblood of the tree, torn open and exposed, withering even as they stood there. Iris watched his fingers and felt a catch in her chest, both for the dying tree and for herself. Her father never touched her so tenderly. He never touched her at all.*

*'Why can't you just fasten it all back together?' she asked. 'Why can't you put a cast on it like the cast on my arm last year?'*

*'Because this isn't like a broken bone, Iris. This is . . .' He stared at the tree for a moment. 'This tree has given up. See that cambium? It was only holding by a thread. All the rest is scar tissue. This tree can't possibly heal. Its heart is broken.'*

He coughed. But no, it wasn't her father coughing. The dream folded back and she blinked, coming out of the tomb, only she wasn't coming out of the Mayan tomb. The light was fluorescent. She was in the hospital room. A man in a white coat was standing at the foot of the bed. His gray hair stuck out from his head like dandelion fluff and he was wearing several pairs of reading glasses suspended from leashes around his neck.

'Oh,' he said as though slightly befuddled. 'Did I wake you?'

'That's all right,' she assured him, willing herself to alertness.

'I saw the detective leaving.' He made a scolding cluck with his tongue. 'I cautioned her about talking in the room and bothering our patient. She could conduct her business in the hall.'

Iris nodded.

His smile was quick and jerky. A puppet smile. His lips were pulled upward by invisible strings, then dropped. 'I'm Dr Milford, the neurosurgeon who's treating your father. Would you like to step out in the hall with me?'

The hallway was deserted except for the man with the mop who was working his way haphazardly toward the end.

'I wish I had better news to give you, Ms Lanier. Your father was struck by a bullet that entered the right side of his face and traveled at an upward angle into the frontal lobe of his brain. We removed the bullet and cleaned out the bone fragments, blood clots, and damaged tissue. He also has a fracture in the back of his skull.' The doctor pointed to an area on the back of his own head, 'in the area where the occipital bone joins the parietal.'

'On the lambdoid suture?'

'Yes.' The gray eyebrows lifted in surprise. 'Are you in medicine?'

'No. Physical anthropology. Bones. Please go on.'

'The fracture probably occurred when he struck his head falling to the pavement, and we can assume a serious concussion would be evident if not for the greater trauma and damage of the bullet wound.'

Iris nodded understanding.

'We've done all we can to relieve the pressure from the swelling and so far we're holding our own. His heart is strong and his respiration is steady but he has no reflexes and doesn't respond to light. He is not clinically brain dead, but . . .' The doctor hesitated.

'What exactly are you saying?'

'I'm saying that the prognosis is poor. If I were to rate

his chances the number would be very small.'

'But there is a chance?'

'A small chance.'

'How long will it be before we know?'

The doctor shrugged apologetically. 'There is no predicting. Frankly, I'm surprised that he's held on this long. The first forty-eight hours are usually the most critical period.'

'Is that encouraging? That he made it through the forty-eight hours?'

'Possibly. I'm sorry. I really don't know.'

'So he could go on like this indefinitely?'

'He could go on like this for weeks or even months. There's no predicting at this point. Except for feeding, he's not on any life support, so that's not an issue.' Milford held up his hands in a gesture of helplessness. 'The brain can be very mysterious. Even to a neurosurgeon. Especially to a neurosurgeon. And, as I'm sure you're aware from cases in the news, the coma state can stretch on for years in some instances.'

He glanced down at his watch. 'I have an emergency coming in so I have to leave now, but I'll see you again when I make my rounds tomorrow. And remember, there's a lot we don't know about coma. Your father may have a certain level of awareness.'

Iris had barely stepped back inside her father's room when the nurse reappeared.

'Thought I'd check on you,' the woman said. 'I called about someone hooking up the phone and TV in here.'

Iris attempted a thank-you but had trouble getting it out. There was a distance between her and the woman. Between her and the room. As though she were watching it all from someplace far away. Or through a tank of water.

The nurse didn't seem to notice. 'I don't get comas very often. Gunshots either. They're usually on another wing.'

She snapped off the overhead lights so that only the fluorescent tube over John Lanier's head was left burning. 'Since he's in a private room you can come and go in here whenever you want. I'll give you a pass to show downstairs. Technically you're not allowed to use the patient's bathroom but nobody's going to yell if you're in there for a few minutes now and then. Just don't try to shower or anything.'

She turned toward Iris and shook her head sympathetically. 'You look done in. I can get you a foldout cot if you want to spend the night here in the room.'

'Thank you.'

'Figured you didn't have a place to stay yet since you were dragging around your suitcase. You must have come straight from the airport or the train or something.'

Iris nodded and the woman busied herself with the catheter bag hanging on the side of the bed. 'So, how'd it go with the detectives?'

'They weren't very helpful.'

The nurse chuckled, keeping her attention on her task. 'Him I don't know, but her . . . She's some piece of work, huh?' With a rush the urine drained from the bag into a plastic container. The nurse held it up, read the volume mark, then carried it to the bathroom and flushed it away. When she came back from the bathroom she resumed talking. 'She's been around a lot the last few weeks. Got a sister who's a patient on Yellow. Right around the corner really. Janelle. That's her sister. Poor girl.'

The woman stripped off her latex gloves and crossed to the window. 'Wonder if the rain stopped yet.' She bent close to look out, parting the blinds with her fingers. Her skin was the color of espresso coffee beans against the starkly white blinds.

'Thank you for looking after my father,' Iris said.

'That's my job.'

'Then thank you for doing your job.'

'Just be glad they brought him here instead of Columbia. That place is so big. You could get lost over there. How much personal attention can a patient get in a place that big?'

'It's bigger than Morningside?' Iris asked.

'Twice as big. Maybe more. We just seem big because the wings go every which way. That came from adding on a little at a time through the years, you know, going where there was room to go. That's why we've got two halls that cross right over the street, because there are really three separate buildings connected together.' She grinned. 'The same way my grandson builds with his LEGO blocks.'

'Don't people get lost here?'

'Visitors maybe.' She chuckled. 'But never patients. That's the beauty of it. All you got to remember to find your father is to ride up on the blue elevators. This is the blue wing. Next one over is yellow. The other two colors take you across the street. Stay away from them or you will be lost.'

'OK.' Iris sank back into the chair. She hoped the cot would come soon.

The woman made several notations on the chart at the end of the bed. 'My name's Helen,' she said as she headed for the door. 'I'm on from four to midnight. You need anything, just ask for Helen. I'll take good care of you and your father.'

'Thanks,' Iris said. There was something. What was it? Something the detective had said. 'Wait . . . Helen . . . The detective said that some of my father's things were at the desk?'

'Oh, that's right. There was a package. After meds I'll get it for you.'

'Thanks. And, something else. I was wondering . . . When I got here there was a woman in the visitors lounge. A thin woman with greyish hair. She said she'd been there for days. Do you know who she is?'

65

The nurse chuckled. 'No. Don't know who she is. Funny thing though, she asked about you.'

'She did?'

'Uh huh. Right after I brought you in here I was walking back to the desk and she stopped me in the hall and asked me who you were.'

'What did you tell her?'

'I told her you came from far away to be with your father.'

'Did she ask my name or anything?'

'No. I wouldn't have answered anyways.'

'I wonder why she was so interested in me.'

'Oh, people sit up here day after day, waiting for their sick relatives to get better or worse, and they get all lonely and bored. They get desperate for company. Maybe she was hoping you'd be someone to pass the time with in the lounge.'

Iris nodded. She watched the nurse leave, then turned toward the bed, toward her father. Slowly, tentatively, she reached to touch his hand, but as soon as the contact was made she drew back. His skin was cool. Like he was already dead. Like he wasn't there anymore. She hadn't been allowed to touch him in life and now he was beyond touch.

'What were you doing in New York?' she asked, raising her eyes to the ceiling because she could not bear to look directly at his sunken half-face. 'Why did you go down to the river in the middle of the night?' The questions hung in the stillness, unanswered, unacknowledged.

A narrow foldup bed was delivered and she lay down on it. Voices drifted in from the hallway. Something metal clanged to the floor somewhere. The beeping of the heart monitor seemed to grow louder.

A vision of Moonsmoke's face came to her mind and she wished she could go to the stela and look at the carved portrait. Study it. Now that she knew Moonsmoke's story, knew the woman had vanished, had left behind a loving husband and children and disappeared . . . Now she wanted to search that solemn countenance for answers.

Had she felt a connection to Moonsmoke from the beginning? Was that why the portrait had been so compelling to her when it seemed to hold only historic and artistic interest for everyone else? She wanted to go to her now, fold back the flap of her tent and cross the nightblack plaza to sit at Moonsmoke's feet. She wanted to touch the weathered stone cheek and look into the timeless depths of her moonlit eyes.

But what would that accomplish? The past was done. Answers to it meant nothing in the present because that was all there was. The present. And maybe the future. The past, and the search for answers to the past, was like quicksand. Never conquered. Best avoided.

She thought of her work. The work that was her life. Or was it that she had made her life the work? Whichever. Work was safe. Work was good.

Back at the dig it was quiet and dark. The women in the chamber were resting, waiting patiently for her return. But then she had a disturbing thought. Had they known they would be sacrificed? Had they also waited patiently for the priests who tore their hearts from their chests or cleaved their heads from their necks? And number six, lying in the mouth of the tunnel with the ceremonial knife in her back . . . Had she stood meekly, head down, waiting for the chiseled point to pierce her flesh?

Maybe they had all been just like her, raised to be well-behaved girls, silent and unquestioning, acquiescent and cooperative right up to the end.

Well, this was different. She would not let these detectives bulldoze her and make insinuations about her father. She would not let it happen again.

What if he died?

What if he never got better?

She curled up on the cot, feeling as small and vulnerable as a child. As helplessly exposed as the women she'd left in the tomb.

Sleep.

Maybe if she got some sleep.

Then tomorrow she would assemble a list of questions to ask the detectives and a list to ask the doctor. She would do research. She would make the detectives see how unreasonable their suspicions were. Tomorrow she would be rested and things would make sense again.

# Four

Iris was jolted awake at six a.m. by a nurse's aide calling out 'Good morning!' and switching on all the lights.

Her first thought was that her father might have improved in the night, during the hours when she was sleeping. She struggled up off the cot, groggy from too little sleep. But he was lying in the bed just as before. Just as still. Just as absent.

The nurse began the routine tasks of his care, humming and talking while she worked, as though she were fussing over an infant. She was a tall woman with the music of the Caribbean in her voice.

After she was gone, Iris sat down in the chair at her father's bedside. The day stretching out before her settled onto her shoulders in a leaden weight. Time thickened and slowed around her. There was no forward progress of any sort within the room.

She listened to the faint hum of the fluorescent tubes overhead and the beeping of her father's heart. She stared out the small window. The sky was relentlessly clear with no clouds to watch.

Finally, the aide returned to give him a sponge bath and Iris allowed herself to go to the cafeteria. She passed the visitors lounge and looked inside, but the strange woman wasn't there.

Luzon, the midnight-to-eight charge nurse, was coming briskly down the hall. She was so small that she looked like a child playing hospital. When she reached Iris, she stopped.

'Helen told me you were asking about a lady in the visitors lounge,' she said in her heavy Filipino accent.

'Yes. She's not there now but—'

'The lady with the turquoise, right? The one who looks like an artist from Santa Fe.'

'Yes . . . Do you know who she is?'

'Don't you?'

'No. Should I?'

'Well, I just thought . . . since she was here for your dad . . .'

'She was here to see my father?'

'That's what she said. She showed up . . . let's see . . . maybe the second day your dad was here. It was my shift. She wanted to go in and see him and I had to explain that only immediate family was allowed.'

'Did she tell you her name?'

The nurse's frown deepened into thought. 'Not that I remember. But she admitted right away that she wasn't immediate family. Sometimes people try to lie about that, but she didn't.'

'Did she say whether she was from here, in the city?'

'Sorry. No. I only talked to her for a minute.'

'Did you tell the police about her?'

'Why? She didn't make any trouble for me. What would I have told the police?'

'Maybe she knows why my father came to New York. Maybe she knows—'

Iris stopped. The nurse's expression was changing from friendliness to skepticism and Iris realized that the woman knew nothing about the police case or about the questions surrounding her father's actions. She could also tell that the woman did not want to know.

The nurse looked at her watch. 'Almost time for meds. Got to get busy.'

★ ★ ★

To help the morning pass, Iris began jotting notes, making lists, trying to impose an order on the situation. She drew up a chart of questions, known facts, and theories. The questions took up most of the chart.

She wondered if the police knew more than they had told her. Wasn't that a common police technique, to hold back information?

She wondered if her father might have traveled to New York on an errand for someone else. But the only person to whom he owed any such loyalty was Yoshi Hirano, and she had spoken to him on the telephone. If Mr Hirano had sent her father to New York, he would have said so.

She wondered if her father was indeed looking for a prostitute that night in Riverside Park. He had seemed monklike, almost asexual, while she was growing up, but what did she know of his needs? What did she really know of him as a male human being – separate from the powerful father, separate from the hard working orchardist. Nothing.

And what about the woman who had spent days in the visitors' lounge, waiting even though she hadn't been allowed in John Lanier's room? Who was she? How did she fit?

Lunchtime finally came and Iris went downstairs. The cafeteria was crowded and noisy so she bypassed it and went to the main lobby. She noticed a gift shop tucked away along one side. The sign on the door advertised newspapers and magazines, but it too was jammed with people.

She went out the building's front doors and started down Amsterdam Avenue. The day was brilliantly clear but there was a blustery wind. People were hurrying on the sidewalks, coats billowing out around them. She ducked into a pizzeria for lunch, then crossed the street to a newsstand. Headlines jumped out from the rows of newspapers.

> LOCKET KILLER VICTIM IDENTIFIED
> JUDGE BATTERS WIFE
> CULT MASSACRE IN IDAHO
> DRUG MURDERS TIED TO GUATEMALA

Drug murders. Was that the reason the detectives had been so fixated on her working in Guatemala? She picked up a science magazine and the paper with the drug murder story. So many alarming headlines. Even on the science magazine. FLESH-EATING VIRUS and THE RETURN OF KILLER TUBERCULOSIS and FATAL NEW STRAIN OF LYME DISEASE FOUND. Hopelessness was apparently a big seller.

The wind rushed through her clothes. She hugged herself against it and walked aimlessly. There was a drugstore advertising a sale on cheap watches so she bought a twenty-dollar man's sport model that was waterproof, shockproof, and, with luck, anthropologist proof. As she walked back toward Morningside she buckled the black rubber watchband around her wrist, wondering if her time in the plastic chair beside her father would move faster or slower now that she had a way to track it.

By that night she could safely say that having a sweep second-hand did nothing to push time forward. Her afternoon and evening had seemed endless. And the exhaustion had returned. She supposed that she had still not recovered from all the lost sleep and travel stresses.

The nurses had advised her repeatedly to leave the hospital and get some rest. Finally, at ten o'clock – head and back aching, eyes like sandpaper – she knew they were right. But she dreaded leaving because the only logical place to go was her father's rented room. She had the keys and it was already paid for. There was no question that she should go there. But she was afraid of what she would find. She didn't want any more surprises or shocks. If her father had any more secrets she didn't want to know them.

She hailed a cab and spoke to the driver through a clear bullet-proof partition. His voice was muffled. She wondered if he felt safe behind the shield and if feeling safe made him happy. She watched the meter turn over. The Plexiglas muted the characteristic sound of the fare clicking upward, but she could still see the numbers advancing. Morningside was on the Upper West Side and her destination was in the lower twenties on the East Side. A cab didn't seem like a luxury, but it was.

In her months at the dig she had been so free of financial concerns that she'd forgotten how inconvenient it was to be constantly short of money. This would be her last cab ride. The subway or bus was all that her budget would allow.

The driver squealed to a stop at the address she had given him. She slid the fare into a small tilting drawer that didn't allow their fingers to touch. Maybe someday everyone would have shields that kept them separate and safe, and there would be fewer headlines.

She wrestled her luggage from the backseat out to the curb and looked up at the building her father had slept in. It was forlorn and grimy in the evening light. Her father had come all the way to New York and rented a room here. That could not be true, yet it was. She looked up and down the block. It was shabby and layered with generations of graffiti. Several of the store windows were papered over with FOR RENT signs, but there were a few lights shining. Right next-door to the building was a window hung with bright neon script – MADAME ZORA PSYCHIC ADVISOR. Down the block a steel-barred liquor store shone like a hospital operating room.

On the sidewalks there were people with briefcases and purposeful expressions, but they were walking as though this was an area to be gotten through as quickly as possible. At the corner an emaciated couple in ragged clothes begged from cars at the traffic light.

Iris tried to push through the revolving brass-and-glass door but it was locked. To the side was another door, a panel of numbered buttons and an intercom. The door had a heavy, recently added lock marring the original ornate brass. She took out her father's keys. One opened the lock.

The lobby was less dismal than the exterior. There was a long transverse crack in the high ceiling. The floor was scarred from the ripping away of built-in furnishings. A staleness hung in the air. But it appeared fairly clean. She headed toward the two small elevators in the back, then noticed a steel door with SUPERINTENDENT in red stenciled letters, and decided to stop there.

She pressed the buzzer and waited. A short balding man opened the door, gasped, and clutched at his chest.

'Are you all right?' she asked, reaching out in case he fell.

He waved her away and leaned against the door until his breathing recovered.

'Sorry,' he said weakly. 'The old ticker I guess.'

'I could call a doctor.'

'No. No. I'm fine now.' He straightened and adjusted his shirt collar as though to prove the point.

He was wearing a dark green work shirt with the name Andretti stitched over the breast and the title Superintendent emblazoned like a family crest on the pocket.

'I'm Iris Lanier,' she said. 'My father, John Lanier, has a room rented here, but he's in the hospital now.'

'Ah, yeah. OK. How's he doing?'

'He's—' She had to clear her throat. 'He's in a coma.'

The man shifted nervously. 'That's bad. That's bad.' He

leaned out the door to look past her, scanning the lobby with quick darting glances. 'You won't get a refund, you know. As far as the management company's concerned, when the room's rented in advance, that's it. If no one stays in it you kiss the money goodbye.'

'I don't want a refund. I thought I might stay here. In my father's room.'

'Great idea!' He nodded and smoothed his little mustache with a finger. 'Great idea.'

'Did you by any chance speak to my father while he was here? Did he tell you anything about the purpose of his trip or . . . anything?'

The man seemed to relax all of a sudden. He leaned against the doorframe and crossed his arms. 'Oh, man, this place is not exactly the Plaza, you know? People come. People go. The management company takes care of renting out the rooms and I usually only talk to people if their toilet overflows or their lock sticks.'

She nodded and glanced around the lobby. 'Is this a hotel?'

'Used to be the Hotel Fitzgerald. It's still the Fitzgerald but now we got rooms by the week or month. Cash only and payment in advance.'

'I suppose it's much less expensive than a hotel.'

'Yeah. The owners don't even care if it stays rented. I think they're waiting to tear it down. Probably gonna build some big office building for foreigners to get tax rebates off of.'

She held out her key. 'I'll go on up then.'

'Sure. Sure. Hey, we got a basement storage room if you want me to stow your suitcases there after you unpack.'

'Thanks but no.'

'Yeah, well, let me know if you got any problems.'

'OK.' She turned and started toward the elevators, passing a door marked STAIRWAY FOR EMERGENCY USE

ONLY and in smaller letters – DO NOT USE ELEVATORS DURING FIRE.

'The elevator with the chain across it is broken,' he called after her. 'And remember, we get all kinds here. You should be careful who you're alone with. Very, very careful.'

She turned to face front in the car and saw that he was still standing there, watching her, staring intently as the old brass doors creaked shut.

At the sixth floor the doors opened onto a long dimly lit hall stretching out in two directions from the elevators. It seemed deserted. She shouldered her carry-on, tugged on her suitcase leash and turned right toward the smaller numbers. The air smelled musty and stale.

Her father's room was at the end of the hall. Number 602. Just as she reached it a man suddenly burst out of the door opposite, slamming into her and knocking her carry-on to the floor. The man whipped around to face her, looming and full of menace, but as soon as he saw the offender who had dared to be in his path his entire manner changed to fumbling surprise.

'Shit,' he said, managing to make the word sound like an apology. He picked up the carry-on and handed it to her. He was all in black. Heavy black boots with ankle chains. Black jeans. A black leather jacket with numerous buckles.

She wondered what would happen if she called for help in that deserted hallway. Would anyone hear her? Would anyone respond?

'Excuse me,' she said, edging past him in the narrow space. He stalked away, heading toward the elevators.

She unlocked the door to 602, stepped inside, and flipped the light switch. Breath held, she scanned the room. It was plain but clean. Anonymous. A cheaply furnished, no-frills hotel room. There were no troubling surprises. And there was nothing of her father in sight at all.

Slowly she walked through, peeking inside the bathroom, glancing out the two windows. Two different views of the city. She wondered if her father had asked for a corner room so he could have two windows. How strange to think that he had rented such a room. She went to the small closet, hesitated a moment, then jerked it open. Clothes. That was all. Just clothes. Nothing terrible. No secrets. Just the same basic clothing he had always worn. Relieved, she closed the door and leaned against it.

Her headache was worse. She turned off the light and stretched out on the double bed, closed her eyes, and pressed her fingertips against her temples. Just for a minute. Just till her head felt better and she was ready to worry about dinner and think what to do next. The bed felt so good. Such a luxury to be in a real bed. From overhead he heard the sound of music, plaintive and low. She closed her eyes and listened to the sad sweet notes.

Hours later there was a sound. She opened her eyes. The window rattled stealthily. She was afraid to move. Her heart was pounding.

Trapped.

She was trapped in the dark in her childhood bedroom. Something was coming in the window. But if she yelled, if she woke her father, he would be so furious.

*'You have too many nightmares! There is nothing to be afraid of. Nothing! If you wake me again I'll shut your door and take your nightlight away.'*

The rattling continued. If she moved, the thing would see her. But she had to move. She had to look. To know what was after her. Slowly, she shifted her head . . . just enough . . . so she could peek sideways.

A face was pressed against the black glass, staring in at her through the open blinds. She screamed.

The scream brought her fully awake. She pressed her hand against her chest, against the hammering of her heart. The room was dark, but she knew immediately where she was. There was no face at the window. The blinds were open as they had been in her dream, but there was nothing outside the glass except the glow of the city night.

She pulled herself up into a sitting position and waited for the shakiness to pass. She was still in her clothes. There was a clock bolted to the bed's attached nightstand and the lighted digital numbers read 1:45 a.m. She couldn't remember the last time she had had such a night terror.

Funny, she had forgotten about all her years of childhood frights. After her mother was gone she had awakened often in the night, drenched with sweat and screaming in terror, calling *Mommy! Mommy!* Always Mommy. Long after she had decided to hate her departed mother, she had still screamed Mommy during nightmares.

She got up off the bed and went to the window. It faced north. She could see part of the Empire State Building through it. The room's other window faced east but all she could see in that direction was the building across the street, or, if she looked down, she could watch the activity on Lexington Avenue.

Both windows were hung with old-style metal blinds. Venetian blinds her mother used to call them. They had strong, wide slats and heavy grayish pull cords. And both were six stories above the ground so no one could have been staring in at her. Still, she closed the slats tightly before undressing and going back to bed. The next thing she knew sunlight was leaking in around the edges of the blinds. It took her several seconds to remember where she was and why. Then she bolted upright.

The digital numbers read 7:00 a.m. Her stomach clenched into a knot. She had been away from the hospital

78

and out of touch for eleven hours. Anxiously, she picked up the phone and called the Blue Four desk.

Luzon answered. 'No change,' she said. 'Your father is the same.'

'Can you take this phone number and keep it there at the desk?' Iris asked. 'It's where I am now . . . where I'll be every night.'

'I'll post it,' the nurse assured her. 'But you relax. There's no reason to hurry over. Dorothy comes on next and she'll make sure he's cared for.'

Iris sat on the end of the bed and willed herself to calm down. A hot bath. Fresh clothes. A quick breakfast *en route* to the hospital. She needed to find a jacket of some kind. The sweatshirts in her digging wardrobe weren't enough against the March weather in New York. But she would worry about that later. For now she would stick to the basics.

She pulled up the blinds and a clear bright light flooded in. The utilitarian starkness of the room pleased her. The plain walls and linoleum tile floor. The simple furnishings. In addition to the double bed, there was a long low mirrored dresser with a hotplate on top, a square table suitable for card games or eating or writing letters, and two wooden chairs that almost matched the table. It was all-purpose furniture. There was nothing frivolous or valuable about it.

She was comfortable in rooms like this where there was nothing tugging at her. Nothing to lose. Nothing to hide from. Not like her father's house, so crammed with ghosts from the past. Memories lurking everywhere.

He had taken years to build the six-room structure, crafting it from a plan he'd designed himself. Every log was perfect and true and straight, and there were almost no nails in the entire building. It was all done with precise fitting and hand-whittled pegs and mortise and tenon. The floors were a beautiful red oak, salvaged from an old

79

gymnasium that was being torn down. And everything was oiled rather than painted.

She had vivid memories of helping him. Holding things. Handing him tools. Carrying the end of a log. Only it wasn't just her carrying it.

*'It's heavy, Clary. Be careful. Don't hurt yourself.'*

*'Don't worry, John. We're fine on our end.'* And then that smile. That secret smile that her mother gave only to her. She could have lived on that smile. Taken it with her to a desert island and survived on it alone. *'We're strong, aren't we, Iris? We can carry our end. We're strong women.'*

Quickly she shook off the memory and got up from the bed to prowl the room. She tried to picture her father bent over the hotplate, heating water for instant soup or instant coffee. It was impossible to imagine. Her father ground and blended his own coffee. When he made soup, he started by soaking dried peas and beans all night. He was not a man who approved of instant anything.

She opened the small closet again. Four clean cotton shirts hung there along with a heavy, quilt-lined, wool jacket. The pockets were empty. There was nothing on the shelf. She pulled the jacket off the hanger and threw it on the bed. That would be her coat. She moved to the dresser, thought about the police, that they had been there before her, pawing through his things, invading his privacy. How furious he would be when he found out.

There were two smaller drawers on top. The first of these held an airline ticket and a stack of the red cotton bandannas he used in place of handkerchiefs. She picked up the ticket. It had an open-ended return. The other small drawer held the pocket knife he usually wore in the leather case on his belt, a folded wide-radius roadmap of the greater New York area, and his wallet.

She picked up the wallet. She had made it for him when she was twelve and she was surprised to see that he still had it. Her fingers traced the worn leather and she remembered the thick slabs of oak-tanned hide that she had carved and stamped and stained, working in the night for weeks so that she would have a surprise to give him for his birthday.

When it was all finished, the oak-leaf pattern burnished to a shine and the letters JL raised on a diagonal banner so that they jumped out, she whipstitched it all together with chocolate brown lacing and it was so stiff and thick that it wouldn't close. She had to wet the spine and force a fold, then weight it closed for days. The finished product had been a big unwieldy rock of a thing. But he had used it. Carrying it in his back pocket had to have been uncomfortable. Like sitting on a book. But he had used it.

Now, after years of wear, the wallet was supple and thin, the oak-tanned leather darkened from his touch, stained with his sweat.

She opened it. There were three hundred dollars in cash, a California driver's license, and a collection of business cards. Inside the acetate window that had been intended for an identification card was a picture of a solemn fifteen-year-old Iris in cap and gown, wearing her high school valedictorian medal. The picture made her angry. She jerked out the cards and flipped the wallet closed.

Her father had always collected cards. Whatever was given to him he kept, sticking it in pocket or wallet, eventually transferring it to his dresser top and then, when that became cluttered, into a shoebox on a shelf. To her knowledge he never got the cards back out of the shoebox or contacted any of the people, but still he kept them.

His current collection contained a card from a California travel agent with New York flight times noted on the back and an orange card printed with the message – I AM A HOMELESS BLIND WAR VET. GOD BLESS YOU FOR HELPING. There was a card for Madame Zora, the psychic advisor, and a card for a New York City coffee shop, THE SEVEN STARS DINER, with an address on the edge of the West Village.

She put the cards on top of the dresser and picked up the bag of personal belongings that the nurse had given her. She had opened it at the hospital but only given the items a cursory look before fishing out the keys to the room. Now she dumped the contents out on the bed. There was a red bandanna, some change, and a plasticized card bearing a miniature guide to Manhattan streets and public transportation. There was a folded rectangle of paper that she hadn't noticed the night before. A receipt of some kind. She smoothed it out. It was from the police department. A receipt for unreleased items. The list was handwritten and difficult to read. Shirt. Shoes. Seven .38-caliber bullets.

She crushed the paper in her hands and pressed her fists against her mouth. Bullets? Her father had had bullets? That was not possible. It couldn't be possible. There was an explanation. Hadn't Detective Kizmin said that the attacker used a .38-caliber gun? That was it. The mugger had dropped some of his bullets and they had been on the ground near her father. He hadn't actually had them himself.

*Don't hurry*, the nurse had said, but there was a ticking in the pit of her stomach, an internal clock counting off the minutes that she was not at her father's bedside.

She went to the bathroom and started the water for a hot bath. There was no shower. Just the roomy old porcelain tub. That was fine. In Guatemala all they'd had was a barrel mounted in a tree, rigged to trickle water down on whoever stood beneath it. A sort of primitive shower. This was pure decadence by comparison.

While she waited for the tub to fill she looked in the old-fashioned mirror medicine cabinet. Her father's toiletries were neatly arranged on the glass shelves. Everything

82

was simple and basic. There was no aftershave or cologne. No fancy hair product. And no medicine at all. This cabinet belonged to the father she knew. But the father she knew would not have come to this room. Or to this city. The father she knew would not have been in Riverside Park in the middle of the night.

She submerged herself in the hot water and tried not to think about him, but it was impossible. There was his old cotton robe hanging on the bathroom door. And there, at the foot of the tub, was the familiar bottle of liquid castile soap. The only soap they had ever used at home. Almond or peppermint. This time it was peppermint. The quirky old-fashioned label declared that it was safe enough to use for anything, tooth brushing included.

There was also a fresh thick cake of regular soap in the wire dish attached to the tub. It was not something her father would have bought and so must have come with the room. Maybe left by the last occupant. Whatever, she was thankful for it. She could not have used that peppermint liquid. The scent carried too much of the past with it.

By the time she was dressed, the ticking in her stomach had become an urgent gnawing. There was only one shoe beside the bed. She knelt to retrieve the mate and in the process of bending and reaching she noticed something on the floor across from her, beneath the window. Something like bits of gravel or grit. Something she hadn't noticed there the night before.

She slipped the shoe on then went to look. The grit was chips of paint. She pulled up the blinds and jiggled the old sash-hung window. A few more slivers of paint broke loose and floated down to the floor.

The thumb lock was open but she couldn't push the window up. The wooden frame had been painted over so many times that it was stuck. She tried to slam it loose with the heel of her hand. More paint chips rained down but the window did not break free. She thought of her father's knife in the drawer.

It unfolded with a snap. The blade was honed to a smooth sharpness and she cut through the layers of paint with barely any pressure. When she pushed on the window again, it opened easily.

The music was back and was clearer with the window up. It was definitely coming from above. Probably out of another open window. She leaned out. Just outside was a fire escape that she hadn't noticed before. It zigzagged from the roof to the first story with a small landing at each floor. The iron railings and landings were covered with years' worth of grime – a thick even coating of grime – except for the smudges on her landing.

Using her elbows for leverage, she hiked herself up into a sitting position on the sill, then swung out onto the landing for a closer look. The smudges were footprints. Someone had been outside her window.

She stared for a moment before accepting what the evidence meant. The rattling. The contorted face pressed against the dark glass. They had been mixed into her sleep but they had not been a nightmare. They had been real.

She climbed back inside, closed the window and forced the thumblock into position, then considered what to do. The telephone had a sticker on the base with the superintendent's phone number in hand-lettering. She dialed.

'Rich Andretti here.'

'Yes, this is Iris Lanier in 602. There was a man on my fire escape last night, looking in my window.'

She thought she heard a sharp intake of breath but when Andretti spoke he sounded casual. 'Yeah, we get a lot of crazies and space cases here. One of them probably stumbled out onto the fire escape trying to find his way to the roof.'

'So you don't think I should call the police?'

'Did he have a Uzi or was he waving a machete?'

84

'No.'

Andretti gave a sarcastic little snort. 'Then don't call the cops unless you enjoy wasting your time. This is New York. What you'll get is a major hassle and no action.'

'Yes, you're probably right.'

'Your window lock works?'

'I think so.'

'Use it. And call me fast if he shows up again. I'll scare him off.'

Iris waited impatiently for the elevator. There was a door beside it, no doubt another door into the stairwell that was only to be used in case of emergency. The door was wedged open an inch with a piece of folded cardboard. Waiting for the elevator made it clear why the forbidden stairwell was so tempting. The grinding and clunking were interminable before the elevator finally creaked open. She stepped inside and the slow journey began. One floor down, the car stopped and a man boarded. Iris eyed the newcomer warily, but then relaxed. Maybe the building held more unnerving types like the biker, but this man was not one of them.

In a glance she took in his polished loafers, khaki slacks, crisp white shirt and freshly barbered blondish-brown hair, and knew that she was safe with him. He even held books. Two large ones tucked casually under his arm.

'Morning,' he said with a tentative smile.

'Good-morning.'

'You must be new here.'

'Yes.'

'I'm Mitch. Mitchell Hanley. 502.'

'Iris Lanier. I'm just above you.'

'Really?' He grinned. 'Well, I promise I won't bang on the ceiling if you dance in the middle of the night.'

Ordinarily she would have ended it there, without a

response. She would have pointedly faced forward and shut him out. But the fact that his room was just below her own made her go further.

'Did anything bother you last night?' she asked. 'At your window, I mean.'

'Are you kidding? I'm on the fifth floor.'

'Someone was out on the fire escape, looking in windows.'

He shrugged. 'Nothing bothered me. Except that damn music. I wish that guy would do his playing down in the basement.'

'That's all you heard? The music?'

'Yeah. Sounds like an alley cat whose girlfriend dumped him.'

'It is sad. It's a saxophone, I think.'

'I like country and western myself,' he said as the doors opened on the lobby.

She walked toward the front door and he fell into step beside her.

'Are you living here in the city or just visiting?' he asked.

'Visiting,' she answered shortly, not wanting to encourage him but not wanting to be rude either.

He zipped his jacket as they went out. Iris could feel his interest. It flowed from him in waves. The same interest she'd learned to recognize in males when she was fourteen years old. But there was something else too. A tense sharp-edged curiosity that went beyond the ordinary sexual absorption.

Mitchell Hanley. She wasn't particularly good at names but his had lodged itself in her mind.

'Where are you headed?' he asked brightly.

'To the subway,' she said, 'but I'm going to stop somewhere first for coffee so . . .'

'Have you learned the neighborhood yet?'

'No, but I enjoy exploring.'

'There's not much that's close to our building, but right

by the subway there's one of those little Korean places that has everything.'

She kept walking, acutely aware of his presence, wishing she could turn a knob and have him disappear. They reached the store and she saw that it was a miniature produce market, grocery, and deli. It did indeed promise everything.

'Thanks for showing me the way,' she said. 'I think I'll take my time and do some shopping.'

'No problem, no problem,' he said and assumed a lounging position against the wall. 'I'm in no hurry.'

She began choosing fruit from the outside bins, keeping her eyes down to conceal her annoyance. The fruit was disappointing. But then, after growing up surrounded by cherry and apricot orchards, and having a front yard full of other varieties, it was hard to be satisfied with the offerings in stores.

When she had everything she wanted, she started for the door.

'I'll wait out here for you,' Hanley said.

Iris turned back toward him, one hand on the door and the other holding her bag of fruit. 'That's OK, really . . . I might be awhile so . . .'

'Take your time,' he said, smiling expansively.

She sighed. It was never a good idea to talk to men. They always assumed too much.

'Please . . . don't wait,' she said.

He straightened, looking puzzled, and then vaguely hurt.

Her relief at having spoken her thoughts made her feel more generous toward him. 'I'm just not in the mood for company,' she explained. 'My father is sick. I'm on my way to see him in the hospital, and I'd like to be alone.'

Hanley nodded quickly. 'Sure. I understand. I know how bad I'd feel if my father was sick. I should be cramming anyway.' He swung the books up as if illustrating his point. 'I'm a law student. Final year. And I've got a major test today. So,' he grinned, 'another time, huh?'

She watched him go. He broke into a loping run as he crossed the street and she heard the leather slap of his shoes on the pavement.

A student. For some reason that made her feel old. Older than Mitchell Hanley. Older than any man who had ever wanted her. And she liked the feeling. She wished for a moment that she was approaching seventy rather than thirty and that every uncertainty, every social discomfort, every raw emotion, was safely behind her. That, she believed, would be the perfect state.

Iris stopped at the Blue Four desk to say hello to the day charge who had taken over from Luzon at eight. Her name was Dorothy and she was pale and blond and pear shaped. She was doing paperwork in the small glasswalled office behind the desk. She waved at Iris, then got up and stuck her head out the door.

'The phone and television are working now. I turned on the TV just in case your dad can hear things.'

Iris nodded and went down the hall. If her father did have any awareness, being trapped with hours of daytime television would probably convince him that he'd descended into purgatory. He had long believed that television and computers were the two most insidiously evil inventions in modern history.

The visitors lounge was empty again. She turned the corner and a man wielding a push broom blocked her way.

'You're Lanier, right?'

'Yes.'

'That woman detective has been hunting for you,' he said. 'And she didn't look happy.'

# Five

Inside her father's room the blinds were open and the fluorescent lights were off. A talk show blared from the small wall-mounted television. Iris set down her bag of fruit and slowly approached the bed. Her father looked the same. Exactly the same.

'Hello,' she said.

She waited, holding her breath, believing that he might blink or move his fingers, that he might give her some sign that was reserved only for her. But there was nothing. On television a man was explaining why he had joined an Aryan supremacy group that wanted to rid the United States of every man, woman, and child who wasn't one hundred percent white, Protestant, and heterosexual. She leaned across the bed to turn it off.

'I'll buy a radio,' she promised. 'New York has a good public radio station.'

The door swung open and Detective Kizmin walked in. She was alone. In her presence Iris felt suddenly and unaccountably guilty. She thought again of calling the Kaliker Foundation. Maybe just for advice. She had no idea what her father's rights were as a crime victim. What her own rights were as the daughter of a crime victim.

'Are you making any progress?' Iris asked, hoping that they might have dismissed all their ridiculous suspicions and begun to track the real criminal.

'Depends on what you mean by progress,' Kizmin said coolly.

'Are you any closer to catching whoever is responsible?'

'You're worried about that, huh?'

Uncertain, Iris stared at the detective and waited. Kizmin nonchalantly dragged the extra chair out of the corner and across the floor.

'The doctor said we shouldn't talk in here,' Iris reminded her.

The detective glanced at John Lanier's still form in the bed. 'You really think we're bothering him?'

Iris looked at her father, then shook her head.

Kizmin sat down so close to Iris that their knees almost touched. 'We've had a full report from California,' the detective said, pulling out the familiar notebook and pen. 'So you can quit playing games and trying to mislead us.'

'Games?' Iris searched the detective's carefully neutral expression. 'You're the one who's wasting time with meaningless questions while my father's attacker goes free to shoot someone else.'

Kizmin watched her impassively. After a moment she said, 'Why did you lead me to believe that your mother was dead?'

Iris's breath caught and she had to look away.

She had a flash of memory. A knock at the door. Running to answer it. Curious because there were seldom any unexpected visitors at their tucked-away house in the trees. Fearful because nothing was right and the unexpected could make things worse.

*She opened the door and looked up at a tall man silhouetted against the bright sunlight.*

*'Is your father here?'*

*She stepped back and let him enter without answering. He was dressed in a police uniform and was holding his hat in his hands. Turning the hat around and around in his thick-fingered hands.*

*Her father came from the kitchen then. He looked at the policeman and Iris saw something pass between them, an adult signal that meant she wasn't welcome.*

*'Go outside and feed Togo, Iris.'*

*She went out through the front door. There was a breeze stirring and the delicate petals of the apricot blossoms were falling like pink teardrops onto the ground. She crept around the house in the back door to hide in the mud room and listen.*

*The policeman was saying something about her being a cute kid. 'What is she, nine or ten?'*

*'Iris is eight,' said her father in a strangely subdued voice. 'She's tall for her age.'*

*'I bet she's taking this hard, huh?'*

*'I don't know. She's in her own world. Just like her mother. She sees things like her mother.'*

*'Yeah, well, I don't know whether this is good or bad news, but we came up empty-handed. We did everything we could. More than we should have really. There's just not a trace of your wife that we could pick up, and she's definitely not Jane Doe'd in any hospital or morgue in the state of California.'*

*Silence. Then her father said, 'That's it? That's all you can tell me?'*

*'Listen Lanier, the chief did this as a favor to you. There's no law against a woman deciding she wants to disappear. We're not obligated to do anything at all.'*

*More silence.*

*'Hey, it's tough. I know it's tough. I don't know what I'd do if my wife suddenly took off. But there's nothing more our department can help you with. The note she left . . . well that cinches it. It's just not a police matter.'*

*'But she was troubled. Disturbed. I told the chief about having to get her last year at this same time. Doesn't that make a difference?'*

*'No. Sorry. The note spells it all out. Your wife left of her*

*own free will and in the state of California she's got every
legal right to do that.'* The policeman cleared his throat.
*'What you ought to do is get yourself a private eye to track
her down. Then, my advice is to find a good divorce
lawyer. She probably won't want to come back, and even if
she does . . . Who needs a woman like that?'*

That was when the howling sound had started. And she
had run out into the orchard to escape it. But she couldn't
get away because the sound was inside her.

Iris turned her head to look at her comatose father. 'My
mother has been gone twenty years. She obviously has
nothing to do with any of this.'

The detective gave no visible reaction. Iris could feel
the sharp eyes probing, analyzing.

'What do you want me to say, Detective? I wasn't trying
to mislead you. My mother's leaving is ancient history. I
never think of it. I certainly don't consider it an important
detail.'

Still, the detective's eyes bored into her. Her hands and
her forehead felt suddenly damp.

*'Nah, nah, nah, nah, nah. Your mother ran away. My
mommy said that only very bad children have mothers who
run away.'*

*'She did not run away! She's coming back!'*

*'She did too run away. She's gone to find another little
girl better than you.'*

'What's going on?' Iris asked, struggling to compose
herself. 'Have you lost interest in Guatemala?'

An odd amusement flickered in the detective's eyes,
then she sobered and leaned forward slightly.

'We're still just doing our job. Collecting information.
That's what detecting is about, assembling all the information so the answers can fall into place.'

'Have you found out why my father came to New York?'

'No. But maybe you have some ideas,' the detective
suggested.

'I can't explain it. I don't . . . Wait . . . There was a woman here. Did you know there was a woman in the waiting room trying to see him? I asked the nurses about her. No one knows who she is but she was definitely asking about my father. And she acted very strangely when she saw me. I'm sure she knows something.'

Detective Kizmin did not reveal whether she had been aware of the woman before, but her heightened attention made Iris think the information was new.

'Which nurses did you talk to?' Kizmin asked.

'Helen, she's four to midnight, and Luzon, she's eight to four.' Iris watched her write the names in her book. 'Do you think—'

'I'll take care of it,' the detective said, like a parent closing off a line of discussion with a child.

Iris crossed her arms. She wondered if detectives were taught to be suspicious, unforthcoming, and authoritarian, or if Kizmin had been born that way.

'Now, according to your father's hired man . . .'

'My father doesn't have a hired man.'

'No hired man?'

Iris shook her head. 'Pickers are hired during harvest season but that's all. There's no one full time or—'

'Then who is Mr—' the detective consulted her notes, 'Mr Yoshi.'

'Yoshi? You mean Mr Hirano. Yoshi is his first name.'

The detective frowned down at her notebook. 'My source described him as an elderly Japanese male who appeared to be the foreman or hired man.'

'He's taking care of things while my father's away, but he's not the hired man. He owns the place.'

Kizmin pondered this a moment. 'Your father doesn't own the orchards?'

'No. Everything belongs to Mr Hirano except for a small piece that he sold to my father. That's where our house is. My father's house, I mean.'

'So your father works for this Hirano?'

'No. He has a lease. Mr Hirano is very sentimental about his land and won't sell, so he leases it to my father.'

Iris watched Kizmin scribble something.

'I'm not going to inherit a lot of valuable land when my father dies, if you were considering that as a motive,' Iris said. She could tell the detective didn't appreciate the joke.

The woman tapped her bottom lip with the end of her pen and eyed Iris speculatively. 'You say your father never owned a gun?'

Iris sighed. 'Except for a shotgun. As I said before, he sometimes fired rock salt at coyotes or stray dogs who were being pests.'

Kizmin seemed relaxed but her eyes were hawklike, waiting for the rabbit to creep out of its burrow.

'Three days before your father came to New York, he took a short driving trip out of the state of California. Know anything about that?'

'That can't be—' Iris stopped herself. She had been about to say 'that can't be possible' but she wasn't sure of anything anymore. 'Where did he go?'

'Where isn't important. It's the why that's important.'

Reluctantly Iris followed the detective's lead. 'Why?'

'To buy a handgun.'

'A handgun?'

'A .38-caliber snub-nosed revolver to be exact.'

'I can't believe that,' she said, but thought of the receipt for bullets that she'd found in her father's belongings.

'He bought it under his own name. We have the receipts. The records.'

Iris shook her head but the detective went on. 'He took the gun home. Mr Yoshi . . . Mr Hirano rather . . . saw him fire some test rounds in the orchard. Then he flew to New York.'

'I don't understand any of this.'

94

'It's possible that he brought the gun with him, checked it through in his suitcase, and was shot with it.'

'You think he was shot with the gun he bought?'

'It's possible. That was a thirty-eight slug they took out of his brain.'

Iris closed her eyes for a moment, trying to block out the image of a bullet penetrating her father's skull and burrowing into his brain.

'Did you find the gun?'

'No. He didn't leave it at home in California though. They searched out there.'

'But why . . .?'

'It's possible that he took the gun with him to Riverside Park to meet someone. There was a struggle. He pulled out the gun but was overpowered and shot. Then the other person took the gun and ran.' Kizmin hesitated. 'There's also a possibility, given the trajectory of the bullet and other evidence, that your father shot himself.'

Iris was so stunned that she could not reply.

'Maybe your father got too deeply involved in something, didn't know how to get out, couldn't face what was happening.'

'That's ridiculous. My father would never shoot himself.'

'People change. You said you hadn't been close.'

'If he shot himself then the gun would have been right there with him, wouldn't it?'

'That area is crawling with prostitutes and pimps and pushers. Anyone could have grabbed the gun and run with it. Guns are valuable.'

'What about the woman that the ambulance driver saw running away? Have you found her?'

'No. And we may never find her. We have almost nothing to go on.'

'So you're not even trying. It's much easier to make up scenarios than it is to go out and find a solid witness, isn't it?'

95

Kizmin rose from the chair and looked down at Iris.

'I stopped by to see you today as a courtesy.'

'Am I supposed to say thank you? You've stopped implying that my father and I are conspirators in some kind of Guatemalan drug ring, but now you're saying that he's either a murderous psycho who bought a gun and came to New York with the express purpose of shooting someone or he's a pathetic suicide who couldn't face the depths he'd sunk to. Well, no thank you detective. Save your courtesies.'

Iris turned away from the woman and looked at her father. There was a moment's silence. She could feel the detective gathering herself, preparing her next verbal assault.

'Did it ever occur to you,' Kizmin began softly, 'that you don't know anything at all about what your father is capable of?'

'No! Never!' Iris didn't turn around to look at the woman. She kept her eyes riveted to her father's slack face.

'The California police considered John Lanier something of a weird character. Maybe your mother left because she was afraid of him.'

Iris clenched her fists so tightly that her short nails dug into her palms. She was shaking. She stared at her father, afraid to speak, afraid to turn and meet the woman's eyes.

'Maybe he was threatening her. Maybe he's spent all these years searching for her. Maybe he bought the gun and came to New York because he'd found her.'

'No!'

'Think about it,' Kizmin said. 'I know you're a very smart woman. So, start doing some thinking.' With that she turned abruptly and walked out.

After she was gone, Iris began to pace. Back and forth. Wall to wall to wall. She thought of all the things she should have said to the detective. 'My father would never hurt my mother. He would never hurt anyone. And he's not suicidal.' Rage built inside her, growing with every circuit of the room. She wanted to shout at the detective. Make her see the truth. She wanted to tell her that the New York police should stop blaming the victim and get out there and find the real criminals.

Iris jerked the receiver off the bedside phone and dialed the hospital operator. 'Could you give me the room number for Kizmin please? I know it's on four, in yellow I think.'

'Would that be Janelle Kizmin?'

'Yes.'

Armed with the number, Iris stalked out and down the hall in the opposite direction from the nurse's station. She went past the custodian leaning against his mop, around the corner and past the tiny kitchen where an aide was filling pitchers with ice. She followed the numbered doors to her destination and went inside. In the bed closest to the door a tiny white-haired woman snored. The divider curtain had been drawn so Iris couldn't see the occupant of the other bed, but she heard the low murmur of voices.

'Detective Kizmin?' she called in a harsh whisper as she moved closer to the curtain.

There was an inaudible reply.

Iris stepped around the curtain. A woman was propped up in the bed. Her head was shaved and an ugly track of welted stitches crossed her scalp. Both her arms were encased in full length casts. One leg hung from a traction bar. Her skin was an ashy color. The low murmur was coming from the television suspended on a metal arm. Detective Kizmin was nowhere to be seen.

'I'm sorry.' Iris began backing away, ashamed of her intrusion.

'No, wait. I'm Kizmin,' the woman pleaded in a weak raspy voice.

'It's a mistake,' Iris said. 'I shouldn't have come in here.'

On the bedside table was a framed photograph of two young women leaning together affectionately. One, in a graduation cap and gown, was probably the woman in the bed. The other was a younger, softer version of Detective Kizmin.

Iris stared at the photo. The faces in it were achingly beautiful. Aglow with the promise of the future.

'Will you change the television for me?' the woman asked.

'Of course. What channel do you want?'

'I want . . .' A look of distressed confusion came over her ashen face and tears leaked from the corners of her eyes.

'Don't cry,' Iris pleaded. 'It's all right. I'm in no hurry. I'll stay till you decide.'

'But I can't remember. All I do is watch this television. Every day I watch it, but I can't remember what's on when or what channel.'

'I'll flip through all the stations for you, and you can see what's on.'

'OK.'

Iris dried the woman's eyes with a tissue and slowly turned the dial through all the choices several times.

'That one,' the woman finally said.

'Anything else?' Iris asked.

'My pillow.'

Gently, Iris adjusted the pillow beneath the woman's ravaged head.

'Are you the minister?' the woman asked.

'No.'

'A lady minister came to see me once but I can't remember what she looked like.'

'It wasn't me.'

'Are you the new teacher?'

'No.'

'I like your eyes. Are they blue or green?'

'A little of both I guess.'

'Mixed-up eyes.'

'I have to leave,' Iris said.

'Everybody leaves. I'm the only one who can't leave. My sister leaves all the time. That's her in the picture. She could be real pretty if she wanted to, but she doesn't care. She doesn't care about anything like the rest of us.'

'I'm sorry but I really do have to leave.'

'Are you the rape counselor?'

'No,' Iris said and then ducked around the curtain. She nearly bumped into Detective Kizmin who was standing just behind the curtain, fist pressed to her mouth and eyes closed.

'I—' Iris began, but Kizmin shook her head and put a finger to her lips. Quietly they left the room together.

'I'm sorry,' Iris said as soon as they were safely in the hall. 'I was looking for you. I shouldn't have gone in there.' She saw the woman differently now. She saw the hardness and the fierceness differently.

Kizmin's hands were shaking and her face was a mask of control. Iris tried to think of something to say that would adequately express her sympathy, but nothing she could think of seemed right.

'I'm sorry,' she said again. 'You must be so worried about your sister.'

Kizmin's eyes lasered into her, ablaze with anger. 'That room . . . that subject . . . is off limits to you. Understand?'

Iris nodded stiffly, her sympathy reverting to resentment.

The detective stared into her face for several long, uncomfortable seconds, then cleared her throat and said gruffly, 'I need to talk to you anyway. I just got off the phone with Detective Barney. We got a body. Some guy's dog got loose and sniffed it out under an old mattress.'

Kizmin seemed to draw into herself then. The fierceness in her eyes faded.

'It's bad timing,' she said wearily. 'Another locket killer victim turned up a couple of hours ago and everybody who's anybody is at that party. There's not much excitement about a stiff who got dumped with the trash in a rough area. Maybe a junkie or a hooker. Maybe an OD. For sure nothing that's going to interest the press or make anybody famous.'

'Why are you telling me all this?' Iris asked carefully.

'Because it's bones. And it's partly buried. That's what you do, isn't it?'

'I don't recall explaining what I do.'

'You didn't have to. I've got a file on you.'

'So what do you want from me?'

Kizmin looked at her and the odd amusement resurfaced in her eyes, only it wasn't exactly amusement. Iris realized now that there was an element of respect or even admiration in it.

'I'm asking for your help,' the detective admitted.

'Are you serious? After all your insinuations and accusations . . . now you suddenly want my help?'

Kizmin inhaled deeply.

'Things go into compartments, you see. On the one hand there's you and your father. Something bad went down in Riverside Park. We don't know what yet, but we're going to find out. We don't know if you were involved. I doubt you were. But all that . . . that entire problem . . . belongs in that compartment over there.

'Now here is a body under a mattress. That goes in another compartment. Completely separate. A body that has nothing left but bones and hair. We don't get bodies like that too often here in New York. This is something unusual.'

Kizmin touched her hand to her forehead a moment. 'You know how it works here in the city? We've got a

100

medical examiner's office. They've already sent the big guns to the locket killer victim so they're going to send us a guy who's got three years of training as a doctor's assistant. He's overworked and underpaid and in a hurry and he's used to seeing corpses on a sidewalk or in a bathtub. Not bones half buried in the dirt.'

'But don't you have an archaeologist or anthropologist you can call in situations like this?' Iris asked.

'Believe me, things are not like in the movies. There's no great expert going to drop what he's doing and come running to help us. Later, after the bones are at the morgue, the ME might call a specialist in to consult, but not now, and especially not now for this body. And you and I both know that this recovery could make all the difference in determining the manner of death or even identifying the victim.'

The woman's intensity was captivating. It was hard for Iris to remain hostile.

'You want advice?' Iris asked.

'I want you to come out and supervise the recovery.'

'You want me to do you a favor? That's quite a request, given the circumstances.'

'I'm not asking you to do me a favor. That's not me rotting out there. That's not me whose family is suffering, searching for their daughter or wife or mother. That's not me somebody will get away with murdering – if it was murder.

'Don't you have any professional ethics? Don't you have a conscience? How can you turn your back on that poor soul who got dumped out there?'

Iris shook her head. 'It's not . . . it's not my responsibility.'

Kizmin seemed not to have heard her. She seemed instead to be considering something. Her brow was furrowed and her expression was suffused with a perplexed wonderment.

101

'I believe in fate,' she said finally. 'I've never had a skeleton before. My partner, with all his years on the force, has never had a skeleton. Now, suddenly we've got bones and at the same time we've got a bone expert right under our noses. That isn't just an odd coincidence. That's fate.'

'I don't believe in fate,' Iris said. 'And I . . .'

Her pulse was thumping and there was a roaring in her head. How could she refuse? She couldn't. But a recently deceased person? A person who had been alive while she herself was alive? Someone she could have walked beside or spoken to? A possible murder victim?

The vision of a dying woman came to her. The woman was holding out a bloody hand, begging for help. She shook the image away, frightened of it.

'I don't . . . have any experience with crime work.'

'Come on. I know your education and work history. I've even had a conversation with one of your old professors. You're supposed to be brilliant, Dr Lanier. An artist with bones I've been told. So, how different can this be?'

'It is different. It is.'

'Maybe so. But with you there we can at least get the excavation part of it right. My partner said he's been calling all over and can't find anyone with excavation experience who's available right now.'

Kizmin leaned closer and looked into Iris's eyes, searching, as though she knew every secret Iris had hidden.

'It's fate,' she said again. 'Things happen that are meant to happen.'

Iris backed up a step.

'The hospital might need me . . . My father . . .'

'I'll fix it where they can reach you through my pager.'

'I don't have any equipment.'

'I know where we can borrow some. The best. Have you heard of Roy Shaw?'

102

'Yes.' Of course she had. The name was a legend in forensic anthropology.

'I do volunteer work for an organization that funds him. They set up a lab for him here in town. We can borrow some of the equipment.'

'Why don't you just call him for help?'

'He's in the Middle East somewhere. Sorting out mass graves.'

Iris pressed her hand against her forehead. The hallway compressed around her, squeezing her, threatening to crush her.

She didn't want to unearth recent remains. She didn't want to get near a murder victim. She was afraid. She was a coward and she would always be a coward.

Just like her mother.

Her mother who had run away. Who had abandoned them. For it was cowardice that was at the heart of abandonment. Running away was a weak and cowardly act. And she was just like her mother, wasn't she? Fearful. Weak hearted. Always ready to turn away. Run away. That was the legacy her mother had left her. Cowardice. How could she do anything but run from this?

'When?' The word came as barely a whisper.

'Now.'

She nodded because her throat was so tight she didn't think she could make another sound.

# Six

The sky was a dull grey by the time they reached their
destination. Iris stepped out of the heated car into the cold
air and stood, staring. Beneath a curve of elevated
roadway a trash-strewn shoulder of sloping ground was
strung with bright yellow crime-scene ribbon. Two police
cruisers sat below on a narrow access road. A cluster of
uniformed men and one suited man leaned against the
cruisers in relaxed conversation. A small knot of spectators, mostly teenagers, milled restlessly nearby, accompanied by the pounding of rap music from a boom-box.

The man in the suit broke away from the group and
started toward them. It was Detective Barney.

'What took you so long, Kizmin?' he called. 'Did your
party invitation have the wrong time on it?'

Kizmin ignored him and went around to open the
trunk. Iris carefully lifted out a canvas bag of equipment
and Kizmin gathered the rest. They had been let into
the forensics lab by a man with a key. Iris had been
awestruck by the facility but had quickly chosen what
she wanted and loaded it into the car. Now she was
there, at the crime scene, with more equipment than she
really needed and no more excuses or delays to keep her
from doing the job.

'You know how long we've been cooling our asses out
here?' Barney said as he reached them. 'The ME's guy
came by once. I ran the plan by him and he said he'd be

105

back. I told him you must have stopped to get your nails done.'

'Say hello to Dr Lanier, Detective Barney,' Kizmin said without looking at the man.

Iris was almost embarrassed by Kizmin's use of the formal title. She was accustomed to being Dr Lanier only on paper. On diplomas and résumés and reports. The dig team sometimes called her Doctor, but there it was a form of teasing, almost a ridicule of the title.

'Yeah. Yeah.' He nodded toward Iris in greeting. 'I still don't know if this is a good idea.'

'Have you got a better one?' Kizmin demanded. She sighed. 'This was a murder,' she said. 'I can feel it in my gut. That woman didn't just crawl under there and die. And I don't think she OD'd on her own and was then just dumped here. I think somebody killed her and then tried to get rid of the body.'

Barney grunted something unintelligible.

'I'm telling you, Barney . . . It was murder and we were meant to solve it. Dr Lanier was dropped in our laps because we were meant to make good on this one.'

'Or this was dropped in our laps so you'd have an excuse to learn some anthro-whatever,' Barney said. He frowned at Kizmin then shot Iris a look of open skepticism.

'Fuckin' fate,' he said. 'Bunch of voodoo bullshit.'

'Be nice, Barney. She wasn't too happy about coming out here.'

Barney muttered several obscenities under his breath.

'Ready, Doctor?' Kizmin said, not waiting for an answer before starting forward.

Iris followed, feeling like an impostor. Like she was playing a role for Kizmin, fooling Detective Barney and the others. She was not at all prepared to step into the scene.

A baby-faced uniformed cop met them at the edge of

the ribboned-off area. 'Watch it,' he cautioned. 'There's needles lying around.'

The remains were partially buried but Iris could see that they were skeletonized. Completely scoured of flesh. A tangle of tiny braids stuck out of the dirt at the top of the head. The braids had small beads woven into them.

'That mattress over there was on top of it,' the young cop said. 'Otherwise nothing's been touched.'

'Box springs,' Kizmin said.

'What?'

'It's not a mattress, MacDonald, it's the box springs that goes under a mattress. Details are important.'

'Oh. Yeah.'

'That's what did it,' Iris said, as much to herself as to Kizmin. 'The moisture was trapped and the insects had a perfect environment.'

Iris stared down at the skeleton. One arm, folded across the chest, was completely exposed. There was a ring still on the finger. A flexed knee protruded from the dirt. The contours of the nose and eye orbits were faintly discernible just beneath the silt. This was no piece of history, no storybook character from some ancient civilization. These bones were all that was left of a human being who could have spoken to her, touched her, laughed with her, who could have been standing beside her on that very spot not long ago.

She felt dizzy and sick. Afraid. She knew that the fear had to be her own but it felt strangely alien to her, as though it was issuing from the grave at her feet.

'Let's get to work,' Kizmin said, breaking the spell. 'We've got plenty of officers here. What do you want them to do?'

Iris looked around. The cluster of uniformed men had moved from the cruisers up to the ribbon and they were all watching, listening, some with expressions of dread or distaste, some with curiosity, some with the neutral stern-ness that all police officers seemed to learn in the course of their jobs.

'How many men do you want to do the digging?' asked Kizmin.

Iris looked back down at the empty eyes and the naked arm, the carefully beaded hair, the ring so obscenely loose on the fourth digit. The woman was so vulnerable. So exposed.

'I think I'd like to do the digging myself, if that's all right.'

Surprise registered in the detective's eyes, then she nodded. 'Whatever you want,' she said.

Iris bent close and looked at the hand. 'We need to remove that ring carefully and put it in a bag. There are hairs caught in it.'

Quickly, Kizmin produced a plastic bag and bent to help Iris collect the ring.

'Should I treat this as a routine dig?' Iris asked.

'What do I know about routine digs? If routine means you're careful and thorough, then yes, go to it.'

Clearly the detective wanted her to take charge and lead the effort, but Iris had no confidence in her ability to be a leader. She wished they would all go away and leave her alone with the woman.

She scanned the scene once again.

'I'm going to mark off a rectangular area with stakes and string. It looks like there was a shallow burial attempt that was eroded during the last rain, so we'll extend the stakes downhill to include grave dirt that washed down.'

'What do you want the rest of us to do?' Kizmin asked.

'All the surface artifacts have to be recorded by position and collected before we start on the grave.' She hesitated. 'And we need to take pictures . . .'

'Where's the photographer?' Kizmin shouted.

'Taking a break,' Detective Barney shouted back. 'He

got tired of waiting so I sent him out for coffee.'

Kizmin gave an exasperated snort.

'That's fine,' Iris said. 'It will take me a few minutes to get my stakes in, map the area, and get my line level.'

She drew in a slow measured breath, then glanced at Kizmin and the others to see if their faces reflected her lack of confidence. They appeared to be fooled. She squatted down to unzip the canvas bag. The borrowed equipment was the best. A Brunton compass. Digital levels. Even a compact satellite map station hookup. She was familiar with such equipment but seldom had the pleasure of actually working with it.

She mounted the calculator on the tripod and began the process of establishing coordinates. It wasn't necessary that she have such exact data for this dig, but the activity was calming. She needed to do it.

The photographer returned and Kizmin put him to work. Gradually, things took on a momentum of their own. Iris became so absorbed that nearly an hour passed before she paused and took stock of the process she had set in motion.

They had formed a team of sorts. The area had been mapped, photographed, and cleared. The photographer was hovering nearby, waiting for further photo orders, and a cop who had admitted to 'some artistic talent' was making a hand-drawn diagram on graph paper. It was all so strange, different from any experience Iris had had, yet so engrossing that she had lost herself in it completely.

'I'll need two people on the sifter,' she called to the uniformed officers standing by. 'And two to carry buckets. We're going to sift all the dirt we take out from around the remains and all the dirt that's washed downhill from the rain.'

A general groan went up but they shifted into position. Iris took the filed Goldblatt trowel out of her back pocket, knelt on a board at the outer perimeter of the grave, and began to dig.

'Can I help?' Kizman asked.

Iris glanced up at the woman's face. There was a hunger in the detective's eyes, as though she wanted to claw the evidence out of the dirt with her bare hands.

'Grab that other trowel,' Iris said, 'and I'll tell you what to do.'

Hours later Kizmin straightened. 'Don't you ever get hungry?' she asked.

Iris looked up. Kizmin's face was streaked with dirt and her wool slacks and silk blouse were a mess.

'Food,' Kizmin said. 'Lunch. Aren't you hungry?'

'Is it lunchtime already?' Iris looked around and saw that all the men except MacDonald were gathered down at the cars.

'It's long past,' Kizmin said.

'We can't quit. It's going to storm soon. Evidence could be destroyed.'

'OK, OK. But how about a five-minute sandwich break? The boys have some take-away. We can go down there, or MacDonald can bring it up.'

'Sure,' Iris said, then turned to MacDonald. 'Just bring me anything. And water. Do they have water?'

She stood to stretch out her back and neck. The skeleton was completely exposed, reclining on a pedestal of soil with everything cut away around it.

There was nothing to remind her of Guatemala, but she found herself thinking of Moonsmoke. Of that solemn, wise, sad face. Her vision of Moonsmoke grew so vivid that she felt as though the ancient queen was there, standing at her shoulder, encouraging her. It was a ridiculous notion, but one she couldn't shake.

'Do you believe in ghosts, too, Detective Kizmin?'

'I certainly don't disbelieve. This job has made me a cynic with an open mind. Ghosts, angels, the devil, the tooth fairy . . . If they're anywhere, they're here in New York.' Amusement filled her eyes. 'Why, is that your weak point? You don't believe in fate but you think there are ghosts?'

'No. I was just curious about you. About how far your superstitions went.'

'My archaic silly superstitions?'

'I didn't say that.'

'You know, the trouble with people who know a lot about something is that they forget how much they don't know about other things.'

Uncomfortable with the direction of the conversation, Iris stared down at the bones. 'What will happen when we get her out?' she asked.

'The medical examiner's office will take over.' Kizmin sighed. 'So it definitely is a her? I thought so, from the hair, and the jewelry, but you never know these days. The way some teenagers dress . . . Wonder if she had kids.'

'I don't think so.'

'You can figure that out too, huh? How about age?'

'Between sixteen and nineteen, I think.'

'You've got reasons, I assume?'

'Oh yes. I'm basing it on Ubelaker's epiphyses union data.'

'Come on – give it to me in English.'

'The epiphyses are at the ends of the bones. Here, look at the radius and the ulna,' Iris pointed to the two long slender bones that ran side by side from the skeleton's elbow to wrist.

'That's the forearm, right?' Kizmin asked, probing her own arm as though comparing anatomy.

'Yes. The end of each of those bones is the epiphyses. When we're young the epiphyses fuse to the main shaft. By twenty-one or twenty-two all epiphyses fusion is complete. That's the big separation point in determining age.

111

'Bones grow and fuse at different rates so if the subject was under twenty-two at the time of death then we can go to individual bones to determine an age range.' Iris pointed to the end of the radius. 'We've got complete fusion on both ends here. That can happen as early as thirteen in females, so we know she was at least thirteen. It can happen as late as nineteen for the distal ends, so that puts her between thirteen and nineteen.

'But then we look at the ulna. The distal end of the ulna is completely fused and you usually don't see that until sixteen. Between sixteen and nineteen. So, now we've moved her youngest possible age up to sixteen, but kept the nineteen as the outer possibility.'

'Why stop at nineteen? Couldn't she have been twenty?'

'No. The head of the humerus isn't fused yet so I'll have to stick with nineteen.'

MacDonald arrived with thick deli sandwiches, wrapped so that they could be eaten without touching anything but the butcher paper. The two women stood beside the grave and ate in silence. Occasional laughter drifted up to them from the men clustered around the cars. Iris had the distinct feeling that some of the laughter was directed at them.

Suddenly, she had to know more about Kizmin. She felt an inexplicable connection to the woman, as though they shared a history or had some other deeply forged bond, yet they were barely acquainted.

'How long have you been partners with Detective Barney?' she asked.

'Not long. We got paired when I was assigned to the homicide task force.' Kizmin regarded the group of men below them for a moment. 'Don't let him fool you. Barney's a good cop and he's not a bad guy. He's just old-style NYPD. From the days when cops were supposed to be "real men". Tough guys. With Irish or Italian names.

112

'He'd been happily partnered for twelve years with a clone of himself. Then the guy died and, bingo, next thing he knows he's partnered with a new-style cop, a law-school graduate who's into brain power rather than muscle mass. Who's dark skinned. And, biggest shock of all, dickless.

'One of the first things he said to me was, "What good is a dickless dick?" '

Iris laughed. 'Think you'll last together?'

'No. But it doesn't matter. I'll be moving on.'

Iris waited for the detective to elaborate. When she didn't Iris said, 'What's a homicide task force?'

Kizmin finished chewing a huge bite of sandwich. 'Sorry,' she said. 'This job breeds bad eating habits. Too much grabbing food on the run.' She cocked her head to the side. 'Let's see . . . How should I explain a homicide task force? Barney calls it the roving band of merry dicks. Basically, it's a small group of homicide detectives who go all over Manhattan, not working out of any one precinct. It's one of the new mayor's brainstorms.'

'If you and Barney are part of a special homicide group then why aren't you two investigating the locket killer?'

'Ahh . . .' The detective's mouth curved into a brief, mirthless smile. 'There's a special locket killer task force for that. And even if there weren't, we wouldn't be called out on it. See, we're what is known in the locker room as the shit smoothers. We catch the stuff that's not important enough to rate any big guns, but that's involved with something that the mayor wants to smooth over or grandstand on.

'Your father . . . that was grandstanding. We were called out because, even though it didn't look like it was going to turn into anything volatile or important, the victim appeared to be a tourist and the city is always

**113**

careful about covering asses when it comes to tourists.

'This today . . . we were called out because things in Harlem haven't been so rosy and the community leaders have been complaining to the mayor. We were sent to make it look like the higher ups are really concerned about another body in this part of the city.'

Kizmin glanced down the slope at the men below. 'That's another reason my partner is in ill humor. He doesn't like Harlem. He doesn't like being surrounded by faces darker than his. And he doesn't like working with boys from the Dirty Thirty.'

'The Dirty Thirty?'

'The thirtieth precinct. It's got a pretty bad rep. Twenty-nine officers indicted for corruption awhile back and more who were just as dirty but didn't get caught in the act. Those guys got modified assignments and other punishments when they should have been arrested too. Not just beat cops either. Supervising officers. Guys with rank.'

'What were they doing?'

'Making money.' Kizmin sighed heavily. 'Stealing from drug dealers. Shaking people down. Dealing drugs.' She shrugged. 'Barney starts to rant and rave whenever we get close to West 151st Street. Bad cops make him feel personally betrayed.'

'But it doesn't bother you?' Iris asked, thinking she heard tolerance or maybe resignation in the detective's voice.

'Sure it bothers me. But I can't help feeling sorry for the guys who fall. It's tough being in a precinct like the three-oh. Slogging away in the muck every day without seeing any real progress, working in a community that mostly hates your guts, watching the bad guys get rich when you can't put braces on your kids' teeth.' She shook her head and then silently finished her sandwich.

'You went to law school?'

'Yeah. Columbia. Compliments of the Kaliker Foundation.'

'You're kidding! I went to school on a Kaliker grant, too.'

Kizmin's face registered surprise, then puzzlement, then suspicion. 'Kaliker only gives grants for law related studies.'

Iris shrugged. 'They paid my way through anthropology.'

'I can check that out, you know.'

Iris had to smile. She wondered if being a detective meant that nothing could ever be taken on faith.

'Why would I lie about something like that?' she asked.

'Because you knew my connection to Kaliker and the foundation, and you wanted an in with me.'

'You sound paranoid, Kizmin.'

The detective shrugged. 'Paranoia is healthy in my job. It keeps you alive.' She smiled then. It was the first genuine smile that Iris had seen on her face. 'Why didn't you tell me before that you were a Kal alumnus?'

'I didn't know it would make a difference.'

'To me, that's as good as someone saying they're a cop.'

'A dubious distinction,' Iris said. She thought a moment. 'So what's your connection to the Kaliker Foundation? Just the scholarship or is there more?'

'That's where I donate all my time. I coordinate their battered women referral services and hotlines.' Kizmin gestured toward the canvas bag that the tools had been carried in. 'We're using these tools courtesy of the Kaliker Foundation. Shaw's lab actually belongs to them.'

'The foundation built that lab?'

'Yes. It's part of their crime solver program. They're trying to get more outside experts involved in solving crimes.'

Kizmin finished her Diet Coke. 'How'd you do it? I mean, how did you get around the law requirement and get a grant?'

115

'I don't know. At the start of my senior year in high school a letter came announcing that I'd won this incredible scholarship. No one in California knew anything about the Kaliker Foundation, much less what their usual scholarship requirements were, so I had no idea that I was an exception. And I didn't ask too many questions. I just wrote back and said yes.'

'That was before Kaliker's work got any national attention,' Kizmin said with sudden intensity. 'Things are different now. People everywhere have heard of Kaliker. Even the White House has taken notice. One day soon Nathan Kaliker will be recognized as a modern hero.'

'He's always been a hero to me,' Iris said. 'Without that grant I doubt that I'd have a PhD, and I certainly wouldn't have been able to afford the schools I went to.'

'Me too. I owe the foundation a lot. That's why I work there, even when I don't have the time to spare.' Kizmin's expression lightened. 'You should go by the office and say hello.'

'Maybe,' Iris said, regretting this whole turn in the conversation. The last thing she wanted to do was go by the foundation offices. Being there, amidst the rooms full of dedicated volunteers, always made her feel guilty. Made her ask herself what she had done to deserve such a generous gift. Made her worry over the debt she owed the foundation. A debt she felt she could never repay.

'They're always glad to see graduates.'

Iris shook her head. 'If they remember me at all it would be as money wasted, I'm sure. My skills certainly haven't benefited the foundation any. Or furthered their goals of improving society. And I'll never be rich enough to give them financial help.'

'That's not the kind of place it is,' Kizmin insisted. 'The grants are absolutely unconditional, and there are some graduates in high positions who don't acknowledge the foundation or give support in any way. Nathan Kaliker

116

never intended it to be a yoke of obligation.'

'Maybe. But being around Nathan Kaliker, being in the foundation offices, makes me feel guilty.'

'Ohhh . . .' Kizmin scoffed.

'Maybe it's all inside my own head,' Iris admitted, 'but it does. I did some volunteer work there when I was living in New York. Nathan himself fired me. Gave me a long speech about how talented I was and how I shouldn't be wasting my time typing and filing when they had plenty of high school kids to do that.'

'Typing and filing?'

'Well, what else was I qualified to do? I didn't have the law background to help with the justice program. I didn't have the counseling experience to work the victim hotline. There was really nothing I could handle there except cleaning or clerical, and I wasn't very good at either of those. I'm probably the only volunteer who was ever fired.'

Kizmin paused in thought a moment. 'I've been out of law school and working at the foundation for about five years. When were you there?'

'Five years ago.'

'What month did you leave?'

'May.'

'And I started in June. We almost met. We came very close to meeting. And now here we are.'

'Fate again?' Iris asked in amusement.

'Some things are, you know.'

'How do you separate fate from coincidence or chance? Or the laws of statistical probability for that matter.'

'When you can't avoid something . . . When you can't run or hide or even turn away . . . That's fate.'

Iris shook her head.

One side of Kizmin's mouth curved into a wry half-smile. 'Call it whatever you want, chance or fate, but the fact is that you were educated by a foundation committed to fighting crime and here you are, using that education to help solve a crime. There's a certain fateful symmetry to that, don't you think?'

'I am here because you pushed me into it,' Iris reminded her.

The discussion was making her uneasy. She wasn't sure why. But then, suddenly, she recalled hearing her mother and father arguing about fate. The exact words eluded her but she remembered that her father had been angry and shouting about fate and magic, calling it all nonsense, and her mother had been crying, insisting that it was her fate to do something, or maybe that she'd already done something because it was fated.

'So,' Kizmin asked with the same smile, 'those important people you threatened to call, was that—'

'The Kaliker Foundation,' Iris admitted.

Kizmin laughed. 'See? It's all fate. If you had called there it would have come to my attention and we'd have gotten straight about each other right away. Then I'd have naturally asked you to come out and help on this. And you'd have come without any hesitation.'

'Would I?'

'You would.'

'But it wasn't just an animosity toward you that made me hesitate. I am honestly not experienced in forensics, and I was afraid to work recent remains . . . especially on a murder victim.'

'Are you still afraid?'

Iris glanced over at the skeleton she had unearthed. 'Yes. I'm still afraid.'

'Of what?'

Iris tried to think of a way to explain. 'Of the power,' she finally said. 'The power of a violent death.'

'But didn't some of your Maya die horrible deaths?'

'That's different.'

'How?' Kizmin asked. 'Murder has been the same since

the beginning of human history.'

'Yes, but it happened so long ago, in a time and a culture that I can learn about but I can't really imagine. Those deaths are just historical footnotes. They don't ever come to life in here.' Iris touched a fingertip to her temple.

'So you're only committed to your work as long as it's nice and distant and unaffecting.'

'I didn't say that. Besides, are you implying that historical research, that archaeology and anthropology, are worthless pursuits?'

'Not at all. For some people I'm sure the ancient Maya come to life in here.' Kizmin tapped her forehead. 'Those are the people who were meant to do that work.'

'Fate again?' Iris asked with a touch of sarcasm.

Kizmin studied her for a moment. 'The only kind of work I want to do is the stuff that eats at my thoughts and my guts. The stuff that grabs me and won't let go.'

'Maybe, detective, the rest of us don't have your courage or passion.'

'Everybody's got it, doctor. Some people just won't use it.'

Iris didn't respond. She stuffed the uneaten half of her sandwich into a bag and went back to the bones, picking up a brush, a spoon, and a dental pick to continue the detail work. Kizmin finished her sandwich and crumpled up the paper. She squatted down on the other side of the skeleton and stared at the exposed bones.

'What do you think happened to our girl here?'

Iris shook her head. 'I'm not qualified to say. Recent death is not my field.'

'Oh, come on, don't dance me around with any more modesty. You could probably write an encyclopedia on this stuff. I'm not trying to pin you down for anything official. Just give me some ideas.'

'Well, there are some suspicious notches in the ribs.'

'Meaning?'

'A knife I'd guess.'

'Any thoughts as to how long she's been here?'

'Since last summer maybe. Judging from the evidence of insect cycles—'

'Stop.' Kizmin held up her hand. 'Don't tell me anything about insects right now, OK?'

'She's about ready to travel. Then we can sift the dirt underneath her.'

Kizmin looked at Iris. 'Thanks. For doing this.'

Iris lowered her eyes, uncomfortable with the detective's gratitude. 'I just hope you can catch the person who put her here.'

'The guy you mean. Chances are it was a guy who put her here.'

'Is that based on your instincts?'

'No. That's based on statistical probabilities. Most violent crimes are committed by males.'

Carefully, Iris freed the bones and packaged them for travel. For a moment she felt it – the fear. Her own or the dead girl's she wasn't sure. Then two of the uniforms went to work digging out the rest of the dirt and sifting it.

'That's that,' she said as she watched the van pull away with the remains of a unknown woman. Girl really. Just a girl.

A curious emptiness settled in Iris's chest. A sense of loss: Who would be responsible for the girl now? Whose hands would trace the symmetry of her bones? Whose eyes would probe her secrets? Who would care?

Did the girl have a mother out there somewhere who grieved for her loss? Did she have a father who was asking himself what he should have done differently to keep her safe?

She tried to shake off the mood, tried to convince herself that it was all rooted in the proprietary feeling she had toward remains that she had excavated. There was always an incompleteness when circumstances prevented her from doing the lab work-up on a discovery. This was no different. It was now someone else's problem and privilege to unlock the mysteries of these bones, and accepting that depressed her.

Suddenly, the present returned. Her father lying so still in the hospital. An unknown attacker. An unexplained shooting. She had been so absorbed in the work that the present had receded, but now, with a sickening rush, it was back.

The van turned out of sight and she sighed involuntarily.

'I'm sorry,' Kizmin said.

'For what?'

'For all the hassles. The questioning.' Kizmin stared off at something in the distance. 'The Guatemala connection really grabbed us. Steered us in the wrong direction at first. Not too long ago we had a dope-related triple murder with a tie to Guatemala.'

Iris nodded.

'Your father was into something heavy, though. Whether he knew it or not. And I think the shooting was related to that.'

'How about the suicide theory?'

'Oh, that was never really serious. The ME did tell us that it was possible. But the evidence is also consistent with your father being shot while struggling over the gun with someone else.'

'And my mother? Do you have any evidence that she's a factor?'

'No. None at all. That was just fishing. But I've gotta tell you, it does make me wonder. And the California guys did paint your dad as a nutcase.'

'He's eccentric. He's set in his ways. But he's not a nut.'

Kizmin shrugged. 'I never met the man myself.'

'What could he possibly have been involved in? He's been leading a completely straight, quiet, and lawful life.'

121

'Shit happens,' Kizmin said. 'No telling what he stumbled into. We'll just have to keep digging and hope that something breaks.'

'What if I wanted you to stop digging?'

'What?'

'Maybe I don't want to know any more. What good will it do, anyway? It won't make him well.'

'I can't believe I'm hearing this. Don't you want his attacker to be caught?'

'Not as much as I want things to go back like they were.'

'You're afraid I'll find stuff that you don't want to know.'

'Maybe. Maybe I just think the whole investigation is a waste of time – that it was a simple mugging and you'll never find the guy.'

'Well, regardless of what you think, I can't give up. I've got my teeth into this and I'm not about to give up.' Kizmin hesitated. 'My partner didn't want to tell you this yet, but an emergency room nurse came forward yesterday. She'd been on vacation since right after your father was brought in. According to her she was walking past his gurney when he suddenly grabbed her arm and said something like, "Tell my daughter hope is the key," or maybe, "Tell my daughter the key is hope." Does that mean anything to you?'

'No. It doesn't sound like something my father would say.'

'Kizmin!' Detective Barney shouted. 'Just got a radio call. There's big trouble at Morningside Hospital. Fourth floor, blue wing.'

Without a word Kizmin ran for her car. Iris was right behind her.

# Seven

Three fire trucks blocked the street outside the hospital. Kizmin skidded the car to a stop in a no-parking zone and both women ran for the main entrance.

'Nobody goes in!' shouted one of the uniformed police officers who blocked the doorway.

Kizmin held up her gold shield, grabbed Iris's arm and pushed through the crowd.

Inside, the lobby was filled with police and firefighters milling about, but there was no sense of urgency. The trouble was obviously over.

Kizmin displayed her shield to a fireman who seemed to be in charge. 'What have we got?' she asked.

'Somebody built a bonfire on the stairs at the fourth floor landing. It made a lot of smoke but we caught it before there was much damage. The arson investigators are up there now.'

'Are the elevators on?'

'Yeah. They're on.'

They rode in tense silence. At the fourth floor the doors opened onto chaos. Firefighters, police officers, and hospital staff seemed to be rushing in all directions. Patients in hospital gowns and slippers were being led down the hall. Bedridden patients were being wheeled through the confusion. The acrid smell of smoke still hung in the air.

Iris ran to her father's room. It was empty. The bed and the IV pole were gone. The heart monitor stood mute and blank with its wires dangling loose.

'I'm going to check on my sister,' Kizmin said from over her shoulder and Iris realized that the detective had come into the room behind her.

Iris went back out into the crowded hallway. 'Where are you taking them?' she called to a nurse pushing a patient on a gurney.

'Back to their rooms,' the nurse answered.

'From where?' Iris asked, but the nurse was already beyond earshot.

She stood in the hallway a moment, people streaming around her, and then she began to walk against the flow. Through the maze of corridors, through the tunnel that crossed over the street and into the west wing. Inside the swinging doors labeled 4 West she found what she had been looking for. Patients in beds and gurneys filled every available space. This was the safe area they had been evacuated to.

She edged through the sea of moaning, frightened people, scanning the faces, looking for her father's bandaged head. An elderly woman clutched at Iris's sleeve with skeletal fingers.

'Don't let me burn,' she pleaded.

Iris bent over to look directly into the frail face against the pillow. 'The fire is out,' she said, pressing the thin hand between her own. 'You're safe.'

'Promise?'

'I promise. Just rest. Try to sleep.' She straightened the woman's blanket. 'Are you comfortable?'

'How can I be comfortable? I'm old. I'm sick.'

'You'll be moved back to your room soon.'

'In time for dinner? I don't want to miss my dinner.'

'No one wants you to miss your dinner.'

The exchange made Iris's chest ache. She continued on through the corridors, soothing people's fears when she could. How did the nurses do it, she wondered. How did they go to work each day without drowning in the heartache?

Finally, she found her father. His bed had been pushed into a corner. A man was leaning against the wall beside him. The man was vaguely familiar but she didn't care who he was. All she cared about was her father.

Relief made her knees weak as she navigated through the crush of beds to reach him.

'He's fine,' the man leaning against the wall said. 'Fine as he was before the fire anyway.'

It was then that Iris realized who the man was: one of the janitors whose responsibility was the hall outside her father's room.

'Thank you for taking care of him,' she said in a rush of deeply felt gratitude.

The man nodded.

They waited in silence while the hospital staff moved the patients around them, bed by bed. Iris felt the man eyeing her with an odd curiosity that made her uncomfortable.

'You don't have to stay,' Iris said. 'I can take care of him now.'

The man shrugged and mumbled something about doctor's orders, but he moved farther away and leaned against the wall near the window. When it came their turn to leave he waved the nurses away and insisted on pushing the bed. The nurses, two young women who were unfamiliar to Iris, were too harried to argue.

After her father was safely settled in his room again, Iris went to Janelle Kizmin's room. Cautiously she peeked around the curtain. Janelle lay in the bed asleep, but the detective was not in the room.

On the way back to her father's room, Iris stopped in the little service kitchen. She filled a pitcher with ice and held it under the water spigot. Outside in the corridor she heard voices.

It was the janitor talking to a man in a suit. Something about the fire. About the fire being a diversion.

She stayed late at the hospital, bought a take-away sandwich for dinner, then went to the rented room. The heat was high in the building and there were no individual controls. She thought about calling Andretti and complaining, then decided against it. There were probably others who called him to complain that it wasn't warm enough.

Since her room was on the end it had two outside walls and two windows, the north-facing one that opened onto the fire escape and another that faced east. She cut the paint seal around the sash of the east window and shoved it open. To reassure herself she stuck her head out and checked. Below was a sheer drop down a smooth brick wall. No one was going to appear outside that window.

As she was drawing back she heard the faint beginnings of the music. It was always the same. Sad and low. She crossed to the fire escape window and pushed it up a few inches. The music was much louder there. It sounded as though it came from just above.

She thought about leaving the window up. Just to listen awhile. But it wasn't safe. It wouldn't be wise.

She soaked in a hot tub, wrote Daniel Becker a letter explaining the situation with her father, then slipped between the soft, worn sheets. So much privacy. After months of living with casual acquaintances it felt good to go to bed in a room of her own. A bath, a real bed, a private room. She tried to hold on to those comforts, to lull herself to sleep, but the pleasure of her small luxuries dissipated quickly. For an hour she stared up at the dark ceiling, straining to hear the faraway music. Then she got up.

She sat at the end of the bed, hands pressed between her knees. The room was suddenly too small, too dark, too hot, too empty. She pulled on clothes and added her father's heavy wool shirt. She opened the fire-escape window and stepped out onto the grated landing. The city lights had a glaring brilliance in the clear, chilly air. She hugged the wool shirt tightly around her and studied the sky, but there were no stars. The lights obliterated them with a man-made glow. What did children here wish on? She had a flash of memory – walking with her mother through the dark orchard in August, on their way for a night-time picnic to watch shooting stars.

The music stopped, then started again. It floated around her. She tilted her head and listened, wondering where it came from. It wasn't a recording. That much she knew. Someone was playing. Playing incessantly. Obsessively. What a grand obsession. If only she had grown up dreaming of musical notes rather than bones. She put her hand on the cold metal railing and took a step. Then another. Until she was on the landing outside the window above hers. This was the source. The music enveloped her in its pure sweetness. She wanted to sink down on the grated metal of the landing, huddle inside her father's oversize shirt, and lose herself in it.

Suddenly she realized that she was no different from the intruder who had pressed his face against her window the night before. She was invading someone's privacy. Luckily, the musician's blinds were drawn tightly, and even though the window was open a few inches she hadn't made any noise to betray herself. As quietly as possible she retreated downward, aware now of every creak in the metal. She climbed back into her own room, closing and locking the window behind her.

The room seemed even less tolerable than before her brief escape. She switched on the light and gathered up her laundry. If she couldn't sleep, she could at least do something productive.

On the ride down, the elevator's noise seemed magnified and she worried that the whole building might be awakened by the grindings and creakings. She regretted being out. It was too late for a trip to the basement. But then the doors opened and she was there, staring into a glaringly white concrete block passageway. She stuck her head out of the elevator and saw that the tunnel-like hall widened into a space filled with recycling bags. Beyond that, through an arch, was a room with washers and dryers. Fluorescent tube lighting flooded the entire area, bouncing off the whitewashed walls with the brilliance of sun on snow. The silence was absolute. It was almost like being inside a tomb.

Clutching her laundry tightly she stepped out into the hallway. The elevator doors suddenly closed behind her, causing a moment of panic. Trapped in the basement! She put her free hand to her chest and laughed at herself. Trapped with the laundry – maybe that was cause for alarm. She would have to do it now.

Quickly she navigated the passageway, passing by the mound of blue recycle bags. Besides the washers and dryers, the laundry room was equipped with a long Formica table and an assortment of wooden chairs.

She stuffed a washer full, not bothering to sort or separate what probably should have been two different loads. Then she plugged coins into the slot. Rushing water echoed in the concrete tomb, cocooning her in sound. The instructions on the box cautioned against pouring the dry detergent directly on fabric, but the water was trickling in at an agonizingly slow rate. She stared down into the machine, watching the water level creep upward, tempted to dump the detergent in and take her chances. The whole process made her think of her father who would have read all the instructions on the washer and all the instructions on the detergent and used a measuring cup and done everything just right. He was such a precise and careful man, such an unwavering rule-oriented man. Or so she had thought. So she had believed.

Had the entire foundation of her childhood been built on lies? Had her father always been a man with dangerous secrets? Or had he changed without her realizing it? She thought back to the brief, uncomfortable phone conversations they had had over the past six years. There had been no clues to a change during those conversations. She didn't believe in people changing, anyway. Not in any fundamental way. Once people were past the formative period of their lives, that was it. They were exactly what they would always be.

*I don't know my father.*

The words echoed in her head over the sound of the water.

'I don't know my father,' she said aloud.

'That's an age-old problem,' replied a voice from behind her. She spun around, heart slamming against her ribs.

Not five feet from her stood a man.

'Sorry,' he said, 'I didn't mean to startle you.'

He was around six foot, with a lean athleticism, an angular face and an intellectual aura that owed a lot to his wire rimmed glasses. She would have run, but he was carrying an armload of clothes and a hardcover book, and his manner was reticent, almost regretful. He did seem to be sorry that he'd startled her.

'I'm sorry,' he said again. 'I was thinking of Odysseus – "Does any person know who his father is?" I shouldn't have spoken.'

'That's all right,' she assured him, though she was still more than a little nervous about being alone with a stranger at 2 a.m. in a deserted soundproof basement.

He crossed to the empty washer beside hers and began putting his clothes in. They looked clean. She dumped the detergent in her own washer and shut the lid. Then she edged toward the Formica table, uncertain as to whether she should stay or leave.

She took a chair near the door. He sat down across the room, stretched out his long legs, and opened his book. She watched him surreptitiously at first; then, when he seemed engrossed in his book, she grew bolder.

He was wearing faded denim jeans and a loose cotton turtleneck that was either black or navy-blue. His dark brown hair was collar length in back and worn carelessly. His face was ascetic, almost gaunt. She could imagine him as a writer or an artist, working in an unheated room, feverishly creating, shutting out the world.

She smiled to herself. When had a man quoted Homer to her? Never.

More relaxed now, she leaned back in her chair and looked over at the washer. The dial indicated that the first cycle had barely begun. There was no telling how long it would take. She wished she too had something to read.

She glanced back toward the man and caught him staring at her. He lowered his eyes to his book immediately, but the intensity of that stare burned in her skin as if she'd strayed too close to a fire.

Without regard for her laundry she bolted from her chair and rushed out of the room. The elevator was standing open, just as he'd left it. She punched the sixth-floor button over and over, unable to relax until the doors finally rumbled shut.

Back in her room the whole episode seemed slightly ridiculous. But she was not sorry she had run away. Her only regret was that she hadn't run from him sooner.

She looked at the telephone, but there was no one to call. Such an American phenomenon, she thought, lapsing into the anthropologist self who kept her safe. To be in a huge city, inside a building that housed so many people, yet to be completely alone. That was unique to American culture.

She crossed to the fire-escape window, opened it, and leaned out. The musician above her was silent. What was

130

that person's life like? Did he or she work a job all day then come home to play their heart out every night? Was the musician alone?

The clock read 3:01 a.m. One thing she was sure of – she was not going back down into that basement again until daylight, regardless of what happened to her clothes. She curled up very small on the bed, the same way she had curled up beside her mother as a child, waiting out the storm with her mother's arms around her. She slept fitfully, dreaming that the face at the window was back, that the face was after her, and it was a relief when the alarm finally shrilled at six-thirty.

She was dressed and going out the door when the phone startled her.

'Yes. Hello. Is this the hospital?'

'Calm down, Lanier. It's Kizmin. I've got a busy day ahead of me so I thought I'd catch you now.'

'What's happened?'

'Nothing to do with the case, but I told Mr Kaliker about your being in town and your father being shot, and he wants you to be his guest at a fundraising dinner tonight.'

'A dinner?'

'Yes. He wants us to go together. It's at the St Regis Hotel.'

'All I have is jeans. And I'm really not interested in going.'

'Listen, I told him you wouldn't have evening clothes and that you probably weren't in the mood for a party, but he insisted. He's arranging something for you to wear and he said to tell you that he needs both of us there to represent his Kal Fund graduates. He says we'll impress the people who count.'

'I don't want to do it.'

'Neither do I. But I'm not going to be the one to call him and tell him, are you?'

131

'No.'

'All right then. Pick you up at the front door of your building at seven tonight.'

Iris stood looking at the phone for a moment after Kizmin had disconnected. Then she pushed Nathan Kaliker to the back of her mind and went down to the basement to put her abandoned clothes in the dryer.

She felt foolish for not having dried them in the night. Someone had probably stolen them all and she would be reduced to the one outfit she had on.

The elevator delivered her down into the glaring white tomb. No daylight reached it so it looked the same in the morning as it had the night before. It was still just as silent and just as deserted.

She went into the laundry area and there were her clothes on the Formica table. Dry and folded. In neat stacks. Incredulous, she turned to survey the area again, looking for the Good Samaritan who had not only paid to dry her clothes but had folded them. Folded them more neatly than she would have folded them. But whoever had done it was long gone.

Something caught her eye though. On one of the chairs was a hardcover book. She picked it up and read the cover. It was a biography of Benjamin Britten, the composer. It was the book that the man in the laundry room had been reading. Was he the one who had taken care of her clothes?

The more she considered it, the more certain she was. She owed him a thank you. And she would rescue his book for him. Return it to him safe and sound. She tucked the book under her arm, gathered up the neat stacks and returned to the elevator. Before she could push the button there was an approaching rumble. Someone was coming down.

Daytime or not it was still a deserted basement and she didn't know who might step out of that elevator. Instinct told her that she shouldn't just stand there and wait to see what happened.

She looked toward the recycle and laundry areas. There was no place to hide. She went around the corner in the opposite direction. There was a large steel door with a massive lock. The exit sign above it had long ago burned out. It was obviously the door to the street but even from the inside she couldn't use it without keys. Another set of double doors led to a storage area behind the elevator, but they were padlocked. She pressed herself into the corner and waited.

She felt ridiculous hiding behind the elevator. What if it was Mr Andretti and he came around to the storage rooms and found her cowering there? How embarrassing that would be. But she didn't move. She waited and listened. It was undoubtedly someone with washing to do. After they went to the laundry area she would slip around into the elevator and they would never know she'd been there.

The doors groaned open and she heard footsteps. It was more than one person.

'See her?' a male voice asked.

'No. Looks like she didn't come down here,' another male voice answered.

'Then where did she go?'

'How the hell do I know?'

The elevator doors closed and Iris heard the car rumble upward. The men were gone.

They couldn't have been talking about her. Who would be looking for her? No. They had to have been looking for someone else. But in spite of her attempts to dismiss the incident she was uneasy until she was finally out of the building and on her way to the hospital.

# Eight

Iris returned to the Fitzgerald after another long, uneventful day at the hospital to find Mitchell Hanley waiting for her in the lobby.

'Iris! Iris!' he called and bounded toward her bearing a large package. 'This came and I signed for it. The messenger said it was really important, something you needed for tonight.'

'Oh, thank you, Mitchell.' She reached for the package but he drew it back.

'Mitch. Call me Mitch. And I'll just carry it onto the elevator for you. We're both going the same direction.'

He seemed determined to carry the box so she started toward the elevator beside him without argument.

'I didn't want it to get stolen or anything,' he said as soon as they were inside the car and on the way upward.

'How long have you been waiting for me?' she asked.

'Not long.'

'I really appreciate it, but shouldn't that have been Mr Andretti's responsibility?'

'That guy? Huh. You can't depend on him. He's a total flake.'

'Well, thank you again.' She took hold of the end of the box, but Mitch still seemed reluctant to give it up.

'I thought I'd take it to your room for you.'

'No, thank you. Really. I'm in a rush. It's a dress that I

have to wear to a fundraising dinner tonight, and I've got very little time to get ready.'

'Sure. All right.' He shrugged and grinned.

The doors opened on six and she realized that he hadn't pressed the button for his floor.

'You missed five,' she said.

'No problem.' He stepped out of the car with her and finally surrendered the package. 'I like the stairs better anyway.' His grin widened and then he disappeared through the emergency door.

At a quarter to seven Iris returned to the lobby and stood just inside the glass doors, watching for Kizmin's car to pull up. She was wearing her father's wool jacket over the clothes that had been sent to her – a perfectly tailored dinner suit in a midnight-blue silk gaberdine and flat-heeled shoes in the same shade.

She would have put on a touch of make-up if she'd had any, but what few cosmetics she'd owned had melted in the rainforest. And she would have worn earrings, but she'd lost the only pair she'd had with her in Guatemala. She had, however, twisted her hair up as a concession to the occasion.

Precisely at seven a sleek black car with dark windows glided up to the curb. A driver in suit and tie got out, walked around to the passenger side nearest her, opened the door and held out his hand as though inviting her in.

She pointed at herself and said 'Me?' though the man couldn't possibly have heard her through the plate glass.

The man nodded, and then Kizmin leaned into view from the dark interior, gesturing impatiently.

'Is this a limousine?' Iris asked, as soon as she was cushioned in the soft leather upholstery.

'A small one,' Kizmin answered. 'Strictly for foundation business.'

136

'Oh.' Iris peered closer at the detective. 'You look like a magazine cover.'

Kizmin appeared slightly embarrassed. 'It's all just for show. The jewelry is all on loan from someone Mr Kaliker knows.'

'Very glamorous,' Iris said. The opportunity to tease the tough detective was irresistible. 'I don't think I've ever known anyone so glamorous before.'

'It's nothing.' Kizmin insisted. 'It's like dressing up for a costume party . . . or Halloween.'

'My parents didn't believe in trick-or-treating. They were opposed to refined sugar products.'

'You never trick-or-treated?'

Iris shook her head.

'No trick-or-treating? No refined sugar? That's un-American.' Kizmin shook her head. 'Anyway, my point is that this is all surface. I don't have a glamorous bone in my body.'

'A glamorous bone,' Iris repeated. 'That's an interesting thought, isn't it? Especially if you consider that the archaic meaning of glamour had to do with magic.'

'What the hell does that mean?'

Iris laughed. 'I don't know. Magical bones. It just seemed like a funny connection.'

'Hilarious,' Kizmin said. 'Is that an example of scientific humor?' She sighed softly in exasperation then tilted her head and studied Iris a moment. 'The hair is nice up. But that jacket stays in the car.'

Iris glanced down at her father's jacket. 'It's cold out though.'

'The driver will deliver us right to the door. You'll only suffer for a few seconds.'

Iris reached out to touch Kizmin's fur. 'What's this?' she asked.

'Mink. And don't start telling me how bad it is to wear fur.'

137

'I won't. I have no information on it.'

'Good. I'm ambivalent myself. The whole nature thing confuses me.'

'Was the coat loaned to you, too?'

'Yes.'

'I don't understand all this – the Kaliker Foundation owning limousines and loaning out expensive clothes and jewelry.'

'It's not actually the foundation's money. Mr Kaliker uses his own funds. He's got family money, you know.'

'I didn't know. I thought he worked his way through law school and built the foundation from scratch.'

'Well he did,' Kizmin explained. 'It's a long story . . . Back then he'd been sort of disowned by his family, but over time, when they saw how much good he was doing, they changed their minds. So he came into a lot of money and now he uses it to cultivate influence, to generate support for the foundation at higher levels.'

Iris ran her hand over the soft leather upholstery. 'When I was in college it was all grimy offices and workers sleeping on couches and fighting with the power company so the electricity didn't get turned off. Every spare cent went into programs or scholarships.'

'That's still the heart of the foundation,' Kizmin assured her. 'But, as Mr Kaliker says, people and organizations have to mature. And they have to make themselves presentable to the establishment if they want nationwide respect.'

'Is Mr Kaliker running for some kind of political office?'

'What makes you ask that?' Kizmin responded sharply.

Iris shrugged and let the matter drop. She admired Nathan Kaliker to such an extreme that he seemed more mythological than human to her and she really didn't need to hear Kizmin's explanations. She took it on faith that whatever Kaliker did was for good and noble reasons.

'You're sure that the hospital can reach me at this thing?' Iris asked.

'Positive. I talked to them myself. They have my pager number and the hotel's direct number.'

Iris nodded. She thought of the skeleton they had unearthed together. 'Have you identified the remains yet?' she asked.

'What? Oh . . . you mean the girl we dug out yesterday. No. No luck. The Chief ME was impressed with your work though. He asked if he could put you on his consult list.' Kizmin glanced over at her. 'I said he'd have to ask you himself.'

'I don't live in this area,' Iris reminded her.

'And if you did live here?'

'But I don't. So it's pointless conjecture.'

'Conjecture is never pointless.' Kizmin leaned forward to press the intercom button. 'Drop us as close as you can to the front,' she instructed the driver. 'My friend isn't wearing a coat.'

The St Regis was an elegant dowager of a hotel from the grand old days of New York City.

'Isn't it beautiful?' Kizmin said as they walked through the public areas on their way to the Kaliker dinner.

Iris took in the expansive lavish decor. 'I wonder if any of this will survive as ruins . . . how much will be left to represent our civilization when archaeologists of the future pick through our dead cities.'

Kizmin sighed and rolled her eyes. 'Maybe it would be better for the foundation's fundraising efforts if you avoided talking to potential donors.'

For the first half of the ninety-minute cocktail period, Iris was Kizmin's shadow. She listened to polite conversations about the problems of crime and violence in urban America and she watched Kizmin's efforts to impress expensively dressed couples with the importance of the Kaliker Foundation's work. The couples were all so similar in age and appearance that Iris couldn't keep them separate in her mind. She suspected that if she were a foreign anthropologist suddenly coming upon this gathering she would believe she'd found a new tribe that had maintained its homogeneity through generations of isolation and intermarriage.

'What do you think?' Kizmin asked when they had a moment to themselves.

'Well, it's certainly not a representative New York group, is it?'

Kizmin laughed. 'No.' She bent closer and lowered her voice. 'This is the power and money élite. These are the people with the most to lose. They're scared of the rising crime rates.'

'But don't they realize that the foundation's object is justice for everyone . . . particularly the less privileged classes?'

'They're aware of the foundation's reputation. But with these people Mr Kaliker stresses his work lobbying for anti-crime measures and his campaigns to strengthen sentences for violent offenders. That's enough for them. That's all they want to hear.'

Iris looked over the crowded room. 'Have you seen Mr Kaliker?'

'I caught a glimpse of him earlier, but he'll be mobbed all night. I doubt that we'll even get to talk to him.'

Iris nodded, feeling some measure of relief at this news. She continued to scan the room. 'Who is that elderly man sitting up on the dais in the front? He looks like the grand old emperor of something.'

'Emperor of eccentricity maybe. That's Mr Kaliker's stepfather. Richer than God and meaner than the devil. Mr Kaliker always invites him to functions but he usually doesn't come.'

140

'He keeps staring over here,' Iris said.

'I don't think he sees well enough to stare this far. But if he did this would be a logical direction for him to stare. He likes young women. I swear he's made a pass at me a time or two.'

Kizmin turned slightly, then stopped, her attention caught by someone.

'That's interesting . . .' she said, pointing out a tall, angular man who looked as uncomfortable and out of place as Iris felt. 'Mr Kaliker brought Vitya. I can't imagine why. This isn't the sort of gathering he belongs in. See him over there? The scarecrow-looking guy? He came here from Russia five or six years ago with nothing. Now he runs the entire foundation.'

'Mr Kaliker doesn't run it anymore?'

'Not the day-to-day stuff. His time is too valuable. He's got to concentrate on meetings and speaking engagements . . . fundraisers . . . all the necessary evils of a successful organization.' Kizmin continued to watch the man as she spoke. 'Vitya is brilliant. And he's idealistic, patriotic, and dedicated to the point of obsession.'

'You sound like you think he's a fool though,' Iris said.

'Maybe I do.' She turned to look at Iris. 'I admire him tremendously. As I admire you. But he's got a very naive view of his newly adopted country, and it's just a matter of time before the system grinds him down and he learns that justice and inalienable rights are only words. That America isn't the bright shining dream he imagined.'

'So, should he quit? Should everyone quit? Should Mr Kaliker give up on the foundation? Should you stop fighting crime?'

Kizmin smiled cryptically. 'The eternal question,' she said. 'Would you quit?'

Iris lowered her eyes, ashamed of what she thought the question implied.

'Uh-oh,' Kizmin said under her breath. 'Vitya is headed

this way. I'm going to leave you on your own to get acquainted.'

'But . . .'

Kizmin faded into the crowd and Iris stood, staring after her, not certain what to do next.

A finger tapped her shoulder and she turned. The man was fairly young – somewhere between thirty and forty – but the concentrated humorlessness of his gaunt face made him seem older. His suit hung loosely from the rack of his shoulders and when he extended his arm for a handshake the bones of his wrist protruded from his too-short sleeves.

'I'm Vitya,' he said in accented English.

'I know. I'm Iris Lanier.'

'I know. I'm honored to meet you, Dr Lanier.'

'Iris . . . please.'

'Yes, and only Vitya for me because your tongue would trip over my family name.' He glanced in the direction of Kizmin's retreat. 'I was hoping to talk with Justine.'

Justine. It struck Iris that she hadn't even known the detective's first name.

'She . . . had to leave.'

He smiled a very sweet smile that made him almost handsome. The corner of one of his front teeth was chipped.

'She is always so busy,' he said, 'always so hard to catch.'

Iris nodded agreement.

'So, may I have your company?' he asked politely.

'Why, yes.'

He smiled again. 'I have heard so many great things about your work with – who is the archaeologist?'

'Becker. Daniel Becker.'

'Yes. With the Maya, correct?'

'That's right. But who told you about my work?'

A puzzled expression came over the man's face.

142

'Nathan Kaliker. But you must know this. How closely he follows your work. He was very pleased when you decided to go on the dig with the famous archaeologist.'

'Mr Kaliker knew I went to Guatemala with Becker?'

'Certainly. And he thinks that now you will finally find a direction for your talents.'

'Are you serious?'

The man looked at her as though he didn't understand the question.

'Vitya! Vitya!' A young woman rushed up. 'We've been looking all over for you. You weren't supposed to leave that spot!'

'What spot?' he asked.

'Oh, never mind. It's time for your presentation. The private room is all set up and everyone's waiting.'

'I must say goodbye, then.' Vitya extended his hand to Iris again. 'I hope we will meet another time, though not at one of these affairs.'

'Not likely you'll be at another one,' the young woman muttered.

Iris moved through the crowd, watching people but taking care not to catch anyone's eye. She didn't want to be drawn into conversation for fear that she might say the wrong thing and offend a potential donor.

After several close calls, she left the huge room and wandered down the hall. There were a number of doors. One was ajar, revealing a smaller banqueting room that was unlit and empty. She slipped inside and went to the darkest end of the room where she leaned into the cold glass of a window and looked out. Below her the street was a silent river of cars. In the building opposite there was a series of lighted uncurtained windows, all to the same apartment. Bold abstract paintings lined the walls and she could see part of a chandelier, the side of a piece of statuary, the corner of a polished display cabinet. It was not the sort of apartment she had ever been in during her year in New York. It was the kind of living space that the city's millionaires owned. The kind of apartment Mr Kaliker's dinner guests would have.

She watched the lighted windows as she would have watched a documentary about life in a foreign country. Wondering how the people lived.

She was roused from her thoughts by the quiet opening and closing of a door followed by the low murmur of whispered conversation. She couldn't see who it was and she was confident that they couldn't see her. There was no graceful way to escape. The only other doors were across the room. While she was considering whether to step out or remain hidden, the voices drew nearer. It sounded like a man and a woman, though the whispering made even gender hard to identify.

'God, you feel good. It drove me crazy when I saw you walk in.'

'Hold me. Hold me. A week is too long.'

'We've got to get right back.'

'Why can't we just walk out there together? Why!'

'You know why. My wife's only been dead two months. It wouldn't look right. People might guess how long we've been seeing each other.'

Iris pressed back into the darkest corner and waited.

There was a heavy sigh. 'Hold me just a minute more.'

'Jeez . . . feel what you're doing to me.'

'Ummm . . . Maybe you should find a way to sneak over to my place tonight.'

'I can't. Oh, jeez . . . Suck me now. Give me your mouth.'

'No, Nathan! I told you. No more quickies in closets. You either make time for me or take care of it yourself.'

Nathan. The whispered name struck Iris as though it had been shouted next to her ear. Nathan Kaliker? That was Nathan Kaliker groping with a woman in the dark?

The whispering stopped. There were soft receding footfalls and then the opening and closing of the door again.

Iris moved back to the window and leaned into the glass. Across the way, framed in the white rectangle of light, a man and woman stood, facing one another. Their faces were contorted with anger. The woman had one hand pressed against her breast and was gesturing wildly with the other. The man's body was wooden and still. Suddenly he raised his arm and slapped her. She lurched out of sight and he followed.

Iris waited, breath held, fists clenched. After several minutes the woman appeared in a different room, possibly the bedroom. She moved close to the window and stood, looking out, one hand resting against her cheek. It was too far away to see if she was crying but Iris imagined that she was. Crying and looking out into the darkness. Feeling alone. Staring out so that it seemed as if she was looking straight at Iris. Though she couldn't be, could she? Was there enough ambient city light to make Iris visible at the hotel window?

She raised her hand and waved at the woman across the street, then left her hand up, flat and open against the cold glass. Nothing happened for a moment. Then, slowly, the woman raised her arm. She pressed her open palm against her own cold glass.

Iris drew back into the darkened banqueting room to escape the woman, then immediately regretted it and returned to the window. But it was too late. The woman was gone.

She stood for a moment, trying to collect herself, trying to reorder her thoughts. Again she had that sense of slipping and she hurried out of the darkness back to the party. When she emerged she learned that only fifteen minutes remained until dinner. The crowded room was exactly as she had left it. Her absence had made no difference. Her reappearance caused no change.

An eerie but pleasurable feeling of invisibility stole over her. She thought about Moonsmoke disappearing. About her own mother disappearing. Was this how it had started for them? Had they too felt the moments of invisibility, the creeping sense of disconnection, until finally there was nothing left to hold them in place?

No. No. They had children! Both of the women had young children who needed them. She could not and would not excuse their leaving.

'Dr Lanier! Dr Lanier!'

It was the same breathless, harried young woman who had taken Vitya to his presentation.

'Dr Lanier . . . Kizmin has been looking all over for you. Mr Kaliker wanted to speak to you before dinner.'

Reluctantly, Iris followed the woman to the front of the room where Nathan Kaliker was holding court. Kizmin was off to the side speaking to a trio of overweight men who were clearly enchanted by her. Iris could see why Kaliker wanted the detective at his fundraisers. The men looked as though they might fight each other for the privilege of handing her their wallets.

'Ah, here she is: our esteemed Dr Lanier.'

Iris tried to smile. Swarms of butterflies dipped and fluttered in her stomach. 'Hello Mr Kaliker.'

Nathan Kaliker had improved in the five years since she'd seen him. His formerly nondescript hair was now beautifully silver. His eyes were bluer than she remembered. His craggy good looks had somehow smoothed. Only his energy remained the same. It crackled and sparked like he had an inner electric field.

'Hello. Hello.' He pressed her hand between both of his.

'This is what the foundation's scholarship program is all about,' he said expansively, still holding Iris's hand. The circle of listeners beamed approval at her.

'Dr Lanier is a renowned physical anthropologist whose work has opened up the field and enhanced our understanding of the human condition.'

Iris wanted to tug her hand free and turn around to see who Nathan Kaliker was talking about.

'Now she is assisting the New York City Police Department in identifying crime victims.'

Iris opened her mouth to correct him, but he suddenly gripped her hand tighter and swung her arm up in a gesture of victory.

'This, my dear friends, this young woman is our future. And the foundation is making that future possible.'

Applause and cheering followed. Iris could feel her cheeks reddening. Finally, Kaliker released her and moved on, leaving her behind as he swept forward to make contact with another group. Kizmin's trio of admirers fell into step behind him and the detective came to stand beside Iris. Together they watched Kaliker's progress until he had gone so far into the crowd that only his trailing wake of followers was visible.

'That was worse than I thought it would be,' Iris said.

'It's all for the cause.'

Iris turned from watching Kaliker's procession and saw that the old man on the dais was staring at her again. Quickly she looked at Kizmin, pretending not to notice.

The detective shook her head. 'I am so sick of questions about the Locket Killer. These people think that being rich gives them the right to know everything. They want information that hasn't been released.'

'What exactly is the Locket Killer?' Iris asked. 'I've seen the headlines, but . . .'

Kizmin's expression turned hard and her voice dropped to a monotone. 'He's been preying on women in and around New York City. He beats his victims, then tortures them with a lot of sick sexual stuff. The tortures vary but he always finishes it off with a long sharpened rod or stake

147

– driven up into them. It penetrates the uterine wall and death occurs from internal haemorrhaging and shock.

'It takes awhile for them to die. He watches. We've had three survivors and we know he sits there and watches.'

'That's enough,' Iris said. 'Don't tell me any more.'

Kizmin looked around. 'Uh-oh,' she whispered, noticing the old man staring down at them. 'Jack has his eye on us. We'll be summoned soon.'

'Is Mr Kaliker's stepfather that bad?' Iris asked.

'Let's just say that caustic would be a compliment.'

But then two well-dressed women approached him and his attention was diverted.

'Come on,' Kizmin said and they dove into the crowd, heading for the far side of the room.

'I just don't remember things this way,' Iris said when they had found a place to stop. 'Mr Kaliker used to be so much more . . .'

'More what?'

'More . . . real. More genuine.'

'Grow up, Lanier. The millennium approaches. People want an actor in the White House. They want simple images and junk-food ideas. If the foundation is going to survive and grow Mr Kaliker has to package it for today. That's all he's trying to do.'

Iris looked down at the hand Kaliker had held. 'I feel like it's all a little sleazy now.'

'How dare you be critical of him,' Kizmin demanded in a harsh whisper. 'After all he's done. Not just for you but for the whole fucking country! How dare you question any of his methods of motives. He's sacrificed his personal happiness again and again for the good of the foundation. For the good of people like you and me. For the good of this ungrateful country of ours.'

Iris studied Kizmin's face, then asked, quietly, 'How did his wife die?'

Kizmin's fierce indignation evaporated. She stared off

148

into a distant corner of the room. Her throat moved. She swallowed several times. 'Suicide. She went into his office while he was away at lunch . . . and cut her wrists.'

Iris crossed her arms and held them tightly against her chest, hugging herself. There was a question haunting her. It wouldn't go away. And she knew that she would not be able to look at Kizmin again without thinking it.

'That was you whispering in the dark with him, wasn't it?' she asked softly.

'I don't . . .' A terrible pain filled Kizmin's eyes. 'You saw us?'

Iris nodded.

'We've been so careful. Nathan has always insisted . . .'

'I'm sorry. I shouldn't have said anything.'

'You would have been thinking it.'

'Yes. But I'm not judging you. I just . . . needed to know.'

The detective looked away, her expression one of profound sadness. 'I'm judging myself.'

# Nine

'Drop me first,' Kizmin told the limousine driver as they were pulling away from the hotel. 'Patchin Place in the West Village.' Then she settled into a stiff pose, facing forward, acknowledging Iris's presence only by her tense silence.

They had been seated at different tables during dinner and then surrounded by a crowd outside the hotel, with everyone waiting for rides and talking excitedly about Nathan Kaliker's foundation. Now they were alone together and it was clear that Kizmin was angry or humiliated or both.

Iris turned her head and looked out the dark glass at the lighted sidewalks. This would simplify matters. She hadn't known what to do about Kizmin as a friend. Now, since she'd opened her mouth and ruined it, now she could forget about having this woman as a close friend.

Instead of the relief she expected to feel, she was suddenly seized by a bitter regret that made her want to smash something.

'Did his wife know about you?' she asked, fully aware of how cruel the question was.

'I never thought so,' Kizmin said hollowly. 'But since her death I've wondered. I can't stop thinking . . . what if . . .'

'What does Mr Kaliker say?'

'I haven't been able to ask him.'

'Doesn't sound like you have a very close relationship.'

'I'm in love with him,' Kizmin whispered, and her words were like blood flowing from a wound. 'I've been in love with him for two years.

'I didn't say anything . . . I didn't do anything. I kept it completely to myself. But then, like a miracle, he came to me. His wife was away and he came to me and told me how lonely he was . . . how his marriage was empty and he'd been lonely for years . . . and he told me he hadn't meant to but he'd fallen in love with me.'

Kizmin covered her face with her hands for a moment, then raised her eyes to meet Iris's. 'You're right to be disappointed in me. To be disgusted with me. I'm disgusted with myself.'

'But that won't stop you from continuing with him, will it?' Iris asked.

Kizmin shook her head.

'I wonder if that's the way it was with my mother when she abandoned us. I wonder if she was disgusted with herself but still couldn't make herself stay. Or say goodbye. Or face us and explain.'

'Iris . . .'

'Do you suppose she loved another man that much? The way you love Nathan Kaliker. Or do you suppose it was that she hated her life so much . . . her life as a mother and wife . . . her life with me.'

'Iris . . . don't.'

'It always thought it was a fault particular to my mother . . . something missing in her . . . some genetic defect that I had no doubt inherited. But maybe I was all wrong. Maybe everyone has it.

'Mr Kaliker seemed so perfect to me. And you . . .' Iris shook her head. 'But maybe no one is as good as they seem. Maybe all humans are capable of the most disgusting, most detestable, most contemptible behavior imaginable. Maybe no one can be trusted.'

'And you thought you could trust me?' Kizmin asked.

'Yes. No! I mean . . . This whole conversation is ludicrous. Tell the driver to stop. I want to get out.'

Kizmin made no move to signal the driver so Iris reached over her, lunging for the intercom button.

'Stop it!' Kizmin grabbed her shoulders and wrestled her back against the seat. 'Holy fuck, Lanier! I'm the one who's supposed to be going off the deep end here.'

Iris stopped fighting and closed her eyes. What was happening to her?

'Maybe I'm going crazy,' she said. 'Remember that mathematician who won the Nobel Prize? The one who completely lost touch with reality for twenty years or something? Maybe that's what's happening to me.'

'We're all crazy,' Kizmin said, 'just in different ways. Once you peel away our civilized veneers we're all raving lunatics.'

'No. I am calm and rational. Usually. That's what makes me a good scientist.'

'Bullshit. You're hiding.'

'So you're suddenly a psychiatrist?'

'A detective. My accuracy rate on human nature is better than a shrink's.'

'Who am I hiding from, then? My inner lunatic? My father's attacker? The library where I still have overdue fines?'

One side of Kizmin's mouth curved up in a rueful smile. 'The hell if I know.'

They rode in silence for several minutes.

'I'm sorry,' Iris said. 'I don't know why I said all that.'

Kizmin smiled. 'It's fate,' she said.

And they laughed together until they had tears in their eyes.

Someone was just stepping into the elevator when Iris entered the Fitzgerald's lobby.

153

'Wait!' she called. 'Hold the elevator! Please!'

The door closed but then rumbled back open and she rushed aboard. There were two occupants in the car – her biker neighbor in his customary all black stood on one side and on the opposite side stood the man she had met in the laundry room. Both were staring fixedly ahead.

The biker, who was closest to the control panel, pushed the DOOR CLOSE button several times with no response; then, muttering a string of curses, he bolted out and slammed through the stairway door.

'Guess he was in a hurry,' Iris said.

The man didn't move or give any indication that he'd heard her.

'Remember me?' she asked. 'From the laundry room?'

The man glanced sideways at her. His expression was carefully neutral.

'I found your book. I've been looking for you so I could return it.'

There was still no glimmer of recognition. And he seemed so different. His shoulders were hunched and he was withdrawn. Was it possible that she had the wrong person?

But then he turned his head and looked at her. 'Keep the book. I finished it.'

'OK. Thank you. I need a good book to read.'

The elevator lurched and the man shifted and she realized that he held an instrument case in the hand closest to the wall. A musical instrument. And he was going to seven. The floor above her. Could he be the phantom sax-player whose music had haunted her nights? She wanted to ask, but kept silent. He obviously wanted to be left alone.

As soon as she was inside her room she called the hospital's Blue Four desk. It was eleven-thirty and Helen was still on duty. She answered the phone.

'I've got all these numbers to reach you,' Helen said impatiently. 'You would'a heard from me if there was something to report.'

'So there's still no change?'

'No change.'

No change. Iris was so sick of hearing that phrase.

'Some guy called here trying to find you though. Long distance. When I wouldn't give out your number he started telling me about how important he was. How I should have seen him on television.'

'Daniel Becker?'

'Yeah. I never heard of him, frankly, but he talked so much I finally gave him your number there just to get rid of him. Hope it was all right.'

Iris had barely returned the phone receiver to the cradle when it rang.

'Helen? Did something happen? Helen?'

'Iris? This is Daniel Becker calling from Guatemala City. We seem to have a bad connection.'

'Oh. Hello Daniel. Are you in the city for your meetings?'

'Yes. I tried to reach you at the hospital and finally someone gave me this number. What's going on? How's your father doing?'

'I wrote, but I guess the letter hasn't had time to reach you yet. My father is in a coma. He was shot.'

'My God! Shot? Was he robbed or—?'

'There's some confusion about the who and why of it.'

'Listen, Iris . . . you don't have to come back. I can have your things shipped to you.'

'Daniel, please. Stop trying to dismiss me.'

'I'm not trying to dismiss you! I'm worried about you.'

'I told you I'd be back and I will. There's not much I can do here anyway.'

'Suit yourself. I know that nothing I say will make a difference.'

Iris let the comment go by without response.

155

'I've got some news for you. After you left, Linda talked us into letting her start the excavation of the tunnel.'

'The tunnel into the chamber?'

'You got it. She wanted to do it as a surprise for you. We thought she'd just be slinging a lot of dirt but a short ways in she hit a bonanza of artifacts . . . jars, plates, jewelry, figurines . . . pretty amazing stuff.'

'Carefully buried? I mean, were they trying to hide the things or preserve them or . . .?'

'No. Everything was broken. Could be that the stuff was considered trash and added to the fill dirt as a way to get rid of it. Or it could be that it broke when it was thrown in.'

'Isn't that odd?'

'Very odd. Could be that the burying of the items had some significance. Maybe they were cursed or defiled.'

'Could they have been used during the sacrificial ceremonies . . . when the women were killed . . . then buried in the tunnel fill as part of the ritual?'

'Sure. Could be. That's actually the answer I'm hoping for. It would add a whole new dimension to the discovery of the chamber.'

'You mean it would be a better story for a news release.'

Becker laughed. 'Why, Iris . . . since when have you become so direct?' He laughed again. 'I always knew you were thinking things like that. It's exciting to hear you come out and say them.'

'Daniel—'

'No, wait . . . there's something else. As I recall you had an interest in Moonsmoke?'

'Yes.'

'When I left the dig the work had just started on the artifacts from the tunnel and there was a long way to go with piecing things back together and reading all the

156

glyphs – but Tim was pretty certain that he saw several different references to Moonsmoke on fragments.'

'What does that mean?'

'Your guess is as good as mine at this point. Listen, I've got to run. I'll call you again before I leave the city. And Iris, think it over. Should you come all the way back down here?'

'I'll be there in time to finish the sixth woman in the chamber, Daniel. And tell Linda to be careful digging out the tunnel. Tell her not to go too far down. She could damage number six.'

Becker sighed. 'Don't worry. I've already set the limit on how far she can dig.'

'You haven't opened Jaguar Eyes' sarcophagus yet, have you?'

'No.'

'Wait for me, Daniel, please.'

'I will. I have been.'


Iris was too agitated to sleep. She paced back and forth in the small room. If she had been at the dig she would have gone down into the chamber and worked all night. She thought of the underground room, the earthy smell of it, the puzzle of the last woman. The memories came to her in an almost nostalgic way, as though that were her home and she was yearning to be there.

She guessed that in a sense it was her home. She had no adult home to miss. She had never made herself a home.

And she never missed her childhood home anymore. Not the house anyway. Sometimes she missed the orchards. The dirt so soft and dark and clean between her toes. The sighing and rubbing of the branches. The clouds of delicately tinted blossoms shivering in the breeze. The fragrance of sun-warm ripening fruit. All that touched a deep chord in her. She missed the cycle of it too. The unwavering sequence. The rebirth each spring. And she missed the night orchard. Leaning against a solid trunk, wrapped up in the darkness, alone but totally secure.

At times her chest ached with missing the orchard. But not the house. Though she had lived in the house motherless as long as she lived in it with her mother, and though it was her father who had dreamed it and built it, the house was none the less connected with her mother.

Quickly, Iris crossed to the north window and pushed it open to better hear the music from above. The air was clear and crisp. Suddenly she needed to be in the darkness. Somewhere safe and sheltered like the night orchard. She threw off her elegant borrowed dinner suit and pulled on clean jeans and a sweatshirt from the drawer. Then she grabbed her father's jacket and went out on the fire escape. How far up did it go? To the roof?

She climbed. Past the window above her, open several inches as before, blinds closed as before, music pouring out in a wailing melody. The laundry-room man. She was sure of it. The man reading a book about a composer. So appropriate. He had dried her clothes and folded them. His hands had smoothed the very clothes she had on. Warmth rushed through her. It was almost as if his touch lingered on the fabric next to her skin.

She shook off the thought, ridiculed herself for the absurdity of it, and climbed faster. The stairway did go all the way to the roof. Iron handrails curved over the parapet. She clung to them, cautioning herself not to look down, and swung one leg and then the other over the low masonry wall.

When she was safely standing on the flat tarred surface, she breathed in the cold night and looked out over the city lights. It was beautiful. Like a shimmer of earthbound stars if she squinted and used her imagination.

The roof area was an open rectangle, empty except for a stairwell housing that jutted up in the center. Probably the culmination of the emergency stairs that ran up from the lobby. She walked the perimeter of the rectangle. The building was situated on a corner, so there were two open sides, a third side abutting a building of the same height, and a fourth side where a taller building presented a solid windowless wall. She sat down and leaned back against the parapet in the shadow of that anonymous wall and she stared out over the sea of lights. It wasn't the orchard but it was good. The best she'd found in New York. Soon she was drifting. Thoughts scattering. Slipping into a meditative state.

The screech of metal snapped her back. She sat up straight, pressing her spine into the masonry. The roof was heavily shadowed. She strained to see. The metal scraped again and a wedge of light appeared at the stairwell door. Someone was coming up.

There was no way she could make it back to the fire escape in time so she froze in place and waited. A male figure was silhouetted briefly in the light, then the heavy metal door thudded shut. The figure crossed to the edge and peered down. His back was toward her. He had on a long coat with a military cut, but she could see nothing of his face. She tensed, ready to leap up and run. If she couldn't reach the fire escape ladder then maybe she could beat him to the metal door and go down that way.

He turned slowly, as though surveying his surroundings, memorizing them. And finally his face was illuminated enough for her to see who it was. The laundry-room man. The musician.

She rose, feeling a tightly wound excitement that was both exhilarating and disturbing.

'Now it's my turn to startle you,' she said.

He turned and peered into the darkness but didn't ask who it was. Did he know?

She moved from the shadows into the light. 'We seem to have the same odd schedule.'

He stood there, looking at her in silence. He seemed

159

taller and more powerful, filling the space around him rather than retreating into it as he had in the elevator.

'Thank you for taking care of my clothes,' she said.

Instead of a reply he nodded.

'Are you sure you don't want your book back?'

'Positive,' he said, speaking at last.

His voice affected her. His speech was educated and so precise that there could have been a British accent in his background. But it was more than that. His voice held a promise of something. She wanted him to speak again.

'I hear you play every night. Are you a professional?'

He was slow to answer. As though he was considering every word before he said it. 'I get jobs here and there.'

In spite of the cold her armpits were dampening, her face felt hot.

'I should go,' she said, backing up a step. 'You obviously came up here to be alone.'

'No. I'm the one who intruded. I'll go.'

'You didn't intrude,' she said but couldn't bring herself to admit that she was glad for his company.

He didn't reply. He didn't move.

She looked out at the sky. 'It's so hard to see stars in the city,' she said, thinking that it was a ridiculous thing to say and that she sounded as foolish as she felt.

'Too many lights,' he said.

'I can't help thinking about all the children without stars to wish on.'

'What makes you think children still make wishes?'

His cynicism surprised her. It was dark and absolute yet without any rancor.

From somewhere uptown came the scream of emergency sirens. The scream rose in pitch until it sounded very near, then it faded. Iris stared down at the streets.

'Are you from New York?' she asked him.

'Yes.'

'Then maybe you won't understand this, but each time I come to this city, to any big city, I hear everything, see everything . . . I jump at sirens and worry about whether there's a fire or an accident or a person hurt somewhere. I meet people's eyes and I'm aware of them . . . I really see them. Then, after a few days, I stop hearing the sirens, and the people melt together so that they're not individuals anymore.'

Why had she said all that? What was wrong with her? Was she turning into Linda? Ready to babble on and on at the slightest encouragement.

She glanced over at him and he was scrutinizing her with such intensity that she felt completely exposed. Quickly, she looked down, pulse beating in her throat, long dormant desires stirring. *We're all crazy*, Kizmin had said, *just in different ways*. And Iris was feeling more crazy by the minute.

There was an awkward silence.

'I'm Iris,' she said. 'Iris Lanier.'

He hesitated. 'Isaac Brightman.'

The awkward silence stretched out and engulfed them. She wanted to run from the roof and from him. She wanted to move closer to him and trace the ridges of his cheekbones with her fingertips. The conflicting urges kept her suspended there, poised for flight but unable to move.

'I have a confession to make.' He looked straight into her eyes, straight into her. 'I heard you on the fire escape. I knew you were up here.'

Iris swallowed hard. This was it. This was the time to say good-night and make a speedy exit. But she stood there, riveted by his eyes, rooted to the spot as if her feet had become embedded in the tar.

Silence again. Only now the silence was so charged that it didn't feel awkward. It felt dangerous.

'It's a saxophone, right?'

'What?'

'Your instrument.'

'Oh. Yes. A sax.'

'Do you play in clubs or an orchestra or . . .?'

'I work wherever I can get a job.'

'Do you play anything else?'

'Why do you ask that?'

She shrugged. 'The few musicians I've known have been able to switch, play other things.'

Again there was the reticence, the hesitation before he answered. 'Clarinet. A little piano.'

'You don't like to be asked questions about yourself, do you?'

'What makes you—' He broke off suddenly and smiled. His amusement had a gentle irony in it.

Smiling with him eased her nervousness a little.

He moved away from the edge to the stairwell housing and leaned against the wall there. She watched him. Now was the time to say good-night. She glanced over at the fire escape railings.

'Tell me about your work,' he said.

'How do you know I even have work?'

'I know.'

'Maybe I'm a student or unemployed. Maybe I fry hamburgers at a fast-food place and have nothing to tell.'

'No. Not you.'

'What makes you so certain?'

'It's in your eyes.'

'What? My profession?'

He cocked his head slightly, studying her as though preparing a diagnosis, not completely serious but not joking either. 'I can't see your profession, no. But I see dedication, commitment, passion – all directed somewhere. Definitely not to the business of everyday life. In fact you seem relatively oblivious to everyday life. So . . . it follows that your energies must be directed into your work.'

She stared at him, uncertain whether to laugh or take offense.

'Am I so transparent?'

'No. But I'm a good guesser.'

She glanced across at the fire escape again, thinking how easy it would be to leave. Ten steps, fifteen at the most, and she could grab the railings and swing over the parapet. She could be on her, way down. Nothing was making her stay. She could go back down into her room and lock the window and never speak to Isaac Brightman again.

'I'm in physical anthropology. Old bones basically. I've been working at a Mayan dig in Guatemala.'

She turned her back on the fire escape and moved to the stairwell wall. To a spot that was as far from him as she could get and still have a piece of the wall. She leaned back, facing out toward the city.

'The Maya . . .' he mused. 'Let's see. Weren't they the peaceful ones who built pyramids for their astronomers or something?'

'That's what everyone believed for a long time.'

'But it's not true?'

'No.' She glanced over at him. He appeared to be interested. 'Do you want a short explanation or a long one?'

'I want to know everything you think is important.'

'That's a tall order. Let me give you the highlights.' She turned so that her shoulder was against the wall and she was facing him. She felt pleasure and a rising eagerness. With the exception of her colleagues, no one ever asked her questions about her work.

So she told him how in 1839, an American named John Lloyd Stephens, and a British artist named Frederick Catherwood saw a mention of 'stone houses' in the Central American jungles. Later, when interviewed, they said that the thought of stone ruins in the jungle had aroused their curiosity, but it had to have been more than just curiosity that drove the two men to hack their way through the Honduran rain forest. Over the span of four very difficult years, traveling by mule and canoe and on foot, with only hearsay and old legends for clues, the two men found forty-four ruined cities. Lost cities. Most of them swallowed by the forest so completely that they were barely identifiable, even at close range.

Stephens wrote journals. Catherwood did exhaustive detailed drawings. And together they brought the ancient Maya to the attention of contemporary science. However, rediscovering the old cities, having descriptions and pictures of them, did not solve the riddles. People were mystified. There were scientists who argued that the extravagant monuments and incredible buildings could not have been created by any native culture, and so must have been built by the Lost Tribes of Israel or by survivors of Atlantis.

'Or space aliens,' Brightman commented wryly. He smiled, fueling her excitement.

She described the other related discoveries that came after Stephens and Catherwood. Old documents found in the Yucatan. A sixteenth-century manuscript, the Popol Vuh, or Council Book, unearthed in the archives of a church in Guatemala. And finally, in Madrid, the discovery of a long-lost book. It had been written three hundred years earlier by a friar and it was a first-hand account of Mayan civilization at the time of the Spanish conquest.

She explained how all of this had opened a window onto the past and people realized that the cities had been part of an astonishing culture. A culture with foundations that dated back thousands of years before Christianity. Scientific expeditions were mounted. Harvard University got into the act. More discoveries were made. Maps were drawn. Information was gathered. And science created a vision of a gentle, scholarly people, a culture that was

164

extraordinarily advanced in mathematics, astronomy, and the understanding and charting of time.

'Sounds like what I remember learning,' Isaac remarked.

Iris nodded. 'You can still go to libraries and find dated books on the shelves that will tell you the same thing. It wasn't until the sixties that the reality of the Maya began to emerge.'

'Wait,' Isaac said. 'Are you saying that scientists studied all the ruins and the documents and everything for more than a hundred years yet still had the fundamental overview of the entire civilization wrong?'

'Exactly! By the fifties there was a detailed body of knowledge on the Maya, but it was based on theories and guesses because so few of the Mayan hieroglyphics could be understood.

'Scientists believed that the populace was rural and scattered, and that the pyramids, the great buildings, and ball fields were ceremonial centers where people from far and wide gathered to celebrate important occasions. It was believed that the only agriculture used was the most primitive version of slash and burn, and that the social structure was divided distinctly between a poor, ignorant, laboring class and an educated, priestly class who lived in the city centers. It was thought that the glyphs found on everything from jewelry to doorways to stone stelae to ceramic jars were primarily decorative – symbolic renderings of religious and astrologic mysteries.'

'What made them change their minds?' Isaac asked.

'The change came slowly at first. Archaeologists developed new techniques for mapping and studying the cities. The glyphs began to be accepted as being more than just symbolic decoration, though most of them were still undecipherable.

'Then, around 1960, three epigraphers made a translation breakthrough—' She stopped. 'Sorry, I'm slinging these terms around without thinking. Epigraphy is basically the study of ancient inscriptions.'

He nodded. His posture was attentive. He seemed to be fascinated. And once again she was filled with the pleasure of sharing her interests, the pleasure of being thought interesting. He smiled, mostly with his eyes, though his mouth curved slowly upward too. It was a very intimate smile.

She touched a hand to her throat, took a deep breath, and shifted so that she turned away from him slightly, looking out over the city skyline.

'Breakthroughs were made and it was learned that a great majority of the inscriptions dealt with rulers and their royal courts. Nearly a thousand different hieroglyphic signs were cataloged. More breakthroughs came. Then, in the seventies, an art teacher from Alabama visited a ruin in Mexico and was captivated by what she saw. She used her artistic background and her intuition, studied the glyphs, and joined with others to make astounding progress.

'Finally, the Mayan code was broken and the door to the past was unlocked. And all the mysterious religious and astrologic symbols turned out to be the written records of the politics, the wars, the great leaders, the vanquished enemies, the celebrations, the complexities of city life. They were, quite simply and eloquently, the history of the civilization.

'Which seems so logical now and makes the early researchers appear thick-headed. But that's the way it was. And there is still so much more to be learned. So much more.'

'What are the big differences, then?' Brightman asked. 'What is the updated view on Mayan culture?'

She laughed a little, her self-consciousness creeping back. 'You mean I've talked this long and I still haven't answered your original question?'

'But it's all fascinating,' he insisted. 'Please, don't stop now.'

'All right.' She composed her thoughts. 'The pyramids and other great buildings were not ceremonial gathering places for a far-flung rural population. They were city centers, equivalent to a modern downtown area, and they were surrounded by streets and houses and aqueducts that stretched out in all directions. The people lived right there. Together. Tens of thousands of people. Over a hundred thousand residents in some cases. Larger than a lot of modern cities.

'They had reservoirs and irrigation systems and permanent farmlands. And the society wasn't divided between extremes of high and low. It was complex and overlapping, just like today. They had rulers and priests, royal families, a powerful and well-connected class, an educated middle class, a lower-middle class, merchants, scribes, tradesmen and so on. All this while our European ancestors were foundering in the Dark Ages.

'The entire vision of an ancient rural paradise filled with peaceloving intellectuals was wrong. It was nothing but a wishful historical fantasy . . . like a myth for the modern world to cling to.

'Oh, they had their intellectuals all right, and they were truly advanced and accomplished. There's no denying that. They were one of the earliest civilizations in the world to symbolize the concept of zero and to calendar with absolute – almost eerie – precision. They had a system called the longcount that goes back to a day that our civilization now identifies as the thirteenth of August, 3114 BC. That's pretty amazing, don't you think? And they were one of the earliest cultures to develop a form of writing and to produce books. But they were not a peaceful people. They were not a gentle people. They were brutal, bloodthirsty, and fiercely competitive.'

'They sound like New Yorkers,' Brightman said.

167

'New Yorkers with a Dracula fixation maybe. They had an obsession with blood. It was sacred to them and spilling it was a reverent act.'

She described the ritual bloodlettings – done in a spirit of worship or prayer, of giving thanks or asking for something. Blood was drawn by piercing the genitals with stingray spines or pulling barbed cords through the tongue; then it was dripped onto paper, burned, and offered up to the gods as smoke. She told how they ripped out hearts and tore off limbs. How they tossed men, women, and children into wells and volcanoes. How they sometimes played their games with decapitated heads instead of balls or played by rules that allowed for the butchering of all the losers.

'And they played war,' she said. 'Cities attacked each other. Plundered each other. Kings marched off to destroy other kings. And it wasn't necessarily to defend territory or water rights. It wasn't necessarily for protection or economic gain. They slaughtered each other for the sheer pleasure of it. They fought to see who won.'

'So much for the myth of the peaceful Maya,' Brightman commented ruefully. 'It sounds like the human race hasn't come very far in two thousand years.'

'Yes.'

'What about the books? You mentioned that they wrote books?'

'Codices. Painted on bark paper. There are only three known codices that survived. They're very elaborately illustrated and very beautiful, with all sorts of information recorded on them. It's hard to imagine burning them all.'

'They were burned?'

'Yes, didn't I say that? When the Spanish conquerors saw them they thought the codices were books of the devil. They burned every one they could find, and couldn't understand why the Maya were so upset about it.'

'So, in essence, they destroyed all the accumulated learning of the culture.'

'Yes.' Iris turned to face him again. 'Some think that they destroyed the culture when they destroyed the books. But it was already crumbling. The cities were overpopulated and they were fouling their water and overworking their farmland. And the wars between the city states had escalated to the point of chaos. The culture was destroying itself. The Spanish just quickened the process.'

'I don't understand though . . .' Isaac frowned in thought and she liked his seriousness. She liked his questioning, searching mind, his intensity.

'Isn't there a large Mayan population still in existence today?'

'Yes. That's one of the most intriguing aspects to all this. The people didn't die out. It was their civilization that died.'

She expected him to make another comment, but he didn't. He just looked at her. But it wasn't the stripped down scrutiny of before. His eyes were gentle and his expression was light, almost smiling, as though he had suddenly been touched by wonder.

'You're exactly as I thought you'd be,' he said.

She didn't know how to respond so she didn't try. Hugging herself, she stepped away from the wall.

'I'm getting cold. And I have to be up early in the morning.'

He nodded. Didn't move toward her. Didn't move at all. Which was good because she felt a strange panic unfurling within her. She started toward the fire escape.

'You can go back on the inside stairs,' he said.

'I'm afraid I didn't bring my key so the only way I can get back in is through my window.'

She expected him to laugh at that but he didn't.

'Let me give you a hand over,' he said. 'It's a long way down.'

Her first reaction was to object, but she didn't. She wanted to touch him. She wanted him to touch her.

He leaned out and held her arms as she swung over the parapet and onto the first step of the fire escape. For an instant their faces were very close. Her cheek brushed the rough wool of his coat. His grip on her arms tightened. She was safely over but he didn't let go.

'Will you come to the roof again?' he asked.

'I don't know,' she told him honestly.

Suddenly, he let go of her and straightened. He took a deep breath and raked his hair back with his fingers in a gesture of agitation.

'Good-night, Iris.'

He turned abruptly and walked away. She listened to his footsteps recede, but didn't move. There was no screeching of metal from the stairwell door so she knew he was still there, somewhere in the shadows.

Her knuckles were white from holding the iron handrail. He was still there. She could climb back over and be with him again. She closed her eyes and held on, imagining his hands, those long sure musician's hands, against her bare skin. Then she quickly went down the fire escape.

When she was back in her room she closed and locked the window, dropped the blinds and stood back to stare at the barrier. Was she trying to keep someone out or keep herself in?

She shrugged out of her clothes and looked at her arms, certain that his fingers had left an imprint. But there was nothing. No sign of his touch.

She went into the bathroom and stood before the mirror to stare at her reflection, curious about what he had seen. She had no clearcut image of herself. The face staring back at her seemed puzzled. *Are you looking at me?* it asked.

The face belonged to someone familiar but separate

from her. A woman with dark reddish-brown hair and eyes that fell somewhere between green and blue – a strong definite color, whatever it was called. Her own eyes were nondescript. Her hair was just brown. She was not remarkable in any way.

She unpinned her hair and shook it out. The woman in the mirror became startlingly unfamiliar. A stranger. Younger than she knew herself to be. Wild and unpredictable.

Quickly, she pulled her hair back and turned away.

Who had Isaac Brightman been looking at? Her or the woman in the mirror?

*You're hiding*, Kizmin had said. *We're all crazy underneath our civilized veneers*. But she was a trained scientist. With a rational, logical mind. She wasn't crazy underneath. At least she didn't used to be.

She turned out the lights and got into bed. The image of Moonsmoke floated in the darkness over her head . . . lucent with a silvery light . . . as though it was made of light. Made of moonlight and smoke.

The image was wearing a ceremonial headdress and a great disc necklace that covered her chest like a breastplate. A great disc with curved edges. Like a breastplate. If she were to lie face down . . . with the necklace on . . .

Iris sat up in bed. The image smiled enigmatically, then vanished into the darkness.

That sixth woman in the tunnel. The woman with the knife protruding from her back. That was Moonsmoke. The missing Moonsmoke. She hadn't run away or been snatched by the gods. She had been murdered.

# Ten

A day passed. Then another. And another. Iris hurried to the hospital each morning, driven by hope, but there was no change. She pored over medical articles about coma. She called in other doctors for second opinions. Nothing changed. Not her father's pallid, stuporous state. Not the prognosis for recovery. Nothing.

She made endless pots of coffee in the small service kitchen, filled endless pitchers of ice water. She read the book Isaac Brightman had given her. She looked in on Janelle Kizmin and changed television stations for her. She called Kizmin's office. She paced the confines of her father's room like a caged animal and made circuits of the hospital's corridors and public spaces, trying to wear away the frustration. Not since childhood had she felt so maddeningly powerless. So dependent and helpless. She felt like she was slipping ever closer to an edge, a precipice, with nothing to hang on to.

She looked down at her father's sunken face, fully exposed now that the gauze wrappings had been removed, and she was stricken by a fierce swelling of love. The feeling was new. While her father was well and tucked away in his orchard thousands of miles from her, she had had no such emotions. She had rarely thought of him at all. And if she had felt any emotion relating to him, it had been relief at her distance from him.

So what was the cause of this bright, hot aching in her

chest? Was it the prospect of losing him? Losing the only family she had left. Losing her ties to the past.

But that couldn't be the explanation because she had no fondness for the past. She had put the past in a box and locked it away. She would be glad to sever her ties to it.

And hadn't she often thought that the perfect intellectual life would be possible only if a person could be unencumbered in the world – free of possessions, free of ambitions, and above all, free of emotional bonds.

She put her hand to her chest and pressed against the ache. Had she felt this same love in her childhood and forgotten it until now? Had it been there after her mother left, during the years when she tried to cling to him – years of neediness and misery when she couldn't sleep or eat, when she hurt inside from all the tears she couldn't cry? Had it been there later, after she had learned the art of detachment so that she could watch him and read his moods, determining in advance whether he was going to glower or teach or ignore, gauging and analyzing him constantly so she knew exactly what was required to keep the peace? Had it been there all along, lurking inside her like a disease, waiting for the right conditions so it could take control of her?

There was no logic to it. No rationality.

Their relationship had become comfortable and predictable over the years since she'd left home. He wouldn't leave his orchard. She was too busy to go to California. They fulfilled their familial responsibilities with holiday cards and birthday phone-calls. They were polite, almost businesslike, and they never reminisced about the past. They never disturbed the calm of the present.

She wanted to shake him, force him to open his eyes and speak to her. To pull away from her touch. To frown and tell her how she had disappointed him, or better yet, to stare out the window and ignore her presence. Anything to restore the balance. To return equilibrium to her careening emotions.

She leaned over his still form to look directly into his vacant, flickering eyes. A tear dripped onto his paperwhite skin and she touched her fingers to her face and found that she was crying.

Carefully she rested her forehead against his chest and the tears soaked into the sheet covering him. He had always been a bear of a man. Now his broad chest felt so frail and insubstantial that she was afraid even her tears might be too heavy.

Useless, childish tears. She straightened and pressed her palms against her closed eyes. Stupid, useless tears. She had learned the pointlessness of tears when her mother left. Tears didn't fix things. They didn't do anything but irritate the eyes.

She went into the bathroom and splashed water on her face. When she came out Dorothy was attending to her father.

'You look terrible. I swear, I could mistake you for a patient.'

'Thanks, Dorothy.'

'What if this coma goes on for months? You just going to hang around the whole time? Think John here wants you to waste away in this hospital with him?'

'Would you rather I sat in my rented room and stared at the walls?'

'No. You need to get out and about. Get some exercise.'

'But what if something happened here and you couldn't reach me?'

'Get one of those beepers. Everybody has them. No reason you can't get one.' The woman paused to scribble something on the chart. 'I could tell you stories . . . Had one case where the patient recovered enough to go home

175

but his wife had worn herself into such a state that she had to be admitted. She wasn't much help to her husband or to herself.'

'OK, I'll look into a beeper,' Iris agreed to pacify her.

'That's good. You get one of those and then you give yourself a break.'

As soon as the nurse was gone Iris began to pace. She didn't want a break. She wanted everything to be over.

She pushed roughly out the door and took her pacing into the hall. Back and forth. Back and forth. In ever-widening arcs. Anything to work off the churning buzz of frustration.

'You all right?' asked one of the ever-present men with a mop.

'Yes,' she said shortly, aiming her pattern away from him.

'There's that detective,' he said.

She turned and saw Detective Kizmin crossing at the hallway intersection near the service kitchen.

'Kizmin!' she called, hurrying forward. 'Kizmin, wait!'

The woman stopped and turned as though reluctant to do so.

'I've been phoning you,' Iris said. 'Didn't you get my messages?'

'I got them.'

Kizmin's striking face appeared almost haggard.

'So what's going on?' Iris peered down the intersecting hallway. 'Were you taking the long way around so you wouldn't have to pass my father's door?'

She said it as a joke but the detective's reaction made her realize that the question had struck a nerve.

'You were, weren't you?'

Kizmin seemed unable to meet Iris's eyes.

'Is it about the party? Are you angry about what I said?'

'No. No.' Kizmin glanced up and down the hall as though checking for eavesdroppers. 'I'm not supposed to be talking to you.'

'What?'

'I'm off your father's case.'

'Off the case! But . . . you promised. You said you didn't give up. You said you had your teeth in it.'

'What the fuck do you know?' Kizmin hissed. 'Up in your scientific ivory tower. What do you know about holding down a job in the real world? I've got people to answer to. I've got to follow orders if I don't want to end up directing traffic somewhere. And let me tell you, your father isn't worth fucking up my whole career.'

The woman exhaled forcefully and sagged back against the wall. Iris studied her face. It didn't seem possible that the cool sharp-eyed detective could be in such turmoil, but it was there, etched into her face.

'What happened?' Iris asked.

'I don't know. Things were moving. One of my snitches thought he had a line on the hooker who ran from the scene. I had an interesting talk with the travel agent who sold your father his ticket. Nothing earthshaking, but Barney and I were clicking along. Then, suddenly, we get the word that the case has been given to someone else.

'Right away I went to the Captain to talk about it. I thought he'd probably jerked it as a favor . . . probably thought our plates were too full and wanted to give us some relief. So I figured I'd just explain to him what I was doing and why I wanted to hang on to it.

'He said it wasn't his doing. Said the orders came from over his head. Said we had to turn in our files immediately and that we weren't to discuss the case with anyone or make any further contact with any of the principals. And he specifically named you.'

'But . . . I don't understand. Why?'

'I don't know why.'

'Who will be in charge now? Does this mean they want to give it more attention?'

'Just the opposite,' Kizmin said bitterly. 'You didn't

hear this from me, but it's going down as a mugging gone bad and some smooth talker from on high is going to contact you and give you a line of official bullshit that they hope will pacify you and bury it completely.'

Iris tilted her head back and stared at the ceiling, fighting against a flood of anger and disappointment.

'I tried everything I could to get it back. But I just had my third reprimand and I've got to let it go.' A quizzical expression crossed Kizmin's face then. 'Wait a minute. I thought you'd be relieved. I thought you wanted this whole thing to be over more than you wanted answers. I thought you were afraid of what more we might dig up.'

Iris lowered her eyes, then raised them to meet Kizmin's again. 'I thought so too. But now . . . This makes me furious.'

Kizmin's mouth curved into a half smile. She waited several beats, then said, gruffly, 'Thanks for looking in on my sister. She talks about you every time I see her.'

'She seems a little better,' Iris said. 'She remembers me at least.'

'Yeah. The doctor says now that maybe the brain damage isn't as bad as they thought.' Kizmin looked off down the hall. 'I can hardly stand it. Being with her. Seeing her. She was a high school English teacher and she really loved it. The doctor says she'll never teach again. Her life is fucked. The entire rest of her life. And that scumbag is still out there walking around.'

'Someone did that to her! My God, I thought she'd been in a car accident.'

'No. It was a domestic dispute. She wanted a divorce so her husband decided to win her affections back with a baseball bat.'

Iris absorbed the enormity of Kizmin's tonelessly delivered words. 'You must want to kill him.'

It was as though an electrical charge passed through

the detective's body. 'I'm a cop,' she said. 'Not an executioner.'

Iris was suddenly tired. She leaned against the wall beside Kizmin and stared down at the linoleum tiles of the hall floor. 'I remember . . . when I was eleven or twelve . . . I was reading a book about the human soul and how everything happens for a reason and our lives are part of a grand design. Not a religious book but a very spiritual one.

'My father grabbed it and tore it to shreds. He said it was dangerous to read such lies. That our lives had no pattern or grand design. That things happened to people the same way they happened to ants and mice and mockingbirds . . . Randomly and by pure chance. And that bad things happened to good people and good things happened to bad people. And there are no rewards or punishments. You can't count on anything. Or anyone.

'Maybe that's truer than your ideas about fate. Otherwise we'd have to accept that your sister and my father were both destined to be harmed.'

Kizmin frowned. 'No. I believe in fate and in the mystery of being human. Even when bad things happen I'd still rather think that it was meant to be than think that it had no more meaning than a rat getting hit by a subway train.'

There was a rumbling hum. Kizmin stiffened. A technician rounded the corner pushing a portable X-ray machine and the detective relaxed again.

'What would happen if you were seen talking to me?'

'I could probably explain it away this time. You caught me and demanded to know what was happening. After this . . . I really don't know. But the order was a serious one.'

The detective shook her head. 'Hell, nothing's going right. Barney says we're jinxed because we spent too much time around the Dirty Thirty. Maybe he's right. We haven't even been able to get an ID on that girl you dug out. Zip. Zero. Zilch. It's like she never existed.'

'How is that possible?' Iris asked. 'Aren't there missing-persons lists, dental records, descriptions . . .'

Kizmin smiled. 'Right. Just like in the movies. But unlike the movies things go wrong or get lost. Reports fall through the cracks. Or people disappear and there's no one to notice they're gone. No one to report it.

'We'll probably never solve her murder. It will be pure luck if we just identify her.'

Iris drew in a deep breath. 'I won't just let my father's shooting drop. After all the speculation . . . with all the unanswered questions still hanging there . . . I can't let it drop.'

The detective grinned. 'I'm beginning to wonder if what you think and feel, and what you think you think and feel, aren't a little removed from each other.'

Iris ignored the comment. 'I won't let them bury it,' she warned.

'Good. Hire a private detective then. I'll give you the name of a good agency. Have them go out to California first. My instinct tells me there are loose ends out there.'

'No,' Iris said, unwilling to admit that she didn't have the money for a private detective. 'I want to check things out for myself first.'

Kizmin gave an exasperated snort.

'What?' Iris demanded. 'You think that I can't possibly find anything that you haven't already found?'

'No. Just the opposite. I'm afraid of what you might dig up. I'm worried about you getting hurt.'

'Why would I get hurt?'

'Why did your father get hurt?'

Iris acknowledged her point with silence, then said, 'I won't get hurt.'

Kizmin glanced around warily. 'I should go.'

'This smooth talker who's supposed to contact me . . .

will he answer questions about the shooting?'

'Probably not to your satisfaction. His job is to sweep it under the rug.'

'Will he let me see the case file?'

Kizmin's eyebrows shot up at the ridiculousness of the question. 'I've told you most of what's in it.'

'All right. Now tell me the rest.'

'Hey. I want to keep my job. I've got things all planned out. I'll get experience in homicide, switch to rape, and eventually head a domestic-violence task force. Getting fired is not in the plan.'

'Have you talked to all the prostitutes in the area?'

'It's not that simple. Those kind of people tend to vanish when they smell cops. Like I said, I had a snitch on it. We're looking for a small blond, probably young, with a short punkish haircut.'

'And what my father said to the nurse in the hospital – about "hope being the key" – are you being absolutely honest with me? He really didn't say anything else?'

'Nothing.'

'The travel agent. You said something about the travel agent.'

'She got a call from a woman who identified herself as Mrs Lanier and asked for your father's flight information.'

'Mrs Lanier?'

'With a story about how she had to make arrangements for him in New York and she didn't want him to know she'd lost the itinerary.'

Kizmin backed away a step, then hesitated.

'There's something else, isn't there?' Iris grabbed the woman's sleeve. 'What else, Kizmin?'

'If you repeat this to anyone, they'll know it came from me.' Kizmin hesitated again as though wrestling with her loyalties. 'Barney really kept the wraps on this. Didn't want anyone knowing about it until we understood it ourselves.'

'What!'

'Your father was wearing a wire when he was shot.'

'A what?'

'He had on a very sophisticated device that transmitted conversation. To listeners or a tape-recorder or something.'

'My father?'

'Yes.'

'Are you sure it wasn't just dropped there by his attacker?'

'Positive. It was fitted to his body. Concealed so that he could be patted down without it being discovered.'

'I don't understand. My father? Someone else had to have put it on him.'

Kizmin shrugged.

'What does it mean?'

'We don't know exactly. But it could be possible that there's a tape out there of your father being shot.'

Kizmin began backing away in earnest. 'I'm sorry, but . . . that's it.'

'What if I need to get in touch with you?'

'I'm not supposed to have contact with you. Maybe, after everything cools down a little . . .'

'Right.' Iris turned away.

'Wait.'

Iris turned back.

Kizmin stood there, arms folded defensively against her chest, teeth worrying the corner of her bottom lip. 'I'm working the foundation's victim advice line for the next two weeks. Nine to midnight, Monday through Thursday. It should be safe for you to call me there. Or, in an emergency, you could call the station and say you're my old roommate from college. Any name is OK. Just specify old roommate and I'll get back to you.'

'You think someone is going to be checking on you?'

'I'm probably being overly paranoid, but this whole thing is feeling weird to me and I just want to be very very careful.'

Iris returned to her father's bedside. She sat down in the chair and stared at his pale, vacant face. Her father was not there within the shriveled body. He was gone somewhere. As absent as her long-vanished mother.

She rested her elbows on the edge of the bed and cradled her forehead in her hands. The nurses were right. Her vigil was useless. Her presence at his bedside was not going to drag him back from his netherworld.

Maybe he was waiting for her to turn the key. Maybe he was trapped and unable to make it back until all the mysteries were solved, all the riddles answered. Until his name was cleared and there were no more questions left.

She pushed out of the chair and stood over the bed. There was a ghostliness to him. As though he were gradually slipping away. Becoming as insubstantial as her night-time visions of Moonsmoke.

She took his hands, gripped them tightly in her own. 'I'll bring you back,' she promised. 'I can find the answers and bring you back.'

# Eleven

Iris went straight back to the Fitzgerald from the hospital. The weather had turned so mild that everyone was preoccupied with it. Strangers on the subway muttered about holes in the ozone and global warming. Even balmy weather had become an ominous sign for people.

She passed Madame Zora's window and caught a glimpse of a shawl-draped figure in the shadowy recesses of the psychic's parlor. She wondered if the spiritualist ever had a customer. Maybe she ought to go in herself, pay the ten dollars, and ask why her father had bought a gun and flown to New York. Why someone had shot him in Riverside Park.

She had her building keys in her hand but didn't need them. The front door had been wedged open with a crushed coffee cup. Mitchell Hanley and Mr Andretti were both in the lobby when she entered. Mitch was waiting for the elevator and Andretti was kicking the stairway door closed.

'Nobody listens!' Andretti shouted. 'The stairs are for emergency use. For coming down when the elevators aren't safe to use. They're not for going up and they gotta be kept locked from the inside.'

Mitch was hunched over in a 'don't look at me' posture. He reached out to stab the elevator button again as if to confirm his innocence.

'We're talking safety here,' Andretti said, turning to Iris

185

to enlist support. 'When that door's left open off the lobby we get junkies and punks sneaking up the stairs and hiding in there.'

Iris didn't bother pointing out that even if the door off the lobby was secured the junkies and punks he was worried about could simply ride up the elevator and enter the stairwell through a door on an upper floor.

'Maybe if the other elevator was fixed people wouldn't use the stairs,' Mitch suggested.

'Hey! It's not my fault the other elevator don't work. I tell the management company every day to get it fixed.'

'The front door was wedged open just now when I came in,' Iris told him. 'I'm afraid your tenants just aren't very security conscious, Mr Andretti.'

'Jesus!' Andretti threw up his hands and stalked away toward the front door.

Iris settled in next to Mitch to wait for the elevator.

He smiled. 'How's your father doing?'

'The same.'

'Thought you spent every day at the hospital.'

'I have been. But I have some things to do this afternoon.'

'Well, how about having lunch with me then?'

'No, thank you. I really have a lot to do.'

'OK, then we'll make it dinner. Ever had German food? Saurbraten and potato pancakes?'

'Thanks, Mitch, but I wouldn't be good company. I'd probably spend the whole evening wondering if the hospital was trying to reach me.'

'No problem.' Mitch pointed to a small plastic object hooked to his belt. 'We'll give the nurses my beeper number.'

'You have a beeper?'

'Sure.'

'How can I get a beeper?'

He looked puzzled. 'You need a beeper?'

'A nurse suggested it. So the hospital can always find me.'

'Oh, yeah.' He broke into a grin. 'And you just asked the right guy. I've got a friend in the business who can fix you up quick.'

'Oh no, I couldn't ask you to—'

'Forget it.' He held up his hand. 'It's done. Now, about dinner . . .'

'I'm really not feeling very sociable tonight, Mitch. Please, let's save it for another time.'

'OK. OK. But I'll hold you to that. Another time.' He pushed the lighted elevator button again. 'This thing is prehistoric. Too bad the super locked the stairs.'

The words were barely out of his mouth when the stairway door burst open and the biker emerged, clad in black leather pants and jacket.

'Hold it!' Mitch called. The biker ignored him and kept moving, leaving Mitch to lunge at the closing door. He was successful, catching it just before it latched and relocked.

'Want to do the stairs?' Mitch asked as he stuffed paper around the latch to keep the lock from engaging.

'No thanks,' Iris said.

She watched him disappear into the dimly lit stairwell. He was good looking. He was pleasant and seemed to be kind. He had to have a reasonable amount of intelligence to have made it to law school. But . . . There was always that unquantifiable 'but' in the back of her mind when she considered his virtues. But. But . . . she didn't want to get involved with anyone while she was worrying over her father. But . . . she didn't like to get involved with guys who were so clearly open to being hurt. But . . . she didn't want to get involved with anyone who expected a commitment. But, but, but. She could come up with dozens of buts. And now she had another to add. And it seemed to be the strongest, most compelling one of all.

But . . . he wasn't Isaac Brightman.

In the four days since meeting Isaac Brightman on the roof she had not been able to stop thinking about him. His eyes, his voice, the gentle irony in his smile. His intensity. His curiosity. His long steady hands. Just the recollection of a movement he'd made or a sideways look he'd given her was enough to cause a visceral reaction. *I knew you were up here*, he'd said. *I knew you were up here*. Remembering that sent a frisson down her spine.

Each night since their meeting she had opened her window and listened to his music, listened for his knock on her door or his footsteps on her fire-escape landing, all the while rehearsing the reasons why she should not see him again. Each night she had struggled with her own desire to return to the roof. But her rational self had always won. Brightman was a part of the craziness she was fighting. He was part of her slide toward the edge.

With Mitchell Hanley her reservations were mostly concerns about him. Not wanting to hurt him. Not wanting to lead him on. Not wanting to build up false expectations. Her reservations about Isaac Brightman were completely different. They were fears for herself. Fears of entering into something that she could neither understand nor control.

She rode up in the elevator, hanging onto the brass sidebar, telling herself that no one else mattered, not Mitch, not Isaac, not Kizmin. Only her father mattered. He needed her. For the first time in her life she was truly important to him. And that was all that mattered.

*California*, Kizmin had said. *There are loose ends in California*. She could follow Kizmin's instincts, Kizmin's suggestions. She could be the detective. Besides, how threatening could a trip to her childhood home be?

Inside her room she went straight to the telephone and called the airlines. The first available seat was on a flight the following morning. She booked it on her credit card, feeling good, feeling positive about making the decision, about having a plan. But after she hung up the phone she was dismayed by the prospect of filling the rest of the day. Every minute counted. She had to do something. What would a detective do next?

She thought for a moment then went to the dresser and thumbed through the collection of cards from her father's wallet. The only New York City card that offered any possibilities at all was the one for the Seven Stars Diner. She picked up her shoulder bag and headed for the subway.

The address on the card turned out to be on the western edge of Greenwich Village, not too far from the forensic anthropology lab where Kizmin had taken Iris to borrow the excavation tools. Iris went into the restaurant. It was a typical New York City Greek diner, long and narrow, with counter service on one side and a line of small booths along the opposite wall. At the back was a wall-mounted pay phone. Iris used it to check in with the hospital. The voice might as well have been a recording. 'No change. No change.'

She sat down on a stool at the counter and glanced over the four-page menu. The place was quiet. Breakfast was over and the lunch rush had yet to begin.

She ordered an omelet with feta cheese and fresh tomatoes. The counterman jotted it down on his pad then called the order back to another man standing at the open grill behind him. Both men were fortyish, dark-haired and robust, more suited to rough outdoor work than to the white aprons they wore.

'Also,' the counterman said, eyeing Iris critically, 'a bagel with the omelet. A nice onion bagel. And a small salad? A nice Greek salad with Kalamata olives and a little feta crumbled over it.'

'OK,' Iris said, wondering if she looked hungry. 'And hot tea with lemon, too.'

The food came within minutes and Iris discovered that she was hungry. The counterman leaned on his elbows and watched her eat.

'Why do so many girls try to be thin?' he said in accented English. 'It is not healthy to be thin.'

Iris smiled and kept eating.

'How can women be soft for children and husband when they are all bones.'

'I'm eating,' Iris said. 'I'm eating!'

'You have children and husband?'

'No.'

'Maybe later. Eat more. Maybe you will find husband.'

'Are all the women soft in Greece?' she asked between bites.

'Are the women soft in Greece?' he called back to the cook with a laugh.

'Yes,' the cook answered in a different accent. 'Beautiful women. Very soft.'

The counterman focused on Iris again. 'He is Greek. He is the boss. I am from Syria. I work here in daytime and drive car service at night. Soon I will have my own restaurant.'

'Like this one?'

He lowered his voice. 'Better. Not a diner. Good Arabic food. Healthy. Taboli, hummus, baba, falafel, kibbeh . . . all very healthy. You know this food?'

'No. I've never had it.'

His face fell as though her admission was the saddest news he had had all morning. Iris finished her tea and he immediately refilled the cup with boiling water and gave her another tea bag.

She took the restaurant's business card from her shoulder-bag and put it on the counter. 'My father had this,' she said.

'Yes.' The counterman gestured toward the cash register where Iris saw a basket of the cards. 'Many people take cards.'

She dropped the card back into her purse. 'That's what I was afraid of, but would you mind looking at his picture anyway.' She handed over the picture she carried. In it her father stood in work clothes, surrounded by trees, only the trees had been cut off when the snapshot was trimmed to fit in her wallet, so no one else could tell that he had been surrounded by trees.

The counterman studied the picture, then shook his head. He carried the picture back to his boss who also shook his head.

'Many people come here,' the counterman said. 'Many people.'

She stood outside the diner on the stone slab sidewalk, considering what to do next. She wished she could call Kizmin and ask for advice, but that was out of the question.

The air was warm and smelled of the river. She breathed deeply. How far could it be to the water? Not more than a few blocks. She started west, toward the Hudson, and it occurred to her that her year of living in the city might as well have been spent underground in Nevada. She had experienced little of New York. She had been closed to everything but her work and her pathetic attempt to help out at the Kaliker Foundation.

A half block from the diner she paused at a stop-signed intersection, waiting for her turn to cross. Ahead she could see a wedge of silvery water.

She looked across the narrow street. It was an old section of the Village, with nineteenth-century brick industrial buildings and newly condo-ized apartment houses. A scattering of small dingy shops were sandwiched in at sidewalk level. Very old New York. Probably historic.

She stopped suddenly and turned to look at the shops again. Covert. The word was in small undistinguished letters but now it jumped out at her: COVERT SUPPLY. Didn't covert mean undercover? As in spying? As in wires to listen to conversations?

She hurried across the roughly cobbled street and went through the door of the shop. An old-fashioned bell tinkled as she entered.

She paused for a moment to let her eyes adjust to the dimness. Single-bulb lamps hung from the high ceiling, casting pools of weak light. The interior was a warren of boxes that completely covered the front window and were stacked almost to the ceiling in places.

'Can I help you?' called a voice from the back and Iris went toward it to find a long glass counter with a man lounging behind it.

'I'm not sure,' Iris said.

'If you're not sure, then you're probably in the wrong place.'

The man was middle-aged and about Iris's height. He had a military brush haircut and a piece of adhesive tape wrapped around the corner of his black-framed glasses. His expression was bored and unfriendly.

'What do you sell here?'

'Are you some kind of reporter?'

'No. Not at all.'

''Cause we're not looking for publicity. That's not the kind of business we run. We're a professional supply house.'

'Professional?'

'Law enforcement, private investigators, corporate security units . . . We don't sell toys. We don't service parents trying to tap their teenagers' phones or wives spying on their husbands. If you're looking for that kind of thing you'll have to go to one of those places with the billboards and the yellow-page ads.'

'Please,' Iris said. 'My father was shot while wearing a wire.'

The man straightened and his boredom evaporated.

'Shot huh?'

He came out from behind the counter and Iris saw that he was dressed in heavy black lace-up shoes with multi-pocketed pants that tucked in to the top of the shoes. From the waist up he looked like a clerk, but from the waist down he was dressed for a SWAT unit.

'He's in a coma. The police said that the device he was wearing was very sophisticated. I was wondering if it came from here.'

'Do you have it?'

'No,' Iris admitted. 'But I have a picture of him. Could you take a look and see if you remember him?'

The man took the snapshot and examined it. His face betrayed nothing.

'Where'd he get shot?'

'Riverside Park.'

'Not where . . .' the man said as though amazed at her stupidity. 'What part of his body?'

'His . . . uh . . . his face.' Iris touched her own cheek with a fingertip.

'Oh, man! How many times?'

'Once.'

'What'd he get it with?'

'I'm sorry . . . I'm not sure what you're asking.'

'What kind of gun?'

Iris was increasingly disturbed by his probing, but she forced herself to answer.

'A thirty-eight.'

'Umm.' The man handed the picture back without commenting on it.

'Well?' Iris said.

'Well, what?'

'Do you remember my father or not?'

193

'We've got a reputation here, lady. This is a closed shop. And by closed I mean closed mouths. We work hard here. We sweep for bugs every week. We have a sound scrambler field so long-range microphones won't pick up from in here. We have special lighting and we pile up the boxes so surveillance cameras can't be trained on the interior. And we have a solid gold rule – we don't talk about our customers. Not ever. We don't take names or keep customer records and my partner and I have very short memories.'

'But . . . this situation is different. You'd be helping one of your customers.'

'So you say. But you could be anybody. Your whole story could be total crap.'

'Here's my identification,' Iris said. 'My father is in Morningside Hospital. You could call there. The nurse in charge till four is Dorothy. Detectives Kizmin and Barney of the Homicide Task Force were the ones investigating the case. It's been switched to someone else, but you could call them and ask—'

The man held up his hand.

'I'm not here to spend my time checking stories. And even if you're legit . . . even if your whole story is on the level . . . how's it going to help you to know where your father got his wire? What would that tell you? You don't think he walked up to me – if it was me he bought from – you don't think he walked up and said he'd like to have a wire and then explained what he was going to do and who he was going to meet and what was going down, do you? Do you?'

Iris shook her head and lowered her eyes to conceal her disappointment.

The man walked back around the counter as though to separate himself from her.

'You say the cops are on this . . . well then . . . let the cops do their job. You've got no business poking your

194

nose into places where it might get bit off.'

'The police have decided it was a mugging.'

His eyes widened. 'The guy gets shot wearing a wire and they're calling it a mugging?'

She nodded.

His blunt fingers drummed a staccato on the glass countertop.

'Your father didn't know anything about wires or covert operations, right?'

'Not a thing. He wouldn't even use an answering machine.'

'Then you gotta ask yourself, who picked out this high-powered rig for him? Who was on the listening end of it?'

'You mean, who would know so much about surveillance devices?' Iris said.

'That's it. That's the way to go with your questions. Zero in on your father's friends.'

Iris stared at him. 'Are you saying that my father came in here with a man who seemed like he was a friend?'

'I'm not saying anything. My mouth is closed. I was just using figures of speech.'

'OK, but could you—'

'Hey! That's all the time I got. Beat it, lady.'

Iris talked to the hospital, got her small wardrobe packed and ready for the trip to California and advised Mr Andretti that she would be gone for a few days but still wanted to keep the room. At dinnertime she went out and found Arabic food. The hummus was creamy smooth, a purée of chickpeas, lemon, and garlic. The taboule was fresh and tangy, almost like a salad, with minced parsley, tomatoes, scallions, and mint in a dressing of olive oil and lemon. She couldn't recall ever giving so much attention to what she ate, but food seemed suddenly important to her. Everything seemed more important. Every smell and taste and sight. Was it the possibility of her father dying that was expanding her awareness or had she changed in some way?

She didn't know the answer. But then, there was another difference she was noticing about herself. Her behavior was becoming increasingly inexplicable. Was it a stage she was entering as her thirtieth birthday approached or was it something more ominous? Was it the inner craziness Kizmin had spoken of? Was she on her way to a breakdown? Was she losing her scientific edge, her objectivity and professional remove? Or was she experiencing some normal aspect of life that she had not previously known about?

She walked for awhile after dinner, then went back to her room and went to bed. Her flight was early the next morning and she wanted to be rested for it. She stared up at the ceiling and tried to coax sleep into coming. Moonsmoke floated in the darkness, smiling her enigmatic smile.

Dead Moonsmoke.

Murdered Moonsmoke.

Iris pressed her palms against her eyes to force the image from her mind but it was immediately replaced by a vision of the unidentified female murder victim she had unearthed, beaded braids attached, empty eye sockets staring down.

Iris sat up and clicked on the light, rechecked the alarm on the bedside clock, switched off the light, and settled down again, determined to think soothing thoughts. Sleep-inducing thoughts.

Suddenly her mind was filled with Isaac Brightman. He hadn't been playing all evening. Was he up there in his room? Did he still want to see her on the roof? She turned over. Tried to relax. Turned onto her stomach. The mattress pressed against her body, heightening her awareness of all the heated tender areas. She flipped onto her back and threw the covers off.

'I will go to sleep,' she said aloud.

When she was young she had tried counting sheep, but since college he had had her own prescription for insomnia.

'The human body has more than two hundred bones. There are . . .' And she began to name them aloud. Every bone. Including all the combinations possible due to fusing. It should have worked. It had always worked before. But an hour later she had gone through all the possible bones in the body, all the joints, and every bone-altering disease she knew. And still she was tense and restless.

'All right,' she said.

In moments she was dressed and climbing the fire escape. The light was on in his window. As usual it was open a few inches and the blinds were tightly closed.

Did he hear her footfalls on the metal? Would he come?

She was barely over the parapet when she heard the scrape of the stairwell door opening.

'Isaac?'

He came toward her, out of the shadows and into the glow from the city lights. Just as she remembered him. Angular face gentle, eyes full of intensity, mouth on the verge of a slow ironic smile. Wearing the same long, square-shouldered, military coat, though now it was hanging open, as though he'd thrown it on quickly over his jeans and shirt. Hands shoved in his coat pockets. Slightly shy. No. Not shy really. Reticent.

'I thought you'd never come back,' he said.

Everything inside her turned upside down.

'I thought so, too,' she said. 'But here I am.'

# III

*Queen of Swords*

# Twelve

It seemed almost inconceivable to Iris that she had not been back to the Santa Clara Valley for more than six years. Oddly, that was harder to absorb than the fact that she had not seen her father face-to-face during those same six years.

She pulled out of the San José airport in her rented car and took Guadelupe Parkway around to the freeway, but as soon as she'd merged with the stream of traffic she decided to get off at Alameda and go locally instead. The freeway would show her nothing and she was hungry for familiar sights.

Everything was brilliantly green and growing, unlike New York where spring was still a promise and most of the trees were bare. She passed Santa Clara University with its pristine mission-style buildings set against lush parklike plantings. The Alameda became the El Camino. El Camino Real actually – The King's Highway – but no one called it by the formal name.

Things hadn't changed much on the El Camino. It was still a typical California commercial mix of drive-up food, motels, doughnuts, and furniture stores, punctuated by the occasional fifties-style strip mall. With plenty of parking. Asphalt enough to ensure that every shopper was always guaranteed a parking place. Iris wondered how many more orchards had been bulldozed and paved since she was last in the valley.

She turned south past the swim center down to Pruneridge, then looped back up, remembering fields that were now housing developments, a Comice pear orchard that was now an office complex. At Saratoga-Sunnyvale Road she turned back toward Santa Clara and finally she made the turns that took her toward her father's house.

The area had become so built-up that the orchard seemed like a mirage, a natural oasis amid the pavements and buildings. She wondered what the developers were offering Mr Hirano now for the land. The offers climbed each year and she had no idea what astronomical figures had been reached, but she knew that years ago there had been offers that made her wonder if the fertile loam that nurtured the trees was made of gold dust. But then, to people like Mr Hirano and her father, the rich alluvial soil of the valley was infinitely more precious than gold.

'Why,' her father said to all who would listen, 'why do we take the Santa Clara Valley with the soil and the micro-climate to grow the finest fruit in the world, and cover the whole damn thing with concrete and offices, and homes for people who wonder why they can't find any of that incredible fruit anymore. Why do human beings always destroy things?'

She had been so embarrassed by him when she was young but she had come to a point where she agreed with him on many things now. Like the fate of the Santa Clara Valley.

She was able to agree with him. She had even come to admire him. But still she could not find peace with him.

As she drew nearer she saw that the cherries were still blooming. The delicate clouds of white blossoms brought a catch to her chest. She wondered if the trees missed her father. She had always had an anthropomorphic attitude toward the trees. It was hard not to. They were so solidly rooted in her life. Some of them were venerable old souls, fifty or sixty years old for the oldest. And they had always seemed to have personalities, not just by type – cherry versus apricot – and not just by variety – Bing or Van or Royal Anne or Tartarian for the cherries, Blenheim or Moorepark for the cots – but also personalities that differed from tree to tree.

She smiled to herself, remembering how she had wandered around the orchard talking to the trees. Talking to everything for that matter. Her father had lectured her constantly about her overactive imagination and fretted over whether she was going to be able to separate fact from fiction by the time she reached adulthood.

At the corner she turned right and drove down the secondary road to Mr Hirano's driveway. His house was partially visible, set back behind a decorative fence and a graceful horseshoe drive. The house was long and low, an elegantly breezy building of cream-colored stucco and curved terracotta roof tiles, a perfect example of mission-style California architecture. It was as clean and perfectly maintained as if it had just been constructed, but the house had been a fixture in the area for close to a hundred years.

Iris parked and went up the walk toward the front door. Hirano thought lawns were wasteful and so all the open ground stretching from his house to the edge of the orchard was filled with plantings. An astonishing sea of specimens. Hirano's agricultural urges had turned to gardening when he retired from his orchards, and his gardens could have been opened as a botanical display. The profusion of color and fragrance was almost disorienting.

She rang the bell and waited. Old feelings from childhood crept through her. She had always been cautious of Mr Hirano and dreaded being sent to his house on errands. Though small in stature and always carefully polite, he had seemed formidable to her, a man capable of roasting children in his oven.

The house was quiet. The bell echoed inside and died.

203

She followed the rock path around the side, past the outbuilding and the old watertank, both in the identical California mission style and both maintained as though new, then she ducked through the break in the evergreen hedge and was surprised to find herself in a beautiful Japanese garden complete with water trickling into a pool. When had that been created? Recently, she was sure.

'Mr Hirano!' she called.

His compact pickup truck was in the drive so she knew he was nearby. She considered leaving her car where it was and continuing her search for him on foot, then decided to drive on around to her father's house and park. If Hirano was in the orchards he would hear her car and come out to meet her.

Her father's house was a straight walk through the orchard from Hirano's, but to reach it by car she had to drive back out to the public road and around to her father's unmarked driveway. The house was situated on two acres that Mr Hirano had carved out of the orchard and sold to her father.

Like Hirano, John Lanier had no use for lawns. There was a cleared strip for vehicle parking and a toolshed, but all the rest of his acreage was taken up by bushes, trees, and plants that produced either food or flowers. Behind the house was her mother's flower garden. On the east side was the vegetable garden. And every other available piece of ground was devoted to his private plantings. Boysenberries and raspberries grew in profusion. Grapes hung on an elaborate trellis. There were two kinds of fig trees, several peaches and a lemon. There were three kinds of pears and two different plums, a walnut, and an almond. And there were the jewels of his collection, his experimental trees, the ones he had grafted together to produce several varieties of fruit on one trunk.

Yoshi Hirano appeared through the trees as she was walking from the car to the house. He did not seem surprised to see her, but then she couldn't remember him ever betraying surprise at anything. He was a short wiry man, slightly stooped from years of physical labor. His hair was as thick as ever but now an iron grey color, and his walnut brown skin was deeply creased from years in the sun.

'Hello,' she called.

He inclined his head in greeting and came toward her. As usual he was dressed in khaki work clothes, which always looked clean no matter how much dirty work he accomplished. Today he also had on kneehigh irrigation boots. He did not look like a man who was worth millions of dollars, but then he never had.

'It is a pleasure to see you, Iris,' he said when he reached her. 'Is there any change in your father's condition?'

She shook her head. 'I probably shouldn't have left him, but I felt so useless just sitting there. I came out to see if I could learn anything by looking through the house. I should have called you, but . . .'

'There is no need for explanation.' He frowned. 'The police were here. I had to let them in.'

'Yes. I know.'

'You will see much more than the police saw so it's good you came.' He rubbed his hands together in what she remembered as a familiar gesture. 'I am busy with the orchard now. Will you join me for dinner at seven?'

She was surprised by the invitation. She had hoped that she could make an opportunity to have a real conversation with him, but she had not expected him to offer the opportunity. Though she had known him and lived near him from birth she couldn't recall ever having exchanged more than a few cursory sentences with him.

'Mr Hirano, here's some bread my mother baked.'

'Please thank her for her kindness, Iris.'

Or sometimes, *'Mr Hirano, when are your grand-children coming to visit again?'*

*'Maybe this weekend, Iris. I'm sure Jeff will let you know the moment he arrives.'*

And after they had their brief exchange his face would close. Or that was how Iris used to think of it. He had a way of dismissing people without making a move.

What a pair Yoshi Hirano and her father had made. The formidable and the taciturn. *'Let's hide from the monsters,'* Jeff used to say, and she'd run with him through the trees.

She watched Hirano disappear back into the orchard, then pulled her carry-on bag from the car and went into her father's house.

He had built it for solid comfort rather than design. It was a basic square girded by a raised and roofed wrap-around porch. The front door opened into a center hall that ran straight back to the mud room and the back door, with only the staircase to keep it from being an open shotgun corridor. On one side of the hall was the living area and kitchen, on the other was Iris's bedroom, a full bathroom, and a room that could have been another bedroom but was always used as a combination office and library. Upstairs was the large loftstyle bedroom and bath where her parents slept together for eight years and where, for the past twenty years, her father had slept alone.

She stood in the hallway a moment, breathing in the scents of the house. She could have recognized the house by smell alone, though she had not realized that while she still lived there.

She went through the door into her old bedroom first. That seemed the safest place to start. As always she felt that she had stepped through a time warp. Everything in the room was just as she had left it when she went away to college at fifteen. Desk, bed, and bookcases still waiting to be used again. And everything very clean, even though

206

her father hadn't been expecting her. She had always assumed that he dusted and shined her old room only when a visit was scheduled, but seeing it now made her realize that he always kept it clean.

She put her carry-on bag at the foot of the bed, stood in the center of the room, and took it in. Strangely, she felt that this was the first time she was really seeing everything. The room had been a haven to her, not only when she lived in the house, but later, when she was home on college vacations, or making an obligatory visit. It had always been her safe place. The one place she felt was completely her own.

But now it occurred to her that the room was full of her father. The bed was not just a bed. It was a beautiful piece of handcrafted oak, sturdy and timeless, with a design carved in the center of the headboard. The bookcases were plain but perfectly constructed, with deep adjustable shelves so that the biggest books could be kept upright. The wooden desk and chair were pieces of art, inlaid along the edges and sides with mosaics fashioned from darker or lighter woods and tiny bits of mother of pearl. Mounted on the wall beside her desk was the specially designed glass-shelved display cabinet for all her childhood treasures, polished rocks and tiny reassembled skeletons and fossils and petrified wood. And all this furniture – the bed, the desk and chair, the bookcases, and the treasure cabinet – all of it had been handmade for her by her father.

The realization was disturbing. How many hours had he invested in the crafting of her furniture? Hours spent sawing and fitting and sanding and finishing. Lovingly attending to every detail. Why couldn't he have given all that loving attention directly to her instead of putting it into furniture to give to her?

She looked out the window that faced the back of the house and saw that her mother's flowers had started to bloom. There were more iris than ever. Spreading each season. Creeping toward the house. She remembered having nightmares about those flowers coming for her.

Abruptly she turned and left the room, crossing the hall into the living area. Everything there was just as she remembered it. Oval rag rugs were still scattered about the wooden floors and the boxy plaid furniture was the same. There was no clutter at all. Nothing decorating the walls. No knickknacks on the end tables. No throw pillows or magazines or half-finished puzzles. Nothing to indicate that the place was currently inhabited.

In the kitchen all surfaces were neat and shiny. She opened a cupboard and was startled to see her mother's favorite dishes, an apple-blossom pattern that had been packed away in the attic for twenty years. She picked up a plate, traced her finger over the raised blossoms, and felt a chill. Why would he have taken the old dishes out of the attic and put them back in the cupboard?

The coffee-maker she had sent him for Christmas was out on the counter so she brewed herself a half pot. When it was finished she searched for something other than an apple-blossom cup to drink from.

She carried the coffee into his office. His imprint was there. The swivel chair behind the desk had the shape of his body impressed in the leather and there was a smooth depression worn into the desk top where he rested his heels. She could picture him tilted back in the chair with his feet on the desk, staring out the window at his trees and dreaming about breeding a new strain of apricot. That was an old picture, though. She realized as soon as the vision came that he had stopped dreaming a long time ago.

As always his shelves were crammed with botany books. She opened the cupboard beneath the built-in shelves and saw a stack of orchard logs, one for every year, stretching back to 1967. She sat down in his chair and searched through his desk drawers but found nothing out of the ordinary. The bottom-right drawer was full of thick telephone directories. When she tried to shove it closed, the drawer stuck. She kicked at it half-heartedly, then, discouraged by the fruitlessness of her search she sagged back into his chair and ignored it.

She sipped at her coffee and let the time pass in brooding. Eventually she realized that it was three hours later in New York and she hadn't called to check with the hospital yet. She dialed and leaned her elbows on the desk. Someone unfamiliar answered and she asked for Helen and the phone was put down with a clunk while Helen was summoned.

She listened to the background noises coming across the lines from three thousand miles away. Idly, she rummaged through the narrow center drawer, picked up a pen, and looked for something to write on. There were no notepads or pieces of scratch paper. She glanced down and saw that he had scribbled all over the telephone directory covers, so she wedged the receiver between her shoulder and ear and wrestled the top directory from the drawer. It was the San Jose book. She colored in the *a* in San Jose and then made the *o* into a skull and the *J* into a cartoonish tibia. She drew random designs. Then, as though her hand had a will of its own, she wrote Isaac.

Immediately, she felt a flush of embarrassment.

Isaac.

He had touched her cheek the night before. He had looked into her eyes and she'd thought he might kiss her but he didn't. He cupped her cheek in his hand then slowly drew his fingertips across the curves and angles as though memorizing her skin.

That was all. Just a touch. But the heat of it still burned inside her. That one touch had been more stirring and more intense than anything she had ever experienced before.

She scribbled across Isaac's name until it was no longer distinguishable, then she turned the phone book over to put it out of her mind completely.

'Hello?' she said impatiently into the phone, but there was still no one on the line.

So she shifted her arm and was about to begin one of her skull sketches when she saw the word that her father had printed across an open space. CLARY. He had printed CLARY. Her mother's name. And he had gone over and over the letters, pressing hard with his pen, making them wide and deep.

'This is Helen,' a voice said in her ear.

She couldn't answer for a moment. She was so disturbed by the sight of her mother's name, so fixated on the letters and the shape of it that she had difficulty asking the familiar questions about her father's condition.

'Same as always,' Helen assured her. 'He's having sweet dreams we hope.'

Iris gave her the number in California and then said goodbye. She put the receiver down on the cradle and stared at the directory cover. What had prompted him to write CLARY there?

She tried to picture him, sitting at the desk, writing the name that he had forbidden in his house for so many years. Had he been looking out at his trees, daydreaming? Or had he been talking on the phone? Had someone said something to him on the phone that prompted his hand to form those painful letters?

She pushed away from the desk and hurried out of the office. Her father's upstairs bedroom was the room she had dreaded most, but now she was determined to see it. Mr Hirano had been right. There were clues that the police would not have recognized. She could see the clues. The problem was that she couldn't understand what they meant.

Her mother's dishes. Her mother's name on the phone book. What did it all mean?

At the top of the stairs was a large sunny landing with a skylight overhead. She could remember her mother sewing beneath that skylight, looking up at her with a smile as she effortlessly guided waves of color beneath the whirring needle of her sewing machine. On one side of the landing was a large bathroom and a walk-in closet. On the other side was the door to her father's bedroom. It was part way open. She pushed and it swung inward.

The room was big. Much bigger than the rented room in Manhattan. It was built under the eaves and the side walls were slanted from the pitch of the roof, with matching pairs of dormer windows and window seats. There were no curtains. He had always said that the trees were his curtains.

Everything was perfectly neat. The huge bed was carefully made. A beautiful quilt with a pattern of patchwork circles was tucked tightly at the corners. She stared at the interlocking circles of color against the white background. The pattern was hypnotic. Familiar. Reluctantly she moved toward it and pulled one of the corners free.

There it was on the back. A patch of muslin embroidered with the quilt's provenance.

Double Wedding Ring
Made by Clary Lanier
1968

She sank down on the end of the bed, gathered the loosened quilt, and buried her face in it. This was the quilt. The quilt she had loved and wanted to snuggle in when she was sick.

'Can I have a quilt just like yours, Mommy?'

'No, sweetie. That's a special quilt for a marriage bed – to bring my marriage good luck. I'll make you a quilt full of animals and flowers. How does that sound?'

The fabric had a sweet, clean smell. He must have taken it from the trunk and washed it and dried it out in the sun. But why? Why? What had happened to make him want to resurrect her mother? Why, after so many years of bitterness and hatred?

She roamed through the room, opening the closets and drawers. Nothing looked out of the ordinary, but she had lost the will to dig very deeply. She went to the side of the bed that he'd always favored and sat down on the edge to look through his bedside stand. The top of it held only a lamp and a small clock. Inside the first drawer was a neat arrangement of pens and notepads, reading glasses, a small calendar and a tube of the antibiotic salve he rubbed on the scrapes and gouges that he so often got on his hands. The second drawer was filled with letters. Iris's letters. They were tied into bundles with white string.

She picked up a bundle and thumbed the edges of the envelopes, then she pulled one out by random, took the letter from the envelope and unfolded it.

Hi,
This museum job is not what I thought it would be. I spend most of my time in a windowless office staring at a computer screen, working with data from bones rather than from the bones themselves. I'm going to give them my notice soon, and I'm thinking about going back to school for my masters. Don't know which school. Am now investigating who's teaching where and what programs are available. Haven't called the Kaliker Foundation yet, but they indicated before that I would be eligible for more assistance from them if I decided to go for advanced degrees.

Sorry I didn't make it home for Christmas. The air fares were unreasonably high. Maybe I'll see you next month.

Whatever happened with the root cancer you were

212

worried about in some of the cherries? Did you have someone out to examine the sick trees? Is it something curable or will they die if they've got it?

I'll be leaving this address after I quit my job so don't write to me here past the end of the month.

Bye,
Iris

She refolded the letter and put it back in the envelope then carefully slid it back into the stack. No doubt he had them arranged by date so she tried to replace it exactly.

She had always resented his letters to her because all he wrote about was the orchard and because there was never anything personal or affectionate about them. But it occurred to her now, after reading one of her own letters, that she was just as guilty of being cool in her writing. At the back of the drawer she found an older bundle from when she first went away to college. She chose the fourth one into the stack and pulled it out.

Papa,
You asked about clubs and social activities in your last letter, but I'm not really interested in any of that. Pre-med is pretty hard with so many science requirements and everything, and I've signed up for a heavy class load so I don't have much time for outside activities. I am going to volunteer for faunal processing out at the anthro lab though. (That's where they process animal bones to use for studying etc. Sounds like what I liked to do as a kid, huh?)

Physical anthropology is the most interesting course I have. I lucked out and got this really top guy for a teacher even though it's an undergrad course.

This Kaliker grant is really something. They've even sent me spending money and a form to fill out if I want to get any books that aren't on my course lists.

Guess that means I can have whatever research books I want. I got a letter about a dinner in New York for the Kal grant students to meet Nathan Kaliker and I think they are going to fly me back there. Won't that be neat? I'll let you know if I go or not.

See ya,<br>Iris

She put the letter back and sat for a moment in puzzled reflection. How vividly she remembered that time in her life. She had been fifteen, going on sixteen, miserably homesick, disheartened by the realization that her younger age and her social clumsiness made her a misfit in college just as she had been in high school. She'd been sleeping with boys in an escalating cycle of self-destruction, and alienating the few people who showed any interest in befriending her. And she had been torn between relief at the separation from her father and hoping her father would insist that she come back, live at home, and attend a local college for her first few years.

When her father seemed oblivious to her misery she had resented him more passionately and taken it as proof that he was glad to be rid of her. Yet, how could he have known she was unhappy if all her letters had sounded like this one? How could he have known that she regretted leaving home at such a young age? How could he have known that she was waiting for him to prove his love by ordering her back?

She saw it so clearly now. How could he have known?

She slammed the drawer shut in frustration and the lamp tipped and she reached to catch it and knocked the clock off. It fell between the bed and the nightstand.

Muttering to herself, she leaned her forearm on her father's pillow and reached down to rescue the clock. As soon as her weight settled onto her forearm there was a cracking sound from under the pillow. Startled, she pulled back and lifted the pillow to peek underneath. There, looking up at her was a framed photograph of her mother, laughing sideways, one hand trying to control a dark curtain of windblown hair. The glass had a crack running diagonally across it.

She dropped the pillow back into place and held her face in her hands. What was going on? Was it possible that her mother had made contact? Or that her father had secretly kept looking for her and had finally found her? Was it possible that her father had been trying to get her mother to come back to him? That idea was so bizarre that she laughed out loud, only the sound that came from her throat was thin and bitter, closer to tears than to laughter.

She resumed her retrieval of the fallen clock. It was after six already. Grateful for the respite, she hurried downstairs to get ready for dinner with Mr Hirano.

She rang his bell promptly at seven and he opened the door immediately, as if he'd been standing behind it, waiting. He was dressed in the usual khaki shirt and pants but these were starched and pressed with impeccable military creases. Instead of work shoes or boots he had soft leather slippers on his feet.

Her palms felt damp and she had the same butterflies in her stomach that she used to get in grammar school when asked to recite for the class.

'Thank you for inviting me,' she said without waiting for him to say so much as hello. 'There's so much I wanted to ask you about my father and—'

'Please come in,' he said, cutting short her nervous rush of words.

As a child she had been invited into the interior of his house only when his grandchildren were there, and as an adult she had not been inside at all, but the routine came back to her immediately and she stopped just inside the door, beside the low shelf of slippers and thong sandals.

The faintest trace of a smile touched his eyes.

'Old habits,' he said. 'They make me fascinating to my great grandchildren.'

'Plural?' Iris said as she bent to take off her shoes. 'The last I knew there was only one great-grandchild. Has Jeff . . .?'

'No, Jeff hasn't married.' He smiled. 'Cynthia had a second child. A girl.'

Iris smiled. 'You must be very proud.'

'Yes! Yes! Very proud. I was an only child and, though I had two children, I ended up with an only child . . . You knew I had a daughter who died, didn't you?'

Iris glanced up at him. She had always thought the daughter was a secret and she wondered if she should admit knowing. He went on though, without waiting for her answer.

'My daughter died, and then, after Stuart was born, my wife could have no more children, and I worried that my family would never take root in America and prosper. But now . . .' He smiled broadly. 'Now I am surrounded by family. I have gone from a single tree to an orchard!'

Iris sorted through the selection of indoor footwear on the shelf. She wondered if her father had the same kind of thoughts. He had no family to surround him, no family at all except her. But then he had never wanted anyone. And he certainly hadn't wanted her.

Iris slipped on a pair of thongs and straightened. Her nervousness had faded. There was nothing formidable about Mr Hirano anymore. In the years since she had last had contact with him he had evolved into a gentler, friendlier man. Or maybe it was her evolvement that had changed the dynamic between them. Maybe he was finally treating her as he treated other adults.

He led her into the house. The living room was still decorated with the furniture and accessories that the grandchildren used to refer to as 'early dude ranch.' The pieces were framed in heavy oak, with cattle brands burned into the wood, and the cushions were covered with heavy saddle-brown leather. They had all assumed that the matched set had come with the house until one day Mr Hirano made a comment about choosing the pieces himself. She had never seen him seated in the living room and she could not picture his small form in one of the oversize, branded chairs.

In the kitchen, which was a wide-open sunny space full of Mexican tile and hanging copper pots, he had put up a shoji screen to separate the dining area from the rest of the room. The house was decorated so thoroughly in early California and ranch motifs that the exquisite screen struck an odd note.

'The screen is beautiful,' she said.

He laughed in his controlled and very polite way. 'A gift from my granddaughter.' He paused and regarded the screen. 'It doesn't seem very practical to me. So flimsy and delicate. But she insisted that I have something Japanese in my house.'

'And your new garden?' Iris said. 'I noticed that you have a Japanese garden now.'

'Jeff made that for me.'

'Jeff?' Iris said in surprise.

Amusement crinkled the skin at the corners of his eyes. 'Yes. My oldest grandson creates fountains and gardens. He claims he inherited part of my farmer's soul.'

The table was set with flatware. There was an open bottle of red wine with two glasses. He motioned for her to sit down, then ducked around the screen. She heard the rattle of utensils.

'Can I help?' she asked.

'No. I'm almost finished.' Appliance doors were opened and banged shut. 'My granddaughter has been trying to interest me in attending a Japanese cooking class with her,' he said. 'I was raised on Japanese food but I

217

married a very American woman. Of Japanese ancestry but very American. Didn't cook Japanese. Didn't even speak Japanese. Her family had been in this country since 1900, you see. Came over from the pineapple fields in Hawaii.'

Iris smelled something vaguely familiar but couldn't identify it.

He appeared from around the screen balancing a TV dinner in each hand. 'Turkey with gravy or Salisbury steak?' he asked.

She took the turkey and he poured their wine. As she ate she thought of how to phrase the questions she wanted to ask. He was certainly being talkative enough.

'About my father . . .' she began.

Hirano shook his head. 'So terrible,' he said. 'That harm would come to such a good man.'

'Did he say anything at all about why he was going to New York?'

'He told me nothing except that he had to be gone for awhile. It's the first time he has asked me for help in all the years he's farmed the orchard.'

'Was he acting strangely?'

'No, but when he came by to tell me he was leaving he shook my hand and said that he felt privileged to know me. That was not like your father.'

'What about the gun? The police said you saw him target practicing with it. How did he explain himself?'

Hirano lowered his eyes.

'I heard the shots and I found your father shooting at cans that he had placed against his toolshed. I asked him what he was doing. He told me he had bought the gun and needed to see how it worked. I heard no more shots.'

'And this was when?'

'The day before he left.'

'Did he have any visits from strangers in the week or so before he left?'

'No. There has not been an unfamiliar car at your father's house for years. But of course he could have met someone away from here and I would have no knowledge of it.'

'Did he say anything at all, give you any hint, about troubles he was having?'

'No. He is a proud man. If he did have troubles he would not speak of them.'

Iris pushed the food around in the compartments of her frozen dinner tray, considering what else to ask. She was reminded of a college professor who had said repeatedly that it was the questions that were important. That in any scientific investigation it was asking the right questions that made the difference.

'Mr Hirano . . . did my father say anything to you about my mother?'

A shadow crossed Yoshi Hirano's impassive face.

'Your father has not spoken your mother's name to me in twenty years.'

There was something bothering Hirano.

'My mother was very fond of you, wasn't she, Mr Hirano?'

Hirano's adam's apple moved in his throat. 'Perhaps.'

'All my memories of her are a child's memories, so I don't know how accurate they are, but I know that she was always baking you bread and sending little things to you.'

'Yes.'

'Were you fond of her too?'

'She was . . . like my daughter. Like the daughter I'd lost had been returned to me.'

'Did she tell you where she was going when she left?'

'No.'

'So she abandoned you, too, didn't she?' Iris asked softly.

Hirano sat very still, with the rigid dignity of a sovereign

219

ruler, but Iris could feel his distress. What were the right questions? What else should she ask? She felt like her own emotions were disrupting her thinking processes.

'You sold my father the land for his house when they were married . . .'

He nodded stiffly.

'But I've never known what was going on before that. When did my father first come to work at the orchard and when did you meet my mother? Do you know how they met? Do you know—'

'They met as all people meet.' His hands fluttered nervously. 'Did I tell you how I met my wife? I met her in the internment camp. She was a most remarkable woman, just a girl then. But the camp made her bitter. She told whoever would listen, "I am as good an American as people with German or Italian ancestors. My family has been in this country four generations. I am more American than people who have locked me in here." My very American wife.

'The internment broke her heart. She saw her family ruined. Their beautiful home and all their possessions were lost. Her father's business was destroyed. And she told me that her mother broke everything as they were leaving, broke all the fine china and the furniture so that the crowd of people waiting outside like vultures would have nothing of value to steal after they were forced from their home.

'My American wife. She seemed just the same when I saw her again and after our families were released, but inside she had a broken heart. Later when our baby daughter died, my wife said it was because there was so much hate left inside her from the camp that it had killed her child. She lost her trust in America, but she knew nothing of being Japanese so her spirit was lost.

'I tried to make her see the good in all that happened. How we had done our patriotic duty by going to the camp.

And how it brought us closer to each other. Closer as families. Closer as a Japanese community.

'Every day I told her, "How can you hate Americans when it was an American who saved my family's land? When it is American justice that made it possible for us to step out of that camp and fight for legal rights in courts? How many other countries would have let us fight in court . . . win in court?" '

'Mr Hirano . . .' Iris said. 'I was asking about my mother. Clary? Remember?'

'You know about debts? Some debts are so great that they carry on and on. They can never be fully repaid.'

'Mr Hirano . . .'

'You know about marriage? Marriage cannot fix what is broken. It cannot save a spirit that has been lost. This is a hard lesson. It turns good hearts to stone. It makes strong men into fools.'

Iris wondered whose marriage he was referring to – his own or her parents'. Or maybe both.

He rose and suddenly he seemed older and frailer than before. 'You must go now,' he said. 'I need to rest.'

# Thirteen

The next morning Iris drove toward the Santa Clara County fairgrounds and Stuart Hirano's San Jose offices. Stuart was Yoshi Hirano's son, but he had not been a presence at the orchard in her lifetime and she considered him only a distant acquaintance. When she was born Stuart was already attending college at Stanford and living on campus. He had seldom returned home for visits. Then later, after he had founded his computer company, he was too busy for visits.

Throughout Iris's childhood Stuart's wife and children had made frequent appearances at the orchard, sometimes staying for days though they lived in a palatial home in the hills near Villa Montalvo and could have driven home in twenty minutes. It had sometimes seemed as if Astrid preferred the company of her father-in-law over that of her husband.

As she approached the turn-off for Stuart's offices, Iris wondered if sunny, outgoing Astrid was still trapped in that monstrous house in the hills, more miserable now with all her children grown and gone. She wondered if Stuart Hirano was still the self-absorbed tyrant she remembered. If he was still as hard on his son Jeff as he had been.

Stuart Hirano's success was legendary, but even so, Iris wasn't prepared for the Hero Systems headquarters. The four buildings were low-slung California modern, an architectural style that attained drama through lavish use of redwood and glass. They were arranged like jewels in a grassy, gently rolling park. Vehicles were screened from sight by evergreen plantings and groupings of flowering perennials. Toward the back she caught sight of a tastefully designed outdoor exercise area. If she had not entered the main gate and been greeted by a guard who welcomed her to the 'Hero Campus' she would have thought she had taken a wrong turn and stumbled into an exclusive resort.

Such a gorgeous location. Such fine, fertile soil. But then she remembered hearing how he had acquired it. How he had bullied and coaxed some orchard owner into selling out. Some elderly man much like his own father. There had been a story about it in the paper because the old man tried to back out of the deal, but Stuart wouldn't let him. Then the old man tried to chain himself to his trees when the bulldozers came. The police had had to arrest him.

Iris scanned the plantings but could not find one fruit tree. The bulldozers had gotten them all. She wondered if the old man was still alive, if he ever came to mourn his trees. Who knew? Maybe he was having a great time with all his newly acquired money. But she doubted it.

Following the guard's instructions, she left her car in visitor parking and walked up a curving path to the main building. Inside was a huge lobby of stone and redwood. One whole side of it was taken up by a mist-shrouded waterfall and miniaturized live rain forest beneath a slanting greenhouse wall. Opposite the forest was a reception desk peopled by several uniformed guards staring down at computer monitors and a smiling, perfectly groomed blonde who barely looked real.

Iris told the blonde she wanted to see Stuart Hirano and was given a stick-on visitor pass for the third floor. Three was as high as the elevator buttons went. That seemed funny to her after so many years spent working in large cities with elevator control panels displaying thirty and forty floors.

The elevator doors opened onto another lobby where she was greeted by a clone of the blonde downstairs. This one was not so friendly, however.

'I'd like to see Stuart Hirano,' Iris told her.

'Did you have an appointment with Mr Hirano?'

'No,' Iris admitted. 'I know I should have called ahead, but I'm a friend of the family and I'm here from out of town, so I was hoping that he could work me in.' Friend of the family wasn't quite accurate but she didn't know how else to describe her connection. And the truth was that she hadn't called because she was afraid he would turn her down if given the chance.

'I'll have to talk to his assistant,' the woman said, coolly. 'What is your name?'

'Iris Lanier.' Iris spelled it for her, then added, 'Dr Iris Lanier,' in an effort to counteract the blonde's disdainful manner.

The title didn't seem to impress her. She swung around to her multi-button telephone.

'Yes, I have a woman out here to see Mr Hirano. Yes. Dr Iris Lanier. She says she's a friend of his family. Yes. I'll wait.'

The woman stared off out the window and tapped the desk top with her manicured fingernails. Iris stood before the broad curve of desk, feeling like a child outside the principal's office. She had feared and disliked Stuart Hirano when she was young, and his office procedures called forth all those old feelings.

She stared out the same wall to wall window as the receptionist, out across the treetops and house tops of the seemingly endless valley. When she was young the foot-hills had still been visible. She had grown up with them as a benevolent presence, a picture-postcard boundary, the barrier that kept everything bad out of the valley. Now they were gone. Obscured from view by airborne parti-cles. No one wanted to say pollution because that called to mind the brown soup of Los Angeles air, and the air in the Santa Clara Valley was still pristine by comparison. But the fact was that the foothills had disappeared from view. Today's children could not ride their bicycles to highway overpasses and stare off at the hills. Adults could not look out their upstairs executive windows and see that the valley was finite.

'Yes?' the woman said into the phone, snapping Iris back to attention. 'Yes. All right.'

She put the receiver down and smiled up at Iris. 'I'm afraid Mr Hirano is at the new Scott's Valley plant today. His assistant suggests that you make an appointment for next week.'

'But I won't be here that long. Can I call out to his Scott's Valley office and talk to him?'

'No, that's a building site. It's still under construction.'

'So there's no way I can speak to him?'

'I'm sorry,' the woman said, but it was clear that she was enjoying herself.

Iris rode the elevator back down to the lobby. Should she drive to Scott's Valley? She had never been there but she knew it was somewhere on the way to Santa Cruz. Maybe forty minutes to an hour of driving on highway seventeen. She was certain that Stuart would see her if she could ever get through his palace guard and let him know that she wanted to talk to him.

The lobby receptionist gave her a warm smile as she relinquished her visitor's pass.

'Is that real?' Iris asked her, indicating the forest.

'Oh yes,' the woman assured her earnestly. 'If you go over and look close you'll see there are even bugs and lizards and things. Mr Hirano is very ecology conscious.'

Iris nodded and started back across the lobby toward the main doors.

'Have a nice day,' the receptionist called brightly after her.

Outside, Iris stopped and drew in a deep breath. The air, even though full of particles, was infused with gentle sunshine and seemed wonderfully fresh. She could drive to Scott's Valley. There was nothing to be discouraged about.

With renewed determination she hurried down the path, brushing by a man who was just emerging from visitor parking.

'Iris?'

She turned. The man was staring at her incredulously. It was Jeff Hirano, son of Stuart, grandson of Yoshi. Her childhood confidant and playmate. At times her best friend. At times her only friend. Until she was fifteen and ruined it all.

He was just as she remembered him, medium tall with an athlete's tapered build, wide at the shoulders and narrow at the hips. Thick black hair with a hint of a wave. Features that blended his Japanese and Scandinavian ancestry giving him a remarkably handsome face that didn't really matter because he was possessed of a gentle charm that made his looks secondary.

'Jeff.' She spoke his name tentatively and with the hesitation that came from fourteen years of avoiding each other.

'Iris! I can't believe this! What are you doing in California? I thought you were off digging up Aztecs.'

'Maya,' she said.

He moved several steps toward her, his eyes fixed on her face as though searching for something.

'I can't believe this. I was just—' He grabbed her arm and started hurrying her toward the parking lot. 'Coffee. Or an early lunch. I won't take no for an answer.'

She let herself be pulled along, let him coax her into riding with him to a restaurant. The vehicle he drove was a

227

mini-van with both rear seats out and a back crammed with tools and pipes and rolls of blueprints. Across both sides H₂O DESIGN was painted in professional lettering.

Once they were on their way to Los Gatos and his favorite Mexican restaurant a silence descended and she wondered if she had made a mistake. They had been close as children but they were strangers as adults. What did they have to talk about? Why was he so glad to see her?

He found a parking place just off the main street in downtown Los Gatos. As they walked to the restaurant he told her about how the area had been damaged by the earthquake in 1989. How it had been close to the epicenter and many of the older buildings had been destroyed.

Andale Taqueria was just beginning to serve lunch as they arrived. They ordered homemade tamales and tropical iced tea and carried their plates back to the empty sun-dappled garden-patio.

'So you created the Japanese garden at your grandfather's house,' she said to break the silence between them.

'Yes. I got into that as a hobby. Even learned some Japanese. Strictly garden talk. I know your name though. Iris is Ayame in Japanese. That means flower of the moon.' He grinned. 'Maybe I'll start calling you Moonflower.' His grin faded into a puzzled expression. 'Did I say something wrong?'

'No. That name . . . Moonflower. It's close to something connected with my work. It startled me, I guess. Did you create the rain forest in your father's lobby?'

He shook his head and laughed. 'Pretty ghastly, huh? A bonsai rain forest. They can't keep it alive but my father doesn't want anyone to know that, so periodically he has guys creep in during the night and replace plants and dead animals.'

'I've been working in a rain forest. In Guatemala.'

'I know! That's so great.'

'How did you know?'

'I always keep up with what you're doing . . . either by quizzing my grandfather or by prying something out of your dad when I'm out visiting the orchard. You mean you haven't been curious about me through the years?'

'I've been curious,' she admitted. 'But I haven't wanted to ask my father about you. Maybe I was worried about what I'd hear.'

He laughed, then settled into a reflective silence, his eyes fixed on the narrow pool of water at the edge of the patio.

'Damn,' he said, 'I feel like a walking cliché. Since the big three-oh hit me all I can think about is the past. Regrets, missed opportunities, lost people.' He glanced at her. 'I've been thinking about you, and suddenly, like magic, here you are.'

Iris sighed. She did not want to rehash the past with Jeff Hirano or anyone else. If she had her wish, the past would be completely wiped away.

He toyed with his food a moment, destroying the shape of his tamale. Then he raised his eyes to hers, expression slightly mischievous, smile self-deprecating.

'Did you know that was my first time with a girl?'

'Oh, come on, Jeff. We're not going to talk about that, are we?'

'Just tell me . . . are you surprised? Did you know then that it was my first time?'

'No. You were older and very popular . . . an athletic star . . . with a hot car. I just assumed . . .'

'Yeah. I was always putting people on. Saying things to make it seem that I'd played around a lot.' He shrugged. 'But I need to know . . . when we did it . . . could you tell? I mean . . . how did I seem to you?'

'I can't believe we're discussing this.'

'Humor me, please?'

'I don't remember exactly what I thought. It was my first time, too. I have to admit though, I probably wouldn't have pushed you into it if I'd known you were . . . inexperienced.'

'Pushed me into it?' He leaned forward in his chair as though excited by the thought. 'Is that the way it happened? I've thought about it and thought about it, and regretted how it all turned out, and it's never made sense to me. I couldn't figure out how it happened.

'We'd been friends for so long. I mean we started out making mud pies together. And we'd always run around through the orchards without any kind of supervision. Remember, a few times we even camped out in that old tent. Slept together! I was closer to you than I've ever been to my sister or my little brother. So why did we suddenly think we had to . . . do it.'

'The fault was mine, Jeff. You weren't to blame, so just forget about it.'

'I can't. When I lost you, Iris, it left a big hole in me. What should I have done to keep that from happening?'

'There was nothing you could do,' she insisted. 'Don't you understand? I pushed you into it. It was all my fault.'

'If that's true, then tell me why.'

She put her fork down and stared at her plate. 'Do we have to go into this?'

'Yes. Please. My life's falling apart, Iris. And I'm trying to figure out where it went wrong. I'm trying to start at the beginning and piece it together.'

She stared down at her half-eaten food. There was no escape. And she had only herself to blame. She'd learned long ago that it was a mistake to go anywhere with a man in his car because that meant you couldn't leave when you wanted to.

'All right. I'll try to explain. You were my first, too . . . but you weren't my last. Remember, it happened in my final year of high school.'

'Yeah.' He put his elbows on the table and buried his face in his hands. 'God, you were only fourteen. A baby. How could I have . . .'

'Stop. I was almost fifteen. I was as tall as I am now. I was getting ready to graduate from high school and go away to college. I knew exactly what I was doing.'

'And what were you doing?'

'Well, I take that back. Maybe I didn't know what I was doing. But believe me, it was a very calculated stupidity.' She shrugged. 'I had decided to be promiscuous and I started with you because you were handy and because I didn't think sex would be any big deal to you. And because you were a nice safe beginning for my experiment.'

'Experiment?'

'OK, tantrum, then. A very ugly tantrum that was somehow supposed to punish my father.'

'Did it? Punish your father?'

'Who knows. I left evidence around all the time. Left my birth control pills out. He never seemed to notice. Now it all seems pretty ridiculous.'

'So he didn't stop you.'

'No. I stopped myself. Which was harder than it sounds. But I got so sick of it all. At first it was really exciting. My father was such a monk after my mother left, and so I was not only bad, I was bad in a way that I thought would be particularly galling for him. And I liked parts of it. Not the actual act, but the touching and holding. I just couldn't get enough of that in the beginning.'

'Your father never was affectionate with you, was he?' Jeff asked as though remembering something aloud.

'What?'

'I can remember my parents talking about it. How your father never hugged you or held you after your mother was gone. How he never showed you any affection.'

All the food she'd eaten turned to stone in her stomach

231

and she was suddenly angry. Had everyone talked about her when she was young? Had everyone amused themselves by discussing the poor pathetic little girl whose mother abandoned her and whose father could barely tolerate her?

'Do you want to hear the end of my promiscuity story or not?' she demanded.

'Yes.'

'After you, I slept with a few senior boys at my high school, then went off to college and moved on to older boys. After awhile I realized that I was disgusted with it. I had reached a point where the thought of another groping hand or even another hopeful glance from across the room made me feel like throwing up.'

'And you didn't catch anything terrible or have an abortion or anything?'

'I was lucky,' she admitted. 'I got it out of my system with no ill effects. And I learned the truth about sex, that it's pretty much just like that famous quote says – ridiculous, messy, and fleeting . . . and ultimately unsatisfying.'

Isaac Brightman flashed through her mind and she wondered if making love with him would change her opinions. Did she want to find out? For that matter, did she want her opinions changed?

'Damn, Iris,' Jeff said. 'That's depressing.' He flipped his fork back and forth on the table. 'So it was nothing personal then? Your wanting me one day and then not wanting me the next?'

'Oh, Jeff . . . I was young and stupid. There was no wanting or not wanting to it. I didn't think it meant any more to you than it did to me. Then, when I realized that it was serious to you, I got scared. I didn't know how to talk about it, so I just backed off.'

He drew in a deep breath. 'I was really confused afterwards. Really worried about what it all meant. I needed to talk to you but you kept avoiding me.'

'I thought you wanted to do it again,' she said softly, 'and I didn't know how to say no.'

He shook his head. 'I thought that I had been either a disappointing lover or a piggish brute who somehow made you do something you didn't want to do. Eventually I settled on disappointing lover. I hated you after that. And I hated myself. It was years before I got up the nerve to try my charms on another girl.'

She moved her hand across the table toward his, then hesitated, and pulled back. 'I am so sorry,' she said.

'Don't worry.' He raised his eyes to meet hers, then quickly dropped his gaze to the table. 'It gave me an excuse to try other things.'

Iris waited. She didn't breathe or make a sound. He was on the verge of something and she wanted to stop him but couldn't.

'I'm homosexual, Iris. I am thirty-two years old, and I am finally facing the fact that I am gay.

'I tried, I really tried to be attracted to women. I like women for friends. I even lived with a girl for awhile. But the bodies and the faces I dream of at night are male.'

He smiled a little. 'I believe in love, you know? Real, true, passionate, lifelong love. But when I think of falling in love, when I imagine finding a perfect life partner . . . I can never imagine it happening with a woman. And I started thinking, what if Iris saw? What if that was the real reason she shut me out . . . Because that day in the orchard she saw through all my macho posturing and she knew the truth and she was disgusted.'

'Jeff . . . Jeff . . .' She reached for his hand again and this time made herself take it.

'You always saw more than other people, Iris. You always had that ability to look past all the falseness and see right into the heart of things. Is that what you did with me?'

'No, Jeff. Not at all. It was just as I told you . . . the

233

blame was mine . . . all part of a twisted phase I went through.'

She gripped his hand tighter, so that she felt the muscle and sinew and hard strong bones beneath the skin. Such a male hand. But what was male and female? Was it in the bones and sinew or in the head and heart?

God, it was too confusing. All she knew was that Jeff, the boy she had loved, the one friend she had had through the horror of her childhood – Jeff was in pain. And she couldn't run away. She couldn't ignore it.

'Jeff, listen to me, you didn't disgust me then and you don't disgust me now. You are one of the sweetest, funniest, most talented people I have ever known. It was my loss that our friendship was destroyed all those years ago. My loss.'

His shoulders shook and a tear slipped down the side of his face.

'What am I going to do, Iris? I'm so afraid of what my family will do when they find out. They'll be so disappointed. So ashamed.'

She leaned across the table and put her hands on his wide muscular shoulders, gripping them hard so that her fingers ached with the effort.

'You are a great guy. A devoted son and grandson. A success in your work. A benefit to society. Your sexuality is a small consideration when weighed against all that.'

He laughed ruefully. 'What a tidy and reasonable view of a messy situation.'

'But it's true. Sexuality is such a minor factor in who we are. It doesn't change the essential elements of who Jeff Hirano is.'

'I don't think my family will take it quite so calmly.'

'Are you certain you want them to know?'

'No, I'm not certain. But I can't stand the lies. I can't keep on pretending that I'm looking for a wife, or that I'm interested in the blind dates my sister is constantly trying to arrange. I can't go on responding to my little brother's nudge and wink routine whenever a sexy woman passes by. The falseness of it all is demeaning. It's . . . perverted.'

'How about if you left a lot of hints and let them figure it out gradually?'

'Like you did with your father when you wanted to get caught being promiscuous?' He smiled sadly. 'I've tried that. Your father didn't catch on and my family isn't catching on. Probably because they don't want to.'

'What are you going to do then?'

'What would you do in my place, Iris?'

'I think I'd come right out and tell them . . . making it as simple and unemotional as possible. Your mother and grandfather will be very supportive. Your father . . . I'd be prepared for a bad reaction from him. But—' she grinned in the same way that she used to grin at Jeff when they were children with devilish secrets, '—given time, I'm sure your father will find a way to make a gay son into an asset for his business.'

Jeff returned her grin but shook his head. 'You were always so brave. I was always awed by your courage.'

'Me? Brave? I'm not a brave person at all! If you were comparing me to the animal kingdom, I'd be right down with the rabbits. Running and hiding all the time. And let me tell you, I am not the right person to give out advice, either. Anything beyond the scope of my work is one big question mark to me. So unless you want to talk about bones you have bought a terrific tamale for the wrong person.'

He grinned. 'I am so glad to see you, Iris. You're just like I remembered . . . tough and funny and smart and totally different from everyone else.'

'Well, that's very nice, but you really don't know what you're talking about.'

He laughed. 'So what are you doing in California? And

why in the world were you at Hero?'

She had been so absorbed in Jeff that she had forgotten about her father for a time, and now it came back like a wound breaking open, the pain as sharp and fresh as if it was brand new.

'I . . .' She had to clear her throat. 'I just couldn't stand it. I told you I wasn't brave. I couldn't just sit there beside his bed any longer and be stalwart. I had to do something. I had to—'

'Wait! What are you talking about?'

'My father.' She searched his face for a sign of understanding. 'In the hospital. In New York.'

'You have totally lost me.'

'Your grandfather didn't tell you?'

'Not a word.'

She filled her lungs with air, wondering if the telling would ever become any easier. 'My father bought a gun and flew to New York. No one knows why. No one knows who he saw or what he did, aside from the fact that he rented a room, went down to a park near the river very late at night, and got shot.'

'My God!'

'He's in a coma. The doctors don't know what the prognosis is.'

'I can't believe that I wasn't told. When was he hurt?'

'It's been weeks now. I flew here yesterday and I had dinner with your grandfather last night.'

'Dinner with my grandfather?' he asked in amazement.

'Yes. He invited me. Fed me a turkey frozen dinner.' She gathered her thoughts. 'Jeff . . . do you think your grandfather is keeping secrets for my father?'

Jeff considered the question a moment. 'My grandfather is very into loyalty. Favors. Indebtedness. All that. There was a lawyer who helped him hold on to the land while he was in the internment camp . . . a real heroic guy . . . and I swear, if that guy rose up from his grave

236

tomorrow and asked my grandfather to jump off the Golden Gate, I think my grandfather might do it.'

'But would he lie for my father?'

'He might. I heard him say once that your father is like a son to him.' Jeff frowned. 'Did he seem like he was lying?'

'Not exactly. But it felt like he was evading me. And then he drifted off into his own past.'

'He did what?'

'It was nothing serious . . . just the kind of thing old people do sometimes. He lost track of what I was asking him and suddenly he was talking about his wife and the internment camp.'

Jeff shook his head. 'Iris, my grandfather has never drifted off course in a conversation in his life. And he certainly doesn't lose himself in the past.'

'People get old, Jeff. Their minds wander.'

'I see him two or three times week. Believe me, if he was drifting or wandering or whatever, he had a very good reason for it. He's sharper than I am.'

She threw up her hands. 'I don't know what to think. There's no one else to ask, but your grandfather is talking in circles and now I can't find your father.'

'Is that why you were at Hero, to talk to my father?'

'Yes. Only he wasn't there. I'm going to have to go out to Scott's Valley.'

'Ahh, who told you that? The glacial blond I'll bet. She's a pretty fierce gatekeeper.'

'You mean he was there?'

'I thought so. He told me to come by anytime today.' Jeff got up out of his chair. 'Come on. We'll go back there together.'

On the walk back to the van he admitted to her that he had brought her out to Los Gatos for more than his favorite Mexican food. He wanted to show her a big job he'd recently completed. She agreed to see it, though she was anxious about getting sidetracked from her purpose.

He drove north on Bascom Avenue to a carved wooden sign that read THE GROVES.

'Here it is,' he announced proudly, pulling the van into a shopping area that would have been impossible anywhere but California. The style was somewhere between Victorian and modern, with lots of decks and terraces of weathered wood in delicate designs. A narrow creek of smooth river stones meandered through. It was charming and extravagant, a tribute to money and leisure, and the little creek set it off to perfection.

'It's beautiful, Jeff.'

'No, it's more than that. What you're looking at is the surface part of it. But my partner and I are doing more than just decorative work. We put together a whole package – an environmentally sound heating and cooling system based on water exchange that – well, I won't bore you with the technical details.'

'So the stream is just an attractive way to use the water for the heating and cooling?' she asked.

He nodded and stared out over his work. 'I guess I've made it,' he said with a touch of wonder in his voice.

'Judging from this you have indeed made it,' she agreed.

'My dad is still asking when I'm going to quit playing around and go to work at Hero.'

She grinned. 'But you've made it, so you won't ever have to go to work at Hero.'

'Yeah,' he said and grinned in pure delight.

They pulled out of the shopping area and started up Bascom again. 'Thought we'd go locally the whole way,' he said. 'So you can see how much the area has changed.'

'I don't recognize anything,' she admitted.

'That strip mall there—' he pointed, 'that was here before. Of course it's been redone so it looks different now.'

He screwed up his face in concentration. 'You know, it just hit me. Your father was around there a lot.'

Iris turned in her seat to stare at the line of stores as they passed. 'That place? Laurel Plaza?'

He nodded. 'When I was working on The Groves I used to go to that strip mall for pizza and saw him several times. I never spoke to him. He looked . . . I guess you'd say he looked like he was trying to keep a low profile.'

'Even if he liked to shop, none of those stores would interest my father.'

Jeff shrugged. 'I'm sure it was him. I saw his truck, too.'

She twisted forward in the seat and rode in silence for several minutes.

'I'm beginning to question whether I knew my father at all,' she said finally.

'Who does know their father?' he said with a trace of bitterness.

'But I thought I knew him. I thought I knew him inside out. I thought I could identify him blindfolded in a room full of strangers.'

'How? You sure couldn't identify him by touch.'

'Not by feeling with my fingertips maybe . . . but I could feel his silence and his disapproval and his unhappiness.'

'Does he still seem like that to you, now that he's in a coma?'

'No. He seems . . . neutralized.'

She clasped her hands tightly together for a moment. Having Jeff there, so familiar and comforting, made her want to open up and talk. She resisted the urge out of habit, but then thought, why not? Who could better understand than Jeff?

'There's more . . . things I haven't told you.'

He waited, carefully keeping his eyes on the road.

'When my father was shot he was wearing some kind of recording device.'

'You mean a wire? Your dad was wearing a wire!'

She glanced over at him.

Jeff shrugged. 'I read a lot of crime stories. That's pretty unbelievable. Your dad is so allergic to technology. I can't imagine him doing that. What else? What other things?'

'I searched the house thinking there might be clues.'

'And?'

'Jeff . . . my mother's dishes are back in the cupboard. My mother's name was printed on the phone book. Her picture was under his pillow. The quilt she made for their marriage was on the bed.'

Jeff looked over at her in shocked silence, then stared ahead at the road.

'My God, Iris. Do you think he finally found her?'

'I don't know what to think.'

'Or maybe she contacted him?'

'I'm afraid . . .'

'He wouldn't hurt her,' Jeff said quickly. 'That's not why he bought the gun.'

'I don't know that!'

'Your father wouldn't hurt anyone.'

'I would have agreed with you a short time ago. But why else would he buy a handgun and sneak it in his suitcase on the airlines and take it with him when he went out at night in Manhattan? Give me some logical explanations that don't involve hurting someone!'

'He needed it for protection.'

'From whom? And why was he there in the first place? And how is my mother involved?'

'You've got to talk to my dad about this, Iris. He'll want to help you. And he's good at finding answers. Or knowing people who can find them.'

240

# Fourteen

Jeff Hirano turned at the Hero Systems sign, waved at the guard, and followed the curving roadway to visitor parking.

'My dad will know what to do. I can't imagine why my grandfather hasn't told him about this and gotten him involved already.'

He led her through the lobby, calling a greeting to the friendly receptionist as they passed. They rode the elevator up and Jeff firmly took hold of her arm, pulling her along with him at a brisk pace, past the cool blond who appeared startled and then angry as they passed.

'How ya doing?' Jeff asked without slowing.

Down a carpeted hallway, past a huge empty conference room and through a set of wooden doors. Inside was a desk and a leather sofa. Jeff nodded to the woman at the desk and continued straight across and through another door.

Stuart Hirano was just hanging up the phone as they entered.

'I'm told you didn't follow proper procedure,' he said, looking directly at his son.

'All for a good cause. Iris is in town. She had dinner with Grandad last night and she needs to talk to you, but your watchdog out in reception was trying to send her to Scott's Valley.'

Stuart Hirano turned toward Iris. 'Good to see you,

Iris. Please, have a seat.' He waved her toward a grouping of chairs near French doors opening on to a terrace.

'I'm sorry to hear you had trouble reaching me. My employees are trained to maintain my privacy. Otherwise I would have a stream of people in and out of my office all day and never get any work done.'

Iris smiled understanding as she sat down, but she suspected that Stuart Hirano had instructed his receptionist to get rid of her.

'I'll find us all something to drink,' Jeff said. 'Tell him what's going on, Iris. And remember to keep it short. He never has more than a few minutes before duty calls.'

Stuart Hirano sat casually on the arm of the chair opposite her as if to indicate the brief amount of time he was allotting for her visit.

'I heard about your father,' he said. 'A terrible thing. Crime and random violence are the plague of our time.'

'This wasn't random violence,' Iris told him.

'Oh? But I thought he was mugged?'

'That's the official version.'

Stuart Hirano abandoned his casual posture and sprang up.

'You don't believe the official version?' he asked, staring down at her so that she felt uncomfortably small in the chair.

'The detective who was originally investigating didn't think it was random either,' she said.

Hirano stood very still for a moment.

'What do you want from me?' he asked finally. His manner was grim and deeply resigned.

Iris was taken aback. Did he think she wanted him to do battle with the New York police for her? Or maybe hire an expensive private detective? Did he think she had come for charity? Suddenly, it did not seem appropriate at all to tell Stuart Hirano everything or ask for his advice.

'I just have some questions,' she said curtly, 'That's all.

242

I spoke to your father last night.'

Hirano nodded, signaling her to proceed.

'Do you know anything about the purpose of the trip to New York? Or anything about difficulties . . . problems . . .'

'Nothing. As you know I saw John infrequently. I rarely have time to go out to the orchard.'

'But what has Yoshi said? I know you two are very close. Has he mentioned any concerns he's had?'

'Your father and mine are not the sort of men to exchange confidences, and even if they were, my father would not betray that confidence . . . even with his own flesh and blood.'

Iris couldn't help sighing. She knew he was right, but somehow it seemed to her that Stuart Hirano was holding back. The right questions. She needed to ask the right questions. But what were they?

'You knew both my parents—'

'Only slightly. I was away at college when they married.'

'Still, you knew them when they were newly married. You saw them every time you went home to visit your parents.'

'I was acquainted with them, yes.'

Iris didn't know which direction to take. This wasn't like probing the secrets of bones where the parameters and possibilities were known to her before she searched out the answers. Here she felt like she was groping in a void.

'Did they seem happy together?'

He shrugged. 'I think so.'

'In love?'

Stuart Hirano shifted as though slightly uncomfortable. 'I suppose so.'

'Did you notice a change over the years?'

'You mean, did I have any forewarning that your

243

mother was going to run away? No. I did not. But, as I've said, I was not around them much.'

Iris thought for a moment. 'Do you know anything about the detective my father hired to try to find her?'

'No. Nothing.'

To her great dismay Iris realized that her eyes were filling with tears.

'I'm sorry,' she said, quickly wiping them away.

She stood. 'I won't take any more of your time.'

'What will you do?' Stuart Hirano asked, his manner softening.

'I don't know.' She straightened her back and blinked hard to control her runaway emotions.

'May I arrange for a private investigator to look into this on your behalf?'

'No,' she answered firmly.

'Please call me if you decide otherwise.'

She nodded, then turned to go. The door was set into a wall covered with memorabilia. She hadn't noticed it when she came in but now it caught her attention. There was a shelf devoted to Jeff Hirano's sports victories, both in high school and college. Baseball and wrestling trophies were draped with swimming medals hanging on ribbons. Framed certificates attested to Jeff's outstanding character, civic awareness, and sportsmanship. Iris felt a twinge of worry for Jeff. What would Stuart Hirano do when he learned his perfect son was gay? Would the trophies still hold the position of honor in the office? Would Stuart Hirano's eyes still glow with pride when he looked at his son?

To the right of the featured shelf display the entire wall was covered with plaques and awards and pictures from Stuart's career. Iris studied them. To her surprise Stuart Hirano had sponsored programs for children throughout the Bay Area. He had founded a 'Reach for the Stars' program to keep teens in high school and motivate them

to make goals for themselves. And he had helped count-
less young people go to college.

She had always thought him a deficient human being.
Not a good man at all. Yet here was concrete proof that he
had done good deeds. Did that make him good? Did that
cancel out the years of neglect and tyranny that his wife
and children had suffered? Did it cancel out the ruthless
way he had acquired the land for his grand office complex?

She scanned the wall again. It was clear that Stuart
Hirano was considered a hero in his public life. A hero.
That was so hard for her to absorb. He was not a good
man at all by her standards yet he was recognized as a
hero.

Suddenly, a troubling question arose in her thoughts.
What about Nathan Kaliker? Was he also a public hero
without being a decent human being? She knew for a fact
that he had been cheating on his wife. She suspected that
he was using Kizmin.

Were all heroes like that? And if so, maybe hero
worship was skewed. For it occurred to her that maybe it
took more dedication and courage and fortitude, more
innate goodness, to attend to everyday life than it took to
perform public acts of heroism. It required more character
to be patient and kind and giving, day in and day out, to
one's own family than it did to make a grand gesture for
the benefit of strangers.

'Would you have given me a scholarship?' she asked
Stuart Hirano on impulse.

'Absolutely, but the Kaliker people beat me to it. You
were an outstanding student, Iris. A real prize.'

So there had been several potential scholarships. And
she had not been competing for them so much as they had
been competing for her.

Hirano turned away from the wall of awards and
studied her.

'You seem very curious about your mother, Iris. Would you like to see the police report?'

'Yes! Is that possible?'

'I'll make some calls. See what I can do.'

'I would appreciate that, very much,' she told him sincerely, but she couldn't help wondering why he was tossing her the favor.

Jeff came through the door then with three cans of soda. He handed one to his father and one to Iris.

'Looks like you guys are about finished, huh?'

'Yes.' Stuart Hirano's entire countenance was transformed at the sight of his son. 'I was hoping you would have lunch with me today, Jeff.'

'Sorry. I took Iris to lunch. Maybe next week.'

'Of course. Of course.'

The men had done a turnabout. Now it was the son neglecting the father.

'What do you hear from Tommy, Dad?'

'The usual. Your mother has his letters at the house if you'd like to read them.'

Jeff looked at her. 'Isn't it amazing, Iris? My bratty little brother turned out to be a computer genius. He's at MIT working on his doctorate.'

Taking Jeff's cue, Iris looked at Stuart Hirano. 'You must be so proud of Tommy,' she said.

'He's a good son,' Stuart agreed though not with any excessive display of enthusiasm. 'Someday when Jeff is in this office, running Hero Systems, Tommy will make an excellent teammate for him.'

Jeff's good-natured expression flattened. 'Gotta go, Dad. I took Iris by that big job at The Groves that I won the design awards for, and now she wants to see some of my gardens.'

Stuart Hirano frowned and shook his head. 'What is this obsession you and your sister have with a culture you've never known? Her with her Japanese clients and her

246

diatribes on internment camps and repatriations. And you with your Japanese gardens – which I've never understood by the way. All that antiquated, stuffy symbolism and structure. Why would you want to build something like that when you have so much space and rich soil here, and such a variety of flowers to choose from?'

'Dad—' Jeff protested.

'And . . .' Hirano shook his finger in his son's face. 'You both seem to forget that you're half Swedish. I don't see either of you out resurrecting or defending your mother's ancestry.'

'Dad! I don't just do Japanese gardens. That's a sideline thing. Like a hobby. I work with water systems.'

'If you're so good with water, why couldn't you build the falls in my reception area?'

'I could have built it. I didn't think it was a good idea. Remember, I told you it wouldn't work?'

'Well, there you have it! Someone else built it for me and did a splendid job. You're obviously in the wrong occupation.'

Jeff flashed Iris a panicky look.

'I really must be going,' she said. 'Thank you for seeing me on such short notice.'

'Any time. Any time.' Stuart Hirano shook her hand then turned toward his son. 'Don't forget lunch next week,' he said sternly.

'Right,' Jeff said.

As soon as they were out of the office Jeff muttered something about lunch that Iris couldn't understand. She didn't ask him to repeat it. That was all he said until they left the building and started down the path toward the parking area.

'Sorry about the lies,' he said.

'You weren't exactly lying. I would like to see your gardens.' She grinned at him. 'Someday.'

He smiled a little.

247

'It's all so crazy. My little brother is a computer whiz who's a carbon copy of dad. And he worships dad. He's dying to make dad proud of him.'

'Maybe you're all the things your father wished he could have been when he was young.'

'If that's true, then why is he trying to turn me into something I'm not?'

'Like you said . . . it's crazy.'

Iris stopped beside her rental car. 'This is mine,' she said.

'Did my father have any useful information for you?'

'No.' Resentment filled her again. 'He offered to hire a private investigator for me.'

'Why does that make you mad?'

'Because . . . we were always the peons out there . . . farming Hirano orchards . . . accepting Hirano charity.'

'What do you mean, charity?'

'Your grandfather gave my parents the land for their house.'

'He sold it to them, fair and square.'

'Yes, but I heard your father and grandfather arguing about it. Yoshi sold it to them for a fraction of the market value: I heard your father yelling about how the sale was really just charity. And I know he was right.'

She crossed her arms tightly over her chest. 'I'm an adult now. I've got the title of doctor. I don't need his help.'

Jeff smiled wistfully. 'I guess we're both still the same deep down. I'm still confused and scared. You're still the same hurt little girl who doesn't want to rely on anyone but herself.'

'No,' Iris said as she unlocked the car door. 'You're projecting your own feelings onto me, Jeff. I am not still the same. That hurt little girl is buried so far in my past that I'm not even connected to her anymore. I've gone beyond all that. It's no longer a factor in my life.'

Jeff looked at her but didn't argue.

'You really should take advantage of my dad's offer. It's nothing to him. He's got several firms who do work all the time on company security and industrial espionage protection or whatever you call it. They're high caliber firms and they do all types of stuff. In fact, I remember that he got one of them to help your father, back when your mother left.'

Iris stared into Jeff's open, sincere face.

'He helped my father get the detective?'

'Yeah.' Jeff shrugged. 'I overheard a whole conversation about getting an investigator to look for your mother.'

'You're sure? This wasn't just a childhood fantasy, was it?'

'I'm older than you, Iris. I was eleven then and I have very accurate memories from that age. Besides, that was such an awful time, having my best friend's mother vanish . . . My memories from that are pretty vivid.'

He peered closer at her. 'What's wrong?'

'I knew my father had hired someone after my mother left . . . after the police said they couldn't do anything. So, just a few minutes ago, I asked your dad if he knew anything about the detective my father used. He said he knew nothing.'

'I don't understand,' Jeff said, shaking his head in puzzlement. 'He wouldn't have forgotten.'

'He lied to me.'

'My father considers himself an honorable man. If he did lie there's a reason. Maybe he promised someone secrecy.'

Iris got into the car and rolled down the window. Jeff bent and leaned in, resting his forearms on the car. 'I'll see if I can find out anything,' he said.

'How?'

'Sneakily.' He grinned and wiggled his eyebrows.

'I can't ask you to do that.'

'You didn't ask. I want to do it.' He sobered. 'Can we keep in touch?' he asked.

'I'm willing to give it a try. But I'm warning you, I'm not a very faithful friend, Jeff.'

'You seemed pretty faithful today.'

'Don't count on too much from me.'

'What do you think I want, Iris? What do you think you have to do to be a faithful friend?'

'Be there for people. Always be there.'

'And you can't do that?'

'I never have. I told you, I'm not courageous. It takes courage always to be there for people.'

He shook his head. 'You underestimate yourself. But I'll save the pop-psych lectures for another time . . . after we've had a lot of vodka.'

'Vodka?'

'Sure. That's what makes the Russians so good at soul searching. Lots of vodka.'

'I hate soul searching.'

'OK, we'll sing show tunes instead. I am invited to come visit you wherever you end up next, aren't I?'

'I'd like that.'

The telephone in his van began to ring and he hurried away to answer it. She saw him writing something, then he looked up and waved at her. She started her car but he signaled emphatically for her to wait so she pulled around next to the van. He jumped out and handed her a piece of paper.

'My father hoped he would catch you. He says to go to this address. The old files are stored there. He says to ask for Sergeant Douglas.'

Stuart Hirano had smoothed the way for her so well that she only had to say Sergeant Douglas's name and she was ushered into a quiet room and handed a slim folder with several yellowed sheets inside. There was a handwritten report detailing the original call from John Lanier, the initial visit to the house, the existence of the note. Two other shorter reports described the morgue and hospital checks, the contacts with other jurisdictions that had unidentified female bodies, the cursory check into John Lanier's story and the record of the visit that Iris had overheard. Tucked behind the reports was a folded sheet of lined paper. Iris opened it.

There, in firm bold strokes written with a calligraphy pen, was the goodbye that Clary Lanier had left for her husband and child.

To my dearest John and my sweetest Iris—
    This is something I have to do. It is best for everyone though it may not seem that way at first. I have been living a lie all these years, thinking that love would make it all right, but now I see that only I can make it right. Please try to understand and remember how much I love both of you.

With all my heart,<br>Clary

Iris's hand was shaking so badly that she had to put the note down. This was the original. She had always wondered what became of it, had always assumed that her father burned it.

She smoothed it out on the table and stared down at the words that her mother had left them. The note was completely different from what she had always imagined and she realized she might never have actually seen it or had it read to her as a child. She must have formed her idea of the contents from overhearing adults talking. The goodbye note everyone had called it, and so she had formed an image of the word *goodbye*. A huge, darkly printed goodbye. But the word didn't even appear on the page.

She closed her eyes and covered her face with her hands. After years of anguish followed by years of hatred followed by years of detachment, suddenly she felt a great wave of sadness for her mother. Sadness verging on sympathy.

She refolded the note and carefully tucked it into a pocket of her shoulderbag. The message was private, personal. It did not belong to the police.

She hurried straight back to her father's house and tried to make a plane reservation for that evening. Nothing was available so she had to settle for a flight that left San Jose the following morning. She was increasingly anxious over the thousands of miles that separated them and certain that she needed to be back in New York. The mystery might have started in California but its end was in New York.

She wandered through the empty house, checking and double checking that everything was exactly as she had found it. She went outside, walked into the orchard, then doubled back and stopped at the garden. Her mother's iris were blooming. Seeing them caused an ache in her chest.

She hurried back into the house. But the ache did not subside. If anything it grew worse.

She went out the front door, got into the rental car, and drove. At first she was driving only to escape, but then she found herself on Bascom and she thought of Jeff seeing her father at Laurel Plaza.

She parked at one end of the old-style L shaped strip mall. They had tried to modernize it with twining art deco pillars and benches, but it was still a tired example of the shopping areas that had sprouted all over California during the fifties. She shaded her eyes with her hand and studied the stores – a pet shop, a music shop, the pizza place Jeff had mentioned, a pharmacy, a diet and weight center, a bookstore, a liquor store, and a beauty shop.

She strolled down the sidewalk, past a window full of frolicking puppies, then past a window of guitars and wind instruments. At the pizza parlor she went inside and bought a cold drink. What could she possibly learn at Laurel Plaza? That her father had developed a craving for pizza or that he was considering the purchase of a guitar? Nothing would surprise her at this point.

She stepped out of the restaurant onto the shady sidewalk and she saw a woman standing between cars in the parking lot. The woman was tall, with long greying hair and prominent silver earrings. It was the woman who'd been sitting in the visitors' lounge in Morningside Hospital in New York.

Heart racing, Iris ducked behind the nearest deco column.

The woman opened the trunk of a car and pulled out a shopping bag. She closed the trunk and looked around, tucking her hair behind her ears, behaving casually, probably thinking that Iris was still safely inside the pizza parlor. She threaded her way through the cars, crossing the parking area toward the other leg of the L shaped strip, where she went inside the small bookshop. From the bookshop the woman probably had a perfect diagonal view of the door to the pizza parlor.

Iris waited behind the pillar. Had the woman followed her all the way from New York?

Iris grew tired of hiding. And the more she thought about the woman, about her father, about all the unanswered questions, the angrier she became. Finally, she stepped from behind the pillar and stalked across the parking area on a direct diagonal for the bookstore.

She threw open the door. It was a quiet little shop with no customers. An elderly man was unpacking books from a box.

'Where is she?' Iris demanded.

The startled man stared at Iris mutely.

'She saw me coming, didn't she? Where's she hiding?' Iris looked behind the counter. Other than that one small empty space there seemed to be no other hiding places in the store.

'Who?' the elderly man finally asked in a timid voice.

'The woman with the long hair. I saw her come in here.'

With wide frightened eyes the man pointed toward a door marked EMPLOYEES ONLY.

Iris approached the door cautiously. From behind it she heard the faint strains of *Nessun dorma*. She tried the knob. It was unlocked. She took a deep breath, then quickly opened the door. The aria enveloped her and she found herself looking down at the woman, who was seated behind a desk, hands frozen in the act of doing paperwork, face registering fright and then acquiescence.

Without taking her eyes from Iris, the woman reached over to a small tape player and pushed a button. The aching sweetness of Pavarotti's voice abruptly ended and a thick silence sucked the air from the tiny room.

'I knew you'd come someday,' the woman said.

It was hard to breathe. Hard to think. Iris felt like she was sinking beneath the surface of very deep water.

'You were at the hospital in New York,' Iris finally managed to say.

'Yes.'

'But . . . why are you here?'

'This is my store.'

'Everything all right in there?' came the quavery voice of the old man from just outside the door.

'Yes. We're fine,' the woman said. 'Would you please answer the phone if it rings?'

He peeked in through the door to assure himself, then quietly closed it and left them alone.

'You can move that stuff off onto the floor,' the woman said, pointing to a slatbacked wooden chair that was stacked with papers.

Iris moved the stack, turned the chair to face the desk, and sat down.

'I'm Iris Lanier,' she said.

'I know,' the woman said bitterly.

Iris was puzzled by her manner. 'Have we seen each other before, other than at the hospital?'

'I've seen you.'

'What the hell is going on!' Iris demanded, suddenly fearful, and angered by the fear.

The woman steepled her hands, bent her head and closed her eyes a moment, then opened them and peered up at Iris.

'I'm Mariette,' she admitted. 'Mariette Miller.'

Iris stared at her, waiting for more.

The woman appeared confused.

'Don't you . . .' She shook her head. 'You don't know who I am?'

'How could I?'

'But I thought . . . I just assumed . . . when I saw you I thought that you had finally found out and—' The woman suddenly began to cry. She searched her desk for tissues, cursing softly under her breath as she fumbled through the drawers.

Iris was numb. Her arms were too heavy to move. She could not have risen from the chair if she had wanted to.

'Found out what?' Iris asked.

The woman laughed, flashing her bitterness again. 'John would die he if he could see this happening.' Then her face crumpled and she appeared stricken by her own words. 'He might die anyway,' she said.

Iris wanted to scream or slap the woman's face or pick up the stack of papers and throw them at the weeping eyes. Anything to stop those tears, to stop the jagged chasms of pain that this stranger's tears were opening in her own chest.

'Excuse me,' the woman said and poured herself a drink

from a bottle of spring water. When the paper cup was drained, she said, 'There. Now . . . let me see if I can sum it up in a short explanation.' She tilted her chin up and studied the far corner of the ceiling. 'Your father and I have been lovers for seventeen years. How's that? Pretty simple and concise, huh?'

Stunned, Iris could not think of anything to say. She stared at Mariette Miller, memorizing her features, absorbing the revelation as she absorbed the physical presence of the woman. Despite the noticeable grey streaks in the woman's long straight hair, her appearance was youthful. She had strong facial features that were classic rather than beautiful, the kind that become more striking with the addition of years. And she had a slender, erect carriage that lent dignity to her movements.

Iris tried to imagine her father's weathered hand touching the woman's face, his solid arms circling her narrow shoulders, his stern disapproving eyes lighting at the sight of her. It was impossible. It could not have happened.

Her thoughts fragmented and scattered. The woman's long silver earrings were like her mother's earrings. Had he been attracted to the earrings? Had he been trying to resurrect his wife? Had he whispered to this woman that he loved her? Why hadn't they married? Was she married to someone else? Had she refused to become a stepmother to his problematic daughter? Why hadn't he introduced Iris to her? Had he been so ashamed of his daughter that he had to keep her hidden?

'I'm sorry for you,' the woman said wearily. 'It must be a shock to find out like this. But my emotions are worn so thin right now that I don't have any sympathy to offer.'

Iris struggled to give voice to a question. Any question. It was hard to know where to begin.

'Why did you keep your relationship a secret?' she finally asked.

'John insisted. He was adamant about your not finding out.'

'Seventeen years?'

'Oh, yes. I could tell you months and days and hours if you really want to pin it down. God, I was so young when I met him . . . only twenty-three. Now I'm forty and he's fifty-two. Where did it all go?' She closed her eyes a moment then opened them. 'What did I do wrong?' she whispered.

She looked around her tiny office as though taking stock. 'I try to tell myself that things are fine,' she said. 'I have my own business. I'm an independent woman. I'm healthy and not exactly doddering into old age yet. I could still have a life with a man. I could still have a baby.'

She stopped and lowered her eyes to her desk top as though embarrassed. 'But you don't want to hear any of this.' She shifted in her seat and neatened the papers in front of her.

'So,' she said briskly, 'Why did you come to California?'

Iris could not speak for a moment. Seventeen years. How would she have felt if her father had brought this woman home seventeen years ago? She would have been twelve then. She would have already had four long years of being motherless and lonely and miserable. Would she have accepted a twenty-three-year-old stepmother? Would she have embraced the woman as a friend and an ally? She honestly didn't know. But, looking back from an adult perspective, she knew that her life would have been very very different if this woman had become part of it, and she couldn't help but believe that the differences would have been positive ones. This woman might have been the savior she fantasized, the angel she dreamed of on the nights when she wasn't having nightmares.

'I came . . .' she began haltingly, 'because there are so many unanswered questions. I was trying to find out why my father went to New York. Why he got shot.'

'But . . . what do you mean, why? It was a mugging, wasn't it?'

'No. The police don't know exactly what it was. But it wasn't random.'

The woman stared down at her desk blankly.

'Did he tell you why he was going to New York?'

The woman continued to stare down at nothing. 'He got a call. We were in the kitchen.'

'At my father's house?' Iris asked.

'Yes. I had been spending a lot of time there lately. I cooked there. Even slept there. That's what we were doing . . . cooking I mean. He picked up the phone, said hello, and then got this terrible expression on his face.

'He looked so bad that I was afraid something had happened to you. Then he changed phones. I was whispering to him, asking him what was wrong, but he waved me away and went to talk in his office.

'He was gone for a long time. Finally I got worried and I went to check. He was off the phone. Just sitting there. Staring at nothing. Looking like he was in a state of shock.

'I asked him if you were OK and he said, "This has nothing to do with Iris."

'I tried to put my arms around him, to comfort him, but he pushed me away. I begged him to tell me what was wrong.

' "It doesn't concern you," he said.'

Mariette Miller's bottom lip trembled. 'Seventeen years of loving that man and he said, "It doesn't concern you," like he was talking to a nosy neighbor.

'I'd been hurt worse by him many times over the years. Every time we had one of our biyearly fights about getting married I'd end up feeling like he'd ripped out my heart and chewed it to pieces. But I'd never walked out. Never. That had always seemed irrevocable to me, and I'd just never done it. But something snapped inside me that day. Something wore completely through. And I told him that

258

if his problems didn't concern me then maybe I shouldn't be with him anymore.

'I thought that would shake him up. It was so unlike me. I'd been so tractable. But he didn't react at all.

' "I have things to do," he said. "I have to take a trip and I'm not sure when I'll be back."

' "Fine," I told him, "I'm not sure when I'll be back either." And I left. I walked out of the house, and that's the last time I saw him.'

Iris watched as Mariette Miller folded forward, as though she was melting, as though the pain was dissolving her bones. She lay face down across her desk and a terrible keening filled the room.

The woman's pain flowed into Iris, joining with her own. And she had to get away. She stumbled from the chair out the door, through the quiet store to the front where she leaned against the counter, fighting for breath, holding herself, pressing her arms against her belly and chest.

The old man watched her from behind a set of shelves, rheumy eyes full of alarm. She shoved away from the counter and pushed through the door. A little bell tinkled with her exit. Had she heard the bell when she came in? She couldn't remember it. Was that a defect she had? Not noticing what was happening around her? Missing the tinkling bells and the seventeen-year love affairs?

She made it down the sidewalk to one of the art deco benches and sank onto it. If only she could wish herself back to Guatemala. Back to the underground chamber. Where all she had to think about was the next cut of her trowel, the next sweep of her brush. Where Moonsmoke waited to give up her secrets. Where her days were full and her nights were deep and dreamless.

She was a coward and she couldn't be trusted and she knew that was true. She knew she was just like her mother. But she knew how to manage her life so that no one else got hurt. Wasn't that what counted? That no one else get hurt? And she knew that she belonged down in that chamber, thousands of years in the past, and not out in California with troubled friends and heartbroken lost strangers who should have been more to her but now never would be, and she wanted to grab her father's shoulders and shake him in his bed and scream, *This is all your fault!*

'Iris?'

She looked up and there was Mariette Miller, standing on the sidewalk, her swollen eyes just vulnerable enough, her stance just helpless enough that Iris was caught. That was the trick in running away. It had to be done when the other person was strong and self-possessed. Or angry. Anger made it the easiest.

'May I sit down?'

Iris nodded.

'What do the doctors say now? Have they seen any change in his condition?'

'No.'

'They wouldn't let me in to see him. Family only, the nurse said. No exceptions.'

'You didn't miss anything. He just lies there. It's terrible to see.'

They sat together in silence a moment.

'How did you find out he was hurt?' Iris asked.

'I was in the store alone when Yoshi Hirano came in. My heart jumped right into my throat because I knew who he was, but I didn't think he knew me. John had always been so discreet.'

The woman drew in a deep breath.

'I asked if I could help him and he said that he had come for a friend. That he was worried about whether his friend John Lanier had ordered any books, and that if he had he wouldn't be able to pick them up for awhile because he was in Morningside Hospital in New York City.'

'Then, while I was still too stunned to respond, he said goodbye and left.'

'So Mr Hirano knew about you?'

'Obviously.'

'And then you flew out to New York?'

'Yes. I left right away. Closed the store completely. I thought . . . I hoped . . . that he might need me. The truth is that I need him. I'm lost without him.'

Iris clasped her hands in her lap and concentrated on them. Then she glanced sideways at Mariette Miller. 'You have no idea who was on the phone that day?'

'None. The only thing I heard John say was hello. Other than that he just listened. And then he changed phones.'

'I wish you'd been a snoop and picked up the kitchen extension.'

The woman ducked her head. 'I considered it,' she admitted. 'I had this bad feeling from the moment his face got that horrible expression on it. I knew that whatever he was hearing would change both our lives.'

'Did he ever say anything to you about hiring a private detective to look for my mother?'

'He mentioned it. He said he went crazy when she first left and he spent a year where all he could think about was finding her. He admitted that he wasn't sure what he would have done if he had found her, but that he never had to face that because the detective didn't get anywhere. She walked out of the house that day and completely vanished.'

'Do you recall the detective's name?'

'No. I don't think John ever said.' The woman flashed Iris a worried look. 'Do you think that's what happened . . . he finally found her?'

Iris could not bring herself to answer. Instead she said, 'He bought a gun. He took it to New York with him and that's probably the gun he was shot with.'

'No. That can't be,' the woman insisted. 'John would

never . . .' She shook her head.

'That's what I thought. But he did. There's no doubt about it. They know where and when he bought it and what kind it was.'

Mariette Miller pressed her fist to her mouth and stared down at the sidewalk as though wrestling with a decision.

'I did hear something else,' she said softly, her fist still against her mouth. 'I didn't think I should tell you, but now . . .'

'What! What is it?'

'Just after he answered the phone, his face got all white and shocked, and he whispered "Clary." He whispered your mother's name.'

# Fifteen

On her flight back to New York, Iris considered what her next move should be, and by the time she landed she had a plan. She dropped her luggage at the Fitzgerald, let Andretti know she was back and then went directly to the hospital. Helen was on duty.

'No change, honey,' Helen called out as soon as she saw Iris coming down the hallway. 'But you had a guy calling from Guatemala day before yesterday and he was pretty mad that you'd gone off to California.'

'Thanks,' Iris said, wincing inwardly.

She had forgotten that Daniel Becker was going to call her again before he left Guatemala City. There was no telling what he had thought when he'd heard she left for California. She might already be out of a job.

Inside her father's room all was the same. She felt almost as if she was entering a time warp where everything was frozen. Where change was not possible.

She took his hand and told him everything she had learned in the course of her trip. She told him she'd met Mariette Miller. There was no response. She could have been talking to the wall.

'Now I'm going to see the place where you were shot,' she said. 'And I'm going to try to find the prostitute who was there.'

Nothing. She carefully put the limp hand back down on the bed and left the room.

★ ★ ★

By the time she approached the exact location of her father's shooting in Riverside Park the afterglow of a spectacular sunset was lingering over the New Jersey skyline to the west. According to the science section of the *Times* there would be many beautiful sunsets, the result of a volcanic eruption in Hawaii. It was predicted that airborne dust from that disaster would hang in the atmosphere for weeks, reflecting the sun's colors and painting the sky.

The park was a long thin strip of greenbelt that stretched out beside the Hudson all along the Upper West Side. Kizmin's directions were not precise enough to allow her to find the exact spot where her father's blood had seeped into the ground, but she knew that she was close.

She stood on the walkway nearest Riverside Drive and studied the people passing by. The early-evening crowd was a mix of dog walkers and people hurrying home from work or school. If there were prostitutes in the crowd, she could not identify them. What next? She couldn't call Kizmin, and she refused to give up.

'Excuse me,' she said to a well-dressed woman with a fluffy little dog on a leash.

The woman slowed and eyed her warily.

'Do you know where I can find any prostitutes in this area?'

With a jerk on the little dog's neck the woman hurried away.

Iris tried this same direct approach on two more people without success. Finally she decided she would have to modify it.

'Excuse me, sir. I'm a reporter and I've been assigned to talk to prostitutes from this area but I don't know how to find any. Do you know where I might look?'

The man tucked his newspaper under his arm and scratched his head. 'Do I look as if I'd know?' he demanded, and Iris realized she had no talent for smooth-talk.

'I didn't mean to imply—'

'I don't want my name used in the article,' he said, glancing around as though worried about witnesses.

'No problem. You don't even have to give me your name.'

'This time of night they're usually up closer to the bridge. They hang around up there for the commuter business.'

'Commuters?'

'Don't they give you any background information for your story? They do round trips over the bridge when the traffic is heavy like this. A blow job on the way over to Jersey and then they catch a return job so they get a ride back.'

'I see,' Iris said, trying to keep her expression carefully professional.

She saw a likely looking trio on a corner, not exactly together but occupying the same space separately. As she walked toward them she passed a man lounging in a doorway. All she really saw of him were his flashy black and white shoes, but she could feel his eyes on her as she passed.

Two of the women were in miniskirts and spike heels with tight little bomber jackets as a concession to the season. They stood near the building line, passively watching the traffic inch toward the arteries to the George Washington Bridge. The third, in red short-shorts and black thigh-high stockings, strutted back and forth along the curb making pouty lips at passing drivers.

'Excuse me,' Iris said, approaching the two women in skirts. They exchanged mute glances, then stared at her with the dull, uncomprehending expressions of deer caught in headlights.

'My father was shot nearby in Riverside Park and I'm trying to find out who saw him . . . who called the ambulance. This was a few weeks ago. Around three a.m. A thin blond was seen in the area. Maybe you know her?'

'Is he dead?' one of the women asked. She was in her twenties with cocoa skin and orange hair.

'No. He's in a coma.'

'We're decent citizens,' said her companion, a very pale, emaciated woman with harsh blue-black hair. 'If we saw anything like that we'd a done our duty and told the cops.'

'This isn't about the cops. This is for my information. I want to know what happened.'

'Sounds like you know what happened. He got shot.'

'Yes, but . . . I don't know why he was in the park so late. If he met someone or was just passing through . . .'

'Or if he was lookin' for a little fun, maybe?' the pale woman said, and her partner snickered.

'I've got money. I'll pay for information.'

Again they exchanged an unreadable glance.

Iris reached in her shoulder bag and pulled out two twenties. 'Look, here's a little something to compensate you for your trouble. If you can remember who might have seen him then tell her there's more money if she calls me.' The bills vanished into the women's clothes.

Iris scribbled the rented room's phone number on a piece of paper and handed it to them. 'Tell her to keep trying till she gets me.'

Orange hair slipped the paper into a tiny purse.

'Hey, what am I missin'?' called the woman in red shorts. Her voice was decidedly masculine. 'You givin' out free samples of something, sugar?'

The pale woman glanced fearfully up the street and gestured for red shorts to be quiet, but not soon enough.

'What's goin' on down there!'

It was the man in the doorway. His menacing voice

made everyone jump, even Iris. Red shorts bolted back to her post. The pale woman jerked a handful of plastic-wrapped condoms from her bag and thrust them into Iris's hands.

The man approached in a sauntering, shoulder-rolling stroll. He cuffed the two women aside roughly, then stood glaring down at Iris, so close that the tips of his fancy shoes were almost touching the toes of her sneakers. She resisted the urge to run and stared right back at him. His overpowering, expensive cologne nearly gagged her.

'What do you want here, bitch?'

'Excuse me? I am trying—'

'She's one of them health workers,' the pale woman blurted out. 'She's saying the same old stuff and peddling rubbers.'

'My girls don't need no health workers,' he growled, glancing down at Iris's handful of condoms. 'I run a clean outfit.'

'I'm sure you do,' Iris said, taking her cue from the woman, who was blinking rapidly and watching Iris with an expression of desperation. 'I'm just trying to do my job.'

'Yeah, well, you done it. Now fuck off.'

She nodded and started walking, slowly at first, then faster and faster. She covered several blocks before she could make herself stop hurrying away from him. Suddenly she realized that she was still clutching the handful of condoms, and she quickly dropped them in her purse. Her hands shook slightly. The man, the pimp, had been terrifying. She tried to imagine what kind of lives those women must have. Did they have a place to call home? Did they have families? Boyfriends? Children? Or did they lead subhuman existences, like they were chattel or slaves. Who said prostitution was a victimless crime?

Iris kept walking until she saw another pair of women.

She repeated her request and her gift of twenties. Then, depressed and disquieted, she headed back downtown.

Madame Zora's sign was lit as usual. Iris stopped and looked in the window. There was one dim little room and it was empty except for a small table and chair. She had never actually seen Madame Zora. Was there such a person?

At the back of the room she could see a dark doorway hung with strands of red glass beads. The beads parted and a woman leaned out. The woman was barely visible in the shadows but she was looking straight at Iris. Watching her. Waiting. As though she knew something.

The shadowy face and the patient knowing expression on that face were eerily reminiscent of Moonsmoke. Iris could not make herself turn away. She stared in and the woman stared back, neither moving, neither breaking eye contact.

Finally, the woman raised her hand. Slowly, almost reluctantly, she beckoned Iris inside.

*This is ridiculous*, Iris told herself as she went through the door. She stood inside, eyes adjusting to the odd blue-tinged light. The woman had disappeared again.

'Come in,' the woman called from the darkened room beyond the beads. The long red strands swayed, reflecting glints of light.

What did she expect? What was she looking for in Madame Zora's parlor? Some of Kizmin's trust in fate or Linda's faith in astrology? Maybe a dose of Jeff Hirano's belief in true love? *Real, true, passionate, lifelong love*, no less.

Why was she there?

'Please,' the woman said, 'you will feel better once you come in and sit down.'

Iris stepped through the beads and found herself in another room lit by small guttering candles.

'I'm sorry. I shouldn't have come inside,' she said. 'I don't know why I did. So, you'll have to excuse me, but—'

The woman moved her shawl-draped arm and pointed at the empty chair across the table from her.

'Sit down.'

'I don't . . . really . . . I shouldn't . . .' But Iris sat in the chair. She felt as if she were separated from herself. Suspended. With no control over her actions.

'Please relax,' the woman said.

She was a very ordinary woman now that Iris had a better view of her. Full-faced and large busted but not at all overweight. Her hair was dyed an unnatural black. Beneath the brightly fringed shawl she wore a plain dress.

'I've never done anything like this,' Iris said.

The woman nodded.

'Do you want me to show you my palm or can I just ask you questions?'

'Relax,' the woman said again. She unwrapped a deck of oversize cards from a silk scarf and shuffled through them.

'What are you doing?'

'This is the Tarot. You are the Querent. You have a question. Hold it in your thoughts. Don't say it.'

'I don't know why I came in here,' Iris said.

Madame Zora ignored her and held up a card. 'This is you,' she said. 'You are the Queen of Swords.'

Zora handed the card to Iris. On it was a beautiful detailed drawing of a regally crowned woman on an ornate throne. One hand was outstretched. The other held a raised sword. The woman was staring out into a cloudy sky, an expression of great sadness on her face.

Iris swallowed hard. She stared down at the Queen of Swords in her hand and realized that she was shaking.

'The queen is quick-witted and has keen powers of observation. She wears the butterflies of the soul on her crown and she bears a weight of sorrow for loved ones

269

who are lost or far away. Her upraised sword warns all who dare approach her.'

Zora took the card from Iris and placed it neatly in the center of the table.

Iris shook her head. 'I don't know why I came in here. Really . . . I . . .'

Zora stared at her silently and shuffled the deck of cards. The queen lay mutely on the table. Staring into the cloudy sky. Holding her sword.

Iris wanted to leave but she could not make herself move from the chair.

'Cut them into three,' Zora instructed, laying the deck in front of Iris. 'Use your left hand and cut to the left. Keep your question in your mind as you touch the cards.'

Slowly, reluctantly, Iris cut the cards. She didn't need to think out her question. It was there in her thoughts all the time. *What happened to my father and how can I save him?*

Zora scooped them back up. 'We will lay out the Celtic Cross and Staff, an ancient method for reading the Tarot. You are in the center – The Queen of Swords. The first card is dealt on top of you. This is the card that covers you. It represents the general environment that surrounds the question you've asked. Deftly, Zora slipped the top card off the deck, flipped it right side up, and placed it over the queen.

'The Eight of Swords,' she said, and there was something in her manner, a moment of startled discomposure, that struck Iris as ominous.

'What is the Eight of Swords?' Iris asked, studying the picture. It portrayed a blindfolded bound woman standing on wet ground with eight swords driven into the earth around her like the bars of a prison.

'The Eight of Swords signifies betrayal, bondage, and fear.'

Zora glanced up at Iris, then looked quickly back down at the cards.

'The next card will cross you and it will show the forces opposing the Eight of Swords.'

She turned the card and laid it sideways across the previous card.

'This is strength. That is what you have to oppose the betrayal and bondage and fear. Strength.'

The card depicted a white-gowned woman with flowers at her waist and in her hair. She had her hands on a lion's mouth, either forcing it open or holding it closed. Above her head was the sideways eight symbol for infinity or eternity.

'With strength you oppose the strife surrounding your question. The Strength card signifies spiritual power, energy, action, courage, force of character, love conquering hate.

'The third card is beneath you. It represents the past. That which has already been part of your experience and forms the basis for the matter at hand.'

She flipped the third card and laid it directly below the queen with her covering and opposing cards. The drawing was bleak and disturbing. It depicted a black sky with a figure lying on barren ground, face turned away. The figure was pierced with ten swords.

'The Ten of Swords,' Zora said with a sharp intake of breath. 'This card signifies a past of pain, disruption, tears, desolation, and ruin.'

'You mean in the past experience of the person I asked the question about?'

'No. No. In your own past experience,' Zora insisted. 'We will analyze meanings after the Cross and Staff are complete. Now, please, just sit back.

'The next card is behind you and goes behind the queen's back. It shows that which you are just passing out of or will pass out of shortly.'

She laid the fourth card to the left of the center. It was the first completely benign picture Iris had seen. The

271

figure was a scholarly looking man holding a globe in one hand and a staff in the other. He was gazing out at mountains and water from what appeared to be a parapet.

'The Two of Wands,' Zora said. 'The Two of Wands signifies the use of scientific methods, sadness in the midst of accomplishment, boldness in work, and a proud unforgiving nature. Notice the red rose and white lily crossed on the parapet. This is pure thought crossed with desire.'

'These are all things I'm putting behind me?' Iris asked. Zora nodded.

'The fifth card crowns you. It represents what is not yours but could be yours. Something you could arrive at soon.'

She flicked the card into position over the queen's head. On it was an elaborate picture of a fierce fire-haired angel, arms spread, wings tinged red by the brilliant sun behind him. He was looking down on a man and woman, both naked. Behind the woman was a fruit tree twined with a long snake. Behind the man was a barren tree with flames for leaves. The roots of the two trees met on the ground beneath the man and woman's feet.

'Ah . . . The Lovers.'

Iris felt her cheeks flush. *The Lovers. Isaac.*

'But wait,' Zora cautioned. 'This card is not so obvious as it may seem. In addition to love it signifies the struggle between the conscious and the subconscious. It represents exposure, trust, temptation, attraction, and of course, choice.'

Iris shifted uncomfortably in her seat.

'The sixth card is before you. It represents the near future, the coming action.' Zora held the deck out and flipped the card into position at the right of the center, then drew back as though stung.

Iris examined the card. On it was a hideous drawing of a creature with the torso and arms of a man, the face and curved horns of a goat, and the muscular shaggy legs and clawed feet of a mythical beast. He had large outspread bat wings and an inverted pentagram between his horns. One hand was raised. The other held a smoldering torch. He was sitting on a block that had a ring fixed to it. Attached to the ring were two chains, one leading to the neck of a naked female and the other to the neck of a naked male. Each of the humans had small horns protruding from their hair.

'That's the devil, isn't it?' Iris said.

Zora did not raise her eyes from the card. 'The Devil signifies violence, force, fatality, extraordinary efforts, and predestiny. His right hand is raised in the sign of black magic. His left holds the torch of destruction.'

'That's supposed to be in my immediate future?' Iris started to rise from her chair. 'I think I've had enough of this.'

'No! No! It's bad luck not to finish. The cross is formed, now we only need the cards for the staff.'

Iris sank back into the chair.

'The seventh card begins the staff. It is you – your attitudes and relation to the matter at hand.'

She put the card low and to the right of the cross. It was a solitary genderless figure against a grey sky. The figure wore a long black cape and had a bowed head. At his feet were three spilled cups of red liquid. Another two full cups stood behind his back. In the distance was a small bridge to a building on the other side of a stream.

'That is the Five of Cups,' Zora said. 'It signifies regret, bitterness, sorrow and disillusionment. Loss, but with something remaining.'

Quickly Zora flipped another card into position over the last.

'The eighth card is your house card, your environment, the influence of others, what others think or what others are bringing out in you. It is the Moon.'

Against a blue sky a three-phased moon with a solemn

273

female face looked down upon two towers and a grassy bank along a river or lake. A narrow meandering path began at the water, went between the towers, and continued on to the horizon in distant mountains. A wolf and a dog bayed at the moon while a crayfish climbed out of the water toward the path.

'The moon looks down over us, body, mind, and spirit, shedding light and leading us along the path. The Moon is a powerful card representing the emergence of latent spiritual powers, of intuition and imagination. But it also signifies darkness, deception and terror. Unforeseen perils. Hidden enemies. Grave danger.'

'I've heard enough,' Iris said, but she remained in her chair.

'Just two more,' Zora assured her. 'The ninth card is your hopes and fears. Your ideals.'

She turned another card, placed it over the last, and smiled. On the card was a golden-crowned woman in red robes. She was between two pillars. In one hand she held an upraised sword and in the other a set of scales.

'Justice,' Zora announced. 'Justice will be done. Rightness. Balance achieved. Vengeance taken.'

She paused and then turned the last card with a dramatic flair. 'This represents what will come. It is the most important card. The card with the highest significance.' Zora smiled as though she had pleasantly surprised herself with the card that appeared.

'The High Priestess.'

Iris leaned across to study the last card. It was a beautiful picture of a seated woman in blue robes and cape with the crescent moon at her feet and a full moon crown on her head. She was holding a scroll. On either side of her were pillars, one black and one white. Behind her was a lush garden of pomegranates and palms.

'I'm going to become a holy woman?' Iris asked.

'The High Priestess signifies mystery and secrets . . .

274

the scientific and the mystical. Power and wisdom. A future that has yet to be revealed to you. Enlightenment. Inner illumination. Tenacity. It can also signify the unfolding or the revealing of the woman who interests you.'

Iris stood. 'How much?' she asked, reaching into her purse.

'But I'm not finished. You're supposed to reveal your question now and we go over the meanings together.'

'No thank you. How much?'

'Ten dollars.'

Iris put a bill on the table and hurried back out to the sidewalk without waiting for Madame Zora to escort her. She rushed through the Fitzgerald's lobby and into the open elevator. Why had she gone into that woman's shop? And why had she stayed there in the chair and listened to all that?

After she was safely inside her room, she realized that she hadn't eaten dinner. Hadn't really had lunch either because the airline food had consisted of an inedible soggy sandwich and an overly sweet wedge of stale fudge cake. She sat on the end of the bed and tried to collect her thoughts.

The phone rang and she jumped for it. To her surprise the caller was Linda.

'Where are you calling from?'

'I'm at an airport, on the way to my parents' house. There's a big family celebration tomorrow night so my dad sent a helicopter to the dig to pick me up. It was so embarrassing. I'm going back as soon as I can escape.'

'Good. I'm glad to hear you're going back.'

'You are?' There was a pause. Then Linda said, 'You sound different.'

'You've never heard my voice over the phone.'

'No. I don't mean that. I mean . . . *different*.'

Iris disregarded the comment. 'Dr Becker told me

about all the work you've done on the tunnel.'

'He did! I wanted to surprise you with that news myself.'

'Well, it was a surprise. And I thank you for it.'

'I suppose he told you about all the artifacts we found in the dirt, too?'

'Yes.'

'And how they had the Moonsmoke glyphs all over them'

'Yes.'

'Shoot! Now I'm sorry I called you for him.'

'You're calling me for Dr Becker?'

'Yeah. He was all flustered when he found out you'd left New York. He wanted me to try to get in touch with you and find out what's going on and whether you're really going back.'

'I am going back. Next week, I think.'

A rush of excitement filled Iris as she thought about Moonsmoke waiting in the chamber. Waiting to give up her secrets. For a moment she wanted to tell Linda what she believed to be true. What she *knew* to be true. The sixth skeleton was Moonsmoke. And she was wearing the disc necklace pictured on the stela. But then she hesitated. Linda talked too much to be trusted with a confidence. And the prospect of telling someone about a revelation that had come to her in the darkness made it seem a little crazy.

'You'll probably beat me back,' Linda said. 'I don't know how soon I'll get away from here. Oh . . . and I probably should warn you, there's an R & R scheduled. Everybody was desperate for a break before the final push so they're all leaving on Monday. Going to a hotel for a few days.'

'To Guatemala City?'

'I don't know where they decided to go. There was talk about that nice hotel over by Tikal. But . . . anyway . . .

you might want to wait to go back because only Tim and one of the hired guys are going to be holding down the dig. Nothing much will be happening.'

'I might plan my return for exactly those days. I'd like a little time to get back into things without someone looking over my shoulder.'

Linda sighed. 'Yeah. I'd like to go back then, too. I've been trying to get Tim alone.'

Iris hung up the phone, puzzling over Linda's interest in Tim. Wondering why she hadn't noticed it before.

The music had started. She could hear the low sweet notes of Isaac's sax above her. She stood for a moment, looking up at the ceiling. Then she crossed to the window and opened it.

Those stupid Tarot cards. All she could think about now was those stupid cards. She didn't believe any of that, did she?

She sat on the sill to hear the music more clearly. There was the fire escape that would take her up to Isaac's window and beyond to the roof where she knew he would meet her. *This is your crowning card, The Lovers. It represents what is not yours but could be yours. Something you could arrive at soon. It is love and the struggle between the conscious and the unconscious. It is exposure, trust, temptation, attraction, and of course, choice.*

It was all her choice. No one was pushing her. Not even Isaac. Except for that first time when he'd asked if she would come back, he never spoke of when they would see each other again or whether they would ever have a relationship beyond the roof of the Fitzgerald. It was all her choice. That stupid card. Why had she listened to that nonsense? *What is not yours but could be yours.*

She swung out onto the fire escape and climbed to his window.

'Isaac,' she called softly and tapped on the glass. As

277

usual his window was open a few inches and the blinds were tightly closed.

The music stopped. The blinds parted a fraction and she saw his eyes.

'Why do you keep your window open all the time?' she asked.

'It's stuck. It won't go up or down.'

'I'm going to the roof.'

'I wish you'd start using the inside stairs,' he said. 'It's dangerous climbing over the parapet.'

'All right. I'll take the elevator and meet you.'

*The Lovers. What is not yours but could be yours. Exposure, trust, temptation, attraction, and of course, choice.*

The elevator opened on seven and he was there. Coat thrown on and hair tousled, as though he'd raced from his room to be there. He smiled and his eyes smiled and the bottom dropped out of her stomach.

'How was California?' he asked, stepping in beside her.

'The cherries were blooming. My mother's iris were starting to open.'

He leaned closer to her as though examining something.

'What?' she asked.

'Your ears are pierced but you never wear earrings.'

'My last pair disappeared in Guatemala. I haven't gotten around to replacing them.'

The doors opened again at the eighth floor and he led her out and into the stairwell. It was dark and fetid and he took her hand for the climb. His skin was warm against hers. Every sensory organ in her body seemed suddenly connected to her hand.

When they reached the metal door at the top he had to slam his shoulder against it repeatedly before it would open.

'I think I prefer the fire escape,' she said.

They stepped out onto the roof and he did not release her

278

hand. Overhead hung a brilliant crescent of moon. *The moon looks down over us, body, mind, and spirit, shedding light and leading us along the path. But it also signifies darkness, deception, and terror. Unforeseen perils.*

'What are you thinking about?' Isaac asked.

'I just had the most bizarre experience. And it was my own fault. I should have gone to dinner but instead I stepped into Madame Zora's psychic parlor.'

'You mean you haven't had dinner?' Isaac asked with concern.

'I'm not really hungry,' she lied.

'You have to eat. I could eat something, too.'

He looked down at the streets below as though measuring distances, and she had to laugh. 'Think someone will deliver take-away up here?'

He smiled one of his slow half-smiles. Gentle yet teasing. It made her breath catch.

'Sit right here,' he said, indicating the wall of the stairwell. 'I'll be back with food in ten minutes. Then I want to hear all about Madame Zora and California and whatever else you want to tell me.'

'Where are you going?'

'To a Cuban-Chinese place. Just two blocks over and very fast at take-out.' He started toward the fire escape then turned back to look at her. 'You will wait, won't you?'

She pressed her back against the stairwell wall and let herself slide down into a sitting position. 'I won't move. I promise.'

She watched him swing over the parapet and listened to the faint metal twang as he descended. The fact that he'd taken the fire escape inside of going back inside the building seemed completely natural. She wouldn't have questioned it if he'd spread his long Russian officer's coat and flown down.

She leaned her head back and studied the moon,

looking for that solemn female face she'd seen in the moon on the tarot card. The more she thought about it the more it seemed that that face had resembled the stone portrait of Moonsmoke. Could that be possible or was it all in her imagination? *The Moon is a powerful card representing the emergence of latent spiritual powers, of intuition and imagination.*

'Right,' she said aloud, wishing she could forget the stupid cards.

Cuban-Chinese. She had never tasted such a thing. She had never had a man so concerned about her missing dinner.

*I want to hear about Madame Zora and California and whatever else you want to tell me*, he had said. And she couldn't wait to tell him. Tonight she would tell him about her father and the police and her long-missing mother. And about the stupid Tarot cards.

*Exposure, trust, and, of course, choice.*

Yes. She would tell him everything.

# Sixteen

Iris was brought out of a dream about her mother. It was something frightening, though she lost the sense of it immediately and was left only with an image of Clary Lanier, shiny dark brown hair, flawless unlined skin, hypnotic eyes. A young woman. Younger than Iris was now. Her mother never aged in her dreams. She was always beautiful and young. Suspended somewhere in time.

The shrilling sounded again. She sat up. What was that? The telephone!

Heart racing, she scrambled off the bed and fumbled for the receiver. Who else but the hospital would be calling her so early in the morning.

'Yes! Hello!'

Silence.

'This is Iris Lanier. Hello! Hello!'

'You're the daughter?' asked a cautious female voice.

'Yes. Is this the hospital? Has something happened?'

No reply. Iris could hear soft breathing.

'Who is this?'

'I'm the girl you're looking for. I was with him.'

'What?'

'Your father is the one who got shot, right?'

'Yes! You were with him?'

'Sort of. I mean I heard the shot and I saw him fall and I ran over there. I stayed with him till the ambulance came.

That oughta be worth something, huh. Like a reward or something?'

'Did you see who did it? Could you—'

'Hey, I ain't answering no more questions on the phone. My time is valuable. And none a this is for the cops. I lose my memory real fast around cops.'

'OK. Do you want to meet?'

'This afternoon. Washington Square Park. Four o'clock. Got that?'

'Yes, but couldn't we meet this morning?'

'Four o'clock. That's when I can be there.'

'OK. How will I find you?'

'I'll find you.'

'How? Do you know what I look like?'

'My friend told me.'

'That park will probably be crowded.'

'Yeah. Yeah, so maybe you should carry something . . . something like . . . a pink purse.'

'I don't have a pink purse.' She thought for a moment. 'I could buy something pink.'

'Yeah. OK. Flowers. Bright pink. And you just wait around till I talk to you. I'll be checking it out real careful so you better make sure it's not a setup or something.'

'Don't worry. I promise I'll be there alone. But how will I know for certain that it's you?'

The woman was silent. Breathing. Thinking.

'Cookie. I'll say that first thing. And don't forget your money. I don't say nothin' about nothin' without a reward.'

Iris lay back down but could not sleep. Finally she got up and decided to go to the hospital. Just as she was ready to leave there was a knock at the door. She looked out through the peephole and saw a distorted version of Mitchell Hanley's face. She stood there, silently, hoping he would go away.

'I've got your beeper for you,' he called as if aware of her presence. 'Andretti told me you were back.'

She had forgotten about the beeper. How could she ignore him when he had gone to so much trouble? She opened the door. His freshly combed hair was still damp enough that it appeared brown rather than dark blond and he was surrounded by a cloud of expensive cologne.

'These are for you,' he said, extending a bouquet of daisies. 'You had me worried. I didn't know where you'd gone or whether you were coming back.'

She accepted the flowers, wishing they were pink, thinking about the pink flowers she had to buy later in the afternoon for her meeting with Cookie. So many hours to wait. Four o'clock seemed like forever.

'I was just leaving for the hospital,' she said.

'I'm kind of in a hurry too. I've got to get to class.' He handed her the beeper.

'When a call comes in for you this will flash.' He turned the small black plastic rectangle over in her hand and indicated a sticker on the back that was printed with a phone number. 'All you do is check in at this number and the answering service will tell you who called and how to reach them. There's a trick with your phone too.' He handed her an instruction sheet. 'You can set it up so any unanswered calls to your number here are automatically forwarded to the answering-service number and then they beep you.'

She examined the little black box. 'I thought these things just flashed a digital readout of your caller's number.'

'That's a different kind. Takes weeks to get one of those because that involves actually hooking into a system where your beeper has its own phone number.'

'OK. Thank you.' She smiled. 'How much do I owe you?'

'You'll get a bill from the service.'

'There was no deposit or startup fee or anything?'

'No. I got it from a friend.' He grinned in his most engaging boyish manner. 'I'm leaving now too. Can I walk you to the subway? Maybe buy you a take-away coffee from the deli?'

She hesitated, but given the favor he had just done for her, there seemed no graceful way to decline. 'I'll put these flowers in water and be right out.'

'You could take them to the hospital,' Mitch suggested. 'That way you'll have flowers in your father's room.'

'Good idea.' She cradled the bouquet in one arm as she locked her door. Then she dropped the keys in her shoulder bag and went with Mitch to the elevator.

On the way down Mitch worked hard to entertain her. His efforts only made her more uncomfortable. She could tell that he was going to be hurt or angry or both when he finally realized that no amount of charm was going to win her over.

Suddenly she thought of Isaac and she had a complete whole-body reaction. Like an all over flush with a catch in her chest and a flutter in the pit of her stomach. God, this was crazy. They'd never even kissed. What would happen if they made love? Would she be passing out at the thought of him? But then it occurred to her that maybe sex would be the cure. Maybe if she slept with him she would be able to put him out of her mind.

'Ta dah!' Mitch sang as the elevator finally settled to a halt and creaked open. He stepped forward, bowed, and waved her out with a playful flourish.

Beyond him Iris saw the mail carrier crossing the lobby. 'Excuse me!' she called out, and hurried past Mitch.

The woman stood by the locked grill that housed the mailbox area, watching Iris's approach with a neutral expression. The superintendent's door opened and Andretti came out, stopped as though surprised, and then rushed toward the mailboxes.

'I'm early,' the carrier announced. 'Had to do my route backward today.'

'I'm glad I caught you,' Iris told her. 'I've been worried about the mail. You see I'm staying in John Lanier's room, 602. My name is Iris Lanier. Is there a form I should fill out or—'

'Hey, let me take care of this,' Andretti insisted. 'What's a super for, huh? You go on to see your father and I'll handle it.'

The mail carrier regarded them both with impatience. 'There's nothing to handle,' she said. 'In a transient building like this we go strictly by room numbers.' She shuffled through the bundle of mail in her hand. '602 you said?'

'Yes. But I haven't received anything yet. There's been no mail at all in the box since I moved in. Not even junk mail. That's why I thought . . .'

'You going to give me some room?' the mail carrier asked Andretti.

The super was blocking the entrance to the alcove that housed the little brass mail boxes.

'It's gettin' late,' Andretti said to Iris. 'You're usually at the hospital by now, aren't you?'

'Move your ass!' the mail carrier demanded and Andretti reluctantly stepped aside. The woman shot him a look that left no doubt as to her low opinion of him, then pushed her mail cart ahead of her into the alcove. She still hadn't responded to Iris and she didn't look as though she would. Her attention was riveted on sorting through the bundle of mail she held.

Iris glanced at Mitch, shrugged, and turned to leave.

'Here,' the mail carrier announced. '602. Don't say you never got anything from me.'

Iris hurried back to take the envelope. It was addressed to John Lanier. The return was a bank in Manhattan. Probably just a credit card solicitation. But maybe not.

Maybe it was something. Iris stared down at it. After a moment she realized that Andretti and Mitch were also staring at her, or watching her stare at the letter, maybe even staring at the letter themselves. The mail carrier had moved on and was briskly stuffing mail into boxes, but the three of them were suspended.

Across the lobby, the door to the emergency stairs swung open and the biker emerged in one of his standard black uniforms. He hesitated when he saw them. For a moment she thought he was going to stop and join the tableau. Then he veered off toward the mail alcove.

'It's getting late,' Iris said to no one in particular. She stuffed the unopened letter into her shoulder bag and started toward the front door.

Mitch hurried to catch up with her. Damn. She had said she'd walk with him to the subway but now she desperately wanted privacy so she could open the letter.

They walked in silence until they reached the deli.

'Here we are,' Mitch said, and held the door open for her.

She was trying to think of a way to get rid of him when he suddenly looked at his watch. 'You know, I hate to do this, but I've really got to run. I'm late for class. Rain check on the coffee, huh?'

'Sure,' she said.

She stood inside the glass door, watching him spring toward the subway stop. She wanted to rip the letter open immediately, but that impulse was tempered by an ill-defined anxiety. What if the letter contained damning evidence against her father? Kizmin had asked about her father coming into large sums of money. What if this letter from a bank was about dirty money?

'You shopping, lady?' asked the tiny storekeeper in nervous, accented English.

'Yes, yes,' Iris assured the woman.

She grabbed a carton of juice from the cold case and

hurried to the counter. With the bouquet of daisies cradled in her left arm she shrugged her bag off her shoulder one-handed and tugged it open. The letter was right there. Waiting. Her hand shook as she fished awkwardly for her wallet. When she pulled it out the letter came too and fluttered to the floor. She dove after it, dropping the flowers and knocking a display of plastic-wrapped muffins from the counter in the process.

'I'm so sorry,' she repeated several times as she rescued muffins and flowers and piled them on the counter.

The clerk was staring at her with an expression of annoyance and suspicion.

'I really am sorry.' Iris picked up several of the muffins. 'I'll take these too.'

She handed over a twenty. The woman behaved as though she was afraid to take her eyes off Iris long enough to take change from the register. Nervous, Iris dropped her wallet back into her shoulder bag and gathered the letter and the flowers. 'Come on,' she muttered to herself as the woman slowly counted the change out onto the countertop between them.

Two police officers came in through the door as the clerk was handing Iris the plastic bag containing her purchases. The woman's face lit at sight of them. Quickly Iris scooped her change into the plastic shopping bag and headed for the door. She could just imagine the clerk accusing her of something and the officers hassling her. Demanding to see the contents of her bag and her purse. Confiscating the long white envelope.

But no one pursued her and when she was out in the open, striding down the crowded sidewalk toward the subway, she wondered at her attack of paranoia. Maybe she was catching whatever Kizmin had. A paranoid virus or something.

She hesitated at the top of the subway stairs. Mitch was probably gone so there was no reason not to go down.

There were benches against the wall. She could huddle there and read the letter.

Downstairs the platform was jammed with commuters fighting their way to work. Iris edged through the impatient crowd, steering her way toward the far wall where she had seen the benches. Suddenly she was jerked backward and a pain shot through her shoulder. 'Watch it!' the man behind her shouted and her first thought was that he was yelling at her for stumbling into him. Her second thought was that her shoulder bag was gone.

She whirled around in time to see a tall man in a jogging suit with her purse clutched to his chest.

'Get him! Get him!' the man behind her shrieked at no one in particular.

She lunged forward, shoving through the wall of people who were all turned, watching the man run away with her purse as if they were spectators at an impromptu entertainment. The thief hit an oncoming wall of people at the turnstile and had to push his way forward. She hurtled toward him, through the open space created in his wake, got close enough to grab at the back of his jacket with her fingertips.

'Give me my purse,' she shouted and beat him over the head with the bouquet of daisies. Then suddenly she was sprawled on the concrete on her hands and knees. Someone or something had tripped her.

'You OK, lady?'

'Hey, you OK?'

Hands reached for her but she pushed them away and jumped up. The man with her purse hit the stairs and sprinted upward, taking them two at a time. People shied back from him, giving clear passage to his escape. Except for one man. Behind him. Running after him. Someone was trying to help.

Iris scrambled through the turnstile and plowed her way to the stairs. The crowd was not intimidated by her. No one moved back so she could run up the stairs unimpeded. By the time she made it to the top the man with the purse was gone. The pursuer was there though, bent over, breathing heavily and cradling a bloody hand.

'Which way did he go?' she scanned the avenue and cross street but saw no sign of him.

'It's no use. He jumped on a bus.'

She raised her face to the sky and blew out several hard, angry breaths. Then she sagged against the railing, weak-kneed in the wake of the adrenalin surge. The purse was gone. Another statistic. Only it wouldn't even be that because she wouldn't bother to report it. She had had a purse stolen before, and she knew that reporting it to the police would be time consuming and utterly futile.

The Good Samaritan started to move away.

'Wait. I didn't get to thank you.'

He hesitated and she took stock of him. He was a conservatively dressed man whose close-cropped, nappy hair was more grey than black. An average man. A family man judging from the gold band on his left hand and the general look of him. A man with so much to lose, yet he had put himself at risk for a stranger. She was deeply touched.

'Did he hurt you?' she asked, indicating his hand.

'No. I slipped and fell.'

'Can I do anything?'

'It's just a scrape.' He kept his head down and did not meet her eyes. A modest hero. Then, without another word, he joined the crowd on the sidewalk and was gone.

As she re-entered the subway her mind raced through an inventory of her losses. Her visitor's pass to the hospital. Her room keys. Damn. Andretti would not be happy about that. Her sunglasses. Her wallet, with her driver's license and money inside. But the driver's license was expired anyway. And there hadn't been much money left. And she still had her passport and credit card back at the room.

Somehow she had managed to hang on to the plastic grocery bag. She shifted it and heard the jingle of coins. A lucky break. The change from the twenty was floating around in the bag so she still had some cash to get around. The lowlife hadn't gotten much profit for his efforts. That was some consolation.

The letter!

She froze, oblivious to the people pushing past her toward the turnstile. The letter. Oh God, the letter.

'Will ya move it, lady.'

Mechanically she let her feet carry her forward with the flow of the crowd. Through the turnstile and over the trampled daisies that littered the floor. Her father's letter was gone. It was gone. It was in her purse and – but wait. Wait. She'd scooped the change into the plastic bag and she'd had the letter in her hand and . . . She jerked open the plastic grocery bag and there it was, stuck between two crushed muffins, the long white envelope bearing her father's name.

An uptown train thundered into the station in a blast of sour, artificial wind and she hurried aboard. The platform no longer seemed like a good place to be. Wary and watchful, she chose a seat near the conductor's booth and hunched there, hugging the plastic bag to her chest. She had come so close to losing the letter.

The car was crowded. She was wedged into her seat without room to move, her shoulder jammed against the thigh of a man standing in the aisle next to her so that if she shifted at all she was in danger of contact with intimate parts of his anatomy. There was no way she could reach into the bag, fish out the letter, and open it without causing a major disturbance, yet she had to read it. She had come so close to losing the letter altogether. So close to never knowing.

Two stops later she bolted off the train and up the stairs into a small croissant bakery and café. The restroom was in the back, a single door marked simply BATHROOM. She locked herself into the tiny, dimly lit cubicle and pulled the letter out.

Mr John Lanier:

Thank you for choosing our bank for your safety-deposit-box rental. We have many services available and would like to have the opportunity to show you the ways in which our bank can help with your financial needs.

It was signed by an officer.

She read the paragraph several times. A safety deposit box. Her father had rented a safety deposit box from a bank in Manhattan. Why would he have needed a safety deposit box for his trip? He wouldn't have carried his will or other important documents with him. He didn't own jewelry.

She had a sinking, sick feeling. A safety deposit box could be used to hide large amounts of cash.

She noted the address of the bank, then put the letter away and stepped out of the bathroom. A pay phone was mounted on the wall next to the door and it occurred to her that she had better alert Andretti about the key to her room being stolen. There was no answer at his number. She bought a cup of coffee and tried again. Still no answer.

The bank was downtown. If she went there first she could stop by the Fitzgerald on the way.

She walked back to the building, telling herself that it was to save the subway fare, but relieved not to have to go down into the subway again so soon. When she arrived she realized that she no longer had a key to get in. To her relief, the front door was wedged open. She knocked on the superintendent's door but got no answer. The lobby was deserted. She rode the elevator to the basement to look for Andretti but he wasn't there either. For fifteen minutes she waited near his door, then she tried knocking again in case he'd been asleep or showering. She considered just leaving. But what if the thief found the building's address in her purse and came there with the keys? Such things weren't uncommon. She got back on the elevator and rode up to the seventh floor.

She knocked on the door to 702 and waited. It felt strange knocking on Isaac's door rather than his window. She had never been at his door before.

'Who is it?' came the muffled reply.

'It's Iris. I'm locked out of my room. My purse was stolen. I can't find Andretti. And I—'

Locks turned and the door opened a crack. One eye and a strip of Isaac's face appeared. The room was dark behind him.

'Oh, I'm sorry. I woke you up, didn't I?'

'Don't worry. What happened?'

'My purse was snatched in the subway. The keys were in it. Both the front door and my room.'

'Have you told the super?'

'That's the problem. I can't find him and I need to leave. I haven't even been to the hospital yet. I was wondering if you might possibly be able to give him the message for me later?'

'Of course. I'll get him to change the lock right away.'

'Great. Thanks.'

'Do you need anything else? Money to get around?'

'No. I'm fine.'

'Your hands are all scraped.'

She looked down at her palms. 'I fell in the subway. Trying to catch the guy.'

'You shouldn't have gone after him. That's very dangerous.'

'I know. I don't know what came over me.'

'He could have had a knife or a gun.'

'Well, I didn't scare him enough to make him use it. He just raced out of the station and vanished.'

She could hear faint sounds coming from inside his room. Something familiar.

'You have a computer set up in there?' she asked. 'Sounds like you're printing something.'

'Yes,' he said, as though ready to end the conversation.

He didn't have on his glasses. His eyes were naked. They were very clear, pure grey with a rim of dark charcoal. Funny, she hadn't noticed his eye color before. But then she had never really seen him in daylight.

He was her vampire lover. Only available after dark. And now he was trapped in daylight with her. And probably half-naked judging by the way he was peering out from around the cracked door.

'Well, thanks,' she said, smiling as she backed away. 'I'll see you later.'

On the way down to the lobby she wondered how he could sleep and run a computer printout at the same time.

The bank was jammed with people waiting in long snaking lines for a turn at one of the two teller windows. A large sign announced that teller windows had been closed in favor of customer service phones that would swiftly and conveniently provide access to a computerized service center. The phones stood in a row along the wall, with no customers using them.

Iris looked around for someone to question about the safety deposit boxes. There was an information desk but it too bore a closed sign with a reminder about the convenient computer that would help via telephone. Finally, Iris saw a small arrow on a plaque with the message that said safety deposit boxes were downstairs.

'Can I help you?' the woman behind the counter asked curtly as Iris approached.

'I'm not sure how to handle this,' Iris admitted. She pulled out the letter. 'This came for my father.'

The woman skimmed it then frowned. 'Is there a problem?'

'Yes. My father is hospitalized. Unable to take care of his own business.'

'You can pay the box rental for him.'

'But can I get access to the box?'

'Not without a court order. And if your father . . . if the box holder should become deceased, then the contents of the box are seized and examined before release.'

'I see. Does my father have a key?'

'Yes. And if it's lost then he'll have to file a request to have the box drilled open. That's an extra charge and my manager would have to take care of it.'

'When did my father rent the box?'

The woman hesitated and frowned again but consulted her records. 'All I can tell you is that he's a new customer and his rental fee is due next week.'

'Do you have records that show when he visited the box?'

'Yes. But I can't give out that information.'

'Can you tell me whether he's been in at all since he opened it. Please. It's very important.'

The woman gave an overblown sigh of exasperation, but flipped through a log. 'I don't see anything,' she said curtly and Iris knew better than to push for more.

Several customers had lined up behind her so Iris paid the rental, thanked the clerk, and stepped aside, uncertain what to do next. She picked up a bank pamphlet and pretended to read while she watched a man produce a small brass key and give his name. The clerk had him sign the log, then took a signature card from a file and compared it for identification. That was it. The key and a signature.

294

All the way uptown to the hospital Iris wrestled with the new questions. If her father had a safety deposit key, where was it? There had been no small brass key in his personal effects.

The locked box held the answers. She was certain of it. At home her father kept his important papers in cardboard boot boxes on the closet shelf. He had never been concerned about deeds or birth certificates or titles or any of the other paperwork of modern life. For him suddenly to rent space in a bank vault in New York meant that he had something vital to protect. Or something terrible to hide.

She was determined not to bring the police into it, not before she knew what the box contained. But without the authorities how would she ever get access to the box?

Even with all that had happened it was still morning when she finally arrived at the hospital. It took her nearly an hour to get a replacement visitors pass. Not only had the thief gotten her purse, he was stealing time from her too.

'The phone in there was ringing a few minutes ago,' one of the ever-present floor cleaners told her as she was going in to her father's room.

'Are you sure it was the phone in my father's room?' Iris asked him.

He shifted his wide broom. 'Yeah. I'm sure.'

She went inside. The room was so familiar to her now that she was barely aware of the smells and the monitor sounds. Her father had been arranged on his side. His eyelids were fluttering erratically and a facial tic had developed near one corner of his mouth.

'Hello.'

Someone had changed the bedside radio to a Latin music station and she turned back to public radio. It didn't matter how many notes she left or how many times she mentioned it to the nurses – the radio was always changed.

At least she had finally gotten the television disconnected and she didn't come in to find him trapped with that anymore.

She sighed and pulled the plastic chair into position. The topic on the radio program was something to do with racial categorization. The guest expert didn't like the way the government was labeling people. Iris tried to follow the arguments for and against. Race was a confusing issue for her. Using it to categorize seemed meaningless because the real differences between peoples were cultural differences. They weren't inborn. They were learned.

Yet, as a physical anthropologist, she had been taught to group skeletons into distinct racial categories – Caucasoid, Mongoloid, and Negroid. So she was faced with a dichotomy. She believed that, under the skin, down deep where it counted, people were more similar than different. But when she was examining a skeleton she used race as an indicator.

She still remembered how disturbing she had found this in college. So much so that she had been ready to change her major. Then her advisor, a wise and patient man, had taken her into the lab and put human bones into her hands. He had shown her the subtle indicators that put a skeleton in one racial category or another. He had said there was nothing wrong with people being different. Then he had rearranged the skeletons, separating them by gender rather than race.

'Now look, Iris,' he had told her. 'The sum total of all the racial variations is insignificant when compared with the biggest division of all – the differences between male and female. The skeletal anatomy of a man varies dramatically from that of a woman. Is there anything wrong with that? I should hope not. Our differences make life glorious. Our differences make the continuation of the species possible.'

'But in our hearts and our minds we're the same,' she had insisted with youthful naiveté.

'Ah,' he had said with total seriousness. 'My field is physical anthro. I'm afraid I can't speak to hearts and minds.'

Over the years she had reconciled herself to seeing racial patterns, but she liked to be fooled. She delighted in skeletons that she could not classify. And she reminded herself that gender was far more divisive than race could ever be.

The speaker on the radio argued that the very act of labeling could be divisive and there would be no labels in a perfect world. But then, in a perfect world, her youthful beliefs would be true – people would be the same in their hearts and minds. That certainly wasn't the case in the imperfect world she lived in. Pain and anger, bitterness and despair. Those could go deep. Bone deep. Scarring hearts and minds so that human connection, that human similarity was gone.

Iris turned off the radio. She had too much to think about already. She couldn't stand more.

'I can't figure it out,' she said aloud. She grabbed her father's hand and squeezed hard. 'What were you doing?'

There was no response. Not a twitch.

Dr Milford poked his head in the door and beckoned her out into the hall.

'Glad to see you're more comfortable with him. That's good. He might sense that.'

Iris kept her doubts to herself.

'We're going to have to make long-term care plans if this keeps up. You understand that, don't you?'

'Yes.'

'This could go on and on.'

'You've made that clear, doctor.'

'And even if he should regain some level of awareness, he's not going to jump out of bed and function normally.

We're looking at months of therapy.'

'I understand.'

'Yes, well . . . good.' A look of puzzlement came over his face and he stared off over her shoulder. She turned but didn't see anything. 'We'll talk again,' he said and hurried away down the hall.

She went back into the room. 'What should I do?' she asked the silent figure in the bed.

At two o'clock she told him goodbye and went back to the hotel. She had to get her new keys and pick up her bank card and credit card, then go to a bank machine to get cash for the 'reward' she had promised to the woman she was meeting in Washington Square Park.

Andretti was in the lobby. He gave her two new keys and said that the locksmith had just left.

'I had them upgrade the lock,' he said. 'Just for you.'

'Thanks.'

Iris escaped quickly into the elevator which was fortunately standing open. Andretti was unsettling. He had not made any passes at her. She hadn't even caught him studying her anatomy. But he was almost too friendly, too helpful, too interested in her welfare, and she was uncomfortable in his presence. He was, in a word, creepy.

The bright shiny brass of the new lock shone like gold in the dimly lit hallway. The tumblers slid smoothly when she turned the key. It was a good, heavy lock. Whatever Andretti's reasons for favoring her, she was grateful for the extra security.

She glanced at her watch. There was no time to waste. But she couldn't stop thinking about the safety-deposit key. Where was it? Had it been stolen? Had her father been shot for that key? If so, if the contents of the box were that important, then why hadn't the attacker faked his way into the box by now? Why hadn't there been any activity?

Maybe it had been stolen without the thief knowing what it was.

Or maybe it was still around. Still safely hidden somewhere. Maybe it was right there close to her.

She scrutinized the room, trying to imagine where her father might hide a little key. The room was so bare. And so neat. Funny, she didn't remember leaving it so neat. The bedspread was perfectly smooth and the pillows were aligned. Her haphazard bedmaking didn't usually yield such results.

Later, she would tear the place apart. That was the only solution. For now she had to go meet the woman who had witnessed her father's shooting.

She crossed to the dresser and opened the top left-hand drawer where she had put her mother's goodbye note, her airline tickets, receipts, passport, and bank cards, and she had to shake her head and blink several times before she believed it. Everything was meticulously arranged, aligned as perfectly as the pillows on the bed. She took out her bank-machine card and credit card and slammed the drawer shut. Then she picked up the phone.

'Mr Andretti?'

'Yeah.'

'This is Iris Lanier in 602. Did you let anybody in here while that lock was being fixed?'

'Not for a second,' he said, sounding offended at the suggestion. 'I watched that locksmith like a hawk and nobody else was around.'

'You didn't surprise me with some kind of maid service?'

'Why?' He chuckled. 'Did somebody break in and clean the place?'

She sighed involuntarily. 'I'm afraid the purse snatcher must have gotten in here before the lock was changed.'

'You missing stuff?'

'No. But someone has been in here. I guess there was nothing he wanted.'

'Thank God for small favors, huh?'

She hung up and turned to look at the room. It sent a chill through her to know that a stranger had been there, invading her privacy. But Andretti was right; she should be thankful that he hadn't taken her passport or her plastic. And now she had the new lock to protect her so he wouldn't get in again. She shoved the cards in her pocket and let herself out. But on the way to Washington Square it struck her – the burglar had gone through things and then taken great pains to tidy up. Why? So she wouldn't know he'd been there?

Why would an ordinary burglar care about concealing a break-in?

# Seventeen

Washington Square Park was more a square than a park. It was a magnet for all manner of people – students from nearby NYU, residents of the Village, and those who wished they were a part of NYU or the Village. Today it had a carnival atmosphere. It was jammed with people watching musicians, mimes, and jugglers on unicycles, everyone out to enjoy Friday afternoon and the start of the weekend. Iris walked the perimeter, clutching the bouquet of unnaturally pink carnations that she'd bought from a street vendor, and questioning whether she should have called Kizmin before the meeting. But she hadn't heard from Kizmin since the detective had been taken off the case and she was determined not to contact the woman unless driven to do so.

The mild weather was still holding and people were out to enjoy the sun. A number of the Roller-Bladers zipping around had peeled off their jackets and were down to T-shirts. She passed an elderly woman sharing a hot dog with a dachshund and a young man feeding a soft pretzel to a big, brightly colored parrot. The bird was secured with a leash that attached to one leg, but he sat on the man's shoulder, tearing at the pretzel, as though he had no interest in escape.

Iris watched the parrot, wondering if it had come from the forests of Guatemala, hoping that it was instead a hand-raised domestic bird.

'He knows you're looking at him.' The man smiled and moved several steps closer to her. 'He's very conceited and he especially likes attention from pretty girls.'

Iris had to restrain herself from rolling her eyes. 'How long have you had him?'

'A couple of years. I got him for a steal because he was so unmanageable. A regular psycho bird. I think it's because he was brought in from the wild.' He stroked the parrot's chest with the back of a finger. 'You were a rough, tough, mean machine weren't you, Jerko? But that's all over now. He's my buddy now. He's used to city life.'

'Is he?'

'Sure. Look at him. How much happier could a bird get?'

Iris looked at the parrot but didn't say anything. She wasn't against pets. She wasn't even against parrots as pets. But the idea of one of those darting, soaring, arrogant forest creatures netted and fighting and having to settle for life on a leash begging for food made her sad.

'I'm surprised he didn't die,' she finally said.

'Yeah, well, it took a lot of patience. A lot of . . . you know . . . empathy.'

'Oh?'

'Yeah. It was tough. They're very intelligent creatures, you know. Way up on the animal IQ charts . . . right up there with dolphins. He's quite a character. Loves to ride in cars. Especially my Jag.'

The eye-rolling urge struck again but Iris just nodded and moved away.

'Hey,' the man called after her, but Iris kept going, continuing her circuit of the park, nerves strung tightly in her chest.

She held the absurdly dyed flowers in front of her like a bridesmaid and she studied the faces of people she passed. A prostitute, even one dressed in teasing streetwalker attire, would not stick out in this crowd. The college students were working too hard at outrageous costumes. Total nudity might have been noticeable, but that was the only state of dress or undress not represented.

The minutes ticked by. Someone jostled Iris's arm and she jumped. Where was the woman? Why didn't she make contact?

An hour passed. People's features began to blur. The crowd in the park was growing. The music was pounding at her head. Guitars and trumpets and steel drums all playing different songs. Each trying to drown out the other and attract a larger share of the audience. And there were radios, too. Dozens of boom-boxes blaring out rap and rock and salsa.

The woman wasn't coming. She was not coming. Screaming laughter erupted and Iris turned to look back. Was that Mitchell Hanley ducking through the trees? No. Of course not. She had to calm down.

A vendor's cart was parked near the entertainers' pit. She stopped to buy a cold drink. There were two women ahead of her in line. 'It's a full moon tonight,' one of them said. 'Do you think we should go?' Her companion shrugged. 'I'm really getting burned out on all this Satan stuff. Let's go to a movie instead.'

One of the women dropped some change as she was paying. Iris bent to retrieve it for her and when she straightened there was Clary Lanier, walking down a path, just beyond a grassy area. Her mother. Just like in the dream. Iris stepped over a small fence and ran after her.

'Hey! Give me my money!' came the shouts from behind her, but she ignored them. That was her mother moving just beyond the trees. Laughing. Long dark hair gleaming. Silver earrings ablaze in the sunlight. But then the woman turned and it wasn't her mother. It wasn't Clary Lanier at all.

303

'Get off the grass, stupid!'

Iris stepped back onto a path beside an old man dozing on a bench. Her appearance startled a flock of pigeons and they flew at her, wings beating so close that she had to cross her arms over her face.

'You're wrecking those nice flowers,' a voice said from nearby. It was a woman in short shorts and thigh-high spike-heeled boots with a cropped fake-fur jacket open over a low-cut stretch-lace top. Standard attire for the park.

Iris held up the flowers and examined them. They were a little bedraggled.

'You have someone in the hospital you're taking those to?'

Iris's head snapped up and she stared into the woman's face. She was a girl really. No more than eighteen or nineteen. With short spiky white hair. Her eyes were bloodshot and her skin had an unhealthy pallor in spite of layers of make-up. Her clavicles stood out in sharp relief above her low-cut top.

'I'm Cookie,' she said, glancing around warily.

'I'm Iris.'

'I was wondering if I should talk to you or not. I've been watching you and you're acting pretty bugged out.'

'I'm nervous,' Iris said defensively. She gave the flowers to a little girl who was being pulled by the hand behind a fast-walking woman. The child smiled in delight. It was a moment before the mother noticed.

'Drop those this instant!' The mother swatted the bouquet from the child's grasp.

'But Mommy . . .'

'Those could be contaminated or poisoned! They could have needles in them!'

'Fuck you lady!' Cookie shouted after them.

'Do you want to go somewhere quieter?' Iris asked.

Cookie's eyes narrowed. 'You think I'm stupid?' She

304

glanced around again. 'There. Those people are leaving. Let's sit on that bench.'

'I was afraid you weren't coming,' Iris said as they took the end spots on the bench.

'I been here. Watching you. Did you bring money?'

'I've got a hundred dollars.'

'That's all?' She huffed in disgust then sat back and crossed her arms.

'I don't even know if you're worth that much,' Iris said, trying to conceal her anxiety.

The girl turned and sullenly looked Iris over. 'I don't see a purse. You sure you got it on you?'

'It's in my pocket.'

'Don't you know ladies are supposed to have purses.'

'My purse was snatched.'

Cookie smiled as though she had suddenly recognized Iris as a friend. 'That's why I don't never keep nothing important in my purse. Just a few rubbers and a lipstick. If some fucker wants that he's welcome to it. But you can't give up and not carry a purse. That's so unladylike.'

'OK,' Iris said carefully.

'I seen that look you gave me when I said who I was. Like you were sorry for me. Well, I don't need that shit from your kind. Understand? I mean look at you.' Cookie swept her with a disdainful glance. 'You're dressed in boy's clothes. With no purse or jewelry or makeup. Bet you don't got a man.' Cookie waited a beat then chuckled. 'You don't. I can tell. Well I got me a fine man who takes real good care of me.'

'Cookie . . . please . . . I need to hear about my father.'

'Let's see it then,' the girl said slyly. She slid one hand down beside Iris's leg and rubbed her fingers together. 'Just give it to me nice and easy.'

Iris slipped the folded twenties from her pocket so that Cookie could see, then she closed her hand over them.

'Tell me about my father first.'

Cookie sniffed loudly, then ran a pointed tongue over her clown-red lips. 'It was a regular night. Real late. Pretty slow. I just got done with a drive around and the guy dropped me off near the park. I was strollin' along, looking for another customer, and I see this guy hanging around in the park. I could tell he wasn't no kind of pro or nothin', but he was kind of staying in the dark parts and I thought maybe he was shy . . . you know . . . wanting a date but shy about it. So, I walked over by him.

'And he kind of whispered, but it was almost like a growl, you know, like he was a wolf or something. He said, "Get out of here you filthy whore. Somebody should put a locket around your neck." Well, I was spooked. I mean, was he the Locket Killer or what? I didn't lose no time gettin' out of there.

'Then along comes this big guy walking down the sidewalk. So I says, "Lookin' for some fun?" and he says, polite as can be, "No thank you," like I was offerin' him a cup of tea of something.'

The girl paused and peered at Iris curiously. 'That was your dad, huh?'

Iris cleared her throat. 'Yes.'

'Well, he passed by me and started into the park like he knew right where he was going. Went straight to that guy out there. They talked for maybe a minute or two, then bang. He got it.'

'Did it look like the man was trying to rob him?'

'No. It looked like they were meeting, ya know? Like they planned it.'

'What did the other man look like?'

'Oh shit . . . it was real dark where he was hangin' out. From what I could see he was just sort of average. Medium everything.'

'Could you hear anything they said?'

'No.'

'Did you actually see the shooting?'

'Sort of. I mean not really, but it was kinda like they were just standing there talking, then they were wrestling, then boom. The big guy crumpled and the other one ran.'

'Try to remember something more about the man you saw.'

Cookie blew air upward so that it ruffled her uneven bangs. 'The guy was not big. Not small. White I think. Like I have this picture in my mind of whitish skin when he ran off. But he was wearing a knitted cap and all that so it was hard to tell.'

'And you're sure it was a man?'

Her brow furrowed in thought. 'I don't know . . . like . . . it seemed like a man, but he had on a puffy jacket and that cap and I guess it coulda been a woman. I guess a woman could have made her voice growl like that. I know some pretty mean women.'

'Did you call the ambulance then?'

'My girlfriend was up the street, so I yelled for her to go call, and I ran over to see how bad he was. I could tell he was alive but he didn't look too good so I stayed there with him till I heard the sirens coming. Ruined my pantyhose kneeling on the ground.'

'Thank you,' Iris said, swallowing hard against a sudden tightness in her throat.

The girl lowered her eyes. 'That's like the whole story. He didn't say nothin'. I tried to talk to him but he just sort of stared up at the moon the whole time.'

Iris nodded. 'Why won't you talk to the police?'

'Don't make me laugh. What I know won't make no difference. I can't ID the guy. And talkin' to the cops could get me hassled or killed or worse.' Cookie wiped her nose on the back of her hand. 'It's probably dumb to talk to you, but I needed the cash.'

'Thank you for staying with him.'

'Yeah, well I didn't want him to be alone. I mean, I

know there's supposed to be angels who come, but, just in case there isn't . . . I didn't want him to be alone.'

Silently, Iris handed over the money. Cookie hunched forward protectively to shield her financial gain. Iris watched her count the bills and refold them, then slip them into a clip. A silver money clip. Her father's missing money clip. How much had Cookie netted for her compassion that night?

The clip and the money disappeared inside the leopard-spotted jacket and Cookie grinned. One of her front teeth was chipped.

'You have my number,' Iris said. 'If you think of anything else . . .'

'Yeah, sure.' The girl bent to adjust the thin chain on her boot. Her top gaped open. There was a garish tattoo of the Virgin Mary between her thin breasts.

Iris watched the girl sway off into the crowd on her three-inch heels. Should she follow? It would be easy. But what would it accomplish? She was convinced that Cookie had told the truth.

For some time Iris sat on the bench, staring at nothing. Her father had flown to New York, rented a safe-deposit box, and met someone in Riverside Park at two in the morning. Why? She had to keep going until she knew. But she dreaded the answers.

Even when she hated her father, she had believed him to be perfect. So unswervingly honest and ethical that he loomed before her like something carved from rock. He had driven twenty miles to return fifty cents to a store clerk who gave him too much change. He had notified his bank that they forgot his service charge one month. And she would never forget the Christmas that the beautiful ham came. She'd been home alone and had accepted it. When her father returned he packaged it right up and took it away, returning it because he said that if he took a gift from a supply company then he would feel obligated to use their products on his orchard. Never mind that he already used their products. That he'd been using their dormant oil spray for years.

She pressed her fingertips against her temples and closed her eyes. What next? What the hell should she do next?

A chirping sound started somewhere close. She sat up straight and looked around. The other people on the bench were staring at her. The beeper! She jerked it off her belt and turned it off, then ran to a pay-phone and called the page operator. There was no message. Just a number.

'This is Iris Lanier,' she said as soon as the ringing was answered.

'Surprise! It's Mitch. Thought I'd give your beeper a test.'

She sagged against the cubicle wall. 'Hi, Mitch. It works fine. Thanks again for setting it up.'

'No problem. Have you had dinner yet?'

'I just had pizza,' Iris lied. It was so easy to lie on the phone with the other person far away.

'Oh. That's too bad. How about—'

'I'm on a street phone, Mitch, and I can barely hear.' This was great. She was going to like the beeper. It opened up whole new possibilities.

'Yeah. Right.' He sounded bitterly disappointed.

'I'm sorry . . . Maybe I'll see you tomorrow morning. We can walk to the subway together.' She shook her head and slapped her forehead with her palm. Why had she said that?

Shadows lengthened into darkness and she walked until she lost track of where she was. Everything seemed so hopeless. She had no idea what to do next. And she had to go to Guatemala soon. That was a promise she had to keep.

309

She came upon a store painted with wild Day Glo designs, stopped, and looked in the window. Every bit of space was crammed with clutter. Howdy Doody dolls and Roy Rogers cap-guns and Flash Gordon space-rays. Lava lamps and Barry Goldwater buttons and carnival glass dishes. Old beaded dresses hung from hooks in the ceiling, draped with fur capes that had the heads and paws attached. New York. Why hadn't she seen all this when she was living in the city? And what had Linda meant about her sounding different? Was she changing?

Again she thought of Madame Zora's Tarot cards. So absurd, yet she could not get them out of her thoughts. *This card represents the past. That which has already been part of your experience.* She recalled again the black sky with the figure lying on the barren ground, pierced with ten swords. *The Ten of Swords signifies pain, disruption, tears, desolation, and ruin in your past experience.*

No. She refused to accept that. When she was eight and her mother left the world had been a terrible place for awhile, but she had overcome that. She had put it behind her. There had been no ruin. No desolation. And the pain and tears were hardly significant because they were the pain and tears of a child. Children were surface creatures. Adaptable and easily contented. She had been fed and clothed. She had still had a parent and a solid secure home. She had had a top-quality education.

Losing her mother had been hard. But many things in life were hard. Much of the earth's population faced death, disease, and starvation regularly. Compared to that, being abandoned by her mother was nothing. Nothing.

And what purpose did it serve to dredge up the past? What possible good could come from examining childish heartbreak? She was an adult now. She was a physical anthropologist. A scientist. A well-educated, experienced, dedicated, professional person. That was all that

310

mattered. Nothing in the past was important.

Her beeper sounded again and she rushed to a street-corner phone. The chirping didn't alarm her quite as much this time but she was nervous as she returned the call.

'How's my brilliant anthropologist?'

'I'm sorry, I don't . . .'

'Ah, of course, I haven't said hello properly. This is Nathan Kaliker.'

'Mr Kaliker?'

'Yes. Yes. How is your father? I tried to reach you at the hospital without success.'

'He's the same. Thank you for asking.'

'I tried to reach you at your room as well, but all I got was pager forwarding.'

'I'm sorry I was difficult to find. I'm actually out on a street somewhere.'

'Somewhere?'

'Well, I've been walking. I can't quite see the street sign but I'm on Avenue D or C, I think. Near Fourth Street maybe.'

'Good Lord! I'll come pick you up immediately.'

'No, really . . .' But Iris surveyed her surroundings and realized that she had strayed into a questionable area.

'I won't accept a no. I happen to be calling you on the phone in my car and I insist that you let me pick you up and drive you to your destination.'

'Mr Kaliker . . . I . . .'

'I mean it. I insist. I'll be there in ten minutes.'

'OK. Hang on. The overhead light is broken and I have to go read the street signs.'

After Iris had reported her exact location to him and hung up the phone she retreated into a lighted doorway to wait.

'Hey . . . baby!' A man called to her from across the street and he made obscene gestures with his hands.

She regretted telling Nathan Kaliker that she would

wait. It seemed that moving on was a wiser course of action. But she waited, wondering how she would know which car was his. When the white limousine pulled up she stopped wondering.

'Hello, hello,' Kaliker called heartily as she climbed into the back of the limousine with him.

'This is very kind of you.'

'Well, I must say, this is very foolish of you.' He gestured toward the street. 'There are areas that are safe after dark for a woman such as yourself, and there are areas that are to be avoided.'

'Yes. I wasn't thinking.'

Kaliker smiled.

Iris was very uncomfortable. She had admired Nathan Kaliker for so long, had held an ideal of him in her mind for so long, that it was hard to accept his human frailties. His intimacy with Kizmin, his emerging political persona, and his preference for the trappings of the rich at the same time that he was championing justice for the poor and downtrodden – all of it was disturbing for her.

'Would you like something to drink?' he asked, opening a built-in service bar with a tiny refrigerator and ice-dispenser.

Iris shook her head, thinking about how ice was such a luxury in Guatemala but here people had it in their cars.

'I need to return those clothes that I was loaned for the fundraising dinner,' she said. 'But I've called the foundation and no one seems to know anything about it.'

Kaliker chuckled. 'That's my own little project,' he said. 'My personal assistant arranged that. Did you like them?'

'Yes. Very much. But how do I make the return?'

'You didn't really think that I wanted them back, did you?'

'But . . . it was supposed to be a loan.'

'Don't be concerned. The expense was nominal. Just part of putting on a function.' He smiled.

'I can't accept a gift like that.'

'Don't be ridiculous, Iris. What am I going to do with the clothes if you give them back? They certainly can't be returned to the store. You did me the favor of attending my function and I did you the favor of supplying you with suitable clothing. Period. Now, we have more important things to discuss.'

Kaliker's expression turned serious. 'I know the full story about your father,' he said, 'and I know about the police shuffling it into the mugging file. You shouldn't have tried to handle this by yourself, Iris.'

She stared at him, too surprised to reply immediately.

'I have influence in this city. Whatever you want to do, whichever direction you want to take this – I can facilitate your efforts.'

Her first reaction was to clutch at his offer and shift all the burdens from her own shoulders to his, but she dismissed that immediately, annoyed at her own momentary weakness. She could not ask Nathan Kaliker to fight the monsters or face the difficulties for her. She already owed him a debt that she could never repay. She would not multiply that debt.

'Thank you for offering,' she said. 'But I think I've taken it as far as it can go. I've been to California and searched through the house. I've even talked with a witness to the shooting.'

'A witness?' He appeared to be stunned by this news. 'Have you told the police?'

'No. She's a prostitute and she won't go near the police. There would be no point to it, anyway, because she can't furnish a helpful description of the attacker. It was dark. She couldn't see him well. And even his voice was disguised. He spoke to her in a whisper, or as she described it, a growl.'

'He spoke to her?' Kaliker asked. 'This is a travesty! You have a witness the police couldn't find and now they aren't even interested!'

'I wouldn't say I *have* her. She contacted me and we met

313

in a park this afternoon. I wouldn't know how to find her again. And if I did, she made it clear that she has nothing to say to the police.'

'Do you think she's reliable?'

'Yes.'

'And what else? Has our Detective Kizmin managed to scrape up anything new?'

Iris wanted to say, *Why don't you ask her yourself?* but didn't. 'I'm not to call her unless there's an emergency, but I doubt she's scraped up anything. I think she was serious about following orders.'

'You know you can be perfectly frank with me, Iris.'

'I am. I haven't spoken to her since she told me that she was off the case.'

Kaliker nodded. 'That's probably for the best. She might feel duty-bound to repeat whatever you told her to her superior officers.'

Iris glanced over at him, wondering if that were true.

'And beware of who else you share your confidences with. If your private little investigation gets back to the police they might be very upset with you.'

'I am naturally reticent about sharing confidences, Mr Kaliker. You don't need to worry about that.'

He patted the back of her hand in a paternal way. She wondered if that was how it had started with Kizmin.

'You know there are other options open to you, Iris.'

'What do you mean?'

'It would be quite easy to arrange a jet, with the proper medical equipment and personnel on board, and to move your father to a facility close to his home. Then you could simply forget all this ugliness. After all, whatever you do, however successful you are in tracking down his assailant – it's not going to cure him, is it? It's not going to erase that bullet's damage from his head. It's not going to undo what happened. And, whatever it was that made him buy that gun and make his journey,

314

might be best left unexamined. Sometimes parents have things in their lives that they don't ever want their children to be exposed to.'

'Are you saying I should give up?'

'Oh, Iris, that's such a negative term – give up. I've lived enough years to have learned that sometimes we simply need to accept what has happened and concentrate our efforts on living with it. Fighting shadows can become an obsessive and ultimately destructive activity. Sometimes we simply need to put what has happened behind us and go forward.'

'Yes, I've been doing that my whole life.'

'You understand what I'm saying then.'

She nodded.

'Call me when you're ready to take him home. We'll find the best facility out there.'

'I'll think about it,' she said.

The limousine dropped her at the Fitzgerald and she watched it pull away into traffic. Nathan Kaliker was not the man she had imagined him to be. But then she felt a stab of guilt. What great things had she done with her wonderful education? Who was she to judge a man like Nathan Kaliker?

He was still a hero. Without him, thousands of bright young people would not have had the opportunity for a quality education. Without him, there would be no foundation to help crime victims or fight the battles of those with no resources.

Mr Andretti was in the lobby when she entered and he hurried toward her as though he had been waiting for her arrival.

'Some wheels,' he said. 'We don't get many tenants who are dropped off in limousines.'

'Hello, Mr Andretti. I really appreciate that good lock you put on my door.' She kept walking toward the elevator and he fell into step beside her.

'No problem. Glad to do it. How is your father doing?'

'The same.'

'Does this mean he's not going to come out of it?'

'The doctors don't know.'

Iris pushed the elevator button, hoping it was nearby.

'How was California?'

'Fine.'

'Any news about anything? I mean . . . have they got any leads on the guy who shot him?'

Iris turned to look more closely at Andretti. Did everyone know her business?

'Exactly what are you asking?' she said.

'Well . . . I'm just worried about whether the police are after the lowlife who plugged your dad. I live in this city too, you know. And I believe in stricter laws. More crime control.'

'Unfortunately, the man who shot my father may never be caught. There's very little evidence to go on.'

Andretti grimaced, almost as though he had a physical pain somewhere. 'The stupid cops,' he muttered, and Iris had the impression he would have said more but the elevator opened and she escaped.

The building seemed very quiet. She glanced down at her watch. Eight o'clock on a Friday night. Everyone was out having fun somewhere. As she put her key in her new lock she thought of Isaac. There was no music. Maybe he was out somewhere on a job.

She switched on the light and saw a piece of paper on the floor. It was a note that had been slipped under the door.

Iris,
Go to my window. Left something there for you on the sill.

Isaac

Quickly she went out onto the fire escape and up to his window. There, peeking out from under his blinds, was a small box with a ribbon tied around it.

The room was dark but she tapped on the glass and called his name anyway. There was no answer. She bent down, slipped her fingers into the two-inch gap, and pushed the edge of the blinds sideways a little, but she could see nothing. The room was totally black.

'Isaac,' she called again, wondering if he was asleep, but there was no sound or movement in response.

She carried the box back to her room, untied the ribbon, and opened it. Inside was another note, folded into a small square.

I couldn't resist. Please accept.

Smiling to herself she lifted out a small velvet pouch. Attached to the pouch's drawstring was a tiny parchment envelope. She loosened the drawstring and poured the contents into her hand. Earrings. Unusual silver earrings set with iridescent blue-green stones that caught the light in remarkable ways.

She opened the tiny envelope and unfolded a certificate.

This certifies the authenticity of the Roman Glass used in this fine jewelry. The glass was discovered at an archaeological site and is two thousand years old. Tone and color in this ancient glass have been developed through the pressure and chemical reactions during burial since the time of the Roman Empire.

She went to the mirror and held the earrings up to her ears. The woman in the mirror smiled at her, eyes glowing with pleasure.

The phone rang.

'Hello, Iris Lanier speaking.'

'Hello. This is Stuart Hirano.'

'Oh . . .'

'I've come to Manhattan to talk with you. Can you see me?'

'Immediately?'

'Yes. I haven't had dinner yet. Have you?'

'No.'

'Would you join me?'

She hesitated, dread filling her. 'Yes. Where shall I meet you?'

'I'll send a car for you. We'll go to one of my favorite places. I always find that difficult subjects are less daunting in pleasant atmospheres.'

# Eighteen

The car that came for Iris was a basic car-service model, just one step above a taxi. Not at all the ostentatious transportation Nathan Kaliker favored. That struck Iris as ironic since Stuart Hirano was the one who had always seemed to her the limousine type.

She wore her dinner suit, which she would forever think of as Nathan Kaliker's suit. And she wore the Roman-glass earrings. Every time they brushed her neck she thought of Isaac.

Hirano's favorite place turned out to be the River Café, which was nestled at the base of the Brooklyn Bridge, on the Brooklyn side. The restaurant was on the water, quite literally, since it was a floating barge that was firmly anchored at the site.

Stuart Hirano was waiting for her at the bar when she arrived, and they were led immediately to a table before a sweep of glass that looked out on the lighted Manhattan skyline and the spangled dark water of New York Harbor.

'This is breathtaking,' she said as they were seated.

'Yes. It helps put things in proper perspective.'

The waiter took their drink orders and Iris stared out at the dark water that mirrored the lights of the city, at the city itself, at the distant shimmer of New Jersey and the stately stone arches of Roebling's great bridge. Stuart Hirano didn't speak and she wondered if he was reluctant to begin or if he was giving her the gift of time, letting her savor the visual feast and settle into the situation before he began.

Their drinks arrived and Hirano finally said, 'I've requested the tasting menu for both of us. That way we don't have to concern ourselves with choices.'

Iris nodded.

'Has there been any change in your father's condition?'

'No.'

Hirano nodded. 'We've had a family meeting. We want to bring him to the Bay Area where we can be of assistance to you, and to him when he begins to improve.'

'Thank you for the offer. Someone else has already offered to move him for me. I'm thinking about it.'

'But my father feels strongly that it's our place to arrange his care.'

'I'll let you know what I decide,' Iris said.

'In the interim I'll begin investigating the medical options available in our area.'

Iris didn't respond.

'That's not the reason I came to see you face to face, however.' He paused and looked out across the water for a moment. 'My son, Jeff, was caught trying to break into my secure computer files. He was after the name of a detective.'

'I'm to blame,' Iris said quickly.

'Yes. And you have caused more trouble than you can possibly imagine. But, it was Jeff's choice. His decision.'

Hirano paused for a moment, as though it was hard for him to continue.

'I asked him how . . . how could he do such a low and disrespectful thing? How could he bring so much shame on the family?

'And I expected him to cower like a dog, whining excuses and begging forgiveness, but instead he stood up to me. He said that I was the one who'd brought shame on the family. He accused me of trying to turn you away when you came for help and of lying to you about arranging a detective for your father. Then he said some things about his grandfather . . . accusing him of being evasive or misleading.

'He told me he was ashamed for me. And for his grandfather. He said he had to try to set things right.'

Stuart Hirano took a long drink of his Scotch.

'I went to my father then, and we decided that something had to be done.

'My father said . . .' Hirano swallowed stiffly. 'He said to tell you that he's been a foolish man. That his determination to honor his pledge to your mother blinded him to the fact that the child is the fruit of the same tree.

'Those were his exact words,' Hirano said. 'He wanted me to give you the message exactly.'

'But I don't understand what it means,' Iris said. A dark heaviness was spreading through her. She was afraid of what he might tell her. Afraid to know any more. But at the same time she wanted to know. She had to know.

'You'll understand everything after you hear the story. That's why I'm here. To tell you. Not by my own choice, though. I've come for my son and my father. To do what they feel is right.'

He took a drink of Scotch and composed himself.

'My father asked that I start by explaining about his debt. That part of the story begins during World War II when my father and his parents were sent away to an internment camp. My father has no bitterness about it.' Hirano shook his head as though contemptuous of his father's lack of bitterness.

'He's always said that he was born in America and he was glad to do whatever had to be done for the war effort, even if that meant being imprisoned. But while the Japanese immigrants and their American-born children were being sent away, California tightened its Alien Land Laws. My father and his parents were in danger of losing the land they'd worked so long and hard for.

'They would have lost it. But a man named Alesker stepped in. A man who remembered that his own ancestors had been persecuted in Russia before fleeing to this country.

'Alesker saved the Hirano farmland. He did it against the advice of his fellows in the business community and he suffered for his decision, but he never backed down. And after my grandparents and father were released from their internment, he helped them get started again.

'Needless to say my father felt an enormous indebtedness to this man. An indebtedness that was compounded by the man's death before my father could do anything significant to repay him.'

Appetizers were delivered to the table and Stuart waited until they were alone again before continuing.

'Now the story jumps ahead,' he said. 'I went away to my first year at Stanford. It was close enough that I could have commuted but of course I didn't. I'd had enough of being a farm boy.

'I became active in school. Forged a whole new life for myself. And I became well-known on campus.

'One day a girl came up to me and asked me where I was from. I told her. This didn't seem particularly unusual because, as I said, I had made a name for myself. But then she asked me if my father was Yoshi Hirano.

'That got my attention. I never talked about my farmer father to any of my friends at Stanford, and I couldn't figure out how she would know his name. She was evasive when I tried to question her . . . said she knew people who had grown up in my area – that kind of thing. I should have been more suspicious of her but I was young and she was good at distractions.

'She played me like a fish on a hook. Leading me on.

Using her looks. Teasing me with little bits of information – her first name but not her last, her home state but not her local address.

'I saw her a number of times . . . always on her terms. I would be walking along on campus and suddenly she would appear. Flirting. Teasing. Making me believe that she was interested in me. Then an acquaintance of mine spotted us together and he told me that she was living with an upperclassman off campus.

'The next time I saw her I confronted her and she admitted that it was true. Then she started to cry. Looked at me with those big dark eyes and said that I was the only friend she had. That she was completely alone and she was only seventeen and she wasn't even enrolled in school.

'She told me that she'd left home for good because her mother was dead and her rich father didn't care about her and she had a stepmother who hated her. She'd run away to California because she knew a boy who was studying at Stanford and she knew he'd take care of her. She said she didn't really love him. Had never loved him. And she wanted to get free of him but he wouldn't let her go. And she had no other place to go. The boy was supporting her.

'I fell for it completely. I thought that being her friend was a good start and would develop into more if I could just help her get away from the other boy. Our impromptu dates turned into absurd little sessions where she told me about her lover – sometimes saying that he was cruel and controlling, sometimes telling me what a great man he was going to be.

'She had me completely off balance. Trying to convince her to leave him . . . that she could make it on her own . . . thinking that any day, any day, I'd be the one she was sleeping with. But she insisted that she couldn't leave him. The reasons varied. She was afraid of him or she owed him too much or she couldn't make it on her own because she was still too young.'

323

Hirano frowned. 'Looking back I can't imagine why I was so taken with her. She was quite beautiful of course, but she had incredibly stupid ideas. Daydreams about joining the Peace Corps and all sorts of nonsense.

'Finally, one day she told me why she had sought me out in the first place. She said that her maternal grandfather had been friends with Yoshi Hirano. His name had been Alesker.

'I was stunned. Totally stunned.

'I had grown up hearing about Mr Alesker. He had sainthood in my household. I told her then that my father considered his debt unpaid and that he would welcome the chance to help an Alesker descendant. I suggested that he would be happy to find her a job or a college scholarship or whatever she needed to get a start on her own. She said she didn't know what she wanted to do, and she made me promise not to tell my father about meeting her.

'She missed several of our scheduled meetings and I assumed that she'd found another fool to buy her lunches. But then she reappeared and said she'd been in Berkeley. That she'd been driving back and forth because there was a new antiwar group forming. That the boy she lived with was starting a whole movement on his own and it was going to be called Red Phoenix.

'She was very excited. And she was back to talking about how great he was. How she was going to help him with his grand plans. And I woke up. I finally realized what her game was. From then on I avoided her . . . ducking behind walls when I saw her looking for me. Eventually she stopped trying to find me.

'I met Astrid then and I started to get serious about my life and my future.

'I realized how lucky I was to be rid of that girl and I put her completely out of my mind. Then, one day I heard that a bomb had exploded at a draft-board office near Berkeley, killing a child. A new group that no one had ever heard of was responsible. The group was called Red Phoenix.

'I was upset, worried that she would get caught and somehow I would be linked to her. I followed all the stories in the newspapers. A young man had also died in the blast, killed in the act of placing the bomb. Her live-in boyfriend I assumed. And I hoped that she had gone into hiding far away.

'The papers broke the news that the federal authorities were searching for a young woman who had driven the bomber to the scene. I knew of course that it was her. The description was vague, but I knew. It was hard to believe, with all her world peace, bleeding-heart ideas, that she would be part of a bombing, but it had to be her.

'I was so nervous about my connection to her that I had to get away from school and from Astrid so I drove to my father's for the weekend. I pulled into his drive and I looked up and there she was. My father was hiding her!

'I flew into a rage. I told him that he was breaking the law, that he was jeopardizing my future as well as his own. But he stood firm. He said that she was Alesker's grand-daughter and he would not turn her away.

'She tried to play on my sympathies again. Oh, she was filled with confusion and remorse, and terrible grief for the dead child. She swore to me that she hadn't known about the bomb, that she had thought she was giving the bomber a ride so that he could put up flyers about a protest. She insisted that Red Phoenix was supposed to be nonviolent.

'I asked why she didn't turn herself in and tell the authorities what she had told me. She said she was afraid they wouldn't believe her. Which was true, I suppose. Why should they have believed her? But then she admitted to me that there was more to her fear. She was pregnant and she didn't want to take the chance that she might be sent to prison and have her baby taken from her.

'I immediately assumed that she was carrying the dead bomber's child, but she told me I was wrong. She had met someone on her trips to Berkeley. A botany student. Someone she said was the exact opposite of the boyfriend she'd been trying to escape. She went on and on about him and how wonderful he was.

'I left and went back to school, furious at my father and at her, afraid of what might happen next. But nothing happened. The stories faded from the news and nothing happened.

'The next time I visited my father's house I learned that she had moved out and was living with her botany student in a garage apartment in a low-rent area. With some Hispanic woman and her no-good husband. Her student had quit his studies to be with her. No one recognized her as the girl who had been described in the papers. I further learned that my father had hired the botany student to work the orchard.'

Stuart Hirano drew in a deep breath and regarded Iris with a grave expression.

'My mother?' Iris asked when she could finally bring herself to speak. 'The girl was my mother?'

'Yes.'

'And my father was the botany student?'

'Yes.'

'And she was pregnant with me?'

'Yes.'

Iris stared out the window without seeing.

'We'll eat now,' Hirano said abruptly. 'After dinner you can ask me questions.'

Iris finished eating without tasting the food. Stuart Hirano didn't appear to enjoy his dinner either. As soon as the plates were cleared he ordered brandy, then leaned toward Iris with a warning glare.

'You understand,' he said in a harsh whisper. 'This is not some college prank I'm talking about. If the authorities find out that he harbored a federal fugitive, my father will be in a great deal of trouble.'

She nodded.

'The child who died in the bombing – her parents moved out to the Midwest and he's a senator now. Gerald Dixon. I hear he puts constant pressure on the FBI to remind them that this hasn't been solved. He's an influential man and I have no doubt that he would try to send my father to prison.'

'I understand, Stuart.'

She didn't want to spend a minute longer in Stuart Hirano's company, but she was desperate for more information. She struggled to order her wildly careening thoughts into questions.

Before she could form one Hirano said, 'I've often wondered about the little Hispanic woman.'

'The woman who rented my parents the apartment?'

'Yes. Do you remember her? She used to come to the orchard with you during the house construction.'

Iris thought a moment. 'I'm not sure.'

'Yes, well, you were only five or six when the woman left town. I couldn't believe Clary would become friendly with such lower-class people, but she seemed to be very close to the woman . . . and I've always wondered how much Clary told her.'

'Did anyone ever talk to her after my mother disappeared?'

'Your father may have. I'm not sure. She was living in the East by then . . . New York or New Jersey somewhere. At any rate, I doubt that Clary would have told her much. Your mother was never stupid.'

Iris stared down into the brandy that Hirano had ordered for her. She didn't like brandy. She hadn't touched it.

'Did my father know about the bombing?' she asked.

'I don't know. Clary was good at manipulating men, distracting men. He might not have known.'

She tried to imagine her father – her principled, upstanding father – protecting an accomplice to a bombing. It was impossible to accept.

'I never heard about any relatives named Alesker,' she said, challenging Stuart Hirano to convince her.

'Your mother was afraid all the time. Afraid of being caught. She kept her past a secret.'

'But what about Ross? I was told that her birth name was Clarice Ross.'

'A fiction. Created for a false identification that was used to get a marriage license.'

'And all that about how she was an orphan?'

'Fiction. She was good at it.'

'So her whole life was a lie?'

'Basically.' His expression softened somewhat. 'I do have to say that she surprised me by becoming a very good mother.'

'Until she abandoned me.'

'I don't know how to explain that,' he admitted. 'She seemed so devoted to you.'

Iris sighed and leaned back in her chair. She could imagine what had happened. Clary Lanier had gotten sick of a life in hiding, a dull life with a dull man in an orchard. She had run away – either to her rich father or to a more exciting man. And she hadn't taken Iris because an eight-year-old child is a liability when a person is running away.

Stuart Hirano finished his brandy. 'There is the possibility that your mother was a little—' He tapped the side of his head with his index finger. 'She'd run off twice before, you know.'

'Tell me about that.'

'Both times she left a note saying only that she had

328

something she had to do. Both times she was found outdoors at night in a state of distress and your father was called to go pick her up.'

'Where did they find her?'

'I can't recall, but it will be in the report. The private detective's report. Which I have brought you a copy of.'

'And what else does it say in the report?'

'Nothing of consequence, Iris. Shortly after I hired the agency, your father fired them. He said that he had decided not to pursue her. That if she wanted to leave he wasn't going to chase after her.'

Iris nodded. 'That sounds like my father.' She thought a moment. 'And did you pursue her on your own?'

'I thought about it. But then I decided that her disappearance was probably the best thing for everyone.'

'OK, Stuart, now what about the present? What do you know about my father's shooting?'

'I have no help for you there, Iris. I know nothing.'

Stuart Hirano gave Iris a ride back to Manhattan. They rode in silence most of the way. When the driver pulled up at the Fitzgerald, Hirano got out and walked Iris to the door.

'What will you do now?' he asked.

'I'm not sure. I think I'll look into my mother's family.'

'That isn't very wise, Iris.'

'Oh?'

'You should just let this drop. Digging around in it could cause trouble for everyone.'

'Are you afraid that you'll somehow be tarnished by all this, Stuart?'

He glared at her without reply.

'You were always a very smart girl, Iris. I hope you continue to be smart.'

'Is that a warning?'

'Not at all. You completely misunderstand me. I'm only

concerned for your welfare . . . and for the good name of my family.'

Iris had a moment of sympathy for him then. Stuart Hirano was a man accustomed to controlling everything around him. It was undoubtedly very hard for him to come up against uncontrollable situations. Or people.

'Thank you again for offering to move my father.'

Hirano seized on that as though looking for a safer subject. 'Will you let me know your decision right away?' he asked.

'Not *right away*. I have to go back to Guatemala within the next few days to finish my work there.'

He nodded. 'I know this is a delicate issue, but my father wanted me to ask . . . Do you have enough money to see you through all this?'

'Yes,' she answered curtly, though the available funds on her emergency credit card were dwindling at an alarming rate.

'So then,' he rubbed his hands together in a perfect imitation of his father. 'You're off to Guatemala soon?'

'Yes. I'd like to arrive there Monday or Tuesday. While the camp is empty. That way I'll get back to work without a lot of interruptions.'

'But you won't be out there alone, will you?' Stuart asked.

'Not completely. A few people are staying to guard the place.'

She looked down the block, to the corner where the familiar couple was begging money for drugs. How could a decent man like Yoshi Hirano have a son like Stuart? How could a wonderful man like Jeff have him for a father?

The thought of Stuart Hirano's award wall drifted into her mind. Stuart Hirano – the great hero. A great hero to head Hero Systems, Inc. What a pathetic bit of hypocrisy that was.

330

She turned back toward Hirano and extended her hand to say good-night. She had felt flashes of hatred toward him during the course of the evening, but she didn't hate him. Not really. In fact she was beginning to feel sympathy for him.

'Good-night, Stuart.'

'Good-night, Iris.' She tried to pull her hand away but he held on. 'And Iris . . . Stay away from Jeff. I mean that.'

She jerked her hand free. 'That's up to Jeff,' she said. Maybe she did hate the man after all.

Iris was barely inside the lobby when Mitch Hanley came through the door. He hurried up to walk beside her.

'Who was that?' he asked as they waited for the elevator.

'Someone I know from California.'

'Oh yeah? You're sure dressed up. Been out on the town? Doing the town with your California visitor?'

'What's on your mind, Mitch?'

'I guess what's on my mind is how come you can't leave the hospital or spare any time to spend with me but you can get all dressed up and entertain men from out of town.'

'That's inappropriate, Mitch.'

'Oh, right. I guess that's me . . . inappropriate Mitch.' He slammed through the stairwell door and left her standing in front of the elevator.

The phone was ringing as Iris unlocked her door but she didn't reach it in time and when she checked the page operator there hadn't been a message left. She called the hospital in case someone there had been trying to reach her. They hadn't.

With some measure of apprehension she sat down on the bed and opened the private detective's report that

Stuart Hirano had given her. The name of the agency was on it with a note inviting her to contact them if she had any questions.

The report was only two pages. She scanned the information. There was nothing new. Except for the paragraph about her mother's two previous disappearances. She had been found both times in the little town of Half Moon Bay on the California coast, 'wandering and in great distress' according to the report. The investigator who wrote the paragraph thought that the incidents warranted a trip to the town. But that hadn't happened. Her father had fired them first.

She put the report on the dresser and was stopped by her reflection in the mirror. She smiled, watching the earrings Isaac had given her. They caught the light in blue-green sparks every time she moved her head.

What did she want? Did she want to pursue her mother? Find out about her mother's family, a family she hadn't known existed, a family that was hers, too? Did she want to know any more than she already knew? There was a whispering voice inside her saying, *Go back to the rain forest, go back to your work. Let the Hiranos put him in a hospital near them, leave word that you want to be contacted if he ever starts to wake up and then go back to Moonsmoke and the past. The safe, quiet past.*

There was no music overhead. She heard something, a rumbling noise, but she couldn't be sure if it was coming from Isaac's room.

She picked up the phone and called the airline, locking in her ticket to Guatemala. The booking agent gave her a speech about the ticket being non-refundable, non-transferable, non-exchangeable, non-, non-, non-. Iris acknowledged the conditions, recited her credit card number and then hung up with a feeling of satisfaction. At least one thing was decided. One dangling end would be tied up and brought to a conclusion.

332

She found paper and pen and wrote a thank-you note to Isaac for the earrings. Then, before she could change her mind, she went out and took the elevator to the seventh floor. Quietly she bent and slipped the folded paper beneath his door. She had barely straightened when the door opened.

'Oh . . . there was no music so I didn't think you were home.'

He had the door barely cracked open.

'Is your door stuck too?' she asked, teasing.

'What?'

'Like your window. Both of them only open a few inches.'

'Sorry, I'm not very presentable.'

'I didn't wake you again, did I?'

'No. I'm working out.'

'Is that what those funny noises are?'

'Probably. Was I bothering you?'

'No.'

'I could shower . . . be ready for the roof in ten minutes.'

She hesitated. But she felt as though a line had been crossed and if she was alone with him again there would be serious decisions to make. She couldn't face any more decisions. Not tonight.

'Thanks, but I'm tired. I've just had a draining evening with someone from California.'

'Maybe it would help to talk about it.'

'No. I don't want to talk or think. I just want to sleep.'

'You look beautiful. The earrings are just right on you.'

She smiled at him.

'I'm leaving for Guatemala day after tomorrow,' she said, suddenly realizing that she might not see him before her flight.

'For long?'

'Just long enough to complete my work down there. A week maybe.'

'Why the day after tomorrow? Is there a rush?'

'Becker is getting anxious over whether I'm coming back and I want to go while the rest of the team is away on break. Thought I could sneak in while they're gone and get some major work done.'

'Does this mean I won't see you again before you leave?'

'I don't know,' she said, backing away from the door.

There was a warmth creeping through her and she was dangerously close to saying yes to anything he might suggest.

'Good-night,' he said softly and his voice was like a caress.

'Good-night,' she answered and hurried away to the elevator.

She returned to her room and found that she was too restless to go to bed. Tomorrow sounded as though it would be busy so she decided to plan ahead and pack for the trip to Guatemala. She took stock. The dinner suit she would of course leave behind. But the earrings . . . She would take those. Just to look at.

There were enough clean clothes that she thought she could manage without doing any laundry. She put her jeans and shirts into the suitcase. Then she picked up her backpack. Toilet articles would go in there but she didn't want to pack them until the last minute. She walked into the bathroom and looked around. Just the basics as usual. And that nice big bar of soap. They were always running out of good soap at the dig and resorting to caustic local substitutes. She put the backpack down beside the tub. So much for packing. That had taken all of ten minutes.

The phone rang and she rushed to answer it.

'Are you going to the hospital tomorrow morning?'

It was Kizmin. Her brusqueness was either due to stress or continued paranoia.

334

'Yes. Will you be there? I have things I need to tell you. Things I've learned about—'

'Hold it. Not on the phone.'

'There's nothing wrong is there?'

'It's the bones.'

Iris knew exactly which bones she meant. They had only one skeleton in common.

'What do you think about facial reconstruction?'

'At this point it's probably a good idea.'

'Good. When can you start?'

'I didn't say it was a good idea for me to do it.'

'She's yours, Iris. You can't say no.'

'No.'

'Come on. You're not going to give me another song and dance about your qualifications . . . I know you've done facial reconstructions for some kind of mummy display.'

'That's different. Reconstructing for a museum exhibit didn't require any real accuracy. I didn't have to create an identifiable individual for that, just a generic human face. This is a real woman. This is too important.'

'Listen . . . nobody knows about this but you, me, and Barney. How about you give it a try and if it doesn't come out right we'll scrap the whole thing.'

Iris closed her eyes and didn't answer.

'She needs you, Iris. You want us to nail her killer, don't you? You want her to have justice?'

'I've already committed to leave for Guatemala day after tomorrow.'

'So, you start on her face tomorrow and see how far you get. I have to fight through some red tape and pick up the skull, so I should be able to meet you at the lab with it about eleven. You remember how to get there? Right on the West Side Highway . . . I can't remember the address off hand but you go to Laight and—'

'I remember where it is.'

'Good. I'm leaving a lab key at the nurse's desk for you to pick up in the morning. That way if I'm late you can go on in and start getting the equipment ready.'

'OK. But don't just bring the skull. Bring all of her. I'd like to give her a more thorough examination.'

'How long do you think it will take?'

'I'm not sure. I'll work all night if I have to. I can always sleep on my flight.'

'So why the sudden trip back down there?'

'It's not sudden. I need to finish my work and I decided to go while the rest of the team is away from the dig.'

'You're not going to be alone out there in the jungle, are you?'

'Why is everyone worried about that? It's a lot safer than here.'

'Except for the poisonous snakes and the wild creatures with big teeth and the various guerrilla armies that inhabit that part of the world.'

'I won't be alone. There are a couple of guys watching over the dig.'

'Good. How long will you stay?'

'A week or so. Whatever it takes.'

'Maybe that's good. Your getting out of town and away from all this.' Kizmin hesitated. 'What you ought to do is have your father moved to a hospital near your home in California, get out of here, forget about the shooting and these bones I'm bringing you tomorrow and the whole nightmare, and concentrate on getting back to something like a normal life.'

'Is that what you would do?'

Kizmin laughed softly. 'See you tomorrow,' she said and hung up without answering Iris's question.

# Nineteen

Early the next morning Iris went to the hospital. She collected the key to the lab and sat with her father for awhile, then she went out to a library and searched microfilms of the San Francisco and San Jose newspapers for the Red Phoenix bombing. She didn't have an exact date so she started eight months before her birth and worked backward.

### NO LEADS IN BOMBING

There are no new leads in the bomb blast that killed an eight-year-old girl and a Berkeley student last Saturday. The description authorities released . . .

Quickly, Iris skipped to Sunday, the day after the bombing.

### BOMB BLAST KILLS GIRL

A bomb blast at a draft-board office in Ebersville claimed the life of an eight-year-old girl last night. The girl was identified as Katina Dixon, daughter of Gerald Dixon, a graduate assistant at the University of California at Berkeley, and Kathleen Dixon, a legal secretary.

The blast occurred at two a.m., one hour after the end of a peaceful antiwar rally on the Berkeley campus, twelve miles north of Ebersville. Authorities have not yet determined whether there was a connection between the two.

Also dead in the blast is an unidentified male. Authorities suspect that he may have been killed by a premature detonation while placing the bomb inside the office.

The Dixons had attended the antiwar rally and were on their way out of the area for a vacation. They stopped for gas at an open service station near the site of the blast and the girl crossed the street to put a birthday card in a mail-box that was located directly in front of the blast site. A hospital spokesman said that the child's injuries were caused both by the concussive force of the explosion and by flying glass. She was still alive when her parents reached her but died in the ambulance en route to the hospital.

A letter postmarked the day before the bombing claims that an antiwar group calling itself Red Phoenix was responsible. Authorities had no comment as to whether they were familiar with Red Phoenix, however a spokesman from the Berkeley campus reported that the area has recently been posted with antiwar messages signed by Red Phoenix.

Anyone with information about this crime is asked to call the police immediately.

Iris made a copy of the article then went on. One paper had a whole page about Katina Dixon with heartbreaking pictures of her impish face, an interview with the grandmother whose birthday card the child had been mailing, and details of her wounds. Iris scanned the page but could not bring herself to read the articles, especially the one with the headline GIRL'S THROAT SLASHED BY GLASS, or the one headed TINA'S LAST WORDS, or HALF MOON BAY MOURNS TINA, accompanied by pictures of grieving relatives and a sobbing former teacher.

She spun the knob of the machine forward.

Authorities revealed today that a young woman was seen dropping off the bomber shortly before the draft-board bombing last weekend. The woman was driving a light-colored late-model four-door sedan, possibly a Ford. She is described as eighteen to twenty years of age, with a fair complexion and dark hair. She was wearing long earrings and a peasant-style blouse. Authorities suspect that she might be a college student.

## BOMBER IDENTIFIED

The body found at the site of the Red Phoenix bombing has been identified as that of Denny Winslow, a nineteen-year-old Stanford dropout who had enrolled as a student at the University of California at Berkeley. Winslow's home address is Bakersfield, California.

Friends say Winslow came to Berkeley from Stanford because of personal problems. He had recently stopped going to his Berkeley classes and had been behaving strangely. He reported having visions and spent all his time distributing literature for the Red Phoenix antiwar group. Winslow was seen looking in the front window of the draft-board office shortly before the blast, but it has been determined that he gained entrance through a back door off an alley. He was seen getting out of a late-model car driven by a woman. Authorities believe that the crude home-made bomb exploded prematurely, killing Winslow as he was placing it near the filing cabinets in the office.

The article naming Denny Winslow was accompanied by his high-school graduation picture. Iris studied the face. He had a crooked, slightly bucktoothed smile, like a cartoon character, and an expression of apology or embarrassment, as though he hadn't been comfortable in a serious pose. It was hard to believe that this boy had held power over anyone or had inspired anyone to believe that he would be great someday. It was also hard to believe that the boy pictured could have had a dark or violent side, could have bombed a building and killed a child. Her mother had been very young at the time, but surely this was not the boy who had had so much influence over her.

She made copies of the two stories and then left the library. She knew enough. More than enough. And knowing made her sick to her stomach. She slipped the copies into the manila envelope with the private detective's report.

Luck was with her and there was a southbound number one train just pulling into the station when she ran down the subway stairs. She hurried aboard and took a seat near the car's wall-map so she could figure out where to get off. It was a long ride. The red line on the map stretched all the way down the West Side.

The car was nearly empty. She settled into the molded plastic seat and pulled the contents of the envelope out. After she had reread the articles she looked over the detective's report again.

Half Moon Bay. That was where her mother had been found both times before. Katina Dixon was buried in Half Moon Bay. Her mother had gone to Katina Dixon's grave.

At Canal Street she walked west toward the Hudson River and then over to the lab. Detective Kizmin was not there so Iris went inside. It was housed in an old industrial building and if she hadn't gone inside with Kizmin before she wouldn't have known how to do it. She wouldn't have known how to operate the open-gated freight elevator. And she wouldn't have been able to find the door on the top floor that was decorated with a playful skull and crossbones.

The lab was big, occupying most of the top floor. The front portion had been partitioned off into living quarters but other than that it was all yawning open space, interrupted only by weight-bearing pillars. She stood, staring, filled with awe. There were old industrial windows, narrow but stretching floor to ceiling, that flooded the space with natural light. In addition there was some kind of shaft built into the center of the building and large panels of glass had been installed to take advantage of the light afforded by the shaft.

She cleaned off a work counter near the windows so the light would be strong and she assembled the equipment she needed. The lab had everything. There was an entire cabinet devoted to facial reconstruction supplies. Most of it looked as though it was brand new. When she was finished she wandered some more, examining the place and trying to imagine herself working there.

Between the living area and the lab space was a doorway that she assumed to be a closet. She opened it and discovered stairs. She went up and through another door. It was the roof. But not like any roof she had ever seen or imagined. Someone had created a garden complete with trellised patio and huge potted bushes. Only the evergreens were alive now but she could envision the garden in spring with the stacked beds and pots and tubs overflowing with flowers and dormant vines around the trellis leafed out and spreading. She walked through it, filled with an almost childish delight. Who had made the garden? Who took care of it?

Near the center was a grouping of potted bushes with red plastic ribbon strung from one to another. Upon closer inspection she saw that the bushes surrounded a large open airshaft that plunged down into the heart of the building. This was the shaft that had been windowed at the lab level. Iris backed away from it. A small child or a person with bad eyesight would not be safe near that.

She ducked out of the maze of shrubbery and crossed to the open side overlooking the Hudson River. There were only short planters there so that the view wasn't obscured. She looked out across the water and then down at the street. Something was happening on the sidewalk below. A knot of people had gathered and more were running to join in.

The gathering shifted and she saw that the nucleus of the activity was a prone form on the sidewalk. People were kneeling or bending over someone. Had there been an accident? Should she call an ambulance? It was too far down for her to shout the question. Maybe she ought to run down with a blanket?

The crowd shifted again and some of the people in the center started pushing those behind them back and suddenly Iris saw that the body on the sidewalk was Kizmin.

She raced down the stairs and through the echoing empty spaces, onto the open elevator, through the metal door, and out onto the sidewalk. Her pulse roared in her ears and she stormed through the gawking crowd, knocking them aside without apology.

Kizmin was on her back, moaning but not fully conscious. There was blood. A lot of blood. Iris couldn't tell what the wounds were. She dropped to her knees and put her ear to the detective's chest. There was a strong heartbeat and the woman was breathing.

'What happened?' she demanded, looking up at the circle of faces. She could hear a siren and knew that someone had called an ambulance.

'She was carjacked,' said a teenage boy. 'I saw the whole thing. She pulled up and was getting out of her car when this dude jumped out from behind that scaffolding over there and started whopping her with a tire-iron.'

'Man!' said the boy's companion. 'He beat her to her

knees, and he grabbed the keys out of her hand and he could'a took off then but he didn't stop. He just kept hitting her.'

'Yeah,' the first boy agreed. 'She tried to pull a gun out of her purse but he was hitting her too hard. If we hadn't run up and started yelling he'd a killed her! We almost caught him but he jumped in her car then and split.'

'He did this to her so he could steal her car?'

'Happens all the time,' both boys assured her.

'What did he look like?' Iris asked.

'Oh, man, he was just your average guy. Had on jeans and some kind of dark jacket.'

'How about hair color? Skin type? Age?'

'He was wearing a knit cap and a face-warmer. And gloves. I think he was light-skinned, and he moved fast you know. Like he was in pretty good condition.'

Kizmin moaned again and opened her eyes. She tried to raise her head.

Iris leaned closer. 'Relax. Lie still. The ambulance is coming.'

'He got my car,' the detective whispered hoarsely.

'Forget your car. You can get another one.'

'The bones were in it. I hope the fucker dies of fright when he opens that box.'

The ambulance screamed to a stop and the crowd parted.

'She's a police officer,' Iris told the paramedics. 'Can you call that in on your radio? Tell them an officer was attacked.'

'What's her name?'

'Kizmin. Detective Justine Kizmin.' Iris realized it was the first time she had ever spoken the woman's first name.

They worked over her several minutes then put her on the stretcher and into the ambulance.

'Where are you taking her?' Iris asked.

'Bellevue Emergency.'

'Can I ride with her?'

'You her partner?'

'No.'

'A relative?'

Iris shook her head.

'You better wait here. The cops are on their way and they're gonna want to talk to witnesses here.'

Iris watched them race off with sirens wailing. The people who remained were talking excitedly and the two boys were repeating their story. Embellishing it. Making themselves even more heroic. Iris eased back from them and slipped away. She wasn't sure what Kizmin would want her to say to investigating officers. The last she had heard the detective had been ordered not to make contact with John Lanier's daughter and she didn't want to cause any more trouble than there already was.

She started walking, with nothing in mind but to put distance between herself and that bloody spot on the sidewalk. As the adrenalin faded she felt increasingly sick and shaky. When she couldn't go any farther she sat down on the steps of a stoop. The West Village streamed busily around her with a Saturday giddiness. A cold front had been forecast for Sunday and everyone was out enjoying the fifty-plus temperature while it lasted.

Iris huddled on the steps. Her throat and her eyes burned.

'Sisters and brothers!' she heard a man call from the corner. 'The end is near! The millennium approaches! Jesus wants you to learn how to save yourself! Only nine dollars and ninety-five cents!'

She walked to the corner pay-phone and dialed the number she had been carrying but had never used.

'Yes.'

'Hello, Isaac? This is Iris.'

'Iris. What's wrong? You sound upset.'

'If I came straight to the roof now, could you come up?'

'Where are you?'

'In the West Village. On Sixth Avenue.'

'Tell me what's wrong.'

'Detective Kizmin was attacked. She . . . someone beat her with a tire iron and took her car.' A sob shuddered through her chest. 'I . . . I don't know how bad she is. The ambulance took her to the hospital.'

'I'm coming to get you, Iris. Don't wait there though. Walk over to the big bookstore at the corner of Eighth Street and Sixth. Go inside. I'll be right there.'

Iris hunched down between bookshelves, pretending she was looking for something, but seeing Kizmin's blood, hearing Kizmin's pain-racked voice.

'Iris!'

She jumped up and straight into his arms. He held her for a moment, the wool of his Russian officer's coat rough beneath her cheek.

'I shouldn't go to the hospital because I'm not sure if she was supposed to be seeing me . . . But I have to know how she is! I should find a phone. That's what I should do. The doctors have seen her by now and maybe someone will tell me something.'

Isaac glanced around the store and Iris realized that they were attracting attention.

'There's a coffee shop with an inside phone not far from here,' he said.

She nodded.

He led her out of the store and down the crowded sidewalk on the avenue. Past the incense vendors and the Senegalese selling umbrellas.

Inside the busy coffee shop they went straight to the phone at the back.

'Hello . . . yes . . . you have a woman named Justine Kizmin there and I'm a friend of hers and . . . could you tell me how she is or . . .'

345

'No information available,' the voice replied shortly and then the dial tone buzzed in Iris's ear.

Frustrated, she slammed the receiver down on the metal hook. 'Maybe I need to say I'm a relative? Her sister? I could say I was Janelle.'

'Let me give it a try,' Isaac said.

Iris moved to the side and watched him dial.

'Hello,' he said in a low bark that astonished her. 'This is Sergeant Murphy. You've got one of my people there. Detective Kizmin. Yeah. How's she doing?'

'Uh-huh,' he said several times and winked at Iris. Finally he hung up and turned toward her.

'Surgery on her left arm, something broken in her shoulder—'

'The scapula?'

'Yes, I think so. Stitches on the side of her head. A mild concussion. And lots of bad bruising. But nothing that she won't get over.'

Iris breathed out a sigh of relief.

'She was lucky,' Isaac said. 'She could have been killed.' He looked at Iris. 'Were you with her?'

'No. But we were meeting. I saw her right after it happened.'

They had to lean close to hear one another over the lunchtime racket in the small restaurant.

'Let's get out of here,' Isaac said and within minutes they were in the backseat of a cab.

Iris tilted her head back against the seat and closed her eyes, feeling almost weak from relief. Kizmin would be fine. She was tougher than a tire iron.

'What are you smiling about?' Isaac asked.

She opened her eyes and sat up straight. She hadn't been paying attention at all as Isaac directed the driver to turn here and there, and she had no idea where they were.

'I was thinking about Kizmin.'

'She's lucky,' Isaac repeated.

'Is that enough sightseeing?' the driver shouted through the Plexiglas divider.

'Take us over the bridge, make a U-turn and come straight back.'

The driver grumbled something but turned onto the Brooklyn Bridge access.

'Where are we going?' Iris asked.

Isaac seemed distracted, looking out the side windows and then the back.

'Nowhere. It's such a beautiful day. And I thought you needed time to relax.' He turned his head and looked into her eyes. 'Are you relaxed?'

Suddenly Kizmin's attack and every other concern melted into the background and there was only Isaac. Sitting just inches away from her. His hand resting on the seat beside her. His shoulder almost brushing hers.

Today his eyes were more blue than grey. Almost the same shade as his blue-grey officer's coat. She wondered if his eyes changed with different colors of clothing.

'I can't believe I'm actually seeing you in sunlight,' she said. 'You're not a vampire after all.'

He laughed then looked out over the water. 'I love this bridge,' he said. 'We should be walking across it though. That's the best way. Walking or running.'

She leaned toward the window to look up at the walkway and the scattering of people there. It was so good to be with him. So extraordinarily good.

He was wonderful. Being with him was wonderful. She took a deep breath. The very air around him was wonderful.

Why was she so afraid of her feelings? So afraid of what might happen between them? Why was it so hard for her to believe?

'So, where would you like me to drop you?' he asked. 'The Fitzgerald or somewhere else?'

'No. I . . .' She stared down at her hands in her lap.

Plain hands with short utilitarian nails. Suddenly she wished she were more elegant. More poised. More something. 'Umm, I was thinking . . . maybe we could have lunch together?'

He hesitated and her heart sank.

'That's OK,' she started to say, but he glanced out the windows again, then leaned forward to speak to the driver.

'Spring Street, between Greene and Mercer,' he said.

'Is that Soho?' the driver asked.

'Yes.'

'You gonna get out there or we gonna just drive past?'

'We'll get out.'

Iris listened to the exchange, afraid to make any assumptions, but hoping.

Isaac settled back against the seat beside her. 'Is Malaysian OK?'

She assured him that it was, though she'd never had Malaysian food and could only guess at what it might consist of.

'Penang is a great place,' he said. 'The owners are really nice people and the food is terrific. And it's not midtown. Midtown is so chaotic this time of day. Soho is . . . better.'

And it struck her that Isaac Brightman, for all his outward steadiness and composure, was just as nervous as she was.

They sat near a rock waterfall. The food was wonderful – not quite Chinese, not quite Indian, not quite anything she had ever tasted.

'From now on, whenever I eat Malaysian food, I'll think of you,' she told him, expecting one of his slow smiles or a wry comment.

'Will you?' He didn't smile. His expression was almost sad.

'Isaac, is it my imagination or do I detect a certain reluctance on your part?'

'I could say the same about you,' he said, amusement returning to his eyes.

'Yes,' she admitted. 'But my reluctance is wearing down while yours seems to be increasing.'

He didn't reply.

'Are you married or ambivalently gay or carrying a disease or . . .' She wound down without finishing, her hands twisted together in her lap.

'No,' he said, pushing his chair back a fraction, closing himself to her as surely as if he'd shut a door between them.

She nodded. 'I'm just trying to understand – you . . . myself . . . everything. I'm afraid I've never learned how to do' – she held out her hands then quickly pulled them back – 'whatever it is we're doing. Or almost doing. Because we're really not *doing* anything, are we? It's not like we have any sort of relationship. Not really. So . . .' She exhaled in a deep sigh. 'I don't know why I'm saying all this.'

'Iris,' he said, speaking in a low voice that was almost angry, certainly regretful. 'I couldn't stop thinking about you . . . from the first moment. And I let myself start something that never should have been started.'

She tried to smile and make her voice light. 'You think a musician and a physical anthropologist are such an impossible pairing?'

'The two of us are an impossible pairing.'

'But we're not talking about marriage here,' she protested. 'Why can't we just go easy . . . let things take a natural course . . . and see what happens . . . see where it goes. See if it's important enough to have these concerns.'

'It's not going anywhere,' he said. 'There is no future for us. And to go any deeper will just make it harder at the end.'

'Oh.' She was trembling inside but she tried to appear calm and purposeful as she stood and gathered her jacket. 'Thanks for the rescue and a great lunch. And thank you for setting me straight. Now maybe I can concentrate on the important things in my life.'

# IV

## The Underworld

# Twenty

Iris was surprised to find Linda aboard her commercial flight into Guatemala City.

'This is great!' Linda said repeatedly. 'We couldn't have planned this any better!' and she asked the man in the seat next to Iris to move.

From the moment she sat down Linda talked so much that it was difficult for Iris to have a coherent thought. Iris welcomed the release from thinking though, the break from worrying over Kizmin who was lying in the hospital all battered and stitched, the break from agonizing over her father and the endless mysteries that surrounded him, the break from imagining little Katina Dixon caught in the bomb's blast.

Isaac was not in her thoughts so she needed no break from thinking about him. She refused to think about him. She was furious at herself for the entire fool's charade that she had played with him.

What was wrong with the man, anyway? All that talk about not going any deeper and not having a future together. What century was he living in? That's not the way it was supposed to work. They hadn't even kissed yet! And all that talk about not wanting it to be harder at the end. Harder for whom? Did he just assume that she was going to fall madly in love with him and be devastated? Who did he think he was with all his assumptions?

But she was not going to think about him. She refused to think about him.

'You seem really distracted,' Linda said. 'Bet you're excited about getting back down in the chamber, huh.'

'Yes. Very excited.'

When the plane landed the skies were dark with hazy smoke. Linda's father had arranged a helicopter to take his daughter from the airport out to the dig site. As Iris climbed aboard the small bug-shaped aircraft, she couldn't deny that money had its conveniences. They lifted into the prematurely darkened sky and traveled inland. The view was spectacular until the smoke became so thick that it was nearly obscured.

'It's that time of the year,' the pilot said in heavily accented English. 'They are burning forest to make more farmland.'

By the time they landed at the site the sky was so smoky that the orange ball of the setting sun looked like it was veiled with mourning cloth.

Tim and Juan came out to meet them, waving and smiling. Then they all went to the club tent to eat the treats that Linda had bought in the airport. Juan joined them enthusiastically even though he understood little of what they were saying.

'The first thing I've got to do is break the bad news,' Tim said after they were settled in at the long table with the lantern lit and the panels of mosquito netting stirring softly around them.

Iris and Linda looked at each other and then back at Tim.

'Dr Becker opened Jaguar Eyes' sarcophagus the day before yesterday. He was convinced that you were never coming back, Iris, and he decided that everything of great value should be packed up and taken out on this trip.'

Linda let out a cry of disappointment. Iris stared at

the lantern. That was it. Now she knew where she stood with Daniel Becker. Now she knew that there would be no job offer. Strangely she felt no disappointment. Only resignation.

'What did you find inside?' Iris asked.

Tim became instantly animated. 'It was great. He was buried with jaguar hide covering his hands and feet, and a huge headdress and mask.'

'Has there been any more work done on the artifacts from the tunnel?' Iris asked.

Tim grinned. 'Has there ever. I made some real break-throughs and you're going to love this story, Iris. It's all been taken into the city, but I've got pictures . . .' He rummaged through a cardboard box and handed her a stack of Polaroids.

'Turns out the officially sanctioned version of Sun Lord Jaguar Eyes' life was the product of considerable histori-cal revisionism.

'It was all a lie. All the stuff in his tomb and on the stelae about what a hero he was and how he was never defeated in battle – the paintings showing him fighting hand-to-hand while he's all decked out in his Quetzal feathers – and that big jade plate with the carving showing him making his triumphant return to the city on 8.14.3.1.12—'

'I can't believe the way you remember those Maya longcount days,' Linda said admiringly. 'What would that be on the modern calendar?'

Tim, basking in her admiration, shrugged as though his knowledge was nothing. 'AD 320,' he said. 'September. The seventeenth, I think.' He cleared his throat and tore his eyes from Linda to address Iris. 'And you know how that plate carving showed him surrounded by adoring followers with his overjoyed wife and daughters bowing at his feet?' Tim grinned. 'Not quite true it seems.

'The artifacts that were tossed away into the tunnel tell

a different story. Seems that Jaguar Eyes took his youngest son and went to battle. The scene shows his wife and daughters weeping. They were either sad to see him go or maybe just sad to see him take the young son. Anyway, neither he nor the son made it home. He was assumed dead. His wife, Moonsmoke, stepped in and became ruler. The people loved her. Things were dandy. One scene shows the gods smiling down on her with the symbols for prosperity and plenty.

'Then old Jaguar Eyes stumbled out of the forest with his butchered son's head in his hands. He'd been a captive slave all that time. He's shown as very ill and being nursed by his daughters. Then he's depicted as sitting in a position of honor next to Moonsmoke. Like they were equals. That's it for the tunnel artifacts.

'That brings us to the painting in his tomb which we didn't understand until we had all this new information. It shows his three daughters offering themselves up as sacrifices in exchange for Jaguar Eyes' return. There are servants clutching at their feet in the picture but—'

'Two servants?' Iris asked.

'How did you guess?'

'I have five female sacrifices in that chamber.' She felt a rising tide of excitement in her chest. 'Maybe it's the three daughters and their two servants.'

Tim grinned. 'Could be! Could be! What a story, huh?'

Iris nodded. 'Yes. But what about Moonsmoke? What does Jaguar Eyes' revised account say happened to her?'

'You sound as though you know something already,' Tim said.

'First, answer my question. Then I'll tell you,' Iris promised.

'According to the stuff in the old boy's tomb, Moonsmoke disappeared from the earth one day and is believed to have risen up into the sky to become a goddess.'

Iris studied her folded hands on the table a moment.

'Tim, I think that the sixth woman down there is Moon-smoke. And she has a knife in her back.'

The next morning Iris stepped out of her tent to another day of darkened skies. Tiny cinders rained down. She stared up at the haze as she walked to the chamber. Around her in the forest the animals were agitated and noisy. She wondered, were they disturbed by the smell of fire or did they have some primitive inner warning that the future of the entire rain forest was in jeopardy?

A giggle sounded from somewhere nearby. She didn't have to worry about Linda wanting to work with her that day. The woman was too occupied with Tim to care about work.

Tim and Linda's affection for one another seemed silly and adolescent to her, but what did she know about affection? What did she know about love? Affection had always been difficult for her. Both to express and to receive. And as to love . . . She had never been in love. Never even close. Hadn't believed it was possible until Isaac. And now she would never know if it might have happened. She wondered . . . but no. She was not thinking about Isaac. Especially not here. Not now.

As she neared the chamber she saw that everything was different above ground. There were numerous plastic flags and other signs of disturbance. A canvas tarp was laid over the newly opened tunnel entrance. Off to one side stretched a long mound of sieved dirt, attesting to the backbreaking hours of troweling and sifting that had gone into opening the tunnel. Assembled chunks of a massive stone stela lay in a line on the other side.

Iris sat down on the edge of her rabbit hole, swung into it, and descended the ladder. The chamber was shadowy but appeared undisturbed. As Daniel had promised, no one had worked inside it in her absence. She stood at the bottom of the ladder, breathing in the musk of the earth.

The day was so dark that she was forced to turn on both miner's lamps to work. That annoyed her. She preferred the natural light. As soon as she lit the lamps, the bones of the star-ray women leapt into stark relief. Their grinning death's-heads seemed to float in the eerie light.

*His daughters.*

He had sacrificed his own daughters to thank the gods for his return. She didn't believe that the women had offered themselves. No. He had killed them.

Maybe their deaths came first and then he murdered his wife because he couldn't stand to be reminded that he had sacrificed his youngest son to war and his daughters to the gods. Or maybe he murdered his wife first – because she was a challenge to his power or because she didn't support his vision of himself. The whole story would probably never be known. He might have killed her for complex reasons, or he might have killed her out of simple hatred. And then, after he'd murdered her, maybe he sacrificed the grieving daughters to silence them. Who knew? Who would ever know?

Iris went around the women to the naked bones at the tunnel's mouth.

This was Moonsmoke.

'Moonsmoke,' she whispered, as certain of the woman's identity as if she were greeting an old friend.

Had this long-dead woman watched her daughters die? The thought sent a chill through Iris. And suddenly she thought of her own mother. She saw her mother's face. Not the beautiful face from old photographs but a frightful shadowed apparition. A tortured face. A face that could have caused nightmares except that there was no menace about it.

She shook off the disturbing image and sat down at Moonsmoke's side. Using a magnifying glass she examined the edge of the disk beneath the woman's chest. As she had expected it was made of jade. A curved necklace,

358

very large, that had been worn almost like a breastplate. A sure sign of her royalty. And she had carried it with her into death. Not even her murderer had dared take it from her.

The necklace was the key to proving Moonsmoke's identity. Iris had to finish cleaning her up and record the *in situ* information, then they would lift her and the necklace beneath would be revealed. And then the world would know who she was and how she had died. That seemed more important to Iris now than any of the scientific data.

She grabbed a stiff brush and set to work on the upper back area above the projecting knife. There wasn't much left to do. Just the neck and head really. And the right hand which was resting near the head. The body had been lying face down in the mouth of the tunnel as it was filled, with the right arm stretched upward.

Moonsmoke.

As she worked the name echoed in Iris's thoughts. It vibrated in the bones beneath her hands. As though the bones were stirring. Or whispering. As though they had been waiting for Iris. Waiting – deep within the bowels of an ancient city where all love, hate, and death had been ground to dust a thousand years ago – waiting for someone to listen to the truth.

Finally, Iris finished the skull, disappointing because it was face down in the dirt. She started on the hand, which was several inches above the skull. The work was clumsy because she had to reach up into the tunnel, but she quickly unveiled the hand and saw that it was lying on something.

She moved a light closer and eased up into the tunnel mouth alongside Moonsmoke. It was tight. Almost claustrophobic. But she wanted to have a better look.

The phalanges were so delicate, and she could see what was under them, and suddenly everything made sense. It

359

was a curve of broken jar, like a scoop, and the right arm was extended because it had been reaching up. To dig. Trying to scoop away the dirt that filled the tunnel. Trying to dig her way out even as they were pouring the dirt in over her. Digging. With that knife burning in her back and her daughters lying dead behind her. Digging while she listened to the men above who were burying her.

Iris jerked free of the tunnel and pressed her hand against her racing heart. Only then did she realize that she was hearing a sound from above.

She cocked her head to listen. The sound was muffled but unmistakably a vehicle of some kind. She had a moment of disorientation, then laughed, thinking of the old Twilight Zone stories where people's lives were sometimes repeated. *The sound of an unexpected vehicle, the question of who was arriving.* Her life was becoming curiouser and curiouser. Just like Alice. Maybe she had dreamed the first sequence of events, including the trip to New York, and now she was about to receive the telegram about her father.

The engine noise grew closer. The team or maybe part of the team had decided to return. Reluctantly, she rose, disappointed that her solitude was about to be invaded.

She heard a shout. Concentrating, straining to hear, she moved to the ladder and stared up at the circle of smoky sky that was visible through the opening. Sounds carried strangely down into the chamber. Maybe it had been a parrot's cry or the call of a monkey. Suddenly there was a series of pops, like a distant string of firecrackers, and the parrots did start screeching, and there were screams, chilling, unmistakably human screams.

Iris grabbed her sharpened trowel and hurried up the ladder. Another scream shuddered through the air. A woman. Linda. It could only be Linda. Iris scrambled out of her rabbit hole and crouched behind the mounded line of dirt. There was nothing to see. Just the jungle and the sooty sky. Overhead the howler monkeys screeched and crashed through the forest canopy. Cautiously, keeping to the trees rather than cutting across the open, Iris ran toward the city's center. The engine rumbled to life again. Then it was joined by the starting of a second vehicle. She heard a shout in Spanish, then another piercing scream that was abruptly cut short.

Her mind raced. The radio set was at the club tent. She could go there and call for help. But help was far away. She was the only help that could make a difference.

There was no sound or movement as she crept forward into the heart of the dead city. The stifling liquid heat flowed with her as she moved. As soon as she reached the intersection of the two grand boulevards she could see the temple pyramid. Its carved demons stared down at her approach, guarding the plaza with their fierce, mad countenances, watching over the bleeding bodies sprawled beneath them.

Tim lay in the center of the plaza, as though he'd been walking out to greet his attackers. Juan had been shot as he emerged from the digging space within the pyramid. His body was slumped against the temple and his blood sprayed across the ancient stones in vivid red arcs.

Terror resounded through her in waves. Were the attackers still nearby? Were they watching her even now?

But what if the men out there were alive? What if she could help them? She stepped out into the plaza, holding her breath, squeezing her eyes shut for an instant against the gunfire that didn't come. Then she ran to Tim and dropped to her knees beside him. He looked so normal, as though he had stretched out on his back to soak up the sun with his arms outstretched and his dark glasses neatly in place. Small red circles decorated his tan shirt. So small they hardly seemed important.

She put her hands against his chest and pushed and counted and breathed air into his mouth but there was no response. No sign of life at all. And each time she pushed down on his chest blood seeped out from beneath his back. Thick, darkening blood spreading out over the worn stones, leaking into the earth through cracks and fissures, pooling around her knees like syrup.

Dead. He was dead and there was nothing she could do. She ran to check Juan. Her pulse roared in her ears and her eyes had a will of their own, darting about, watching, certain that the monsters would appear at any moment.

Juan was dead. Definitely dead. His head was half gone.

Blood. Blood on her hands and the knees of her jeans. Dead. Lost. Both dead. Butchered. Massacred. Monsters. There were monsters here. The monsters were everywhere. No place was safe. No place to run. Hide. Where to hide?

She gripped her head, squeezing her bloody fingers into her own flesh, fighting back the panic and hysteria.

Wait. Where was Linda?

She heard a noise from inside the pyramid. They were in there! Looking for the entrance to Jaguar Eyes' tomb.

'Linda!' she called softly. 'Linda, where are you?'

She ran from the plaza, down the boulevard to the tent compound. Her footfalls were completely absorbed by the moist earth and the still air and the dark forest. As though she was insubstantial. Already disappearing into history.

'Linda!' she called, running from tent to tent. Everything was silent.

She ran to the club tent. It yawned, open and empty, the long swaths of netting hung limply. She sank onto a bench, knees suddenly too weak to stand, stomach churning. A lizard scampered across the planked wooden floor, something alive, a blur of motion that was oddly heartening to her.

The radio was smashed. Tim's Jeep was gone. She stared down at her hands. The blood had turned dark and rusty on her skin. It was black beneath her fingernails. Tim's blood. Tim who had been alive just minutes ago but who was now dead and could not be saved. Tim who had laughed at breakfast and talked about the future. No more laughing. No more future.

Iris went to her tent. She wanted to cower there. Crawl beneath her cot and curl up and close her eyes. She dropped to her knees on the plank floor. All dead. All dead. They would come for her soon.

No!

She jumped to her feet. They wouldn't get her. She would hide. Find Linda and hide in the forest.

She grabbed a bottle of water and some Granola bars, dropped them in her backpack, and strapped it on. The engines were still running somewhere. Two Jeeps. They had come in one and they were stealing Tim's. There had been a woman's scream. Could Linda be near the Jeeps?

She crept along the edge of the forest, hiding and searching. There! The Jeeps were both idling. A man sat in the back of Tim's Jeep. He was laughing. Having a great time. Running his hands over Linda's body. She was bound and gagged. Her eyes were squeezed shut.

Silently Iris edged toward them. She found a heavy tree branch and carried it with her, her approach masked by the sound of the engines. She lifted the branch and brought it down on his head with a ripe melon thud. He collapsed sideways. Linda opened her eyes and looked at Iris with a blank stare.

Iris ran around to the other vehicle and stabbed the tires with the point of her trowel. Then she pushed the slumped man out of Tim's Jeep, jumped behind the wheel, and headed into the forest.

'Hang on, Linda. Hang on. You're safe now. Everything is going to be OK.'

But, as she bounced out over the forest floor, Iris realized that she didn't know where she was going.

# Twenty-One

Iris was lost for hours, driving around blindly in the forest until she stumbled on a logging road and finally found an Indian village. Linda was still dazed and staring fixedly when they were finally taken to Guatemala City.

After the police finished with her, Daniel Becker rushed in and took her to a hotel room.

'My God, Iris. My God,' he repeated over and over, with an expression of horror on his face. Several times he seemed as though he might take her in his arms, but each time he stopped himself.

Iris felt numb. Wooden. She wouldn't have protested a hug. She wouldn't have responded at all.

'Jesus . . . Bandits! My God! And to think we just moved all the valuables . . . I mean – Not that that's the most important thing here. I mean . . . losing Tim and Juan . . . nearly losing Linda . . . My God . . . if it hadn't been for you . . .'

'I'm very tired, Daniel.'

'Of course. I just wanted to say how sorry I am that I opened the sarcophagus without you. I shouldn't have given up.'

'It doesn't matter anymore.'

'Iris . . . you're very important to me. Do you know that?'

Slowly she turned her head to look at him.

'I'd like you to work with me. I've been waiting. Trying

to find the right time to say this. But the right time never seems to come. I think we'd make a great pair, Iris. Like the Leakys.'

'The Leakys were married, Daniel.'

'Yes . . . well. We might not want to go that far, but I think that combining work with a relationship might create a lot of energy for both of us.'

She stared at him, not quite believing what she was hearing.

'Think about it, will you?' Daniel said, backing towards the door. 'Get some rest and think about it.'

As soon as Becker was gone Iris called the airport and asked when the next available northbound commercial flight was. To anywhere. As long as it was headed north. Then she walked out of the hotel, found a taxi and left. The police were finished with her. Linda was under sedation, waiting for her father to arrive. There was nothing keeping Iris in Guatemala and she needed to get away. Far away.

Luck was with her and she had good connections. She felt a strange mix of emotions. Detachment combined with a heightened awareness. There was an ache in her chest that wouldn't go away. She was hungry but food made her sick. She was exhausted but she felt that she might never sleep again. On the final leg of the journey, a red-eye flight into New York, she fell into a deep dreamless sleep and when she awoke she looked around and saw that the rest of the world was exactly the same. Only she had changed.

As soon as she had cleared customs, Iris went to a pay-phone and called the Blue Four desk at the hospital. There had been no real change in her father's condition, she was told. He was moving around more but, she was warned, that did not necessarily mean anything. The nurse's words gathered weight in her head and sank though her body.

'Don't go getting all depressed,' the nurse scolded. 'You haven't been gone that long and the important thing is that he's holding his own.'

'I'm still at the airport,' Iris told her, 'but I'm coming straight there.'

'No hurry,' the nurse assured her.

She considered how best to find out about Kizmin's condition. She didn't know whether she should make direct contact. As a precaution she called the Kaliker Foundation offices and asked if they knew how the detective was doing. Someone there told her that Kizmin was still hospitalized. That she was having surgery on her elbow.

'She's not having visitors yet but she called here at the office this morning. Sounded pretty groggy.'

'The next time she calls could you give her a message for me?'

'Sure.'

'Just tell her Iris is worried about her.'

She swung her backpack to her shoulder and went out toward the taxi stand. Her perceptions had completely reversed. New York felt like the safe haven to her now. A picture of the ruins flashed in her mind, red blood against ancient stones, lifeless stares, faces frozen in terror. She pressed her palms against her eyes till it hurt and the image was wiped away.

The bodies were gone from the plaza now and an army of officers and team members and politicos had swarmed over the dig. The bandits might never be caught, the police had told her. They suspected that it was a new trend. They suspected that someone close to the dig had tipped the robbers about the team's leaving. They had spoken to her as though they thought she knew the answers.

She tried to push it all out of her thoughts. She wished her mind would go completely blank for awhile. Later she would worry about contacting Daniel, about having her belongings shipped to her, about telling him that she wasn't interested in his proposal. Later she would worry about the fact that all she had was the contents of her backpack and the clothes on her back, plus the few items she had left at the room. Later she would let the horror of it all replay . . . if she could just have a break from thinking now.

The taxi line was long so she took a chance on a gypsy cab, a battered Pontiac sedan driven by a smiling, over-weight Arabic man.

'You like music?' the driver asked, and switched on the radio. *Strangers in the Night* blared out of the speakers. She was about to ask him to turn it down when the news came on. Nathan Kaliker was mentioned. He was among a group of people invited to the White House.

There was something about a drunk driver with twenty-seven license suspensions who had plowed into a sidewalk full of people. Then the news commentator said, 'Police are still searching for information about a young woman who was killed last week when she either fell or was pushed to the tracks in front of a subway train. The woman had short blond hair and a tattoo of the Virgin Mary on her chest. Anyone with information about the crime or about the victim's identification is asked please to call the Crime Beater's Tip Line.'

Iris sat very still. She felt cold. Shivering with cold. How many women were there in Manhattan with the Virgin Mary on their chest?

When she arrived at the hospital she went straight to the pay-phone in the lobby and considered who to call. She finally decided on Detective Barney, Kizmin's partner.

Barney was not happy to hear from her.

'This isn't a social call,' she told him. 'I heard on the

368

radio about the woman who was killed in the subway . . . the one with the tattoo.'

'Yeah.'

'I think it's a girl I talked to last week.'

'Keep going. Tell me more.'

Iris described her meeting with Cookie.

Barney blew up and muttered a string of obscenities, then took her number and said that someone would get back to her.

'How's Kizmin doing?' Iris asked.

'Ah, the poor kid's had it rough. Her left elbow's a mess. The doctor says she'll never play tennis as a leftie. She says, "What the hell, guess I'm stuck with being a cop." ' He laughed heartily.

'Would it be all right for me to visit her? Or at least give her a call?'

He hesitated. 'How's about I ask her first?'

'OK.'

'I'm going to see her tomorrow. Check with me after that.'

'Thanks.'

The phone went dead in her ear.

Iris walked into the stillness of her father's room. The blinds were slanted open and slender bars of sunlight striped the white cotton blanket that covered him. His hair had grown to nearly an inch long. Had there been that much grey in it before? Had he aged so much without her knowing?

'I'm back from Guatemala,' she said aloud.

She stared down at him. Slowly, haltingly, she bent over and touched her lips to his forehead. Then she pulled up the chair and firmly took his hand. He had always done what had to be done. He had always been strong. And in his own narrow, unflinching way he had been very good to her. He had loved her.

369

Maybe that was enough. Maybe that had always been enough but she'd been too stubborn and self-centered to see it. Or really to see herself. Because in those rare moments when she took a thorough, dispassionate self-inventory she had to admit that every aspect of her character that she valued had been forged under his influence.

His empty, unfocused eyes blinked several times. She knew it meant nothing, but it was comforting to see movement. It made him seem more alive.

'Oh, Papa,' she said. She leaned into his chest and pulled his free arm around her neck, tears streaming unchecked down her cheeks. 'Oh, Papa. I saw people get killed.'

A faint tremor went through his arm.

'Can you hear me?' she asked, pulling back to look at him. 'Move your eyes if you can hear me.'

Nothing.

She turned away from the bed and cradled her head in her hands. After awhile she picked up her backpack and walked out.

When she exited the elevator on the main floor a strange lethargy came over her. Eventually she would go to the rented room but there was no rush. There was no need to hurry anywhere. For anything. There was no point in racing around New York, back and forth from the hospital. No point at all. She could not save him. She could not bring Tim or Juan back. She couldn't make a difference at all.

She wandered into the lobby gift shop, a square room jammed with artificial flowers, stuffed animals, candy, toiletries, and reading material. Two of the walls facing into the lobby had been constructed of glass so that the small room wouldn't seem claustrophobic, but the store was so overstocked that shelf units and displays covered the glass, destroying whatever illusion of openness the architect had intended. Iris edged past the customers lined up at the register and went to the magazine and newspaper shelves. She wanted to see if there were any newspaper stories about the woman killed in the subway.

She bent to look at the papers on the lower tiers. At about knee level a piece of shelf was broken away, exposing a rectangle of the glass wall behind it. She glanced through the tiny window, stopped, and leaned closer for a better look. Across the lobby in the archway of the pay-phone alcove was a man who looked just like the Good Samaritan from the purse snatching incident.

A nameless anxiety filled her. Was she having another episode like the one in the park? Would she turn around now and imagine her mother's face on a stranger? She darted a glance behind her but everyone inside the store was just as they had been before. A child screamed out in the lobby and her heart leapt in her chest. The screaming went on and she had to cover her ears. Her hands were cold. A chill sweat broke out on her forehead.

*Stop it!* she ordered herself silently. *This is not the rain forest. It's New York. The bandits are not out there. The bodies are not out there. I'm safe. I'm fine.*

And she was suddenly filled with a rueful amusement. How ironic it was to feel safe because she had reached New York City. People were killed in Manhattan every day. Her father had been shot in the city.

She shook her head at her own absurdity and looked out the little triangle window again expecting to see that she had been mistaken about the man by the phones. He was still standing there. A pleasant-faced brown-skinned man whose nappy hair was going grey. A man who looked as though he had a wife and kids in the suburbs. The Good Samaritan.

He was focused intently on the door to the gift shop, standing half inside the phone alcove so that he was not directly visible from the front of the store.

371

The coldness in her hands spread throughout her body. He was watching the gift-shop door. Waiting. She glanced around the store again. It had temporarily emptied of customers. Besides the wizened little clerk, Iris was the only person left inside. He was waiting for her. Hiding and waiting. Stalking her.

She stood and slipped both her arms through her backpack straps. Her breathing was short and shallow. She didn't know what he wanted but she knew she had to get away.

She left the shop, glancing casually around the lobby as she stepped out. At least she hoped it appeared casual. From the corner of her eye she caught a glimpse of him drawing back out of sight. There was no question. He had been watching for her and he didn't want to be seen.

Three women were approaching. They wore clip-on office IDs. Her mind raced. She pictured the layout of the hospital. Remembered the office and the door in the back that led into the emergency room.

'Excuse me, I've forgotten how to get to the office,' she said.

'Just come with us,' one of them offered.

Iris fell in with them and tried to make small talk as they walked. She wanted to look normal so that he wouldn't be alerted or on guard when she made her move.

Nothing made sense. Where had he come from? He couldn't have followed her from Guatemala. Maybe the whole thing was perfectly innocent. Maybe he'd seen her in the hospital lobby and wanted to speak to her and was just waiting for the opportunity. Maybe he had seen her and was hiding from her, embarrassed to meet her again and hear more gushing thanks. That had to be it. He wasn't stalking her. He was hiding from her. She wanted to look back but wouldn't allow herself to.

By the time she reached the office with the women, she

had convinced herself that the man's behavior was innocent. She continued to play out her charade because it
gave her a sense of security, but she was certain that she
had overreacted.

In the company of the women she was able to walk
through the office waiting area and pass by the counter
without being questioned.

'Did you need to see someone back here?' one of the
women asked, realizing that Iris had tagged along into the
warren of cubicles behind the counter.

'Fran,' Iris said, conjuring up the name of the woman
whose desk she had sat at to talk about her father's
financial situation.

'Is she expecting you?'

'Oh yes. But I can't remember how to get to her desk. I
know it was near a door to the Emergency Room.'

'Right. Just follow the grey carpet to your left then
make a right at the end.'

'Thanks.'

Iris walked quickly. No one else questioned her. The
door was right there where she remembered it: EMER-
GENCY ROOM was stenciled on it in big red letters.
Underneath it said STAFF ONLY.

She pushed through and found herself in the emergency
treatment area. Gurneys full of moaning people lined the
walls and spilled out into the aisles. People in surgical
scrubs and uniforms scurried through the fluorescent
glare. Monitors beeped. Little knots of relatives huddled
here and there. No one seemed to notice her.

She found her way out to the emergency waiting area. It
was pure chaos. A bleeding, coughing, sobbing mass of
humanity complaining in a dozen languages. There were
several doors to choose from. The closest one looked as
though it might open into the main corridor outside the
office. It was metal with a small square of glass set in at
eye level. By now all the caution felt unnecessary, but she

still needed to reassure herself so she went closer and peeked through the window.

The sight of him slammed through her like an electric shock. He was near some soda machines, trying to look inconspicuous, his attention riveted on the door to the office waiting-room. Just then the door swung open, bumping into her.

'Sorry, sorry. You OK?' It was a young woman with two small children.

'I'm OK.'

Iris looked up. The woman let go of the door. She saw the man's head turn. And just before the door swung shut she saw the startled look of recognition come over his face.

She turned and ran. Dodging wheelchairs and crying children. She raced the length of the room and out through the glass doors onto the sidewalk. There was a taxi stopped right outside letting off passengers. Iris pushed into the backseat while the man was still paying.

'Watch it, bitch!' the passenger shouted at her as she pulled the back door shut.

The taxi driver turned around to look at her with a look of resigned disapproval.

'Go!' she shouted. 'It's an emergency!'

He pulled out into the traffic. 'Where to?'

She gave him her address at the Fitzgerald and then turned to watch out the back window.

'You know lady, this is the first time I had an emergency run away from the hospital.'

'Just go,' she said. 'Please.'

'What'a ya got, a crazy doctor with a saw after ya?'

He chuckled, then swerved around a corner and she could no longer see the Emergency Room doors. Maybe she had lost him.

She wondered if she should go to a police station instead of the Fitzgerald. But what would she tell them?

*There was a man looking at me in the hospital*. They would laugh her right back out onto the sidewalk.

She decided she would go straight to her room after all. She would be safe there. Mr Andretti would be in the building. And maybe Isaac. Maybe Mitch. She'd lock herself in and call for help. Call who? She couldn't call 911 and say that there was a man following her and she was sure it was the same man who'd chased a purse snatcher for her. Kizmin would help her but Kizmin was out of commission. Detective Barney maybe? She could just imagine what his reaction would be.

Nathan Kaliker? He would be happy to help her, but what could he actually do? What could anyone do? Hold her hand? Tell the bad man not to bother her anymore? The man hadn't threatened her or broken any laws.

When the taxi reached her building, Iris shoved money at the driver, told him to keep the change, and dashed across the sidewalk to the door. It was unlocked and there was gum jammed into the mechanism so that she couldn't lock it behind her. She thought she'd lost the man but she didn't want to take any chances.

'Damn, damn, damn,' she breathed as she raced across the lobby. The elevator doors were closed. She hit the button several times, her eyes darting back to the entrance and the small piece of the street that was visible through the front glass.

A taxi pulled up. She saw the passenger lean forward to pay. It was him!

She bolted across the floor to the superintendent's door and pounded frantically. 'Mr Andretti!' she shouted, 'It's Iris! Please let me in.'

Silence.

The man was stepping out of the taxi now. She saw him look through the glass and stiffen as he caught sight of her.

He lunged for the front door and she turned and ran to the emergency stairs. She jerked the forbidden door open, kicked the matchbook wedge away, and heard the satisfying click as the lock engaged behind her. Only then did she realize that the stairwell was completely dark.

With her hand lightly skimming the handrail for balance she hurried upward into the blackness. The stink of urine burned her nose. Glass crunched beneath her feet. Someone had broken out all the light bulbs.

The door to the first floor was slightly ajar, admitting a sliver of light. She passed it and ran until the blackness closed in again and she had to slow down or fall. There was more broken glass and another foul odor joined with the urine. Through the wall came the rumbling whine of the elevator on its way down to the lobby. Her pursuer would get on that elevator. She had to beat him upstairs.

Or maybe she should turn around and go back down? Maybe she could escape the building while he was inside the elevator?

But what if she went back down and opened the door and he was standing there? What if he didn't get on the elevator at all? Which was a possibility because he might not know which room was hers . . . which floor she was headed for. He might—

Suddenly her toe caught and she pitched forward into the darkness. Her knees and outstretched hands slammed into something on the concrete steps. Something that cushioned her fall. She groped blindly. One hand sank in wetness and she recoiled. But even as she did, the realization hit her. She was touching a body. The smell was blood.

She regained her balance and got to her feet.

A groan shuddered through the darkness and she felt her way to a kneeling position on a step.

'What happened?' she cried. 'Where are you hurt?'

She found an arm, then ran her hands over the chest. A man's chest. Her fingers traced the outlines of the face.

He turned his head slightly and his lips moved against her skin.

'Can you talk?' she asked.

There was another groan, then a word she couldn't understand.

'I'm going for help. Don't try to move.'

'Iris?' he whispered.

'Oh, no! Mr Andretti?'

'Iris . . . they got me. Just like your dad. You gotta run . . . They . . .' He coughed with a liquid, bubbling sound.

'I've got to find you help,' she cried, lurching to her feet.

'No,' He grabbed her ankle. 'I gotta tell ya first. Take my keys.' He shoved a heavy keyring at her. 'It's in the trunk. You gotta get it. I didn't tell him. The tape's there, too. He didn't get nothin'.' The cough rattled again in the darkness. 'You gotta stop him or . . .'

His body shuddered.

'Oh God, please let me go get an ambulance.'

'No. Listen first. You gotta . . . talk to Paula for me. Paula Cruz. Atlantic City. Can't remember . . . number. She's a dealer at . . . Oh, Jesus . . . Oh bless me, Father . . . it hurts. Tell her . . . the girl gets everything. Tell her . . . I was a hero. And tell Zora I'm sorry.'

His grip weakened and Iris jerked her ankle free. The stairs were slick and wet.

Through the wall she heard the elevator rumbling upward. But she couldn't think about that now. She had to get help. She went upward. She had lost track of what floor she was at but that didn't matter. When she reached the next landing she felt for the door. Her hands slipped on the knob and she had to wipe them on her pants before she could open it. She burst out of the fetid darkness into the hallway and drew in a lungful of air. The door numbers all began with five.

'Call an ambulance!' she shouted into the empty hallway. 'There's been an accident on the stairs! Call an ambulance!'

Frantically she pounded on doors without response. Finally one cracked open and an old man peeked at her over a security chain.

'Mr Andretti's hurt! The building super . . . he's hurt badly. Please call an ambulance. He's on the stairs.'

The chain rattled and the door opened wider. 'You better come in and do it. I might get it wrong.'

Iris hurried past stacks of yellowed newspapers and bags of empty soup cans. As she picked up the phone she heard the old man talking to someone out in the hall, announcing that the super had fallen down the stairs.

She dialed 911. Her hands were covered with blood. She looked down at herself. The knees of her jeans were soaked with blood. There was a red circle where he'd held her ankle and red streaks where she'd wiped her palms. The front of her blouse looked like crimson abstract art.

The 911 operator wanted explanations. Who was she? Where was she calling from? What was wrong with the injured party? 'I don't know!' she shouted, finally losing her composure. 'He's lying on the stairs and there's blood everywhere.'

'The ambulance has already been dispatched, now if you would—'

She slammed the phone down and ran out into the hall. It was deserted. She raced back to the stairwell and went in. Below, people were gathered on the stairs around Andretti. Some were squatting and some were standing, expressions somber in the flickering yellow glow of hand-held cigarette-lighters.

'He ain't breathin' too good,' someone said. 'Must'a got stabbed in the lungs.'

Stabbed! Iris pressed back against the wall just out of the pool of light. Stabbed! Mr Andretti had been stabbed?

378

'Let me through. Let me through,' ordered an authoritative voice from the darkness below. Thank God, the paramedics had arrived. But then the man stepped into the light and she saw that it was the biker.

'Keep those lighters on,' he ordered as he bent to examine Andretti.

Iris could tell by his reaction that Mr Andretti was already dead.

The biker looked up at the faces around him. 'Anybody see anything?'

'I saw her,' volunteered the old man whose phone she had used. 'She was all bloody and she came into my room to call the ambulance.'

'Was it a good-looking woman?' the biker said. 'Late twenties . . . long reddish-brown hair?'

'That's her! That's her all right.'

Iris's heart lurched. She backed up silently into the darkness then spun and ran up the stairs. All she could think about was locking herself in her room and washing the blood off. At the sixth-floor landing she cracked open the door and looked to see if the hallway was clear. She looked toward the elevator first. The hall was empty that way. She looked toward her room and froze. Her Good Samaritan pursuer was there and somehow he had opened her door. She saw the gun in his hand as he disappeared inside.

Panic struck her and she ran blindly. Up to the seventh floor. She burst out into the hall without looking first and she nearly ran into Isaac.

'Iris!' He closed the space between them in two lunging strides and grabbed her shoulders. 'You're bleeding!'

She shook her head. Tears burned behind her eyes at the sight of him and the urge to break down in his arms was strong. But she stepped back instead.

'It's not mine. I've got to hide. Andretti's dead on the stairs and there's a man in my room and—'

Isaac grabbed her hand and yanked her back into the stairwell. 'The roof,' he said, and she knew immediately what he meant.

Noise from the growing commotion in the stairwell drifted up to them. 'Seal off the building!' she heard someone shout.

Isaac threw his weight against the heavy door to the roof. It didn't budge. 'Damn, it's never been locked! We'll have to go back down to eight and go through someone's apartment to the fire escape.'

'Wait!' Iris fumbled with Andretti's ring of keys. 'These are for the entire building. It's got to be here.'

The fourth key worked. They slipped through the door quietly then locked it behind them. As soon as they were safely out on the roof she put her hands on her thighs, bent forward and gulped in air.

'They'll check up here eventually,' Isaac said.

She shoved Andretti's keys into her pocket, straightened, and looked around. Dusk was settling over the city and there were grey shadows gathering.

'If I wait until dark maybe I can sneak down the fire escape.'

'Don't count on it,' he said and motioned her toward the edge to look down. Below, at the bottom of the fire escape, the sidewalk was swarming with police.

She pulled back sharply. 'Maybe they won't think to look up here. Especially with the door locked . . .'

Isaac took off his long coat. 'Put this on,' he said.

'I'm not cold.'

'You need to cover up the blood.'

She glanced down at herself, then quickly slipped out of her backpack and put on the coat. He picked up the backpack and slung it over one shoulder.

'I can carry my own backpack,' she protested.

'They might have a description of you carrying a green backpack.'

She nodded, understanding. 'Maybe I could make it to the basement on the elevator . . .' she began. 'Or maybe I should just go down and give myself up. I'm not the murderer. Why should I be so afraid?'

Isaac stared at her searchingly. As if he was crawling into her thoughts.

'I know a way,' he said finally. Without explanation he led her across to the side where the roof adjoined another, slightly shorter building. 'Are you afraid to jump?' he asked.

'What happens after I get down onto that roof? Won't I still be trapped?'

'There's a fire escape going down the opposite side of that building. It's accessible from the roof.'

She nodded and sat down on the top of the parapet.

'Wait!' Isaac called in surprise. 'Let me go first and then—'

She swung around and slipped over, holding on until she was hanging, her hands slipping, skin burning over the rough brick. Then she let go. She thudded onto the tarred surface, stumbled and fell to a sitting position. Isaac followed, landing easily on his feet near her.

'If you'd let me go first I could have caught you,' he said.

'I didn't need to be caught.' She scrambled upright and brushed the grit from her hands.

The fire escape was just where he said it would be but the steps and handrail did not extend all the way up to the roof. She looked down, trying not to betray her fear.

Without waiting for discussion he swung over the parapet and dropped the eight feet to the grated metal platform. He was very agile. As before he landed with easy confidence. She followed. The metal rang when her feet struck and she felt herself pitching backward, but Isaac caught her.

They hurried down the flights of steps. No one on the

381

ground paid any attention to them. When the final section lowered to the sidewalk with a clang there were some curious glances from passersby, but no one shouted for the police. No one so much as slowed their pace.

She walked as fast as she could without running. Isaac matched his stride to hers.

'Are you going to explain all this?' he asked.

'I don't know if I can.'

He yanked her into an apartment doorway.

'Now,' he demanded. 'Whose blood is it?'

'Mr Andretti's.'

She held out her hands and stared down at them. Against her skin the blood had dried to rust. Suddenly she could not remain still. She spun and ran, dodging through the crowds. The light at the corner was red but she kept going. Cars honked and brakes screeched around her.

When Isaac caught her she nearly collapsed. Every muscle in her body began to shake as soon as her forward momentum was stopped.

He clamped one arm tightly about her shoulders and pulled her with him to the curb where he used the other arm to signal for a taxi.

'Show us Central Park,' Isaac ordered the driver.

'Why Central Park?' she asked after several moments of silence.

'To give us time to think.'

A wave of nausea swept over her. She let her head fall back against the seat and closed her eyes. But they were all there waiting. All the dull, sightless stares. All the bloodied, ruined bodies. She jerked upright and pressed her hands over her mouth.

'Are you feeling sick?' Isaac asked.

She nodded.

'We'll get off at the Plaza,' Isaac called to the driver. Then he turned toward her with a look of compassion and concern. 'Hang on. It's only a few blocks.'

She felt better when she was outside again in the air. They sat down at the edge of the fountain and watched the water. Iris was grateful for something hypnotic and calming to focus on. All around them tourists brandished their cameras and unfolded their fluttering maps in the breeze.

She knew he wanted to know everything and she thought she probably owed him more than she had given.

'I flew in from Guatemala today,' she said, speaking softly and keeping her eyes on the water. 'I went straight to the hospital. A man was there watching me. Following me. He was the same man who chased the purse-snatcher in the subway.'

Isaac frowned in thought.

'I panicked and ducked out through the Emergency Room. I made it back to the building, but somehow he followed me. I ran up the stairs and tripped over Mr Andretti's body. Then, suddenly there was the biker – you know, the guy from my floor with the black Hell's Angels wardrobe – and he started talking about identifying me and going after me . . . as though I was the killer. So I ran up to the sixth floor. Then I saw the man who'd been following me. He was going into my room. With a gun! That's when I went up to seven and saw you.'

She drew in a deep, ragged breath. 'I don't know what's happening. Nothing makes sense. I keep thinking I'll wake up and none of this will be real. All of them will be alive again and—'

'All of them? Who else got killed?'

'In Guatemala. I was working down in the chamber and bandits came. They killed Tim and Juan and they almost took Linda.'

Isaac stared off toward the park for several minutes, deep in thought.

'We need to know what's happening,' he said. 'I think I should go back to the building. No one saw us together. They won't be looking for me.'

She nodded.

'The safest thing for you to do is stay right here. This area will be full of tourists all evening. Just mingle.' He pointed down the avenue. 'Right there is Trump Tower. They've got public bathrooms. You can go wash your hands there, but don't open your coat. All that blood on your clothes could draw too much attention.'

She nodded again.

'I'll be back as soon as I can. Then we'll go from there, decide what to do. What it's safe to do.'

He scribbled something on a scrap of paper. 'Here's my phone number again, and just in case you need anything . . .' He pulled out some bills and handed them to her with the number.

He stood then and started to swing one strap of the backpack over his shoulder.

'I want to keep that.'

'OK. But don't put it on. Carry it low.' He studied her a moment. 'I wish you had a hat,' he said. 'You're too recognizable.'

She stared up at his face. And in spite of everything that had happened, in spite of the turmoil and terror that gripped her, she felt an almost visceral reaction. *Oh God, was this love?*

'I'll meet you right here,' he said. 'Two hours at the maximum.'

She watched him walk away. What did she know about the man? How did she even know she could trust him?

She looked down at her hands again and thought of Mr Andretti. It came back to her then, Andretti had said to tell Zora he was sorry. Madame Zora. What a fool she had been! That whole Tarot reading must have been a hoax. Zora was connected to Andretti and had known things about her.

She put Isaac's phone number and the money in the zippered pocket of her backpack, then she stood and walked toward Trump Tower. Inside the building she rode the escalators down and followed the signs for the bathrooms. After three soapings there was still a thin line of black blood under her fingernails. She tore at it, jammed paper towels into her nailbed, tried everything she could think of but still the lines remained. She pulled Andretti's keys from her pocket and looked to see if there was a thin one that might work like the tip of a nailfile. There wasn't. Sighing, she opened the main zipper of her pack and dropped the keys inside. There was a clink of metal as the keys struck bottom. Her own keys were floating around down there somewhere, too.

Suddenly it struck her. Her own keys. She had slipped the key to the forensic anthropology lab onto her keyring and she hadn't had a chance to return it to Kizmin yet. She thrust her arm deep into the pack and fished along the bottom until her fingers snagged the plain metal ring. She pulled it out. Yes. The lab key was still there mixed in with her building keys – front door, mail box, and room.

She gripped the ring tightly and went out into the long marble-tiled hallway. A bank of phones was set into the wall. She hesitated. Should she call Isaac? Not much time had elapsed since his leaving. He probably wasn't at his room yet. She left without trying the number, went out into the crowds on Fifth Avenue and went in search of the E line to the West Side. She would hide at the lab until she figured out what to do next. No one would find her at the lab.

# Twenty-Two

Iris stood under a hot shower for as long as she could. Until her skin was hurting. Still, she didn't feel clean. It was as though the blood was permanent, even after she could no longer see the stains.

She moved through the lab, wrapped in an oversize bathrobe she'd found. Everything was quiet and dark. Most of the windows had no coverings so she was afraid to turn on lights. She allowed herself only one small, heavily shaded desk-lamp on the counter next to the telephone. The pool of light from it was so contained that she didn't think it would show from outside the windows. She sat down at the counter and thought about what Andretti had said.

*It's in the trunk. The tape's there, too.*

What was in the trunk? What trunk? Where was the trunk? And what tape was he talking about? Could it be the tape of her father's shooting?

*Take my keys.*

That had to mean that the trunk was locked. Or the trunk was locked inside somewhere. If it had been in his room the police would have it by now, but she didn't think he'd had it in his room.

She buried her face in her hands and tried to think coherently. Her thoughts were fragmented and racing in all directions.

She called information in Atlantic City, New Jersey for

Paula Cruz. There was no listing.

The trunk. She had to find the trunk. What about the basement storage area behind the elevator? That was the perfect place to keep a trunk. A trunk wouldn't be noticeable in a storage area. She visualized the basement again. Remembered the locked side door to the street. Surely one of Andretti's keys would open that door.

There were three bedrooms carved out of the living quarters section of the huge loft. In one of them Iris found some women's clothing in the closet. Everything was two sizes larger than what she wore but she cinched in a long flowing skirt with a belt and rolled up the sleeves of a boxy blazer and achieved the slouchy look. She French-braided her hair tightly into a pattern high on the back of her head and pulled on a floppy velvet hat. There was a large leatherette satchel in the back of the closet. She picked it up, thinking it made her look more legitimate.

She rode the bus until she was within blocks of the building, then she approached it on the sidestreet. She moved normally with the other pedestrians. As she neared the basement door she checked up and down the side-walk, then she stepped out of the pedestrian flow to dart down the three steps to the service entrance. The lock was an odd brand and easily matched to a key. She had it open in an instant. No one was in sight. She let the door latch shut behind her. Quietly she eased past the storage room and along the wall of the elevator housing, then peered around the corner. The basement stretched out in bright white silence just as before.

She went to the storage doors and unlocked them. The room was bigger than she had expected. It stretched out like a railroad car, narrow but very long, with industrial shelving along one side, heavy-duty hooks and pulleys on the other. The forgotten possessions of several decades had accumulated there – bicycles of every size, strollers and high chairs and collapsible playpens, odd pieces of furniture, cast-off appliances, air conditioners and giant floor fans, exercise machines and weight benches. Cardboard cartons and large suitcases filled one whole section of shelves. Beneath them marched a line of trunks.

She waded through the clutter to the trunks. Everything was thickly filmed with sooty dust, as though it hadn't been touched for years. She started at one end and worked her way down. No key on Andretti's ring fit any of the trunks. Two were unlocked and she lifted the lids. One held yellowed baby clothes. The other was packed with Broadway Playbills and dance programs. She searched through the room, moving and lifting and getting down on her hands and knees to look underneath, but there was nothing else that remotely resembled a trunk. Should she break open the locked ones?

She stood there, thinking. Andretti had said, *It's in the trunk. I hid it*, and she'd had the distinct impression that he'd done it recently. These dusty trunks hadn't been disturbed for a long time.

She stepped out of the storage room and relocked the doors. A quick tour of the basement proved what she had already suspected. There were no other hiding places.

At the elevator door she stopped and considered what to do next. Her change of appearance had seemed successful to her and she doubted that any casual observer would recognize her. If there were watchers outside the building, they wouldn't be expecting her to sneak in through the basement. Surely one quick trip up to her room ought to be safe.

She pushed the elevator button, then dashed back around by the storage room to hide. If she heard anyone get out of the elevator she would spring for the basement door.

As she waited, listening to the approaching rumble of machinery, she recalled the other time she had hidden in that position and listened to the two unidentified male voices. They had been looking for a woman. They had been angry about losing track of a woman. A chill coursed down her spine as she realized it had been her they were after. How long had she been pursued? What else had she missed or overlooked or discounted in her role as unsuspecting prey?

The face at her window? Undoubtedly that watcher was a part of the plot. The neat search of her room? Of course. That hadn't been the purse-snatcher. Or maybe it had. Maybe the purse-snatcher was part of it all too. The Good Samaritan certainly had been. But why snatch her purse?

The letter!

That was the morning she got the letter for her father and when she was still in the lobby she had put the letter in her purse. It was only by chance that she'd dropped it in the deli and ended up slipping it into her shopping bag. Whoever was out there had been after the letter! But she still had the letter. She had tucked it and the note from her mother into an inner pocket of her backpack and they were still there.

The doors opened on six. Cautiously she checked the dimly lit hall in both directions. It was empty. Totally quiet.

She hesitated, afraid of losing the elevator. If she could keep the doors from closing it wouldn't be able to leave. She looked out in the hall again, looked down at herself. The leather satchel. That would work. She positioned it on the floor and pushed the button to close the doors. Just as she'd hoped, the doors nudged impotently against the satchel then opened again. She hurried down the hall to her door. There were no police seals on it or any other sign that the authorities had been there. She unlocked both locks, wincing at the noise. Then, with a last look behind her, she slipped inside. And froze. Stunned.

The mattress and box-springs were sliced to ribbons. The pillow was shredded. Drawers were upended and tossed in all directions. There were holes in the walls and ceilings.

She took a few steps forward, over a tangle of torn clothing and around a broken drawer. Her long skirt made her clumsy so she gathered handfuls of the hem and tucked them into the heavy belt at her waist. She bent to retrieve her father's wallet, then gathered all the papers and cards and meaningless bits that had been strewn across the floor. The nylon carry-on case she used for travel was lying near the window, pulled inside out and gutted of lining. She prodded it back into shape and pulled the shoulder strap over her head so that it rested diagonally across her chest and left her hands free. She shoved the wallet and papers inside, then numbly picked through the rubble, rescuing whatever caught her eye. She searched but couldn't find her computer disks. Other things were missing too, though she wasn't able to say exactly what. Several minutes passed before she snapped out of her shock and the fear returned. She had to get out of there.

The building had seemed so safe and quiet, but now she wasn't sure. She opened the window and looked down the fire escape. Maybe she should go out that way? But there was a man loitering on the sidewalk underneath. Was he one of them? Waiting there to catch her? And how about the roof? What if they had discovered her previous escape route and had someone waiting up there too?

Suddenly she heard the rasp of a key in the lock. She dived behind the wrecked bed, crouched there, heart crashing against her ribs.

The door exploded inward and a man rushed past her toward the window shouting, 'Fuck! She's gone!' In the split-second glimpse she had of him she saw that it was the same man who'd followed her from the hospital. The man who'd posed as a Good Samaritan and stalked her since the purse snatching.

He climbed out onto the fire escape, leaned over to look down and called out to someone on the ground. She had been right. They were everywhere.

She peeked around the end of the bed. There was a second man, standing just outside the open doorway, facing toward the hall as though keeping watch. She took a deep breath and bolted to the window. The man out on the landing turned in surprise as she threw her weight against the sash, slamming it down and sliding the lock into place.

The man from the hall spun around, then advanced slowly, arms outstretched, eyes glittering with excitement. 'Don't make this hard,' he warned. 'I'm with—'

But his words ended in a grunt, knocked out of him by the force of a blow from behind. Iris stood there, gaping. Isaac had leaped into the doorway, swung from the frame, and hit the attacker solidly with both feet, sending the man sprawling and gasping to the floor.

'Come on!' Isaac shouted, but she was already moving.

She raced toward the elevator. Behind her she heard glass shatter. The man on the fire escape had broken her window.

'The roof!' Isaac called, motioning for her to run ahead of him.

She kicked the satchel aside and stabbed the eighth-floor button. Isaac hurtled through the doors just as they started to close. She stabbed the eighth-floor button again and pounded the close-doors button, but the mechanism rumbled at its same slow pace.

The doors were inches from meeting when a hand pushed through. Isaac kicked the hand with such speed that the movement was a blur and only the disappearance of the hand and the accompanying yowl of pain assured Iris that it had happened.

When the door was securely closed, Isaac pushed the seven button too.

'Decoy,' he said. 'Soon as it opens start hitting for eight.' And she understood immediately because she had been about to do the same thing herself. Their pursuers couldn't make it up the stairs to seven in time to catch the doors opening there and maybe, just maybe they would be confused by hearing the elevator stop.

As the gears engaged and the faintest rumble of upward motion began, Isaac jumped toward the ceiling and punched open a square trapdoor that Iris had not noticed was there. He leaped again, gripped the edges of the opening with his fingers, and strained upward, pulling himself completely out of the car. The doors rumbled open on the empty hall of the seventh floor. Iris slammed the door-close and the eight buttons until the doors groaned shut. She could hear muffled shouts from somewhere in the stairwell. Isaac leaned down from above and extended his hands to her. She threw herself toward him, grabbed him, felt his fingers lock around her forearms. The muscles of his face were tight as he pulled and she fought for her own purchase, using her elbows for leverage as soon as they were through the opening. Finally she was clear and kneeling on the top of the moving car, face close to the snaking oiled cables.

He dropped the trapdoor into place just as the machinery lurched to a halt. He gripped her hand and she squeezed back. She could hear the doors opening.

There was a flood of cursing, a loud sound as though someone was kicking the car's wall, then voices. 'They must'a beat us on seven and headed up the stairs to the roof!'

'Yeah, they'll get a surprise up there.'

'Who was that fuck, anyway? He nearly broke my ribs.'

'I don't know, but I got a good look at him. If he does get away I'll find him.'

'They're not gettin' away. Wanna go up and watch the party or go down to the lobby and wait?'

'Lobby. I need to get a towel. Cut my arm on that window.'

There was the sound of the doors closing and then the car rumbled downward and the men's words were no longer audible over the grinding and whining. Iris searched Isaac's face in the half dark of the elevator shaft. His expression was intensely focused and very angry.

'I'm sorry,' she whispered but she didn't know if he heard.

The car settled to a stop at the lobby and it occurred to her that it was programmed to sit there with the doors open until a button was pushed or it was called to another floor. She heard one of the men call out to someone across the lobby, something about action on the roof.

She looked at Isaac. 'If we can make it to the basement we can get out of the service door,' she whispered.

He nodded.

'How did you know I was in trouble?' she asked.

'I heard the guy out on your fire escape so I went down to check it out.'

The soft inhale and exhale of their breathing joined together in the stillness.

'I'm sorry I got you involved,' she said.

'It was my decision,' he said. 'My choice.'

From above them came a distant ping and Iris tensed. Someone on a higher floor had called the elevator. She listened to the doors close and braced herself for the upward movement.

As soon as the ascent began Isaac jerked open the trapdoor and dropped down. She heard him punching a floor button, then she swung into position, dangled her legs through the opening and followed, thudding to the floor just as the doors opened.

'Come on,' Isaac urged, pulling her by the hand.

They ran to the stairs and started down. The bulbs had

been replaced so there was a jaundiced light in the stairwell. Iris breathed a sigh of relief when she saw that they were only on the second level. Far from the site of Mr Andretti's murder.

The lobby door was partially open and she could hear several male voices. Isaac put a finger to his lips. She nodded. They crept silently down the final flight to the landing then darted past the door. When they reached basement level, Isaac cracked open the door and put one eye to the opening.

She heard his sharp intake of breath and pushed forward to look. There was a man not six feet from them. He was standing in front of the elevator doors, lighting a cigarette. There was the crackle of radio static, then the man lifted a small black handset to his mouth and said, 'No. It's quiet down here.'

Isaac nudged her and she tensed, ready for flight. She was gripping Andretti's keys so tightly that the metal cut into her skin. She forced her fingers to relax, to flex slightly, and she checked once more to assure herself that the key she had separated out was the key to the basement service door.

The radio crackled once more and the sentry responded with a grunted affirmative. Then he lowered the radio from his mouth and Isaac lunged out of the door toward him and she ran. She jammed the key home, fumbled it in the wrong direction, then twisted it and jerked the door open so hard that she nearly fell. Isaac was right behind her as she stepped onto the sidewalk.

'Careful,' he breathed. 'Act normal.' But a man on the corner shouted something and she knew they'd been spotted.

She ran beside him. The sidestreet was nearly empty of pedestrians. They ran east. She glanced back once and saw a line of men strung out in hard pursuit. At Third Avenue Isaac stepped into the traffic and waved at passing taxis. One screeched to a halt and they jumped into the backseat.

'Go! Go! Go!' Isaac shouted.

The driver muttered something in Hindi but sped up the avenue. Iris turned to watch out the back window. Several blocks behind them she saw a car take the corner on two wheels. Another car behind it stopped and picked up the foot pursuers.

'They're behind us,' she said. 'Two cars.'

'Turn here!' Isaac ordered, then peppered the driver with a terse series of instructions.

Iris didn't recognize anything until they reached Union Square and Isaac shouted, 'Stop!' He threw a twenty-dollar bill into the front seat as they slid out, then they ran again. Down the stairs into the labyrinthine Union Square subway terminus.

She was lost. Running blind. Resigned to letting him lead and trusting in his judgment and knowledge. Her heart and lungs felt close to exploding and the muscles in her thighs were burning. She focused all her strength and determination on continuing forward. More stairs. Down into the bowels of the station. Up to another level. Through the racketing roar and the stale artificial wind from the trains. Zigzagging through the maze. Across a walkway fenced with slender metal bars like an old-fashioned lion's cage, looking through the bars at her pursuers running down below. Them looking up at her. Down again. Onto a platform where a long silver train stood, ready to go, chimes sounding, engine revving, doors sliding closed.

Isaac lunged forward. Threw himself at the doors and got a hand and foot through. Strained and pulled until he forced them open, held them open for her to squeeze inside.

Then the train was moving. Three men ran up to it, slammed their fists against the glass. Shouted curses in inaudible streams, veins throbbing, faces red. Like crazed dogs biting at rabbits in a glass cage.

She sagged against the pole as the train plunged into the dark tunnel and they were safe.

'Hold on,' Isaac said. 'Don't go down yet. They'll call ahead. Have all the stops covered. Try to trap us.'

So she gripped the pole and gritted her teeth and tried to keep collapse at bay.

'What have you got in there?' Isaac asked, indicating the carry-on.

She looked down and was surprised that she still had it. The velvet hat was long gone. The scarf was gone.

'Things from the room,' she said, lacking the energy to elaborate.

'Any clothes? Something you could change into?'

'A pair of jeans.'

'Good. Lose the skirt.'

'Here?' She glanced down the crowded subway car.

'Just pull the jeans on under your skirt. They'll enjoy the show.'

She shifted the carry-on around so she could reach the zipper, then pulled out the jeans.

'Hurry,' he urged.

Leaning against the pole for balance, she awkwardly worked a sneakered foot into one pant-leg. She could feel her cheeks turn red but she clenched her jaw and kept her eyes down. When she had the jeans snapped, she unbelted the skirt and slipped it down.

'Now get rid of that jacket.'

He held up the carry-on while she shrugged out of the jacket, then she let the strap settle back into place over her T-shirt.

'You sure you need to hang on to that bag?' he asked.

'There are papers . . . receipts . . . things that might be clues.'

He nodded.

'Do you think they'll be fooled by my changing clothes?'

His eyes were puzzled, then her meaning registered and he almost smiled. 'That's not why you changed. Loose clothes could be dangerous where we're going.'

A flutter of apprehension went through her stomach but she didn't ask what his plan was. So far he had been an artist at escape, and at the moment he was her only hope.

'Get ready,' he said, as the train screeched into a lighted station.

He wadded her skirt and jacket together and tossed them to a bag lady who grinned toothlessly and squirreled the garments away with lightning speed. Then the doors opened and people jammed together to push their way out through the crowd pushing its way in. She took a step toward the flow but Isaac grabbed her hand and pulled her with him through the back door, over the couplings and into the next car, through that car and another door, and suddenly there was no more train. She was suspended over the gaping black maw of the tunnel.

Isaac jumped down and held his hand out for her. She wanted to ask him where the hell he was leading her, but her mouth was too dry to speak.

'Come on!' he hissed.

And she made the leap into the rank, stinking darkness, where she knew there was a third rail that would electrocute her if she touched it and there were trains coming and going that would slice her apart in an instant and there were rats the size of dachshunds, and in that moment she realized that she had handed her life over to Isaac Brightman.

'Put your hands on my waist,' he instructed, 'and follow exactly in my footsteps. Exactly. And don't let the wildlife scare you. They're the least of our problems.'

She held on to him with a steel grip and moved in sync with him to the center divider, a thick masonry wall that separated the trains going one direction from the trains going the other. The train they had been on roared out of the station with a thundering blast of sound and a whoosh of air that swirled trash around her and flung grit into her eyes. Then they slipped through one of the arches in the divider and they crossed the opposite tracks and relief flooded through her because they were just feet from the lighted platform and safety. But instead of climbing onto the platform Isaac turned and edged along the wall into the tunnel. Several feet in he pulled her into an alcove in the wall.

'This is a safe spot,' he explained. 'In case a worker gets caught down on the tracks when a train comes. He can jump in here and get away.'

She pressed herself back against the rough wall. There was an oily dirt smell underscored by something foul. Something rotting. All around was the sound of scurrying. Thousands of tiny clawed feet running about in the darkness. Occasionally there was a squeak or the snarl of a confrontation. She tried to block everything out.

Air stirred in the tunnel where they were hiding. A distant rumble began to build and the wind picked up and the walls vibrated and the ground shuddered and she pressed her hands against her ears and squeezed her eyes shut. Then Isaac's arm was around her and he pulled her head to his chest and she buried her face in the thick weave of his sweater as the train's passing engulfed them.

It had barely shrieked to a stop when Isaac pulled her from the alcove. They ran along the wall to the beginning of the platform. Isaac boosted her up, then swung onto the platform beside her. Quickly they joined with the crush of passengers boarding the train and slid into seats against the wall.

'The windows,' Isaac cautioned, and she followed his lead, bending down to fuss with the laces on her sneakers.

Remaining bent over until the train had pulled out of the station.

'Think we've lost them?' she whispered as she straightened in her seat.

'Maybe. There were two of them across the platform but they didn't see us get on this train.'

'Aren't we going back to Union Square now?'

'We'll go a stop past it, then get out of the subway.'

Her leg muscles trembled and her chest ached. She was covered with so much grime that she could have passed for a street dweller. She glanced sideways at Isaac and wondered how he had learned to be so tough and resourceful.

'You're pretty good at all this,' she said, and the question hung, unspoken.

He studied his soot-streaked hands for several long moments. 'I grew up on the streets,' he said finally. 'Running away was the major survival skill.'

'Here?'

'All cities are alike.'

A garbled announcement sounded over the public-address system.

'Duck,' Isaac ordered, and they bent to their shoelaces again.

'Think they're still watching here?'

'They probably left a man here just in case.'

'There could be someone at the next stop couldn't there?'

'Anything is possible.'

But the next stop was clear and they hurried up to street level without incident. They walked for several blocks, pausing to wave for taxis whenever an unoccupied one approached, but they were so filthy that drivers sped up and passed them. Finally, they made it onto a crosstown bus.

'Stay down,' Isaac cautioned, and they huddled

together away from the window.

'What now?' she asked.

'We hide.'

She hesitated then. Did she want to take him to the lab? Did she trust him with her secret place? But she was immediately ashamed. How could she not share her safe hiding place when he had put himself in jeopardy for her. When he had saved her several times over.

And how could she have the slightest bit of hesitation when she had followed him into the tunnels and over the third rail?

'I have the key to the forensic anthropology lab,' she said. 'No one will think of looking there.'

The ride was uneventful. On the West Side they transferred to another bus, then they walked. They went into a coffee shop and ate, not so much because they were hungry but because Isaac wanted to watch the street from the window to make sure they weren't being followed.

It wasn't until after they were locked safely inside the lab that Iris allowed herself to consider the enormity of all that had happened.

She gripped her head between her palms, pressing hard enough to feel the skull underneath, and she stared up at the ceiling.

'Who are all those men! Why are they after me?'

In spite of her exhaustion and her aching leg muscles, she began to pace. Back and forth. In and out of the small circle of lamplight.

Isaac caught her, held her by the shoulders, forced her to meet his eyes.

'You must have some idea what's going on.'

She took a deep breath. 'It has to do with my father. With something he was involved in. And with my mother, I think.' She tried to look away but his grip tightened on her shoulders and he held her with his eyes.

'If I tell you everything then you'll be in as much trouble as I'm in,' she protested.

He threw up his hands and laughed in a sharp sarcastic bark. 'You think I'm not in trouble now? You think all those goons will let me go back to my room and my life and pretend none of this happened?'

She turned away from him. 'I'm sorry.' As soon as the words were out she pressed her knuckles to her mouth to keep from saying more. She felt guilty and grateful, but vaguely resented him, vaguely feared him even. She had trusted him with her life but she didn't trust him emotionally.

Wearily she sank into a chair. 'What do you want to know?'

'Everything you haven't told me.'

When the questions were finished she sat back, exhausted, and closed her eyes.

'Someone wants to kill me, Isaac. And somehow . . . I don't really understand this . . . but somehow it seems like the police are involved. Or covering up.'

He didn't answer. Worse, he didn't try to argue.

'If only I could call Kizmin. I don't know who else to trust. I don't know . . . Mr Kaliker. I could call him. But I'm afraid he'd insist that I turn myself over to the police.'

They sat in silence for awhile.

'Mr Andretti said I had to talk to Paula Cruz.'

Isaac nodded.

'I'm going to Atlantic City.'

# Twenty-Three

Iris jerked her head up and looked around. The digital clock on the dashboard read 2:00 a.m. They had turned off the highway into a rest area. Isaac drove past the restaurants and pulled up to the gas pumps.

'I must have fallen asleep,' she said in wobbly voice.

Isaac smiled. The implications of that smile annoyed her and made her sit up straighter.

She cleared her throat. 'You should let me drive now.'

'You don't have a current license. That's all we need. Being hauled in by some eager cop because of an unlicensed driver.'

She knew he was right but still it annoyed her.

'How much longer till we get there?' she asked.

'Another hour or so.'

They were on their way to the home of Monopoly streets and glittering casinos and long sugary beaches. The home of the Miss America Pageant. Iris had been there once before to a conference. She still recalled how shocked she had been, after days of the ocean and the boardwalk and the spectacles, to wander past the casino and into the actual city. It was like stepping behind carefully constructed movie scenery. In back of all the glitz and fun was a sprawl of pathetic urban decay. And somewhere in that two-faced city was Paula Cruz.

She tried to relax and let the annoyance fade, but she couldn't. Paula Cruz had neither a listed nor an unlisted number in Atlantic City or any surrounding area, but Andretti had been so specific. Iris was certain she would find the woman there.

She had had just enough credit left on her card to buy a roundtrip bus fare to Atlantic City and that had been her plan, but immediately Isaac had started revising. In the end she had agreed because his revisions were reasonable and he had borrowed a car from someone and now he was driving her. He was becoming more and more involved. Not just involved. It seemed to Iris that he had taken control.

When they came out of the flat marshy area and into the outskirts of the city Isaac said, 'I called ahead for a room at Resorts.'

'I like the Sands,' she said, naming the place she had stayed on her previous visit.

'What's bothering you, Iris?'

She thought for a moment. 'Everything. You were so worried that I might trap you. That you might be sucked into a future with me. Now here you are all tangled up in my nightmare and . . . I don't want you to help me anymore.'

Without another word he pulled into the Sands self-park garage.

At the check-in desk he asked for connecting rooms.

'You're not buying me a room, Isaac.'

'Excuse me,' he said to the check-in clerk who was working hard at maintaining a neutral expression. Then he pulled Iris to the side.

'You don't have enough money left to buy your own room,' he said carefully.

'I know, but you're not buying me a separate room. It's four in the morning, Isaac. All we're going to do is sleep. Can't we be practical . . . and adult . . . about this?'

He raked his hair back off his forehead and stared across the lobby. Then he went back up to the desk.

★ ★ ★

The room was in the middle of a long carpeted hallway. It was very quiet. Four a.m. appeared to be a time when even rabid gamblers needed to sleep.

Isaac opened the door with a plastic cardkey. Inside there was a large bed and a couch.

'I'll take the couch,' Isaac said.

'You should have the bed.'

'No. The couch folds out. It's fine.'

She started to object, to say that it would be just as fine for her, then decided not to. She didn't want to argue. She didn't want to talk to him anymore at all.

Twenty minutes later she lay in bed listening to Isaac's rhythmic breathing. He was right across the room, lying in a tangle of sheets in the middle of the fold-out bed that had popped out of the couch complete with linens and blankets and pillows. He had said good-night to her but she had pretended she was already asleep.

She wished she could fall asleep. But there was no comfortable position in the king-size bed. And she was too hot. Her skin felt flushed with heat.

What would it be like to have his hard lean body against hers? Those long steady hands touching her face. Her neck. Her breasts. Sliding down her stomach.

She groaned softly and turned over. What had happened to her? She was in the grip of total lunacy.

Finally she slept, but there was no escape in sleep. Isaac came to her through the blowing white curtains of a tent, came to her on a bed that was draped in layers of silk, came to her from out of the ocean, dripping with starlight. Came to her over and over again and she pressed herself against him, heat building and centering, need mounting to explosion. And over and over his image faded and she was left alone in frustration.

Then there was a figure kneeling in the distance and she

ran to it and the figure had long dark hair and there was a spreading lake of red with a body in it. The body was her father's but he had Isaac's eyes. And the figure turned. It was her mother. Crying. Holding a knife. Then her mother became Moonsmoke and she held the obsidian knife. She came toward Iris through smoke and cinders. 'I've been waiting,' she said, and she handed the knife to Iris.

They slept until their nine o'clock wake-up call, then took turns in the bathroom. Iris was carefully polite. Isaac seemed preoccupied. They went down to a food court and Iris looked at the pay-phone, wondering if she should call the hospital and check on her father, wondering if she should try to get hold of Kizmin.

'So what's your plan again?' Isaac asked her over a quick breakfast of bagels and coffee at a wrought-iron table under a skylight.

'He said Paula Cruz was a dealer so I'm going to go from place to place, asking if they have a dealer by that name. It shouldn't be too hard. There are a limited number of casinos here and gambling isn't allowed any-where else.'

'What makes you think a casino will tell you if she works there? I imagine they're very protective of their employees.'

'I'll say there's been a death in her family and I've come to notify her.'

He nodded. 'That might work.' Then he looked her up and down and frowned. 'You need to be dressed more seriously to have a chance.'

She glanced at her jeans. 'This is all I have.'

'You don't look credible.'

'But this is all I have.'

'There's a mall nearby on the boardwalk. Something tailored and black would be good.'

'Isaac . . .'

'I know . . . I know . . . but money is not a problem for me right now, and you can consider it a loan. Pay me back later.'

'I couldn't.'

'Look at yourself. That subway grease didn't wash out and there's a tear in your shirt. These casino security types are trained to be suspicious and skeptical. You'll never convince them of anything looking like a panhandler.'

'All right. All right.'

'I need to make some calls,' he said. 'Take care of some business. I'll do it from the mall pay-phones while you shop.' And she realized how little she knew about him. What business did he have? How could he leave town so suddenly? What about his jobs? And if money was no problem for him, why did he live at the Fitzgerald?

The mall was built so that it looked like a giant ocean liner docked at the boardwalk. She went into the first women's shop that looked appropriate and found a striking black trouser-suit with a fitted jacket. She took no pleasure in the clothes and when Isaac returned to pay for them she had a moment of self-disgust watching him pass the cash across the counter.

Next she had to have shoes because her dirty white sneakers ruined the effect of the suit. She chose the first black flats she saw. When they left the mall and returned to the boardwalk she was wearing the new clothes. They went straight into a casino.

As Isaac had predicted, her inquiries were met with instructions to go to the security office. It was a time-draining process. Her explaining. Them consulting in whispers and making phone calls before finally revealing that there was no Paula Cruz employed there. Isaac wandered through the slot machines and left the whole process to her.

They went from casino to casino, walking from one to the other along the boardwalk, moving from breezy sun-spangled sea views and the soothing lap of the surf, into glittery fantasy halls where everything was artificial and every sound was the sound of money.

It was late in the afternoon before Iris found Paula Cruz.

'You can wait in here,' a husky man in a suit said as he opened the door to a small but comfortably furnished room. 'We'll send her in as soon as we get a replacement dealer for her table.'

'Thank you,' Iris said.

'Uh, is this news going to put her out of commission? I mean, should we plan to replace her for the whole shift?'

'I don't know,' Iris said honestly.

The minutes ticked by. Iris realized that she didn't know what Andretti was to this woman and she didn't know what effect the news of his death would have. She hadn't thought beyond finding her. Now she had to decide what to say.

But before Iris could think any further a petite woman in a dealer's uniform walked in. She had a pretty, heart-shaped face and a cap of shiny brown-black hair. Her physical appearance was quite youthful but something about her eyes gave the years away.

She stopped just inside the door and stared at Iris as though stricken.

Iris rose. 'Are you Paula Cruz?'

The woman didn't answer. She crossed herself.

'Are you all right?' Iris asked.

The woman put a hand over her eyes a moment, then went to a chair and sat down. 'I should have known it would come to this,' she said.

'What?' Iris sat so she was facing the woman.

'I told him to keep me out of it. But he didn't, did he?' She laughed unhappily. 'Obviously, he didn't.'

'You know who I am then?' Iris asked.

Cruz laughed again. 'I'd have to be blind not to.'

'I'm sorry, but I'm confused . . . Do you also know why I'm here?'

'I could make a pretty good guess.'

'Then, you knew he was in danger?'

'What?'

'Mr Andretti . . . you must have known he was in danger.'

'Andretti!' This time her laugh was laced with ridicule. 'God, he was really dreaming when he picked that one, wasn't he.'

Iris sat back and considered how to proceed. She was baffled by the woman's reactions.

'I am so sorry . . . I know I'm going about this clumsily . . . but . . . I can't tell whether you know or not.'

'Know what?'

'That Mr Andretti is dead.'

Cruz's expression went from disbelief to anger to a sad resignation. 'How did it happen?' she finally asked.

'He was stabbed.'

The woman covered her face with her hands.

Iris felt terrible. 'Would you like to be alone?'

Cruz dropped her hands and shook her head firmly. 'It was just a shock,' she said. 'I hated the little prick.'

'I'm sorry,' Iris said because she couldn't think of any other reply.

'Don't be. He asked for it. And as for me, I put sorry behind me a long time ago.'

Iris studied various spots around the room in an agony of discomfort. This was not how she had expected the meeting to go, though she couldn't have said what she had expected.

'I would have called, but I couldn't find a listing for you,' Iris said.

'The phone is in my roommate's name. She had the apartment first.'

Iris nodded.

'What led you to me?' Cruz asked.

'I . . . I was the one who found him. He was still alive but he knew he was dying and he was trying desperately to talk. Some of it I couldn't make sense of, but he was very clear about your name and about telling me to find you.'

Cruz sighed. 'That's just like him. Pulling one last sneaky trick on me.'

'He said to tell you that the girl gets everything.' Iris studied her hands a moment. 'He also wanted me to tell you that he was a hero.'

A bark of bitter laughter escaped the woman. 'A hero, huh? That will be the day.' She shook her head. 'The *girl* is my daughter. I won't say our daughter because all Richie ever contributed was a few squirts of sperm.' Cruz cradled her chin in her palm as though thinking. 'Richie was always a car nut. Classic cars. Race cars. Whatever. I know he had the '57 Chevy left. Maybe he's got more. Maybe there really is something he wanted to leave her. I hope it's valuable. My daughter is in pre-med and we need every dollar we can find.'

Iris nodded. 'I wish I could tell you more but that's all he said.'

'Knowing him he's got cars garaged in Manhattan and the storage bill is more than the cars are worth.'

Iris started to say she was sorry again but caught herself.

'Go ahead,' Cruz said bitterly. 'Ask me everything. I know what you really came for.'

Iris studied the woman's face a moment, wondering how to proceed. 'Mr Andretti said—'

'Oh, no more Andretti, please. Mario Andretti is a famous race-car driver. The little jerk you're talking about's named Malik. Richie Malik. Just Richie will do.'

Iris took a deep breath. 'OK . . . Richie. Richie talked like he was involved in something with my father.'

Cruz gave a soft snort of sarcasm. 'Did you ask your

father about that? If Richie was involved, you can bet it had something to do with quick money and I can't imagine John joining up.'

'I can't ask my father. He was shot. He's in a coma.'

The woman appeared stunned, then genuinely sorry. 'How did it happen?'

Iris told her.

'I knew he'd dragged John into something bad but I never, never thought he'd get him hurt. He liked John.'

'But how did they know each other? How do you know my father?' Iris searched the woman's face and suddenly a thought occurred to her. 'Were you my mother's friend? The one she rented an apartment from before the house was built?'

Cruz looked at her watch, avoiding Iris's eyes and leaving her question unanswered. 'The pit boss said to take all the time I needed, but I don't want to push it. This is the best job I've ever had.'

'Please,' Iris pleaded. 'People have been killed and I've been chased and my father has been shot and I don't know what's going on! Please, tell me what's going on! Who's doing all this?'

'I don't know. But the trouble started with Richie finding Clary.'

'My mother?'

'You heard me.'

Iris stared at her. 'Richie found my mother?'

'Listen, I really don't know what was going on. I didn't want to know. I still don't want to know.'

'Please. I'm begging you. Tell me whatever you know. *Please*.'

Cruz eyed her in suspicious silence, then the suspicion gave way and the woman became agitated.

'Let's go out to the lounge,' she said. 'I need something to drink.'

# Twenty-Four

The lounge was big, dimly lit, and nearly empty. There was a small stage in the center but it was dark and Seventies soft-rock was oozing from hidden speakers. Cruz ordered hot tea.

'You never know around this place,' Cruz said as the waitress departed. 'That room we were in could have been monitored. You could be a fake, pretending to be Iris Lanier to pump me for information. You could be casino security trying to nab me for my connection to Richie.'

Iris was too surprised to reply.

Cruz sighed. 'No. I know you're not a fake. Like I said before I'd have to be blind and deaf not to know you're Clary's daughter. You look like her. You sound like her. I know you're legit. But, whatever Richie has done – I don't want to be involved. I've spent my whole adult life trying to swim out of the shit he dragged me into and I'll be damned if I'm going to let him pull me under now.'

'Listen,' Iris said, leaning forward and pinning the woman with her eyes, 'People are after me. Dangerous people. I need to know what's going on and I'm desperate. I'll keep after you until you talk to me.'

Cruz lit a cigarette and inhaled deeply. 'You're not anything like your mother,' she said, flinging it like an insult.

Iris felt like thanking her.

The woman studied her cigarette. 'Filthy habit. My

413

daughter thinks I quit. She'd kill me if she found out.'

Iris waited.

'OK. It had something to do with your mother and the old boyfriend she lived with before she met your father.'

A heaviness started in Iris's limbs and moved in toward her heart.

'You know where my mother is?'

'No. Not me. I refused to listen to any of it.'

'Was Richie helping my father look for my mother?'

'Richie had been looking for Clary, but not for your father's benefit. He had a scheme to make money . . . as usual.'

'But . . . I don't understand.'

Cruz gave her a measuring look. 'Your father never told you anything, did he? I'm not surprised. He probably didn't want to upset you.'

She took another lungful of smoke and blew it out. 'I can tell the smoke bothers you. John probably raised you to be totally organic. Lots of brown rice and free-range chicken.' Cruz chuckled. 'We sort of lived together, you know. We were like one big family for years. Your father liked to cook and he did a lot of it. His food was good, but sometimes I had wet dreams about french fries and chilli dogs.'

'I lived there too, didn't I?'

'Sure. Until John built the house. You were about four when you guys moved out of my place.'

'And then we lived in part of the house while he was finishing the rest, didn't we?'

'Yeah. You remembering now?'

'Bits and pieces.'

'You used to call me auntie.' She smiled wistfully. 'You were pretty cute. I think that's what made me weaken and want to have my own kid . . . being around you. Otherwise I'd never have been stupid enough to get pregnant by Richie.'

414

'So Richie was there too?'

'Oh, yeah. Richie and I had been together for a couple of years when I first met Clary and John. I was a stupid little *chica* from the migrant labor camps when I met Richie and I thought he was big stuff. Such an important guy, with his fancy cars and his high-school diploma.' She snorted sarcastically.

'Richie was selling used cars and I was waiting tables and we rented this house with a garage apartment. We turned around and advertised the apartment to help us pay our house rent. Clary answered the ad. Seemed like she was asking about it just for herself when she first came out and looked, but then John showed up and moved in with her.'

Paula Cruz's expression softened.

'Clary helped me a lot with the house. She seemed to get a kick out of substituting and scrimping – trying to make do with what we could afford. It was sort of like a game to her. Figuring out ways to cut up those cheap Indian cotton bedspreads and make curtains. Rushing to the Goodwill store every morning to see what new furniture or appliances had been collected the night before.

'I think part of the reason I stuck with Richie as long as I did was that I was so happy during those years with Clary that I didn't realize how miserable I was with Richie.'

She stabbed out her cigarette and lit another.

'I guess I was kind of blind to Richie's true sleaze factor then, too. I mean, I knew that he wasn't a good guy like John and that he didn't treat me like John treated Clary, but I don't think I understood what a worthless scumbag he really was.

'And you've got to remember that it was the Sixties. In spite of what you hear, those were bad times for females. All that peace and love bullshit was just a way to brainwash girls into thinking that they had to open their legs for every guy who asked. And all the craziness with drugs . . . guys made you feel like an idiot if you didn't take whatever they offered. The last thing I wanted to do was to be out in the single jungle again. I wanted to have a guy and a home. I wanted something real.

'I think Clary had that same feeling, too, because she used to talk about her life before John . . . how she'd been like a slave to this guy who pushed her around and thought he owned her. Thought he could make her do anything. She said it made her sick to think of what he might have talked her into doing.

'But she lucked out and found John. And John was . . . the best. Solid as a rock. And sweet. And so crazy about her that he treated her like a queen. I used to get green with envy, seeing what she had.

'And to think . . . she pitched it all. Threw it all away to go back to that other guy. I never would have believed it if I hadn't seen it with my own eyes.'

She took several deep drags and blew the smoke over her shoulder, away from Iris.

'What do you mean, saw it with your own eyes?' Iris watched the woman's face. 'You moved away years before she left us. You were living here, on the East Coast.'

'Yeah. That's right. Richie convinced me to move to Jersey because he had a big aluminium-siding scam cooked up with some guy. I didn't know that then. The song and dance he gave me was completely different. But after we got out here it didn't take me long to catch on.'

She chuckled bitterly. 'Especially after I had to drag my baby daughter down to the courthouse in the middle of the night and post bail for him.

'I tried throwing him out, but he kept coming back, full of apologies and stories about how things were going to be different. And I was really struggling, trying to support my daughter, and I wanted her to have a father. I didn't want to be a single parent, you know. So, like a fool, I kept taking him back. And he was there when Clary came.'

Her cigarette had burned down to nothing and she lit another.

Iris sat very still, breath held, almost afraid to speak. 'My mother came here, to Atlantic City?' she finally asked.

'No. Not here. We were New Yorkers then, living in Queens, out by La Guardia Airport. Things were OK and I thought I might finally have my life on the right track. I was going to school for my high-school diploma and working full time at a printing plant. Richie was bringing money in pretty steady, supposedly by selling appliances.

'By then I never heard from Clary any more except for Christmas cards. When I first moved away we kept in pretty close touch and wrote a lot of letters, but we kind of drifted apart over time.

'Then, suddenly, out of the blue, I got a call from her. She said she was coming to New York and she wanted to see me.

'I was so surprised. And so excited. I said sure. Richie had a car, as always, so I told her we'd pick her up at the airport. I told her she was welcome to stay with us and she said that she liked that idea. So the two of us would really have a chance to talk.

'Two days later we drove out to get her. It had been years since I'd seen her but she was more beautiful than ever, and she seemed . . . strong. Really together. Like someone who's made their peace with God and is in a blessed state.'

Cruz fingered the cross at her neck and blinked hard, as though on the verge of tears.

'We played with my daughter, then sat up late, talking about the old days, and she told me how John was doing. She talked about what a wonderful man he was and how fate had really favored her when she was steered toward

417

him. She said that he had really shaped her life, taught her what was right and good. Then she started telling me about you. How you were so perceptive and bright and wise and on and on, until my eyes glazed over.

'We were in the living room and Richie was supposedly glued to the television in the bedroom, you know, so we could have private girl talk.

'And finally she admitted to me that she had problems. I was really shocked, because she didn't seem like a person with problems. Just the opposite.

'I asked her what was wrong. She was real vague. Said that the past had been tearing her apart and she finally saw that she couldn't hide from it anymore.

'I asked her what exactly was she talking about, and she said more vague stuff. She said that I hadn't ever known the whole truth about her and the old boyfriend. That nobody knew the whole truth. And then she said that she had a lot of regrets about the way she had run away from her old life.

'I asked her what the hell that meant and she laughed that great laugh of hers, just like when we were younger. "This is a new beginning for me, Paula. That's all I can tell you right now."

'Well, she went into the bathroom to take a shower and I went out to the all-night deli for cigarettes and when I got back I caught Richie going through her purse.'

Cruz shook her head. 'What a slime he was.'

'I grabbed it away from him and he started whining about how he was only trying to find out what was wrong so he could help her.

' "What makes you think something is wrong?" I asked him, "Were you listening to everything we said?"

' "Oh, no. No," he said, real innocent like. "But I can tell she's got some kind of trouble."

'The next day I had to go to work so Richie drove her into Manhattan. She had him drop her off on a corner.'

Cruz turned the ashtray around and around on the table. Around and around until Iris had to look away.

'He dropped her off and nobody ever saw her again. But I know what happened. She left you and John . . . she left us all for that rich boyfriend she'd always claimed she wanted to get away from. And everything she told me about her wonderful husband and perfect kid was just a story, like a smokescreen, so I couldn't see the truth of what she was really planning. And everything she told me about missing me, all the promises she made about helping me move back to California . . . Those were all lies, too. I never heard from her again. She didn't give a damn about me or you or anyone else.'

Cruz narrowed her eyes. 'I thought she was something special. I thought she was what the rest of us should try to be. Instead she turned out to be the worst kind of hypocrite.'

Iris sat back in her chair, clasped her hands and pressed them against her mouth. What was there to say? Hadn't she thought the same things herself? Hadn't she always thought that her mother's abandonment of them was a selfish act, an act of cowardice? So why did she have the urge to defend her mother against Paula Cruz's criticism?

'Anyway . . .' Cruz pulled another cigarette out of the pack. 'A few months later Richie got busted. He hadn't been selling appliances. He'd been involved in a bunch of illegal gambling parlors. He got sent to prison and that was it for me. I'd had enough of him.'

She smiled ruefully. 'Lucky for me we were never legally married. My name was still Cruz and when I walked away that was it. No divorce hassles. He'd done me a favor by sidestepping the marriage question all those years. And let's face it . . . if we had been married . . . there wasn't going to be any child support or none of that. He'd a probably ended up robbing me blind.'

'But then,' Iris asked, 'what happened? Why did he

start looking for my mother?'

'Well, first he did time in prison, then he got out, then he screwed up again and got sent to a more serious prison. I didn't see him for . . . I don't know . . . sixteen or seventeen years. But he'd call me every once in a while. Ask how my daughter was doing. Ask for money. Cry about what bad luck he'd been having. Didn't matter where I moved, he always managed to track me down.

'Then, about six months ago he showed up at my door, dressed to kill and driving an expensive classic car. He told me he'd finally found his calling in life. He had become a snitch for the feds. Said he got paid for all the things he was good at – sneaking around and tricking people and lying.

'Well . . . he didn't exactly describe it that way, but that's what he meant.

'He wanted to see my daughter but I told him she was away at college. I asked him if he wanted to contribute anything toward her expenses and he puffed out his chest and said, "Not yet, Paula. But soon. I'm onto something big and when I hit the jackpot I'm going to take care of both of you."

'Right.' Cruz snorted her disgust. 'Like I was dumb enough to believe that.

'Then he started to brag to me about how smart he was. About how he'd always known there was something fishy about my friend, Clary.

'I asked him what the hell he was talking about and he said that when he went through her purse in our living room that night he'd seen some letters she wrote, and he'd seen an envelope full of newspaper clippings about an antiwar bombing in the Sixties. Some group called Red Phoenix.

'Then, he said that one day he was going through old wanted posters that the feds had in their office. He said he was looking for guys he might have met on the street, trying to get ideas for a big reward score. And he saw a poster with a drawing of a college-age girl and a description of her. She was wanted in connection with that old Red Phoenix bombing. And the poster said that anyone connected with Red Phoenix was wanted. His greasy mental wheels started turning and he remembered the clippings in Clary's purse and he asked the guys he was snitching for how much it would be worth for them to get something on Red Phoenix and they told him it could be worth a lot, depending on who he was talking about. They said there was a senator who bugged them about the old case all the time.

'Well, needless to say, that got Richie all fired up and he did some digging on Clary. Figured out that her maiden name was a fraud. Couldn't find any records on her before her marriage to John . . . which was shortly after the whole bombing thing. And he decided he'd found his golden goose. He was also convinced that the guy she'd gone back to was the one behind the bombing.

'Richie thought he had it all worked out. He thought that they'd broken up and gone their separate ways only because they were so scared of getting caught, and when nothing happened after eight years they decided it was safe to get together again. Basically, he was saying that Clary's whole time as a wife and mother had been nothing but a cover for who she really was.'

Cruz shook her head and tucked the cross necklace down inside her shirt.

'I didn't know what to think. I sure as hell didn't want to believe him but it all fit, you know? It all fit. And it explained a lot of things.

'I kinda felt bad, thinking that he was going to rat Clary out, but then I thought, hey . . . why not? Look what she did to John and Iris.

'He kept wanting to know if I could think of anything she'd said that might help him find her. Like if she'd ever mentioned her old boyfriend's name or anything. 'Cause all his brilliant ideas were worthless if he couldn't tell the feds how to put their hands on her or the guy.

'The more he talked, the worse I felt about what he was going to do. I started thinking maybe I should try to warn Clary some way, so I encouraged him to shoot off his mouth some more, thinking maybe I'd hear something that would help me figure out how to contact her.

'He admitted then that he hadn't just dropped Clary on a corner and left that day he drove her into Manhattan. He hid and watched her. She was picked up by a guy in a Mercedes, which really got his interest, so he followed them. He said they drove around the city for a while, then pulled over and went into a clinch. Then the guy drove north. Richie followed them all the way up around Bear Mountain, over a lot of little country roads and into a private drive beside a big old mailbox. Out in the middle of nowhere. He said he remembered everything about the mailbox, but he couldn't remember how to get there exactly. He was really kicking himself for not having written down the license number and kept it all those years.

'The sleazebag.

'I went ballistic when I heard all that. To think he knew where Clary went all that time, but he never said anything. With everybody going crazy trying to find her, he just played dumb. John and I must have talked on the phone every night for two weeks, both of us mad at her and worried sick about her, but Richie never said a thing about seeing where she'd gone.

'Anyway, I exploded at him and told him to do the world a favor and go drive off a bridge somewhere—'

'Wait,' Iris said. 'Before you go any further . . . You said that you'd been talking to my father every night after my mother disappeared?'

Cruz nodded.

'So he knew that she'd flown east and been at your house?'

'Sure. I had to tell him the whole story. A few days after she left I got to thinking about it and decided I should call him. He was frantic. I had to tell him, then.

'After that we talked every day, each of us hoping the other had heard something. Then after a while we stopped calling each other. I think we both got to where we wanted to put it behind us.'

The woman cradled her forehead in her hand as though she was suddenly feeling ill.

'Are you OK?' Iris asked.

'Yeah, sure. You want to hear the rest?'

'Please.'

'About three weeks ago I came home from work to find this mint condition '57 Chevy parked in front of my apartment. I knew immediately that it was Richie's.

'I went up to it and he was inside, all slouched down like he was hiding. I knocked on the window and it nearly gave him a heart attack. He was so hyper and crazy acting that I wouldn't take him into the apartment. I made him talk to me outside.

'He started blubbering about how everything went wrong. That was no surprise to me. When did he ever do anything right?

'Then he went into this thing about how he'd found the old boyfriend and followed him and then he'd found her and he shouldn't have called John but he did and he shouldn't have tried the blackmail, he should have stuck to the feds' reward, and he didn't know John had a gun and now the feds didn't believe him and he was going to get killed before he could get the reward.

'I tried to calm him down and get him to tell it to me straight, but he was totally crazed. He kept jerking his head around, looking up and down the street like someone was after him.

'Then he threw himself to his knees and hugged my legs and begged me to keep something for him. Just for a little while, he kept saying. Just hide it for a little while.

'He jumped up and started to get this box out of the backseat and I said to hold on because I wasn't hiding anything. I wasn't getting involved. I told him he was the scum of the earth and I refused to let any of it rub off on me and I was through. He could get killed for all I cared.

'He crumpled right down to the ground then and sat there crying. Big tears rolling down like a baby. So I told him just to sit and get himself together. That I would go inside and get him a beer and when I came back out I expected to hear him making more sense.

'But when I came back out he was gone. And I was glad. I mean I was worried about him saying John was mixed up in it, but mainly I was just glad to be rid of him.'

Cruz shrugged. 'That's it. The whole story.'

Iris tried to think it all through.

'You say Richie had a box he wanted you to keep?' Iris asked.

'Yeah.' Cruz held her hands approximately three feet apart. 'A plain cardboard box.'

Iris's thoughts raced. A cardboard box was not the same thing as a trunk but maybe he put the contents of the box into a trunk later. How did it all fit together?

'What could Richie have told my father that would make him buy a gun and jump on an airplane for New York?' she asked.

'Probably that he'd found Clary. What else would it be? The thing is, John was wise to Richie. He knew what a prick Richie had become. So it has to have been something pretty heavy for John not to laugh in Richie's face.'

Iris thought a moment. 'These feds that Richie was working with – which agency was that? The FBI?'

'I don't know. He just always said the feds.'

'What he said about blackmail . . . do you think he was

blackmailing my mother and her . . . lover? Or just my mother?'

'It couldn't have been just Clary. She didn't have any money.'

'But she did, Paula. Her father was rich. If she had gone back to him and assumed her old identity, then she would have had money.'

'Man, I never would have guessed that. Clary never seemed like a spoiled rich kid.'

'I don't think she was spoiled. I think she was very unhappy.'

'Yeah, well, anyway . . . it could be either one, you know? Whether she ran off to her rich boyfriend or her rich daddy . . . whichever . . . somebody must have had the money to outbid the feds for Richie's silence.'

'Would my mother . . .' Iris hesitated. 'You knew my mother better than most people, Paula. Do you think she could have been involved in my father's shooting?'

'Who knows? A lot of years have passed. A lot of water under the bridge. She might be some rich society lady now with a whole new set of kids and everything. She might have a lot to lose.'

Cruz looked at her watch. 'I'm sorry but I've got to get back to work.'

Iris nodded.

'Listen,' Cruz said hesitantly, 'I don't know what's going to happen. I don't know who else you're going to talk to . . . but if you happen to meet my daughter . . .'

'Yes?'

'She doesn't know all the bad stuff about Richie.'

Pride and love softened the woman's face. 'My daughter was the salutatorian at her high-school graduation. I raised her to be above people like her father. I don't want her having the burden of knowing what kind of man he really was.'

'I'll be careful if I talk to her,' Iris promised. 'But don't you think it's wrong to keep lying to her? She's old enough now to deserve the truth.'

'The truth, huh? The truth can be pretty ugly stuff. Does she deserve all the pain and disappointment that goes with it? And do I deserve to make myself a liar in my daughter's eyes when everything I did, I did to make life better for her?'

'Hard questions,' Iris admitted.

'Parenting is full of hard questions. It's the hardest job there is.'

They left the table and walked toward the exit.

'You seem like you turned out pretty good,' Cruz said at the entrance to the casino. 'I'll bet John is real proud.'

Iris had to clear her throat. 'You'd have to ask him.'

'I hope I get the chance. I mean, I hope he gets well and I see him again.'

Iris nodded.

'You're like my daughter in some ways. You're strong like she is. We were all such passive doormats when we were young. Even Clary. As lively and smart and funny as she was, she still had a submissive streak when it came to love. You girls aren't like that. Sometimes I'm amazed at the strong women we gave birth to.'

Iris watched her walk across the casino floor toward the blackjack tables. She was such a small woman. From the back she could have been mistaken for an adolescent.

Suddenly Isaac was there, standing in the doorway, close enough to touch.

'She's like the rest of us,' Iris said. 'She loved my mother so much that she can't do anything but hate her now.'

'Your mother?' Isaac asked.

'Let's go find something to eat,' Iris said wearily. 'I'll tell you everything.'

# Twenty-Five

They ate dinner at Dock's restaurant on Atlantic Avenue and they talked it through, turning it every direction. Iris held back nothing. She was beyond worrying about Isaac's involvement. She was grateful to have someone on her side.

'You think it all goes back to the Red Phoenix bombing?' Isaac asked. 'That they were blackmailing your mother or your mother and her lover?'

'Not they. Just Richie. My father would never blackmail anyone,' Iris said firmly. 'He would never be a party to something like that.'

'Your father might not have known what was really going on. Richie sounds like one of those smooth characters who concoct stories and manipulate people.'

'I don't know. I don't know.' Iris shook her head. 'I've got to find that trunk.'

'We could go back to the Sands, check out, and be back in Manhattan by midnight,' Isaac suggested.

'We won't accomplish anything in Manhattan in the middle of the night. Besides, you're already committed to the room for another night. And we know it's safe here. We might as well stay over and go back in the morning.'

Isaac didn't say anything but she could read his reaction in his face.

'What's the difference?' she asked him. 'You're forced

to be alone with me all night whether we're here or at the lab.'

He looked at her. 'I'm sorry,' he said.

It was totally unexpected and she didn't know how to interpret it.

They walked back to the Sands along the boardwalk. With night the temperature had fallen some, but the air was still mild. Like liquid silk against her skin. A bright moon hung low in the sky, reflected in the mirror-smooth sea, and there were faint pinpoint stars visible. She inhaled the briny air and thought about how long it had been since she'd taken the time to enjoy the ocean.

Neither of them spoke. She glanced sideways at him. He looked thoughtful. But then he usually looked thoughtful. Was he silently twisting the puzzle, trying to make the pieces fit? Was he regretting his involvement in the whole mess? Or was he thinking about her. Just as she was thinking about him.

Inside the room the maid had left one small lamp burning. Isaac sat down and stared out the window at the beach below. 'We should try to get some sleep,' he said without taking his eyes from the beach, and she knew he was discreetly trying to give her first turn in the bathroom.

'Isaac . . .' she said, but he did not turn and look at her. 'There's something between us and it's not going away. I feel it more strongly than ever and I know you feel it, too. What is so wrong with just accepting it?'

He didn't say anything.

She sat down in the chair beside him. Still he wouldn't look at her. His eyes were riveted on the beach below.

'Can you look at me?' she asked softly.

He turned his head and she saw herself reflected in his eyes. She saw that he wanted her. She saw the intensity of his hunger for her.

It made her breath catch, made her pulse speed, made warmth spread inside her. Now if he would just lean forward and kiss her so she would know that everything was all right and then she would kiss him. Wasn't that the way it was supposed to work?

The moment stretched out, pulling her nerves taut and twisting them into knots of uncertainty in her stomach.

Suddenly he jumped from his chair and headed for the door.

'Where are you going?' she asked in surprise.

'For a walk on the beach,' he said as he slammed out.

She sat for a moment, stunned. Alternating between rejection and anger, between feeling hurt and feeling stupid. She considered crawling into bed and pulling the covers over her head. She considered getting on a bus and running back to Manhattan.

Then suddenly it struck her that this was something valuable. This was something important. And she would not give up without fighting.

She jumped from her chair and followed him. On her way outside she stopped at the hotel gift shop.

'Those,' she told the elderly woman behind the counter, as she pointed at a three-pack of condoms.

Armed with her purchase she ran out to the boardwalk and stood at the rail, scanning the broad expanse of moonlit beach. There was a dark ribbon of fresh footprints leading from the bottom of the stairway nearby. She ran down the wooden steps to the sand, pulled her shoes off and followed the tracks. Fitting her feet into his prints, stretching her legs to match his stride.

She spotted him up the beach. A solitary dark figure against the pale expanse. Sitting just out of reach of the water. Staring into the gently lapping surf. She approached him from behind thinking that the surf would drown the faint sounds of her coming, yet he didn't seem surprised when she dropped to her knees beside him in the sand.

'Why did you run away?' she asked.

He continued to stare out across the moon-spangled water and she remembered seeing him in a dream, coming to her from out of the sea, dripping starlight.

Without reply he rose and started to walk up the beach. Her confidence faltered a little, but not much. He was still afraid to look at her. That was a good sign.

She fell into step beside him and noticed that he was adjusting for her, matching himself to what was comfortable for her. That had to be a good sign, too.

They walked in silence, on and on. The lights of the commercial strip dimmed and they walked toward the shadowed hulk of an old pier. He turned at the pier to go back in the other direction but she blocked his path, facing him, close enough to feel the feathery touch of his breath against her skin.

'Iris . . .'

'Why is it so hard for you? As a male you are biologically programmed to want this to happen.'

He almost smiled. Took a deep breath. Shook his head.

'You're not like anyone I've ever met, Iris.'

'Then make love to me, while you have the chance.'

'We'll both regret it.'

'Maybe I'll regret it but I know I'll never be sorry.'

Another almost-smile. 'That doesn't make sense.'

She moved closer. So their bodies brushed against each other. 'Who says things always have to make sense?'

And there it was, that slow half-smile that started in his eyes then tugged at his mouth. He took her wrists, held them up and looked at each one, then circled them so that his fingertips touched. He kissed the centers of her palms, then her closed eyes, then her mouth.

He pulled her against him and their bodies curved together. She felt a tremor go through him and it was matched by one of her own.

'You'll hate me one day,' he whispered.

But she threw her head back to the moonlight and did not listen.

Later that night, sleeping close beside Isaac in the hotel bed, Iris dreamed of her mother and Moonsmoke. She dreamed they were both trying to warn her of something but she couldn't hear them. The wind got louder as she strained to hear and they got farther and farther away. 'Wait!' she called and woke herself up.

'You OK?' Isaac asked and slipped his arm around her.

'Mmm.'

She found the perfect spot for her head to rest on his shoulder. The scent and warmth and solidity of him stirred her and she wanted him again, needed him urgently.

'I never imagined it could be like this,' she whispered as she pressed her body against his. 'I never believed . . .'

And when she took him inside, she took him deeply – into her heart and mind and soul – changing herself forever.

Later, after their hunger was spent and they were curved together like spoons, Iris's thoughts went back to Paula Cruz and the story she had told.

'Can't you sleep?' Isaac asked.

'No. I keep thinking about Andretti – Richie, I mean. He was despicable . . . but so pathetic. What could he have told my father? How could he have gotten my father to wear that wire and carry a gun?'

'He was smooth, Iris, an accomplished con artist.'

'He certainly didn't seem that way. He seemed just like a . . . a building super. I can imagine that funny little balding man behind the wheel of a classy car, trying to look tall and important but instead looking like a fool.'

'That's probably a pretty accurate picture,' Isaac said. 'You could title it *Machine Dreams*.'

431

She smiled in the darkness, then suddenly sat bolt upright.

'Wait a minute! Isaac . . . What about the cars? When Andretti said it's in the trunk, maybe he meant the trunk of his car! He put the box in the trunk of his car!'

# Twenty-Six

They were back in Manhattan and safely inside the lab by ten the next morning. Isaac looked up phone numbers in the directory and Iris made the calls. They started with the garages closest to the Fitzgerald and then worked outward from there. Iris asked about cars under the names Andretti and Malik. She also tried describing the cars. When she was questioned she gave a story about her brother being deceased.

Finally they reached a man who said, 'I don't know no Malik or Andretti but we got a Richie Petty who keeps two classic cars in here and one of 'em is a '57 Chevy.'

'I'll be right over,' Iris said.

She hung up the phone. 'We've got it!' she cried, hugging Isaac.

'Now,' she turned away so abruptly that he nearly fell. 'Where are Andretti's keys?'

She grabbed her backpack off the floor and thrust her hand inside but didn't find them. Frustrated she upended the pack onto the counter. The keys fell out with a solid clunk.

'This is it. I know it. Whatever he had in that box he tried to get Paula to hide, whatever he's so worried about somebody finding . . . it's in the trunk of one of those cars.'

They drove cautiously to the garage and pulled inside before getting out of the car. A stoop-shouldered dark-skinned man with crystalline blue eyes came over to greet them.

'How long ya wanna park?'

'We don't. I just talked to you on the phone about my brother's cars and we've come to see them.'

'Yeah, well, I don't know about this. I talked to my boss after you called and he said we ain't lettin' those cars out of our sight before the bills are paid and you oughta have to show us some kind of legal papers to take possession of 'em.'

'No problem, friend,' Isaac said. 'You're exactly right and we have no intention of trying to take the cars. We're just checking to make sure they're all right. No one wants to move those cars until after the estate is settled. You tell your boss that.' Isaac slipped him a folded bill.

The man looked around. 'Guess it wouldn't hurt nothin' to show them to you. Follow me. We keep 'em in a real safe spot.'

They walked down a spiraling ramp to a dingy underground parking area. One corner was fenced off. It contained a vintage Rolls-Royce and a shiny '57 Chevy.

'Here they are,' the man announced proudly. 'I gotta admit, I'll be sorry when they do go. They brighten things up around here.'

Iris and Isaac circled the cars, peering in the windows. Both were spotless and empty inside. Iris got out the keys and began sorting through them.

'Whoa there,' the man said. 'What do you think you're doing?'

'Just looking,' Isaac assured him.

Iris opened the trunk of the Rolls. It was empty. She unlocked the trunk of the Chevy and pushed it open. There was a rectangular cardboard carton, something scavenged from a grocery store, twice as long as it was tall or wide. It was sealed shut with heavy-duty packaging tape. Iris exchanged a look with Isaac.

'We better get this out of here,' she said, feigning disgust. 'I can't believe he'd put rotten stuff like that in this nice car. It's a wonder the smell hasn't started.'

'What?' the garage man said nervously. 'What's in there?'

'Should we tell him?' Iris asked, trying to buy time as she thought of an answer.

'Dead rats,' Isaac said calmly. 'He worked part time at a science lab and one of his jobs was rat disposal.'

They put the box in the trunk of their own car and drove straight back to the lab. Iris's hands were shaking with anticipation by the time they finally had the box on a counter. Isaac cut the tape and she opened the flaps.

She frowned in puzzlement as soon as she saw the contents.

'It's Kizmin's missing bones,' she said.

Isaac looked in. 'Then the carjacking was connected to everything. The guy didn't really want Kizmin's car – he wanted the bones.' He frowned. 'But how does the timing work on that?'

Iris stared down into the box. 'The timing doesn't fit. Richie had the box in the car and tried to give it to Paula weeks before I helped Kizmin dig the girl out of the ground.'

She shifted the box. 'Hold that light up so I can see better.'

Isaac picked up the lamp and held it over the box. Iris peered inside. She picked up the skull, cupped it in her hands and studied it in the flood of light.

'This isn't Kizmin's missing murder victim.'

The empty orbits stared back and sent a chill through her.

'Can you put it away now?' Isaac asked, and she looked up and realized that the skull was disturbing him.

'I'm sorry,' she said, slipping the skull gently back into

the box. 'I forget. They're so familiar to me.'

They stared at the box in tandem for several minutes.

'I don't know what to think,' Iris said finally.

Isaac wandered to the other end of the long counter where the contents of her backpack were still scattered about. He began picking things up and putting them back into the pack. Iris knew he was just trying to keep himself busy and away from the box.

'What's this?' he asked her, holding up a small brass key.

She moved around to look closer. 'I don't know what it is. Did it come from my pack?'

He nodded and upended the pack again, spilling out everything he'd just put away. Iris picked through it. Everything was familiar. The beeper. Her personal items. Everything except the key. She picked up the cake of soap that she had carried to Guatemala. The one she'd taken from her father's bathroom. She had thrown it into her pack but hadn't used it so the bar had been banging around down there ever since. Now it was broken neatly in half. There was an impression of a small key in the inside center of each half.

'I thought your father was such a simple guy,' Isaac said as he took the two halves of the soap bar and studied them.

'No,' Iris assured him. 'Private, self-contained, principled, obsessively organic, and peaceful . . . but never simple.'

'This was a pretty good trick.' Isaac put the key back into the impression and fitted the two halves together. 'Looks like he used a thin blade to cut it in half, notching it a little so the halves would seat in together perfectly. He shaved out the area where the key would rest. Then he probably wet the halves, stuck the key in, held them together with something while they dried.'

'Rubber bands,' Iris said.

'What?'

'He always held things together with rubber bands when he was woodworking.'

Isaac nodded. He held up the assembled bar. 'Then maybe he wet the outside a little so he could smooth over the line.'

'Oh!' Iris exclaimed suddenly and gripped her head with her hands.

'What?'

'My father told an emergency-room nurse to tell his daughter that "hope was the key" or "the key was hope" or something like that. I think he was trying to say that the key was in the *soap*. Literally.'

Isaac opened the two halves and Iris picked up the little key with her fingertips. 'Isaac . . . this is the key to the safety-deposit box.'

It was already past one and the bank had a three o'clock closing time. The plan was for Isaac to impersonate John Lanier and get access to the box.

Iris gave him her father's wallet and its contents, the letter from the bank, and a folded red bandanna for good measure. Isaac studied John Lanier's California driver's license picture and practiced his signature.

'You're good at that,' Iris remarked, watching Isaac perfect her father's scrawl. 'But what about your appearance? What if the clerk on duty remembers him? Or what if they ask to see ID? You're far too young and you're built so differently from him.'

'I'll figure out something,' Isaac assured her. 'Maybe I'll go buy some overalls and a cowboy hat.'

'My father would never wear a cowboy hat.'

'But the bank clerk won't know that. And I can always say I just came out of a long illness in the hospital. That's certainly an acceptable reason for losing body bulk.'

Iris nodded. She trusted him completely now and she

knew he would do his absolute best.

'You are coming, aren't you?' Isaac asked.

'No. The same clerk I talked to might be there and seeing me would jog her memory and make her notice you more. I think it would be best for you to go in alone.'

She turned from Isaac and looked at the box on the end of the counter. 'I'll stay here and take a closer look at the bones. See if I get any ideas about how they tie in to all this.'

'You're sure?'

She nodded.

He came up from behind and circled her with his arms. She closed her eyes, absorbed his scent, his warmth, the strength in his gentle embrace. Suddenly she wanted to tell him not to go. She wanted to run away with him. Go someplace safe. Not just safe from the threat that stalked her, but someplace where nothing between them would ever change. Nothing would be lost.

'I'll be back as soon as I can,' he said. 'Should I take the keys so I can let myself back in?'

'Yes. And be warned. There will be bones out when you get back.'

After he was gone Iris sat awhile by the window, looking out over the Hudson River. Her father was slipping away. Her own life was in jeopardy. Everything was upside down. Yet, she had been led to Isaac. Maybe Kizmin's fate had been at work after all.

She stood and shook off the dreaminess. There were bones to be examined and she wanted to work quickly. She wanted to try to finish before Isaac returned.

The area she had been using as her central point was actually the eating counter that divided the kitchen and living room. She did not want to examine the bones there. She picked up the box and carried it through the door of the living quarters and on into the lab. There was a work table near the airshaft window and she put the box there so she would have plenty of natural light.

She lifted out the large bones first and saw that there was a small brown envelope buried beneath them. She picked it up. As soon as her fingers made contact she knew it was an audio tape.

Quickly she searched through the lab. In a drawer she found a battered portable tape recorder, probably used to record observations during work. She snapped in the tape, rewound it and listened. The noise level was bad. There were odd crackling and whooshing sounds. Then there was a voice.

'Where is it?'

'I don't want a go-between. I said I wanted to do my business directly.'

She thought the second voice was her father's but she couldn't be certain. The man sounded as though he was speaking from the bottom of a well with a high wind blowing by.

'You'll have to do business with me.'

The first voice again. A male, but who?

'No. It's either a face-to-face meeting or the whole thing is off.'

'Oh? Think you're tough, huh? I hear you have a very pretty daughter. Maybe I should talk to her instead of you.'

'You can't get near my daughter.'

'Oh no? Think I don't know where she is? Wrong! And Guatemala's not so far away.'

'Leave my daughter out of this!'

'Is that a threat? Are you trying to threaten me?'

'Get away. Get—'

'Is that—'

There were several seconds of grunts and loud fumblings, then boom. She jumped. She closed her eyes and pressed her hands against her mouth. That was the sound of the bullet entering her father's brain.

439

Suddenly there was a microphone squeal and a very loud voice said, 'John got stupid. If you want the money you better be smarter.'

The whooshing sound returned and she listened to it for several seconds, then reached to turn the tape off. But there was something else. A faint noise, like the click of approaching high heels.

'Oh, baby . . . you don't look so good. Hang on there, the ambulance is coming.'

Silence.

'Damn, I ruined my pantyhose. That's OK. It ain't your fault.'

Silence.

'My name's Cookie and I'm gonna stay here with you. Everything's gonna be OK.

'Oooo . . . what's this bulge in your pocket? Cookie's gonna check.'

There was a shuffling sound.

'Cookie's just gonna keep this for you so the ambulance dudes don't rip you off. When you get out you just come on down and look me up and I'll give it back. Or you can take it out in blow jobs.'

Silence.

'There it is. I hear the ambulance. Gotta run now. Good luck baby.'

Iris stared at the tape for a long time before she could make herself rewind it and listen again. Richie must have been set up somewhere, listening, taping it all while her father was supposed to meet the target. But the target didn't show up. Instead he, or she, sent someone else.

They must have been trying to get the target on tape and her father didn't want to carry on with the business of the meeting when he saw that it was someone else.

She set the recorder off to the side. Maybe Isaac would have some ideas when he got back. At least she had the

440

bones to occupy her. She couldn't have sat there, waiting, with nothing to do but listen to the tape over and over.

Slowly she began the process of laying the bones out, placing them on the table like puzzle pieces, starting with the body's anchors – the pelvic girdle, femurs and tibias and fibulas, humerus and radius and ulna, clavicles and scapulas, the sternum – and then on to the more challenging pieces, lining up the ribs, piecing together the vertebrae, assembling the seven tarsal bones of each ankle, the five bones of each foot, the fourteen tiny toes on each side, then the elegant hands, the eight pebble-like carpals of each wrist and the five bones of each palm, the fourteen phalanges that formed each set of fingers, the patellas at each knee, the delicate hyoid bone, broken in this case but easily fit together. Then she crowned it all with the skull.

She stood back. As always, when she beheld the miracle at the core of humanity, the awe struck her. She smiled down at her new acquaintance. 'Who are you?' she asked out loud.

There were a few tiny bones left over. Iris swept them aside. They could be animal bones. Sometimes that happened. A skeleton was recovered and with it came bones from an animal that had died nearby. There was, however, no sign of animal damage, no gnawing marks at all.

Sometime later, after taking advantage of the lab's luxurious tools and computer, she knew that it was a woman, five foot six inches tall, probably Caucasoid but with a tantalizing hint of Mongoloid in the facial features. The woman had been adult but young at the time of death. She had been in good health and there had been no ravaging disease earlier in her life. There was a well-healed fracture line on the right ulna. Her pelvic girdle showed signs of childbirth.

That triggered a thought for Iris. She turned to the tiny

bones she had put aside. She picked each one up and examined it with a magnifying glass. They were fragments of fetal bones! The woman had been pregnant when she died.

Iris paced for awhile, thinking. Who was this woman? Why did Andretti have her remains in a box in the back of his car? How did she fit into the nightmare?

She crossed to an outside window and stared at the view without really seeing it. Then, she went back to the skeleton and picked up the skull. The dark orbits seemed sad to her now. She could imagine tears falling down the hard white cheeks.

She carried the skull to the area that she had prepared before, when she was waiting for Kizmin to bring her victim for reconstruction. Carefully, she mounted the skull on the stand and went to work cutting rubber markers. Each marker represented the depth of muscle tissue at a given area in the face. When she had all the markers glued in place she opened a package of quick-drying clay and began the sculpting.

Her hands flew. She hadn't done a reconstruction for some time, but it was a skill that came naturally to her. After she had the basic contours she molded lips, a nose, and ears.

She backed up and studied the naked unfinished face. The angle of the chin, the delicately pronounced cheekbones, the high forehead, the smooth lift of the brow-bone. She touched her own face, ran her fingertips over the planes and angles, traced the lines of her own cheekbones.

A monstrous foreboding gathered within her and she could feel the pull, feel the urge to run away, to hide, to find another chamber where she could seal herself off. To go back to Moonsmoke with the knife in her back. To go back to that plaza in Guatemala. To go anywhere. To do anything but this.

She went to the cabinet and pulled out a drawer of glass eyes. Chose the dark brown. She set them into the orbits. She refined the eyelids and smoothed everything. Carefully. Lovingly. Then she looked through the assortment of hair materials. She needed something very dark. Not black but deep sable brown. Painstakingly she fitted eyelashes and eyebrows to the face. Then she put on the wig. Not perfect, but almost. A deep rich brown, long, like silk against the face.

'Mama,' she whispered.

Never aged. Frozen in time.

'Mama!'

And she rested her cheek against the cold clay forehead. She brushed her lips against the cold clay cheek.

'Mama. Mama.'

Her tears wet the shiny hair.

'You meant to come back, didn't you? You wanted to come back.'

And she felt the pain. Felt the terror. As though it were happening to her. She felt the pressure increase on her throat and there was no air. There was no hope.

That was how the fragile hyoid bone from her mother's throat had been broken. She had been strangled.

Something roused her. She wasn't sure what. She sat up and realized that she had fallen asleep. How late was it? Why hadn't Isaac returned?

She rubbed her eyes and drew in a deep breath. After finishing the reconstruction she had sat there and stared at her mother's face. The afternoon had passed with no sign of Isaac. She went into the living room and stretched out on the couch. And now it was late. It was dark outside. Where was he?

She stood and glanced across the room at the kitchen counter. The small lamp burning there was the only light in the room. There was a large purse on the counter that hadn't been there before. She crossed the floor to look and saw that there was also a note from Isaac.

Iris,
I came in and didn't want to wake you. This is what I found in the box. I have to check into something but I'll be back in the next few hours. I'll bring dinner with me.

He hadn't signed it. She wondered if that was because he didn't know how to sign it. He didn't know whether to write just *Isaac* or *Your Friend, Isaac* or the loaded *Love, Isaac*.

She slipped the note into her backpack to save, then she examined the purse. This was what her father had been hiding in a safety deposit box?

There was a noise from somewhere. Just the wind outside, she thought, too focused on the purse to bother with checking the source.

The leather was very old and so dry it cracked when it was opened. Inside there were the standard odds and ends that collect in a woman's purse, plus a wallet and some envelopes. She pulled out the wallet and unsnapped it. On one side was a picture of a beaming eight-year-old face with a dusting of freckles. Her own face. Back when the world was good and her mother loved her. On the other was a California driver's license in the name of Clarice Lanier.

She closed the wallet and tried to swallow the painful catch in her throat. The envelopes were tucked down into the purse's inside pocket. She pulled them out, knowing that this was what Richie Andretti-Malik had sneaked a look at all those years ago in Paula's living room.

The first envelope was stuffed with old newspaper clippings about the Red Phoenix bombing. The second was addressed to a Mr J. DeVries at a Manhattan address.

It had a folded sheet inside. She pulled the sheet out, stared down at it for a moment, then slowly unfolded it.

Dear Dad,

I don't know if you want to hear from me after all these years but I have some things to tell you. I am getting ready to turn myself in to the government for something that happened nine years ago. I'm sorry but it will cause you trouble because my real name will come out and they will find out I'm your daughter. Also someone else close to you is involved. (I'll let him tell you in his own way.)

If I could keep you out of this I would, but I can't. You don't deserve it. I know that I hurt you a lot when I ran away and disappeared. It's hard to explain. Sometimes I don't know if I understand it myself even though it seemed to make sense when I was seventeen.

When you married a woman I didn't like I guess I took that as a message that you didn't love me. Then you were always gone or busy and I was miserable living in that house with her and I only had one friend and when he went away to college I decided to show everyone and run away to join him. I would have called you eventually and probably come home except that I got involved in something terrible then and I've been hiding ever since. You'll know all about it soon enough.

I have kept track of you as best I could. I know that Louise died and I am sorry you had to go through losing another wife. I know how hard it was for you when Mama died. I still think about those first months after her death when we stayed in the country for the whole summer and I hid in my cave and you hid in your cabin and neither one of us knew how to make the other one feel better.

I have miraculously found love and happiness. I have a wonderful husband and a darling eight-year-old girl. You will be crazy about her when you meet her (which I hope you will want to do soon).

I deeply regret the pain I caused you and I regret robbing you of the joy of your granddaughter's love. I didn't understand about being a parent until I became one myself. Now I realize that you did love me after all and I forgive you for not being a perfect father. Can you forgive me for not being a perfect daughter?

I don't know where I'll be but shortly after you receive this I am sure you will be reading about me in the newspaper and you will find out how to reach me.

With love,
Your daughter,
Clarice

Iris could hear her own heartbeat in her ears as she picked up the last envelope. It was addressed to John Lanier in Santa Clara. She pulled two sheets out and unfolded the first.

My dearest John,

I know that I should have talked this over with you beforehand, but I was so afraid you would try to convince me not to do it, or that I would weaken and convince myself not to do it. You see, during these nine years of your loving me I have learned a lot, not just about love but about right and wrong and what makes a good person.

You are my hero, John, and I want to be just like you. I want to show you that I can do what's right and that I am strong. I want to show Iris that, too. I want to be an example for her like you have been an example for me.

I know that you've always suspected I had run

away from more than just my father and that I had more to hide from than an unhappy family background. I'm so sorry that I never told you the whole truth. I was afraid that you would stop loving me and that I would lose Iris.

I was the girl they were looking for after the Red Phoenix bombing. I didn't know there was a bomb and I never would have let it happen if I'd known, but I'm probably guilty of something just for supporting the group, and I'm sure I'm guilty of the crime of keeping silent all these years.

You're probably thinking, why now? It's hard to explain but as Iris grew I kept seeing that poor little Katina Dixon in her, and I kept thinking about what it must be like to have your child die in your arms. I can't bring that little girl back to life or undo the terrible tragedy of it all but I can stand up and be an example for my own daughter and for this new baby growing inside me.

I know you are hurting right now but I hope you'll be proud of me and I have faith that it will all turn out right. By the time you receive this I will probably be in custody but I will call you as soon as they let me. That is, if you still want to talk to me.

With all my love,
Clary

Iris pressed her sleeve against her tearfilled eyes and unfolded the final sheet of paper.

To my sweet, sweet Iris,

You are Mommy's big girl now and so I know you can understand this. I have to be away from you for a while. I'm not sure how long. That doesn't mean I don't love you. Mommy loves you more than the moon and stars and the world and everything in it.

I will explain more to you when I know exactly what is going to happen. I will call you on the phone when I can and I will write you letters and I want you to write me letters. And please draw me some of your beautiful pictures.

You and your papa have to take good care of each other because I know you will both be missing me a whole bunch and I know how hard it is when you're sad. Some day soon I am going to tell you about my own mama and how sad I was when I lost her. I was a much bigger girl than you are now but being bigger didn't make it hurt any less, so I know what it feels like to miss your mother. The difference is that my mama couldn't ever come back to me and that's not the way it is with us. I will come back to you no matter what. Cross my heart. You are my heart.

I love You,
Mommy

Again, Iris heard noises. This time louder. Coming from the direction of the lab. Had Isaac come back without her realizing it?

She put down the letters, wiped her eyes, then padded barefoot through the door and into the lab area. All the lights were off but there was reflected city light filtering in through the tall outside windows. The airshaft glass was dark. She peered into the shadows.

'Isaac?' she called hopefully.

She went forward, toward the silhouette of her mother's head. There was a flicker of movement, a dark form outside the airshaft window, the reflection of moonlight on rope, and then the crash of shattering glass and a body hurtled into the room. A sleek dark human form with a ski-mask instead of a face.

She stood frozen for a moment. Then the figure leaped at her and she spun and ran. He tackled her from behind, and she crashed sideways, falling so hard that the breath was knocked out of her lungs. She gasped for air. There was a burning in her arm. A needle. Drugs.

'No!' She clawed at him. The mask came off. Mitchell Hanley's face stared down at her.

'Mitch?' she whispered.

There was a blackness at the edge of her vision. It flowed inward until there was only a tiny pinpoint of light. Then there was nothing.

# Twenty-Seven

**H**er mouth was dry and tasted of metal. She tried to swallow but it hurt. There was a faint moan. Someone was sick. It was her. She was sick. Everything was moving in a circle around her. Making her sick.

She was dreaming. That was it. She was dreaming and if she could just break out of the dream she would be fine. She forced her eyes open and everything was on tilt, skewed crazily, like a view through a broken lens. She blinked and concentrated on one spot until it straightened out and she could focus. All she saw was wood. Old varnished pine, aged to the color of saddle leather. Above her was a pitched wooden ceiling. Around her were walls of wood. The only relief was a stone fireplace with the remnants of a fire glowing on the hearth.

She moved slightly and realized that she hurt in dozens of places. Suddenly she froze, recalling in flashes the attack at the lab, the hurtling figure, the sting of the needle and the helpless panic as the drug pulled her down and away.

Mitch? Had it really been Mitchell Hanley?

Stealthily she flexed her hands. They weren't bound. The room was cool and shadowed. What windows she could see were narrow and admitting a grey, stormy light. She was lying on a soft leather couch beside the fireplace. There was a blanket over her with ducks woven into it.

A wave of nausea crashed through her and she gripped

the leather and held on. No noise. She squeezed her eyes shut and ordered herself to be still and silent. Her attacker could come back at any time. She didn't want him to know she was awake.

When the nausea subsided she carefully eased herself upward to look over the back of the couch. The room stretched out into an L shape. At the farthest point from her was a long dining table. Her mother's head rested on the table. A man was sitting at the end, studying the head.

It was Nathan Kaliker.

'There is aspirin and water on that table beside the couch,' Kaliker said without looking up.

She swung her feet to the floor and inched down the couch toward the table with her head throbbing. The tablets looked like the extra-strength pain reliever that the bottle claimed they were, and the water looked like plain water. Besides, if someone wanted to give her more drugs they could have been administered while she was still unconscious.

Her hands shook as she gulped down the tablets and the entire glass of water. The water sloshed threateningly in her stomach and didn't cure her dry throat. She cleared her throat several times before she could speak.

'Is it morning?' she asked.

'Yes.'

'I've been out for a long time.'

'Yes.'

Though she was still groggy, Iris's mind began to dart around, weighing possibilities. Were they alone in the house? Where was the man in black? Mitch. Or had that been Mitch? The fuzziness in her brain made her uncertain.

'You don't know how glad I am to see you,' she said. 'How did you get me away from him?'

Kaliker turned in his chair so he could look directly at her. His face had aged in the days since she had last seen him. 'Please, Iris. Don't pretend that you don't understand.'

She thought for a moment. 'But Mr Kaliker, I *don't* understand.'

He sighed and looked back down at the sculpted face of her mother. 'This is beautiful work. You are extraordinarily talented.' He sighed again. 'And you are so much like her it sometimes takes my breath away.'

Iris massaged her forehead and tried to think. She had to distract him. Keep him talking. While she figured out an escape.

'Were you her Stanford boyfriend?'

He smiled a little. 'Yes. That was me.'

'Why didn't you two stay together?' Iris asked, wondering how the drug hangover would affect her coordination.

'Surely you know the answer to that already.'

'I don't know anything.'

She measured the room with her eyes, estimating distances. How fast could she make it across the open expanse of planked floor?

'Did you love my mother?' she asked.

He smiled and shook his head as though recalling something with nostalgia.

'God, yes. She was everything I'd ever wanted. From the first moment I saw her – she was only fourteen years old but she was already enchanting and pure as a flame. And she wanted me, too. She was desperate for a friend. It was perfect. It could have been perfect.'

'Then what went wrong?' Iris asked, flexing the muscles in her legs and trying to judge their strength. Would she be shaky when she stood?

Kaliker stared at the clay face in front of him.

'She ruined it all! She had to run away and come to California. She couldn't wait. She wouldn't listen to reason.'

'You didn't want her in California?'

'Of course not. I barely had enough money to take care of myself. And I had college to worry about. My grades. Making contacts. I didn't have time for her.'

'And you were busy creating Red Phoenix,' Iris said, moving ever so slightly on the couch.

He shifted, becoming suddenly agitated. 'I had to make something happen. I was a nobody at Stanford. I was just another face in the crowd. Jack paid my tuition but kept me penniless otherwise. He enjoys that you know, having people under his thumb, using his money for control.

'Jack?' Iris said. 'Your stepfather?'

'Yes. Jack DeVries. The self-righteous bastard. He's the master of alienation. Even Clary . . . as devoted as she was to him . . . even she was driven away. I have tried my damndest to please that man!'

Iris stared at him. The pieces of the puzzle slowly fell together. 'My mother and your stepfather were . . .'

Kaliker's head swiveled toward her. 'Father and daughter, of course. Jack DeVries is your grandfather.

'I have to say it had me nervous the other night when he decided to attend the fundraiser and I'd already arranged for you to be there. I saw him staring at you several times. The old bastard probably thought he was seeing a ghost.'

'You slept with your fourteen-year-old step-sister?'

'Don't look so shocked. It's not as if it was incest. Jack married my mother when I was seventeen. Clary and I weren't raised together. Not even close. My mother was one of Jack DeVries' secretaries. I was poor white trash. I wouldn't have been allowed to shine Clary DeVries' shoes when the two of us were children.

'It was lucky for Clary that I came along. I was her only friend. The only person in the world she could turn to. And if things had worked out right I'd have graduated from Stanford and proved myself to Jack, and Clary and I would be married now.

'But things didn't work out. It was all wrong from the

beginning. Jack put me on a miserly allowance to *teach me about money*, and I had to go out there to Stanford and compete with all those rich boys . . . boys who'd gone to exclusive schools their whole life . . . boys with expensive cars and wardrobes and money to toss around. Boys like that Hirano jerk who used to sniff around Clary all the time.

'And even though it was the Sixties – the age of non-materialism – believe me, torn jeans or not, those boys stunk of money. And they knew each other. They could smell each other. And they could tell that I wasn't one of them. They'd look at me and see right through to the secretary's son who used to wear hand-me-downs.'

Iris began inching, a fraction at a time, toward the end of the couch. She had to keep him talking. If he was talking he might not notice.

'So you started Red Phoenix to be somebody at Stanford?'

He sighed. 'I didn't realize then that good works gather more power and prestige than threats.'

Iris took a deep breath. It made her slightly dizzy.

'Did my mother know about the bomb?' she asked.

'Oh, no. She wouldn't have understood. Even though the bomb wasn't actually supposed to blow up. She still would have been upset with the plan.'

'What was the plan exactly?'

'I put the pieces of the bomb in a package and gave it to Clary. I told her it contained flyers, and asked her to take it to Denny over at Berkeley. That way I had an alibi because I was still on campus at Stanford. The plan was that Denny would tape the unassembled pieces to the back door of the draft office. I had already mailed a letter to the newspaper saying that the unassembled bomb was a warning from Red Phoenix, showing what could happen if no one listened.

'Denny was not supposed to ask Clary to drive him to

Ebersville. The bomb was never supposed to be put together. And that idiot Denny wasn't supposed to go inside the office.

'It was all engineered to be a show of power. To give authority to the name Red Phoenix. So I could build the organization. Go beyond having just Denny and Clary as my followers. The last thing I wanted to do was commit a serious crime.'

'Didn't you feel responsible for that child's death?'

'That was an accident, Iris. If she'd dashed out in front of the truck delivering my mail, would that have been my fault, too?'

He shook his head sadly.

'I know the dead girl's father, Senator Dixon. He's a big supporter of mine. Isn't that ironic?'

'No, it's tragic.'

'You sound like your mother. I told her that it had all been Denny's fault. I laid it all in Denny's lap, but still, she was so upset. And felt so guilty. She kept talking about turning herself in. She wanted to, but I convinced her that even after we told the authorities how it was all Denny's fault, they would throw the book at both of us. That my future would be destroyed and her father would be devastated and all our lives would be ruined. And for what?

'Of course she had her own secret reasons for agreeing – which I learned of later.'

'She was pregnant with me.'

'Yes. And she'd fallen in love with someone else.'

He shook his head. 'I adore women but you're all alike. So emotional. So . . . soft hearted. If you had a weapon in your hand right now, you'd run away rather than hurt me . . . That's the way women are. That's why they make the wrong decisions. That's why they always lose.'

'Maybe that's why the world is in such a mess,' Iris said.

He looked at her with something close to tenderness.

'You might have been my daughter if circumstances had been different. I might have married Clary and you might have been mine.'

Iris reached the end of the couch and Kaliker leaned to the side and peered out the narrow window. 'Mitchell is out scouting the perimeter with his dog. I don't know how long he'll be.'

Scouting the perimeter? Would she run into Mitch and his dog if she made it through the door?

'And that's who brought me here? Mitch Hanley? That's who killed Mr Andretti? That's who shot my father?'

'Yes.'

'Did he set that fire at the hospital, too?'

Kaliker sighed. 'Yes. That was a failed attempt to get to your father.'

'And he's the one who beat Kizmin and took her car?'

'Yes.'

'Why?'

'He had your phone tapped and he heard Kizmin call you and arrange to meet you with the bones. He thought she was talking about Clary's bones. He thought they had finally surfaced.'

'How could you let him hurt Kizmin so badly?'

Kaliker lowered his eyes. 'Mitch thought that Justine had become a liability. She wanted too much from me.'

'So he meant to kill her?'

Kaliker looked away without answering.

Iris strained to see the locks on the door. Was there a dead bolt or chain that was on? Would she be able to get out quickly once she got there? What did that tiny red light on the wall beside the doorframe mean?

'And my mother . . . why was she killed?'

He reached up and gently stroked the clay cheek with one finger. 'I never wanted to hurt her. Never. I knew where she was all that time.'

He stared at the clay face in silence for several long moments and Iris was afraid that he wouldn't start talking again.

'I was worried at first, worried that she might change her mind and confess, but she seemed so steady in her new life. I didn't think she'd ever want to jeopardize it. Over the years I stopped worrying. Then one day I got a call from her. She said she was coming to New York to see me. Immediately an alarm went off in my head, but then I thought maybe she had missed me all those years. And I thought . . . maybe . . . she wanted me again.'

Kaliker focused on the dead face and Iris bolted from the couch and sprinted across the floor. The door wouldn't open. She threw her body against it and twisted the lock knobs.

'It's the new security system,' he said. 'Mitchell had it installed. Nobody gets in or out without codes when the doors are activated.'

Iris straightened and turned back toward him. She saw then that there was a gun lying on the table near him. He made no move to pick it up or threaten her with it though. She stood very still for a moment, watching him, fighting down her fear.

'There's nowhere to go,' he said. 'Don't you see? We're all trapped in this.'

Reluctantly she sat on a chair at the opposite end of the table from him. He resumed talking as though there had been no interruption.

'I met her on the street . . . didn't let her come up to the office. Thought it would be safe that way. I surprised her by arriving with my car. She didn't want to get in. She asked me if I couldn't park the car and go to a restaurant with her. She was nervous.

'I drove around to put her at ease. I pointed out the foundation offices and told her about them. She didn't seem interested.

'She told me how much she missed her father. Not me. But Jack! Then she started talking about you. Said you were eight years old – the same age as the girl who died. She told me she had visited the girl's grave. Told me that she couldn't look into her own daughter's eyes anymore without seeing the dead girl there.

'Then she said, "I have to set things straight, Natty. I can't run from it anymore."

'I told her that confession wouldn't raise the dead or undo the past. I told her that I would be ruined. That my fledgling foundation and all its good works would be destroyed. She said that people were more forgiving than I thought. She said that her father would help me.

'Hah! Her father! He'd have made sure I lost everything!'

Kaliker scrubbed at his face with his hands.

'I've worked so hard. And I've won him over. The foundation has won him over. He's making me his heir. Not me directly, but the foundation. Which will be almost the same as inheriting directly because I control all the foundation's assets. People already think I have some of his money. Soon I will.'

He stood and walked to the window to look out, then he returned to his chair.

'I tried to explain to her that being a just and moral person does not mean that you have to behave stupidly. I told her she was a fool if she thought the authorities were ever going to let her return to her husband and child.

'She demanded that I stop the car and let her out. I said I would, but I knew that I couldn't let her go.

'I asked her why she hadn't gone to the police already, and she said it was because she wanted to give me the chance to go with her. She didn't want me to look bad. She said then that she knew about the foundation and she was proud of me.

'I saw an industrial side street and I pulled over between some parked trucks.

' "Why are we stopping?" she asked me, but she wasn't afraid.

' "I just want to sit with you awhile," I told her.

'Then I grabbed her, I caught her neck in the crook of my arm, and I squeezed. I kept squeezing until she went limp.'

He drew in a deep breath.

'I propped her up in the seat like she was asleep and I started to drive again.

'I kept driving and eventually I headed here. I don't remember deciding to come. I just did.

'The place was deserted. Jack hadn't donated it to the foundation yet so we hadn't started the retreats or the victims' camps, and there was never anyone up here.

'I sat in the car with her for awhile, trying to decide what to do. Finally I carried her into the woods. To a spot that she had showed me once . . . a favorite spot from her childhood. A little cave just big enough for a child to crawl into and hide.

'I put her inside. With her purse. I curled her up like she was sleeping.

'Then I piled rocks up over the entrance. Tried to make it look like it was never there. I even transplanted some vines to grow over the rocks.

'She rested there all that time. And I always thought of the camp as a tribute to her.'

Iris heard a dog bark somewhere outside. How much time did she have before Mitch returned? The doors were electronically locked. The windows all had security bars. Should she try to fight Kaliker for the gun? He was older, but he was bigger than she was and he was extremely fit.

'Why did you arrange for me to get the scholarship?'

He winced. 'Clary was so proud of you. I wanted you to have the best. For her.'

'Did you think an expensive education made up for losing my mother?'

'It was a gesture.'

'So how did my mother's bones get out of the cave?'

'Through my stupidity,' Kaliker admitted. 'All was well until one day a few months ago when I got a phone call at my office.'

There was a noise from the kitchen and Kaliker turned.

Mitchell Hanley appeared in the doorway. He was dressed in combat boots and clothes that resembled battle fatigues.

'Everything looks good out there,' he said to Kaliker. 'Colonel Ollie only barked once and that was at a rabbit.'

Kaliker sighed wearily.

'It's time,' Mitch said.

Kaliker nodded.

'Wait,' Iris said. 'You haven't finished the story.'

'Shut up, Iris!' Mitch shouted.

'Enough, Mitchell,' Kaliker said softly. He turned to Iris. 'It's only fair that she hears the rest.'

Iris's pulse was pounding in her ears and she was furious at herself. Why hadn't she made another move while she was still alone with Kaliker? Mitch's appearance made it two against one. But she knew that it was partly because of the story Kaliker was telling. She needed to know.

'Some months ago my assistant gave me a message slip that had a local number and said simply *Call Clary's Friend*. I was shocked. I couldn't think what to do. I'd felt safe for twenty years . . . !

'I made the call and was told to assemble a large amount of money or the authorities would be notified. I tried to ask the man questions, but he had a set script and wouldn't deviate from it. He kept saying over and over, "I know everything and the cops will know it too if you don't come up with the cash."

'I panicked. I thought that he must have found Clary's

remains somehow and pieced together the story. I rushed up here and went straight into the woods to check. But nothing was disturbed. I was dumbfounded! I went back to Manhattan and decided to take Mitchell into my confidence.'

'Yeah!' Mitch said angrily. 'After it was too late. After you'd already been screwed.'

'Mitch insisted that we return immediately to the lodge and get rid of the remains. I led him through the woods to the spot to find that she was gone. All the vines were torn away and the rocks were moved and the bones were gone.'

'And the purse,' Mitch put in.

'I knew then that the caller had tricked me into leading him there.

'We went back to the city and waited to hear from the blackmailer again. He was very emotional this time. Raving about how he had me by the balls and how it was going to cost me every cent I had to buy my way out. And suddenly I realized that he had suspected me only of the Red Phoenix connection and had used the phrase Clary's friend to establish his knowledge of that time in my life. He had had no suspicions about Clary's death.

'He'd followed me, seen me check my hiding place, and then opened it after I was gone because he thought I'd led him to evidence of Red Phoenix. What he found was evidence of another crime instead.'

Kaliker looked at Mitch and the younger man shook his head as though disgusted with the way things had evolved.

'I was very careful each time on the phone, in case he was taping. I never admitted anything. Never incriminated myself. Mitch worked at trying to trace the calls but couldn't. Then Mitch had the idea to check out John Lanier.'

Kaliker glanced at the younger man with a pleased expression.

462

'He thought that Lanier was the logical cause of all the trouble. So we checked and sure enough, Lanier wasn't home in his orchard. We tracked him to New York but didn't know where he was in the city.

'Finally a pay-off was arranged. By that time we were sure Lanier had a partner but we didn't know who. And we knew that there was only one way to put an end to the threat. We had to get rid of both men. But we also had to find the evidence and destroy it.

'The voice on the phone insisted on a face-to-face meeting with me. It was set for late at night by the river. Mitchell went in my place. He wore a hat and a heavy coat and kept himself in the dark. We thought he could get away with impersonating me, and if he didn't, then he was going to say that he'd been sent to lead the man to me.

'Mitchell had a case with money in it – not all the blackmailer demanded but a large payment – and he was going to stall him, say that the rest would be available soon. The case had a tracking device in it.

'Mitchell went to the meeting spot early. Everything seemed safe. But when Lanier came he guessed immediately that it wasn't me.'

Kaliker glanced at Mitch and the younger man exploded. 'Then the fucker pulled a gun! He attacked me and the gun went off. And he went down and something fell out of his ear and I heard noise. I checked him out and the fucker was wired!

'Everything had been transmitted somewhere. And I heard this guy's voice saying "John! John! What's happening?" So I got down close so he'd be sure to hear me and I said, "John got stupid. If you still want the money you'd better be smart."

'I found a paper in his pocket. It was a receipt for turning on a phone service. I grabbed that and the gun and took the money and got out of there fast.'

Kaliker shook his head as though saddened. 'Your father was very foolish, Iris.'

'He wasn't foolish. He wanted to catch you. He wanted justice.'

'And look what he got instead. Well, he won't suffer much longer. After we're through here Mitchell is going to put him out of his misery.'

'You'll never get near him,' Iris warned. 'They watch him all the time.'

'Mitchell has charmed one of the younger nurses and learned when your father is scheduled for a visit from a lab technician. Mitchell will be that technician.'

'You won't get away with it. Don't you see? You've gone too far. It's spread too wide to control.'

'Shut up,' Mitch growled. 'Tell her the rest so we can go.'

Kaliker rose and glanced absently out the window. 'From the phone receipt we learned the location of your father's room. We sent the message to you, thinking that you would attract your father's blackmail partner. You came. Mitchell moved in below you. He bugged your phone and your room, and we waited to see who you flushed out. Andretti caught Mitchell going through your room that day you came back from Guatemala. Mitchell chased him down the stairs and fought with him. Unfortunately we didn't learn till later that it was Andretti we were looking for all along.'

'And Guatemala? Was that you too?'

Kaliker nodded. 'By then we realized that we had to get rid of you, too, or you would never stop nosing around in things. Mitchell thought that the box from Kizmin's car contained Clary's bones and purse.' Kaliker sighed. 'When he heard about your plan to be at the dig with only one or two men, he hired South American thugs to play bandit. They were supposed to dispose of you. Unfortunately they mistook the other woman for you and botched the whole thing. Which was just as well because we learned we didn't have the right bones, or the purse.'

'You listened to everything on my phone?'

'Yes. And Mitchell also had a transmitting device. So he could track you wherever you went. He's good with electronics.'

'Very clever.'

Mitch grinned. 'It was in the beeper,' he said. 'I couldn't believe it when you asked me for that beeper. It was perfect. And without it I never would have found you in that lab.'

'Now you know everything, Iris. That's more than your mother could say at her death. And we have what we need. Clary's bones and her purse and the letters, every piece of incriminating evidence is now in our possession. And it will all be destroyed.'

'So it was just the two of you . . . all this time?' Iris asked.

'Mostly me,' Mitch said.

'Then who are all the other men who were chasing me?' Iris asked.

Kaliker and Mitch exchanged a glance. 'You mean the cops,' Mitch said. 'They're after you for killing Andretti.'

'No. Not the police. Those other men in the suits who started after me before Andretti.'

'She must mean detectives,' Kaliker said to Mitch. 'The detectives wear suits rather than uniforms.'

'No,' Iris insisted. 'The guys who—'

Mitch slammed his fist against the wall. 'She's stalling. That's it.'

Kaliker looked at her sadly, then turned his back.

# Twenty-Eight

Mitch lunged forward and grabbed her arm. She raked his face with the fingernails of her free hand and he grunted in fury and slammed her to the floor. He pinned her with his knees and yanked her wrists together in front of her, then taped them again with the same silver tape he'd used in the lab.

'You're going to be famous,' he told her. 'You're going to be one of the Locket Killer's victims. Nathan has an in at the prosecutor's office and he got a copy of the police report. I've got it all . . . the same tape, the same brand of cigarettes for the burns, the same style of locket.' he smiled. 'And the metal rod of course. Can't forget that.'

Desperately Iris twisted and struggled. 'He's screwed up other things, Kaliker! What makes you think your hired thug will get this right?'

Mitch slapped her so hard the room spun.

Kaliker flinched. 'Careful,' he warned. 'I don't think he slaps them.'

Mitch put a length of tape across her mouth, then sat back on his haunches to look at her.

'He's not a hired thug, Iris.' Kaliker rested his hand on Mitch's back. 'He's my son. Born under unfortunate circumstances and to a woman who should never have been a mother . . . but that's all in the past. He's with me and we're going to smooth everything out together.'

467

Mitch looked up at the older man with an expression of adoration.

'Remember, son, you've got to do it where you're going to leave her. He doesn't move their bodies.'

Mitch nodded.

'You've got everything in the car that you'll need?'

'Yeah.'

'The locket. You have the locket?'

'Yeah.'

Iris's brain screamed in silent terror. Mitch was going to make her into a victim of the Locket Killer. He was going to beat her and torture her. Then he was going to shove the metal rod inside her. And she knew, she knew without a doubt that he was going to enjoy it.

'You haven't left prints on anything?'

'I'm telling you, I got it covered. Now, clean up here and then go back to the city and stay cool.'

Kaliker pulled the younger man into a rough embrace. 'Take care, Mitchell.'

A piercing squawk suddenly filled the room. Kaliker rushed to a bifold door in the wall and pulled it open. There was a control panel and several monitors. 'Which one is it?' Kaliker shouted covering his ears.

Mitch ran across the floor and hit a button. The squawking stopped.

'It was the front alarm,' Mitch said. 'Damn, what did I tell you! This security system is great. If we'd have had this before, then that little creep couldn't have sneaked in here and got the bones in the first place.'

Iris carefully rolled over and crawled toward the kitchen, thankful that her wrists had been bound in front rather than in back. The two men were totally engrossed in their electronics.

'Will we be able to see who it is?' Kaliker asked.

'Give me a minute. I'm panning the cameras. I hope he's not in that blind spot where the creek cuts through.

There! There's somebody heading off through the trees.'
Mitch's voice was wild with excitement. 'You call the
security company and tell them it was a false alarm. I'll go
out and shoot him. What the fuck . . . look at that! It's the
musician from Andretti's building.'

Isaac! Isaac was out there! Iris made it into the kitchen
and struggled to her feet. The little red light beside the
back door was unlit. *Please, please, please*, she repeated to
herself silently. There was a butcher block full of knives
on the counter and she grabbed one as she passed.

'Hey!' she heard Mitch shout. 'She's gone!'

The door knob twisted awkwardly with her bound
hands. Then she was out and running. Across the open
area and into the trees.

'Ollie!' she heard Mitch yelling behind her. 'Ollie,
catch! Catch, Ollie!'

She heard the dog crash into the forest behind her.
There was no way she could outrun him. She dived behind
a huge rock, crouched low, heart thundering in her chest,
hands sweating. She wedged the knife handle in a crevice
and sawed the tape clumsily over the sharp edge.

She ripped through it and stood in one motion, just as
the dog reached her. She held out her left arm, bent at the
wrist as though protecting her face, and the dog leaped in
a silent, graceful arc. His mouth opened and his lips pulled
back and his teeth sank into her forearm, and she thrust
with her right hand, shoving the knife into his belly, his
own momentum driving it deeper and wrenching it sideways as his body slammed into her and carried them both
to the ground.

She scrambled out from under him. A sob tore her chest
and she realized her mouth was still taped. She ripped the
tape away, then bent to the bleeding animal, closed her
eyes, and pulled the knife out. He shuddered and cried
out, snapping wildly at the air with his teeth.

She clutched the handle of the knife and crept on

through the trees. Isaac! She had to warn Isaac! But she didn't know which way to run. She didn't know how much land there was or where the entrance lay. She didn't know what other security traps there might be.

They had said Isaac was coming in through the front. The drive would lead to the front. If she circled the house in the trees she would have to cross the drive at some point. Then she could follow it. She hunched over and tried to pad quietly but every step she took vibrated with the crackling of leaves and breaking of twigs.

Isaac was out there and Mitch would kill him.

She could see the house. She dashed from tree to tree just inside the forest, keeping it in sight. It took her just minutes to find the graveled drive. She ran alongside it, keeping to the trees.

A boom exploded nearby. Then another. Rifle shots! She dropped to the ground, thinking she was the target. Then she saw a figure ahead of her through the trees. It was Mitch, rifle relaxed, looking down at something on the ground.

'Mitchell!' she heard Kaliker shouting. 'Mitchell! Ollie is hurt!'

Mitch darted through the trees to the drive and ran toward the lodge. Quickly Iris went to the spot where she'd seen him. Isaac lay face down in the leaves. Two perfect little circles marred the back of his windbreaker.

'Isaac, Isaac,' she moaned and dropped to her knees beside him. She touched his face, put her ear to his back. His heartbeat was faint but it was there, and his lungs were working. She rolled him slightly onto his side and arranged his arms so that he seemed to breath easier.

'I'll get help,' she whispered and hugged him fiercely, willing him to live.

There was something hard under his jacket. She slipped her hand inside. It was a gun. She pulled it out and stared at it. Isaac had been so determined to save her that he'd found a gun and followed her right into hell.

Her hands shook, red with dog blood, holding the sleek black gun. Sobs building in her chest, shoulders quaking, so close to the edge that she didn't know if she could hold on. But she had to. There was only her. And if she didn't fight, then Isaac was lost and her father in the hospital was lost and there would never be any justice for her mother.

She rose and looked around, battling the terror, pushing it down deep inside her. If she made it to the road, how far would it be to help? Where was this place? Could Isaac hold on long enough for her to go for help?

There was a telephone inside the lodge. That would be the fastest way to summon help. That would be Isaac's best chance. She had the gun now. That was all Mitch had. Just a gun. That made them even, didn't it?

She studied the thing. It was not so straightforward as a revolver, but she could see how it worked. She checked to make sure it was loaded, thought about firing into the ground to try it out. No. That would alert Mitch. She didn't need to practice. It was a simple tool. A simple killing tool.

She looked toward the lodge. But there were two of them. How could she handle two of them?

She ran parallel to the drive, looking for the entrance and the road. What she found was a fresh swath cut through the trees, like a narrow pathway, only it wasn't meant to be a path. It had been cleared to build a brand new ten-foot link fence. Spaced along the fence were shiny signs reading DANGER! THIS FENCE IS ELECTRIFIED TO KEEP OUT INTRUDERS. The warning was repeated in several languages.

She followed the fence toward the drive and saw the entryway. It too had an electrified barrier in the form of a tall metal gate on wheels. How had Isaac gotten through? She followed the fence, looking for a clue, and spotted something draped over the top. It was in a densely shaded area with large trees growing right up to the fence path. She moved closer. The thing looked like the rubber backed floor mat from the back seat of a car. Then it hit her. It was a floor mat. Isaac had thrown it there to protect himself from the electricity. He had climbed a tree on the outside, stepped onto the mat and swung into the tree limbs above her.

But the alarms had picked him up right away. That meant that they were all around. Not just at the entrance. She tucked the gun into the back of her waistband and put her hands on the rough barked tree. It would be nothing. Tree climbing was like riding a bicycle. Her childhood skills would come back.

But there was nothing across the road. Absolutely nothing. And the road was nothing. And she didn't know which way to go. This was wilderness area. State Parks all around. Hadn't someone said that it bordered parkland? What if she went the wrong way? She could walk for days without finding help. And Isaac would die. Isaac would surely die. Mitch might get to her father, too.

She dropped her hands and looked around. They might be watching her on the monitor at that very minute. Or Mitch might be running through the trees, shouldering his rifle.

She drew a deep breath and ran back toward the lodge, crouching low and ducking around big trees so she was less of a target. She stopped to listen for a pursuer, held her breath to hear better, and thought she recognized the faint sound of running water.

A creek?

The creek where the surveillance cameras had a blind spot?

She ran toward the sound and came upon a narrow stream of water, running in the bottom of a deeply eroded cut. She jumped down and followed it.

She was nearing the area where she had stabbed the dog

472

when the creek turned sharply away and she had to abandon it. She edged toward the lodge, running from tree to tree. The first bullet struck beside her head, gouged out a chunk of wood and showered bark in her hair.

'Go ahead and run, Iris,' Mitch called to her. 'This isn't the twenty-two I used on your friend. I got out something better to hunt you down with.'

Another chunk of the tree disintegrated.

She cursed herself for her stupidity. Even with a gun she was no match for Mitchell Hanley. She should have gone over the fence when she had the chance.

There was a loud crack of thunder and the rain that had threatened all morning began to fall, peppering her with fat cold drops. She could hear Mitch moving closer. Another thunderclap boomed. A dagger of lightning sliced through the sky and the rain began to fall harder, pouring down in sheets of water.

She heard Mitch cursing and she wheeled and ran, sliding down the muddy wall of the creek crevice on her butt. The thin ribbon of water had grown to fill the width of the crevice and risen to several inches in depth. She waded against it, the water sucking at her shoes and slowing her progress.

When the crevice got shallower she scrambled upward, digging her fingers into the mud for purchase. She pulled herself out and Mitch was at the top, water sluicing down his face. He clubbed her with the rifle butt and she pitched sideways, then sprawled on her back, stunned.

'You've ruined everything!' he shrieked. 'Women ruin everything!'

He dropped the rifle and fell on her, straddling her, face contorted, hands circling her throat. She clawed at his eyes, bucked and writhed and tried to break his hold but he held on and darkness crowded into her brain, like a picture growing smaller on the screen.

Suddenly there was a tremendous explosion nearby, a cracking and crashing, then a sizzling flash and the singing of ravaged metal. Startled, he pulled back and looked toward the sound. She worked her right arm behind her and slipped her fingers around the gun. Moving by instinct and will, her brain cells gasping for oxygen.

The rain slackened. She dragged the gun out and held it in front of her chest, pointing it straight at his heart, gripping it so tightly that her fingers were like white talons. He turned back to her and smiled slightly when he saw the gun, as though it was a toy, a joke, a silly feminine threat. Then he jerked his hands up, whether to swat the gun away or lunge again for her throat she never knew because she fired and kept firing until the trigger brought only blank clicks.

He fell on her like a lover, face nestled in the curve of her neck. She lay there, sobbing, tears streaming from her eyes and mixing with the rain.

Isaac.

She struggled with the dead weight until she was free, then she dragged herself upright. Isaac. Isaac needed help. She started to walk toward the drive. The rain stopped. She was covered with mud and Mitch's blood. Her left arm throbbed unmercifully where the dog's teeth had sunk into the flesh. She pushed herself forward. Toward Isaac.

There was a metallic twanging, then a cry and a string of obscenities. It was a woman's voice. Iris hurried to the drive and saw Detective Kizmin picking herself up from the gravel just inside the gate. One arm was casted and in a sling but she had obviously climbed over. Her car sat on the other side.

'Lanier! Oh Jesus, Lanier! Don't try to run!'

'I'm not hurt,' Iris said. Her voice was a rasp that had to be wrenched from her throat. 'It's Isaac. He's shot. And Mitch is dead. I killed him. And I stabbed the dog.'

'Jesus.' Kizmin looked back at her car. 'The radio's no good up here. I'll have to call for help from the house.'

'Kaliker's still around somewhere,' Iris said. 'Isaac is right over there.' She pointed into the trees. 'Shot twice. Get a doctor. Get a—'

Iris swayed and Kizmin caught her.

'Jesus! Your neck! It's all bruised.'

'I'm OK,' Iris insisted, pushing away the supporting arms. 'Hurry. Hurry.' And she forced her legs to carry her toward Isaac.

# Twenty-Nine

Isaac was still alive. She lay down on the wet ground and held him gently in her arms. Pouring herself into him. She breathed with him. Matching his labored breath. She pressed his hand against her heart so his own heart would feel her strength. Everything hurt. Her head, her neck, her ribs. Shadows gathered around them. And then she saw female figures. They circled and keened softly. The women from the chamber. The sacrificed daughters. And Moonsmoke came to sit beside her, eyes filled with sorrow, mouth shaped into a warning.

Then her mother stepped into the circle. Radiant with light. Eyes glowing. Mouth curved into a tender loving smile. She knelt, cradling Iris in her light, melting away the years of bitterness so that Iris felt her entire body liquefy and flow into a new form. *You are my heart.*

'Not me,' Iris whispered. 'Save him. Save him.'

'There they are! Get those stretchers over here!'

Iris opened her eyes to see unfamiliar men looming over her. Hands reached. She tried to sit up but they pushed her down.

'Take it easy. Everything's going to be fine. We've got a chopper out there on the lawn and we'll have you to the hospital in no time.'

'Not me,' Iris croaked. 'He's shot.'

'We know. We're taking care of him, too.'

They carried her out on a stretcher even though she felt certain she could walk. Isaac was taken first. She insisted on it. She turned her head to watch.

When they carried her to the helicopter he was already inside with IV tubes snaking from his arms and an oxygen mask on his face. Kizmin was there. Her expression was grim. There was blood smeared on her shirt.

'Iris,' she said, 'He's in there, too. He—' But her words were snatched away by the whine of the chopper's engine starting. The rotor began to spin and Iris was handed up inside and she saw that there was another stretcher next to Isaac's. Nathan Kaliker was lying on it. His breath was ragged and wheezing. Saliva ran from his mouth. The right side of his face was wet with blood. There was a hole in his temple, the edges blackened by powderburn.

She closed her eyes and tried to summon her mother again, but the vision wouldn't hold. It shimmered like dust behind her eyes then disappeared. Instead, she saw her father. He was holding out his arms to her as he had never held out his arms in his life and she jerked into a sitting position, shaking and clammy with sweat.

'What is it?' a paramedic asked, trying to ease her back down.

'My father,' Iris rasped. 'I'm afraid my father is dead.'

At the hospital Isaac was carried out first, then Kaliker, then Iris. Two doctors examined her. She begged them to let her call Manhattan and check on her father but they told her she would have to wait. She was stripped and poked and prodded, sponged clean of blood, taken for a CAT scan of the head and an X-ray of the arm, and diagnosed as having a bad dog bite, a severely bruised neck and larynx from the attempted strangulation, a concussion from the rifle-butt blow, and an assortment of minor injuries. The prescription was bed rest and no talking.

Finally she was taken to a patient room. Detective Kizmin was waiting inside.

'It's about time!' Kizmin said as the orderlies pushed the gurney through the door.

Iris attempted a smile. As soon as she was settled into the bed and the two young men had gone, Kizmin pulled the chair up to the bedside and leaned close.

'I called about your father, Iris. One of the doctors said you were concerned so I made the call for you.' The detective hesitated and Iris squeezed her eyes shut against what she knew was coming.

'Your father looked at a nurse and asked her where you were!'

Iris covered her face with her hands and wept. The weeping made her throat and her head hurt so she started to laugh. That hurt worse.

Kizmin poured her a glass of water. 'Here. Drink. I know it hurts for you to talk so I'll do all the talking.'

Iris nodded.

'Isaac just got out of surgery. He's going to make it. The doctor says he's a very lucky guy.'

Again the tears threatened. She pressed the heels of her hands against her eyes and smiled with quivering lips.

'Kaliker died. And you were right about Mitch . . . you damn sure shot him dead.'

Iris closed her eyes. A scream built inside her and crashed silently through her body. She had killed him. It could never be undone or taken back. She had taken a life.

She felt something and then Kizmin was squeezing her hand, holding it as though there was something desperate between them.

'It never gets easier,' the detective said softly. 'I've been through it twice and it was hell both times. They're with me, you know. I'm never free of them. That's the price you pay. That's the curse.'

Kizmin drew in a deep breath and straightened. 'The good news is that we've recovered the bones Mitch stole in the carjacking. So you can have another chance at identifying our girl and catching her killer.' Kizmin grinned. 'I like it when you can't argue with me.

'The bad news is that the feds have arrived. They're here in full force. Can't wait to descend on you with thousands of questions.'

Iris frowned and shook her head.

'Afraid you can't say no,' Kizmin said.

'Why me?' Iris mouthed.

'Why do they want to talk to you? Mmm, guess you're the only one left with answers at this point.' Kizmin's eyes brightened with sarcastic amusement. 'It seems Richie Malik, aka Andretti, had gotten them all excited about a Red Phoenix score and then he backed off. Insisted he'd been wrong. They didn't trust him so they'd been keeping an eye on him. As soon as your dad was shot they tied it to Richie because Richie had been seen with him.

'They had your dad under protection at the hospital. That's who all those men with mops and brooms were. And they had Richie under surveillance. You too. Though they do admit that they were confused about whose side you were on.

'They just never guessed that Nathan Kaliker was behind everything.'

Kizmin bowed her head a moment, and Iris knew that the woman had been devastated by the loss of her hero. She reached out and touched Kizmin's shoulder. The detective raised her eyes to the ceiling. 'It's still so hard to accept.' She cleared her throat and squared her shoulders.

'Anyway, from piecing it together they think Richie called your dad and told him he'd found Clary's bones and he knew who the murderer was. He asked your dad to help him nab the murderer. Unbeknownst to your dad he planned to get money out of Kaliker and then, with your

480

dad's help, turn Kaliker in to the feds and collect all the rewards, too.

'Of course the feds never consulted with us lowly local cops. In fact they were the ones who pulled the strings and got me off the case. They didn't want any NYPD types getting in their way.

'Mitchell Hanley, who was right under their nose all the time, never was noticed at all.

'After Andretti was killed you were their only link and they pulled out all the stops to catch you.' Kizmin grinned. 'Boy, did you embarrass the hell out of them by getting away. Not just once, but twice!' The detective chuckled.

'They tracked down Richie's ex-wife, and bingo, you'd beaten them there. Another black eye for the feds. They found his cars but you'd been there too.'

Kizmin could hardly contain her amusement. 'My partner, Detective Barney, is so impressed he's ready to adopt you. Make you a task force mascot or something.'

Iris frowned, pointed at Kizmin and held out her hands in a gesture of puzzlement.

'How did I get back into it?'

Iris nodded.

'My boss made me stay home after my carjacking and the elbow surgery and all that. I didn't know any of the stuff that had happened. Believe me . . . if I'd known you needed help . . .'

Iris nodded and touched the woman's arm.

'The first I heard of trouble was when a fed came to see me at home. He'd heard that I got to know you and he wanted to pick my brain about where you might be hiding. He gave me a sketchy outline of the situation, including the part about you getting to the bones before they did, and that triggered me. I knew that if you had those bones you'd want to work on them and then I remembered that you still had a key to the lab.

'After I got rid of the fed I went to the lab. You were

481

gone and I could tell there had been a struggle. I got into my car and there was a message for me. Someone named Isaac said that you were in serious trouble at the foundation's upstate camp. I'd been there before with Nathan. I knew how to find it.'

Kizmin bowed her head for a moment and blinked hard, then shook her head as though annoyed with herself.

'I called it in to the feds and barreled right up the highway. They couldn't use a chopper because of the thunderstorm so they tried to find the place by car. Never made it. They were completely lost.'

Kizmin held out her arms. 'That's it. Case closed. Just like television.'

Questions filled Iris's mind. How had Isaac known she was in trouble? How had he found her? But she would have to wait and ask him. There would be plenty of time for them to talk. All the time in the world.

Iris used her finger to draw a K on the palm of her hand. She repeated it several times before Kizmin understood.

'Nathan was fine when I went into the lodge. He was shocked to see me there with my gun drawn. I called for an ambulance, had to wait on the phone while they decided whether the storm was over and they could send the chopper. All the while Nathan just sat there slumped in a chair.

'When I got off the phone he asked me about Mitchell Hanley. I told him that the guy was dead. It hit him hard. The med chopper service called me back to clarify directions and Nathan went over to one of those antique roll-top desks and opened it with a key. I was watching him and had my gun out so I wasn't worried.

'He started writing. He must have sat there writing for ten minutes. I stopped paying very close attention. I was aggravated with the guy on the phone because they weren't in the air yet. Next thing I knew Nathan had a little pistol in his hand. I shouted for him to drop it but he . . .' She rubbed her eyes. 'Well, you know what he did.'

Iris used her finger again to pantomime writing on her palm.

'What did he write?'

She nodded.

Kizmin sighed. 'I was going to wait and tell you when you felt better.' Her eyes wandered the room then finally returned to Iris. 'He wrote an open letter to his supporters and staff, thanking everyone, apologizing for failing everyone. He said he hoped that Vitya could lead the foundation through the disgrace he'd brought upon it.

'Then he wrote out a will. First he gave burial instructions for himself and Mitchell Hanley. He acknowledged Mitchell as his son and expressed regret that he hadn't made the relationship public before.'

Kizmin hesitated and Iris motioned for her to go on.

'And he wrote to Jack . . . expressing regrets . . . and saying how much he had loved your mother.'

Iris pressed her hands over her ears and shook her head until the throbbing inside it filled her entire body.

# Thirty

On the second day that Iris was in the hospital a nurse came in, smiling, and told her to pick up the phone when it rang. She did and was surprised to hear a weak version of Isaac's voice.

'They let me call,' he said. 'But I promised to keep it short.'

'Isaac,' she rasped.

'No. You're not supposed to talk.'

There was a charged silence.

'I'm so sorry, Iris. I should have known. I should have been there. I should have—'

She made a noise of protest.

'All right,' he said. 'I'll stop. But I am sorry. And I'm full of admiration. What you did . . . I know what it took to do all that . . . to save yourself and to save me. I am . . . awestruck. And so grateful.'

'Time!' she heard a nurse's voice call in the background.

'They want me to rest some more,' he said. 'But don't worry about me. I'm mending quickly.'

'I love you, Isaac,' she whispered as loudly as her throat would stand.

There was a click as he hung up. She didn't know if he had heard her or not. She hoped he hadn't. She couldn't imagine what had possessed her to say it.

On the fourth day that Iris was in the hospital the doctor came in and said that she could leave.

485

'I'd prefer to keep you another day but I understand your concerns about your father and your need to go to Manhattan. Detective Kizmin has volunteered to drive you there and has promised that she will keep you from overextending yourself.'

Iris nodded eagerly in response to everything the woman said.

'I've written you a prescription for pain reliever – the same one you've been taking here – and also a muscle relaxer. Sometimes the combination is effective on concussion headaches because the neck is involved. Your bouts of nausea should stop soon. Try to keep food in your stomach or the medicine will upset it and the nausea will be worse.'

Iris nodded and the woman smiled. 'OK. I can tell you've heard enough for now. Remember, no talking till the end of the week and then do it with care. Get plenty of rest. No alcohol. Don't hesitate to call if you need anything. If you have questions write them out and have your detective friend read them to me over the phone.'

As soon as the woman walked out, Detective Kizmin walked in. Iris was already out of bed heading for the closet. The room spun around her and she grabbed Kizmin's arm to keep her balance.

'Maybe you should spend another day in here,' Kizmin said.

Iris shook her head and stood up straight to show that the dizziness had passed.

'Just what do you think you're going to find in that closet?'

Iris turned and looked at her.

'Those things you had on were thrown in the trash.' She smiled and held up a shopping bag. 'But I've got something here.'

Iris dressed in the luxurious silk shirt, black jeans, and leather slip-on flats that Kizmin produced from the bag.

The silk against her skin made her feel sexy, made her think of Isaac. She picked up the small notebook and pen that Kizmin had brought her and wrote *How much do I owe you for the clothes?*

'Nothing,' Kizmin said. 'Yesterday a nurse brought me an envelope full of cash from Isaac with a note asking that I buy you something nice to wear out of the hospital.'

Iris considered this. Before, her reaction would have been to take the clothes off and write him a note saying *No thanks*. But now? She stroked the silk at her shoulder and realized that she was not threatened at all by the gift. She was pleased. She smiled and put her hands over her heart.

'Yeah, it was sweet wasn't it,' Kizmin said and rolled her eyes. 'But it was me out there tromping through the stores, and there's not much I hate more than shopping.'

*Thanks*, Iris wrote. *Everything is perfect. How did you know what I'd like?*

'You are an open book to me, woman. An open book.'

Iris cocked her head in a puzzled expression.

'I guess you remind me of myself a few years back.' The detective shrugged. 'Let's get out of here.'

*Isaac*, Iris wrote.

'Right. I'll take you by his room.'

Isaac was asleep. Iris sat down quietly beside his bed and watched him. He was lying on his back. Beneath the sheets and the hospital gown were the faint outlines of padded dressings on his chest. The sight sent a sharp contraction through her. Was he in pain still? Had there been any permanent damage? There were no intravenous lines or monitor hookups. That had to be a good sign.

He had lost weight. His face was gaunt, a pale study in planes and angles. An overpowering swell of tenderness rose in her breast and overflowed, filling every part of her and burning in her eyes so she had to blink back tears.

Was this really it, then? Was she in love?

His hair looked different. She peered closer and realized that the roots of his hair were a few shades lighter than the rest. He must have started greying at an early age and been so self-conscious that he covered it up. Even this imperfection seemed dear to her.

Suddenly she realized she was afraid of him waking up. She didn't want to face him yet. She was afraid he might start talking about there being no future for them.

She slipped from the room. At the nurse's desk she left him a note.

*Gone to see my father. Back either tonight or tomorrow. I'll stop by your place and get you fresh clothes, etc.* Her hand wavered. Should she sign it: Love, Iris? She glanced up. Kizmin was waiting a discreet distance away, barely concealing her impatience. *Thank you for the new clothes. Love, Iris*.

Quickly, before she could change her mind, she folded the paper and handed it to the nurse.

Her head was pounding so she took a pill and slept most of the way to Manhattan. Kizmin stopped for take-away chicken schwarmas, insisting that Iris eat and insisting that Middle-Eastern food was needed. The detective made her laugh. Kept her distracted with wry jokes.

'Look at us,' Kizmin said, as they approached the hospital doors. The two of them were reflected in the glass. Kizmin with her left arm still encased in a sling and Iris with her left forearm wrapped in gauze. 'What a pair we make, huh?'

When they reached the fourth floor Kizmin turned to go visit her still convalescing sister and Iris was left alone in the wide corridor. She approached her father's room and was stricken by a formless apprehension that stopped her and made her unable to go through the door.

There was no longer a man with a mop in view. The

protectors were gone. Everything was back to being safe and normal. Back to making sense.

But maybe that was where her anxieties lay. She didn't want to go back. She couldn't go back. She had changed too much ever to go back to anything that had been before. And she did not know what was left of the old relationship with her father. She felt like she was balanced on a tightrope with her eyes closed, about to fall, without knowing what was underneath.

She breathed deeply and pushed the door open.

'Iris,' a faltering voice said.

It was her father. He was propped up on pillows, his eyes open and focused. The fluorescent lights were off and the blinds were slanted open so that he could look out at the huge billowing clouds that sailed across the sky.

'Iris,' he said again. One side of his mouth did not move in concert with the other.

Slowly, heart speeding, she crossed the room to his bedside.

'Papa?' she whispered, swallowing hard against the new tightness in her aching throat.

'You look . . .' he said, and struggled to finish the sentence. She thought he would say terrible. That she looked terrible. But the word he finally forced out was 'wonderful.'

'I saw . . . your mother. She . . . came to me . . . surrounded by . . . moonlight. She . . . took . . . my hand . . . and . . . led me back.' He attempted a crooked half-smile. 'No one . . . believes me. They say . . . it was . . . part of . . . the . . . coma dreams. But . . . it was . . . real.'

'I believe you,' Iris whispered, tears streaming unchecked down her face. 'I saw her, too. She came to me, too. And I could feel the light.'

'That . . . was . . . love.'

Iris nodded. 'She loved us.'

'She . . . still . . . loves . . . us. Love . . . stays. It's . . . in . . . the . . . bones.'

Iris wanted to touch him as she had when he was unconscious, but she held back. This was the same father who never folded her in his arms. Never took her onto his lap as she had seen other fathers do with their children. Never held her hand or smoothed the hair back from her forehead or kissed her goodnight.

This was the father who had taught and guided her obsessively, attended to her health, exposed her to art and music and the vast wealth of wonders beyond his orchard even though he himself preferred a life of seclusion. This was the father who had raised her as though the job was a sacred obligation, a duty he had sworn to devote himself to, but not one that he had chosen. Not something that came from his heart.

How could that be different now? If she had not engaged his heart as a child, at a time when love usually flows so naturally, then surely there was no chance for anything more now.

She looked upon his face, ghostly against the pillow yet somehow more alive than ever before. Suddenly a pure silvery light engulfed them, as though the sun had come from behind a cloud, or as though the moon was shining on them. And Iris was filled with a sense of peace because she realized that her love for her father was deep and unshakable. It was indeed in her bones. And it was strong enough to survive alone, unanswered. It was strong enough for both of them.

John Lanier smiled his new crooked smile. Slowly he lifted his arms, stretching them out in a jerky movement like a bird learning to fly. 'Iris,' he said tenderly. And she leaned close and she felt those arms close around her just as the light subsided.

She stayed by her father's bedside all afternoon and

through dinner. He slept then. She kissed his forehead and crept out. Kizmin had made her promise to call when she wanted to leave but she was feeling strong so she decided to ride the subway to the building and call the detective after she was finished in Isaac's room. The trip was a good test. She wanted to prove to herself that she was well.

A new superintendent answered her knock. He was a heavyset man with an accent that might have been Polish.

When she whispered who she was to him his face lit up. She was famous in the building, he said. She wrote him a note explaining her mission and her need to enter Isaac's room. He read the note carefully, moving his lips over the words. Then he expressed sympathy about Isaac being in the hospital and gave her a key to get into 702.

She went by her own room first. Kizmin had had someone go in and straighten it up. There was little left that she wanted. And the mattress was ruined so she wouldn't be able to sleep there. The super would probably find her another mattress. But then it occurred to her that she could sleep in Isaac's room.

Her heart quickened at the thought of lying in his bed and inhaling the smell of him. Resting her head on his pillow. Twining her legs in his sheets.

Suddenly she couldn't wait to get to his room. She hurried out to the elevator and up to the seventh floor. As soon as she got out the doors closed behind her and the car groaned downward to answer another call.

She went down the quiet hallway to his room. She tried to unlock the door, but the key that the new super had given her would not go into the lock. She tried it repeatedly, turning it over, jostling it, feeling the edges with her fingers to make sure the key was smooth and well-cut. Puzzled, she stood there, staring at the door. It was the right room: 702.

She heard the elevator returning and thought that she

should probably go right back downstairs and tell the super that he'd given her the wrong key, but she had a premonition of trouble, of something not being right, and so she hesitated.

'Iris,' a ragged voice said softly.

She turned and saw Isaac coming down the hall toward her. He looked like a refugee from something terrible.

'What are you doing here?' she rasped in a painful whisper.

He tried to smile but winced instead. 'I hate hospitals. After I woke and read your note, I had to get out of there . . . So I hired an ambulance service to deliver me here.'

'The doctor thought you were ready to leave?'

'I didn't ask his opinion.'

Disapproving and incredulous, Iris shook her head. 'We've got to get you in bed. Then we'll call a doctor here in Manhattan.'

Once again she struggled with the key. It still didn't work.

She turned to him, held the key up and whispered, 'Something's wrong. Have yours?'

'Yes,' he said, and opened his hand to show her. 'I'll be fine. I'll go in and lie down. You should be at Morningside with your father.'

She shook her head and held out her hand for his key, determined not to let him shoo her away. She wanted to take him in and make him comfortable. She wanted to take care of him.

'No, Iris. I'll do it. Please go.'

She shook her head again and reached for the key. He was proud. Just like she was. But she would show him that it was all right to trust her. To depend on her.

A look of agony crossed his face and she reached for him, thinking that he was in pain.

'I can't let you go in there,' he said and she realized that his agony was not physical.

492

'Why?' she mouthed.

'Please go. None of this should have happened. I told you . . . I told you it was the last thing I wanted . . . I told you we'd both regret it. I . . .'

He sagged against the wall and she angrily ripped the key from his hand. She didn't care what he wanted; she was not going to let him collapse out in the hall. The key slid into the lock with surprising ease.

She opened the door onto a room that was the size and shape of hers downstairs, but not at all the same. It was filled with electronics. Four televisions grouped on a shelf. Complicated tape-recording machines and various sizes and types of speakers. A video-tape player and monitor. Computer equipment. Strange-looking microphones. On the inside of the door, the standard lock had been replaced by a sophisticated high-tech device.

Her first thought was that he was a thief and she was seeing his stolen goods. That was why he'd been so adept at eluding pursuers.

But no, this wasn't an assortment of stolen goods. This was something more like . . . She searched her memory to recover exactly what it was that this scene reminded her of.

She stepped further inside. There was his saxophone lying on the bed. That made her smile. Some weights and work-out equipment. But why did he have four pairs of differently styled eyeglasses on the bedside table? Along with several contact lens cases? She opened a case. The lenses in it were dark brown. She opened another case. The lenses in it were blue. She crossed to the small closet and threw it open. On the shelf were two wigs and several hats. There were shirts on hangers with heavy padding sewn in.

She looked up. He was leaning in the doorway watching her. His eyes were filled with a profound sorrow.

'Who are you!' she demanded, hand flying immediately

to her throat in response to the pain. Tears stung her eyes, blurring her vision. She blinked them back and crossed to the wall with the shelving and the four televisions and the other unrecognizable machines.

'No one you could ever imagine, Iris. No one you would want to imagine.'

Suddenly the connection was made. Seeing the televisions grouped there reminded her of the surveillance equipment at Kaliker's lodge. She pressed all the power buttons. Pressed the power buttons of everything near them.

The screens sprang to life. Each had a different picture. A different view of the same place. The same place from every angle. Iris's room. The bed, the door, the windows, the chair. He had seen everything. He had spied on every private moment. The bathroom door was pictured but apparently there was no camera inside the bathroom. He had spared her that, at least.

She spun to look at him. His face betrayed nothing now. He was watching her intently but his eyes revealed nothing.

'This whole time you've been spying on me? Lying to me? Using me?'

He was very still.

'I was only going to watch you. But then . . . suddenly, watching wasn't enough. I can't explain it. I've never stepped out of bounds before. I meant it to be just one time, but then I couldn't stop. I thought about you constantly. I wanted to be with you again . . . and again.'

'You were spying on me! The whole time! That's how you followed me to the lodge, isn't it? You had me bugged. You were tracking me just like Mitchell Hanley tracked me!'

'I couldn't let you be hurt. I couldn't—'

'I trusted you! I let myself fall in love with you!'

'Iris—'

494

'No! There's no excuse for what you did. You betrayed me!'

'Iris—'

She grabbed the saxophone from the bed and swung it, smashing screen after screen in small electronic explosions. Smashing the sax in the process. Then she threw down the mangled instrument and walked out.

# Thirty-One

The funeral service was held on a beautiful crystalline spring day. Iris stayed near the back of the church but at the cemetery she walked up to stand beside Detective Kizmin.

Kizmin glanced sideways. There was a brief flicker of surprise in her eyes then the sad cynicism of the day returned.

'I thought you might show up,' the detective said in a lowered voice.

Iris didn't reply.

'Does this mean you're out of seclusion now?'

'I haven't been in seclusion, Kiz. I've been with my father and my grandfather.'

'Could have fooled me.'

Again Iris chose not to reply.

'How's it going with Jack? I still can't believe that you are Jack DeVries' granddaughter.'

'It's . . . difficult. He alternates between affection and anger. He wants to smother me with love, but I think he also wants to punish me for the pain my mother brought him.'

Kizmin nodded. She rocked gently back and forth on her heels and looked out over the headstones. 'You know that guy whose name we don't mention?'

Iris stared straight ahead at the open grave and the meager display of flowers. *Isaac*. Even to think the name made her hurt inside.

'I talked to some people. Called in some favors. Slept with the Pope . . . that kind of thing.'

'I don't want to hear this,' Iris said.

'Yes you do,' Kizmin said flatly. 'The unnameable man, who truly is unnameable by the way, is a major free-lance operator in the world of espionage. His name certainly isn't Isaac Brightman. No one knows what his name is. He goes by Gabriel . . . like the angel. He's very expensive and very choosy about what he does.

'Rumor has it that he was hired by Gerald Dixon, the father of the little girl who was killed in the Red Phoenix bombing. Dixon is a senator. With important connections. He was tipped that the feds had a possible lead on the bombing, and apparently, having little faith in the bureaucracy's ability to solve it after so many years, he immediately hired the Angel Gabriel to make sure justice was finally done.'

Kizmin waited for several moments, then said, 'Who knows, doc. Maybe the poor angel lost his professional cool and fell for your charms.'

'Sure,' Iris said bitterly. 'Or maybe he just likes to sleep with women he's been watching undress.'

Kizmin shot her a look of serious concern and fell silent.

Iris let the silence stretch out. Isaac was still with her. A constant ache in her chest. A constant burning behind her eyes. A visitor in her dreams.

He had disappeared after the scene in his room. Disappeared without a trace. Leaving her with a weight of anger and sorrow. Leaving her to wonder . . . What would have happened if she hadn't smashed everything? If she had let him say more? If she hadn't been so uncompromising and unforgiving?

Could they have worked through things and held onto each other? She would never know. Unless . . . But no. No! She would not try to find him. She would not pursue him. Never. She would not allow herself. She would not!

She forced her mouth to curve upward, turned to Kizmin and demanded, 'If Mr Gabriel is such a hotshot operator then how come I had to save his ass?'

The detective laughed and the worry eased from her face. 'So how's your dad doing?' she asked.

'Terrific. He's making incredible progress with the therapy. And Mariette is with him all the time. I think she's really good for him.

'Great.'

'And your sister?' Iris said. 'How is she?'

Kizmin shrugged. 'Her body is healing fine, but her brain is still pretty scrambled. Some days are good. Some are bad.'

Iris put her arm around her friend's shoulder and squeezed.

Kizmin shrugged it off as though embarrassed.

'So what's the plan now, Lanier? I hear that Jack DeVries wants to buy the forensics lab for you. Are you going to accept, or are you going to crawl back into your Mayan tombs?'

A minister stepped to the head of the grave and began a service. To the side three generations of women and two small boys clung together in dazed grief. The family of the murdered girl she and Kizmin had recovered.

Iris watched them, hurting for them, wondering how people could go on believing that the world was a beautiful benevolent place. When the service was over she turned to go, but Kizmin put a restraining hand on her arm.

'What . . .?' Iris started to say, then saw the family of the mourners headed in their direction.

'Oh, Kiz . . .' she protested.

'They wanted to meet you. What could I say?'

The middle-aged woman reached them first. She gripped Iris's hand in her calloused palms and said, 'Thank you, Dr Lanier. You are an angel. Without people

499

like you what would happen to all the girls like my daughter?'

Iris exchanged a glance with Kizmin over the term angel but the woman didn't seem to notice. She went on expressing her thanks.

'It was a living hell not knowing what happened to her. Now she's at rest and our family can move on. And Detective Kizmin has caught the animal who did it. And it's all thanks to you. If you hadn't found those hairs in my baby's ring, that animal would still be free.'

Yes, Iris thought, they had been lucky. The man had been seen talking to the murdered girl just before she disappeared, and those three slender hairs snagged in the setting of her birthstone ring had proved the man a liar and trapped him. One more animal off the street. But there were so many others . . . the Locket Killer for one. He was still out there somewhere.

The oldest of the grieving women leaned in and grabbed Iris's other hand. 'The Lord has chosen you for some powerful work, child. You must be proud to have such a calling.'

Iris had no idea how to respond. 'I'm so glad that we were successful,' she said. 'It's not a sure thing, you know. With work like this there's always an element of luck and then there are so many factors to contend with, so many variables and possibilities and . . .' She looked at Kizmin for help.

'Dr Lanier has to go now,' Kizmin told them. 'She took time off her schedule for the funeral but now she's got to go.'

'Of course, of course,' the mother said.

'I can't believe you didn't warn me,' Iris said under her breath as she walked away beside the detective.

'I was afraid you'd run if I did, and what could I do. It was the girl's mother and grandma and sister . . . and they were so set on thanking you.'

'I didn't know what to say to them.'

'I noticed. You're not much good at public relations.'

'I belong in a lab, not in public relations.'

'That's exactly what I've been telling you. You belong in that lab.'

Iris refused to reply.

Kizmin's expression turned cool and hard. Iris had almost forgotten that expression. It was the one the detective had worn during their first few meetings.

'So you're running away from it,' Kizmin said. 'You're turning your back on the forensics lab and going off to hide somewhere.'

They stopped on the circular drive beside the detective's car. Iris watched the mourning family arrange the few small sprays of flowers to the side of the grave, out of the way of the backhoe that was lumbering into place as the area cleared.

'No,' Iris said. 'No more hiding. No more running away.'

# Acknowledgements

I am most grateful to the following people:

Heather York, Anthropologist, for her many contributions, and Ben Fenwick for his patience.

Dan Brodt, Anthropologist, for sharing his enthusiasms with me and being such a good teacher.

Kent Buehler, Archaeology Lab Manager – Oklahoma Archaeological Survey Lab at the University of Oklahoma, for the fascinating stories, and Dr Lesley Rankin-Hill, University of Oklahoma Department of Anthropology, for her generosity.

Gerri Snow, for her time, and Dr Clyde Snow for his kindness and inspiration.

Deborah Olson of C. J. Olson Cherries in Sunnyvale, California, the fourth generation of the dedicated fruit growing family that I have admired since childhood.

Elaine Koster for her continuing encouragement and support.

Peter Lavery and all the terrific people at Headline.

Audrey LaFehr and Aaron Priest who try to keep me on the right track.

And Michael Bradley for so many reasons that I could fill another book.